FALLING OFF THE CLIFF

FULL THROTTLE
BOOK ONE

KANITHA P.

Falling Off The Cliff

Full Throttle Series Book 1

Copyright © 2023 by Kanitha P.

All rights reserved.

This book is a work of fiction. Names, characters, organisations, places, events, and incidents are either products of the author's imagination or are used fictitiously.

Song lyrics and/or references are used fictitiously and belong to their rightful owner.

This book contains explicit sexual content, foul language, and mentions topics that could be triggering such as loss, grief, death of a parent (off page), and anxiety.

Editing by Hannah G. Scheffer-Wentz, English Proper Editing Services.

Proofreading by Nyla Lillie.

Cover design by Ivy N. Isles.

To the ones who have always dreamed of experiencing that kind of all-consuming love, the thrill, and exhilaration of falling in love with their soulmates.

And to the ones who hide behind calamitous clouds; I see you, and daylight is on its way to you.

PLAYLIST

MIDNIGHT RAIN | Taylor Swift
SPARKS | Coldplay
MUST BE LOVE | Laufey
STYLE (Taylor's Version) | Taylor Swift
IRIS | The Goo Goo Dolls
FADE INTO YOU | Mazzy Star
MAYBE | James Arthur
YOU ARE IN LOVE (Taylor's version) | Taylor Swift
DAYLIGHT | Taylor Swift
FEARLESS (Taylor's version) | Taylor Swift
LOSIN CONTROL | Russ
OLD MONEY | Lana Del Rey
NOTHING'S GONNA HURT YOU BABY | Cigarettes
After Sex
JUST A LITTLE BIT OF YOUR HEART | Ariana Grande
PEACE | Taylor Swift
SEVEN | Taylor Swift
SEEDS | Yoke Lore
UNTIL I FOUND YOU | Stephen Sanchez, Em Beihold
MEDDLE ABOUT | Chase Atlantic
I WANNA BE YOURS | Arctic Monkeys

"FALLING OFF THE CLIFF"

Moment where the tyres degrade rapidly during a race, rendering them uncompetitive.

CHAPTER ONE

📍 *MONTE CARLO, MONACO*

THE CHANCES OF surviving this evening without letting her fury explode into a cacophony of curses were low. Extremely low.

She was on the cusp of showing how infuriated and anxious she was. She was on the brink of—

"What the hell are you doing, Kam?"

Indy's voice became audible through the loud music. The sounds swirling around, as well as her surroundings, instantly shifted into vague semblances.

Though she had evidently heard Indy's question, Kamari didn't look up, keeping her phone in one hand and holding the stem of her empty glass in the other. A deep frown was etched between her brows, but she didn't care if she looked confused in a place where only euphoria was supposed to radiate.

She felt a nudge on her foot but still maintained her gaze on the screen of her phone.

Three dots appeared, then disappeared—as if her interlocutor didn't know what to reply.

She was expecting a simple and effective response: yes or no. Why was he taking his damned time to type either two or three letters then?

"Kamari," she heard from her side. Her friend's tone was laced with exasperation. "You're not texting *him*, are you?"

She rolled her eyes, annoyed. "Why would I do that?"

"Who are you texting, then?" Diana interjected, leaning towards the centre of the table to snatch the phone from Kamari's grip, making the latter grumble in frustration.

Kamari leaned back into the velvet bench, exhaling a loud huff before bringing the rim of her glass up to her lips, only now noticing it was empty.

"Don't tell me you're doing business right now," Indy exclaimed, outraged, before glancing at Diana.

Diana, who had put her sunglasses atop her head—yes, she was wearing shades in a dimly lit bar—narrowed her eyes. "She *is* working."

"Kam!" Indy cried out, throwing her hands up in the air, irritated by her friend's behaviour.

"Indigo," she mimicked, unfazed.

Diana put Kamari's phone in her small purse. "You're forbidden from touching this until tomorrow. No work, no ex-boyfriend, no Instagram, no nothing."

Indy agreed with a nod of her head, her short blonde hair slightly bobbing in sync with her motion. She pivoted in her seat so her torso would be facing Kamari's side. "I'm sure your brother is doing fine managing your café."

"Yes, but—"

Diana raised a hand in the air, and Kamari pursed her lips in disdain. A huff escaped her mouth and then, with a long exhale, she let her shoulders slump. With a small sigh, she could feel the pent-up stress disappear, evaporating into the air and mixing with the loud bass of the music reverberating off the walls.

Kamari drifted her gaze down, pivoting the red squared napkin so it would be aligned and parallel to the edge of the table.

She didn't have to say a word for her friends to understand her dismay.

Indy placed a gentle hand on her upper arm, forcing her to look up and stare into her striking blue eyes. Her rouge lips then curled into a smile, her gaze bright with golden sparks. "Kam, we're in Monte Carlo."

"This trip," continued Diana, a gleam of mischief alighting her eyes, "is for you to forget about that excuse of an ex-boyfriend—"

"Diana," Kamari warned. It was a fact that her ex was not a good man. Still, there was no place for rudeness tonight or for unwanted memories to resurface in her mind.

"Sorry," Diana said, though she didn't sound sorry at all. "Never liked him." Kamari only shrugged, well aware of the resentment her best friends shared towards James. "As I was saying, you are going to have fun this weekend, *capisce*? No stressing about your café and your brother taking care of it, no wallowing or no dwelling on your past, no thinking about what's-his-name."

Whilst Kamari's two best friends had managed to convince her to go on a getaway weekend, after numerous excruciating minutes of begging, pleading, and pouting, she couldn't spend her time acting miserable and being a burden.

"You're right." She straightened herself, a wicked grin ever so slowly spreading across her lips. "I'm making this trip about *me.*"

Indy's cheer was loud as she clapped her hands. She draped an arm around Kamari's shoulders, pulling her tightly into her side and sighing happily. "We're going to have so much fun!"

Kamari wasn't fond of physical touch—apart from shaking hands after sealing a deal with business partners, of course—but she didn't push the blonde away, regardless of the shiver threatening to skitter down her spine. Indy had already engorged too many margaritas whilst Diana had drunk one Aperol Spritz—not counting the bottle of white they had emptied together during dinner. Kamari had just finished her caipirinha—too quickly for her own liking, by the way.

Kamari lifted a finger, her tone turning authoritative, making Diana scowl. "Let's make one thing clear, though—"

"You can't be serious, Kam," Diana grumbled, irritatingly. Flames of annoyance were burning in her gaze, pinning Kamari with unyielding wrath. "I know what you're going to say. You're going to be all, like,"—her voice shifted as she narrowed her eyes into thinner slits, squaring her shoulders and flipping her copper hair away from her face—"no sneaking into random parties, no hooking up with random guys, no drinks after—"

"I don't sound like that." Kamari was obviously offended as her lips parted before a soft gasp escaped.

"You do," both Indy and Diana said.

"Do not."

"Do too," Indy continued, slightly tipping her mouth into a grimace in a silent apology.

"Okay," she said, the word strangled in her throat. She was vexed, but she knew she was too self-conscious; withdrawn from her youth. In fact, it had taken *a lot* of effort and convincing for her friends to compel her into leaving London for three short days. She folded her arms across her chest, lifting her shoulders in a half-shrug. "So what?"

"So?" Diana scoffed and stood up, causing her chair to screech against the floorboards. The room was barely lit, the sound of the music was incredibly loud, and no one cared about them. Still, Kamari didn't like her friend's impulsiveness, afraid to draw unnecessary and unwanted attention to the trio. "So, Kamari Monroe, this has to stop. We're going to sneak into a party after I give you another drink to loosen up. Indigo, search for the closest private party."

"On it," Indy exclaimed eagerly, already on her phone.

Kamari exhaled and watched Diana walk towards the bar,

ignoring the glances thrown her way and nearly pushing everyone out of her path.

"Get some shots," Indy ordered firmly.

Diana didn't even turn around as she raised a hand, showing a thumbs-up in agreement.

"What did she mean by 'we're going to sneak into a party'? Please tell me we won't get in trouble."

Indy didn't look up from her screen, its light casting a soft glow on her nose. She snorted softly. "Do you want the lie or the truth?"

"The truth?" Kamari wasn't even sure herself.

Indy's lips curved upwards—a devious witch planning her worst and best coup all at once. "We'll get in trouble, and it'll be worth it. Kam, you're 23. It's time you become a delinquent for a night."

———

"Hurry up, Kam! Don't make me drag you by your hair—or worse, by your Jacquemus purse."

Clutching her bag to her chest, she glared at Diana, the sound of her heels tapping loudly on the cobblestones as she tried to keep her balance. "You're not laying your filthy hands on this bag. It cost me over seven hundred pounds."

"Exactly," Diana hissed through gritted teeth. "Come on, the boat isn't going to wait for us."

Boat?

Indy and Diana had managed to drag Kamari out of the club. Truthfully, she was thankful they left because it was starting to get cramped, loud, and busy. Though they hadn't told her where they were headed, Kamari knew they had an evil plan in mind.

The walk from the bar to the harbour of Monte Carlo was quite short, but the streets were filled with locals and tourists. The August air was still warm at this time of the night. The sky was no longer azure like it was when they had arrived earlier today but replaced by a canvas of navy and midnight blue, and the crescent moon started to glow amongst minuscule, radiant stars.

Kamari was regretting her choice of shoes. Were those heels the right move? Surely, she and her friends attracted people's attention, but she hadn't planned on running after some boat whilst getting ready a few hours prior.

Kamari kept her gaze fixated on Diana's flamboyant hair as she walked hastily, dodging people who were solely admiring the yachts filling the horizon.

Indy was walking ahead of them when she abruptly stopped before a luxurious yacht that could welcome a dozen people. She squealed in excitement and ran towards the edge of the deck.

A man was standing on the footbridge, grinning down at the blonde with a bottle of beer in hand. As Indy stood before him, she lifted herself on her toes to wrap her arms around his shoulders.

"God," Diana grumbled as Kamari reached her side. "Does this girl know everyone, wherever we go?"

Indigo Bailey was a social butterfly. The life and soul of the party. The most outgoing person to ever enter a room. As a digital influencer, she was innately gifted with kindness and grace. She knew how to socially interact whilst ingraining her wildness and natural beauty into everyone's mind.

So, yes, it was no surprise to see Indy encounter one of her acquaintances in the small country of Monaco.

"Indigo!" Kamari exclaimed when she witnessed her friend step onto the yacht, her eyes widening. "What are you doing?"

Indy waved her hand frantically, urging her friends to join the party. "Come on, you guys. They're leaving right now."

"That's perfect," Diana quipped, grabbing Kamari's wrist.

Being pulled towards the boat, albeit against her will, Kamari released a small grunt. "But—"

"You can't live a life without partying on a yacht in Monaco."

Despite already gravitating towards a state of carefreeness because of the drinks she had consumed, Kamari could still feel a ball of uneasiness forming in the pit of her stomach.

She couldn't fathom the fact she was about to break a rule— or several. And Diana could see right through her as if she had the ability to read her overpowering thoughts.

"Stop overthinking," her friend gritted. "We'll deal with the consequences tomorrow."

What was she getting herself into?

She followed Diana while silently cursing her two friends. They pushed past tourists who were photographing the harbour and the dark starry sky in the background, apologising whenever she collided with someone.

"Hurry!" Indy shouted. The guy whom she had embraced a few moments ago was still standing next to her, grinning and laughing softly when the two girls picked their pace up.

Diana stepped first on the bridge, letting go of Kamari's wrist to take her shoes off.

Kamari stopped in her tracks. Her heart ceased to beat for a fragment of a second. Her breath caught inside her throat. Fear of the unknown clouded her mind—even though inviting herself to a party wasn't the worst thing she could do.

"Kamari," Indy and Diana pressed impatiently.

She took a step forward.

Her two friends cheered, and she blinked.

When she looked behind her shoulder, Indy's friend had already pulled the footbridge up, and soon enough, the sound of the boat's engine roared through the loud music and laughter.

There was no turning back.

Unless she wanted to jump off the yacht. And with her luck, she would either break a leg or fall into the water.

And she wasn't going to hurt herself or get soaked in that outfit.

Getting drunk was the safest option—to make the anxiety disappear, to have fun, to be young and free, to forget about the turmoil and pain that had been obliterating her heart for what felt like an eternity now.

What was the worst that could happen, anyway?

CHAPTER TWO

⚐ *MONTE CARLO, MONACO*

"HOW DO YOU think the rest of the season will go for you?"

There were three reasons why Thiago hated when strangers attended his parties:

1. They were always too fucking nosy about his private life.

2. They always asked millions of questions about Formula 1 when all he wanted was to take a minute to breathe. Summer break was *meant* for disconnecting, rewinding, and relaxing. Don't get him wrong, though; Thiago loved his life. Loved being a high-performance athlete, racing on the most beautiful circuits around the world, and living each thrilling race like it could be the last one. Loved all this attention and admiration he received from fans and people he encountered, but not during parties. Not during a time when all he wanted was to be a normal person —just for one night.

3. They always left the party with too much gossip on the tips of their tongues, turning whatever they had heard or seen into stupid rumours running all over the internet.

He responded with a shrug, taking a swig of his beer as he leaned an elbow atop the cold railing. "Good, hopefully." He had decided to keep his answers short and simple, not wanting to elaborate too much and carry a conversation he genuinely didn't want to have.

"I'm really hoping it turns out to be better for you, man."

Thiago offered a tight-lipped smile to the man. He didn't even know his name. Only that he was one of his friend's co-workers. "Me too."

Before the man could carry the conversation with more intrusive questions or remarks that only stirred the knife deeply in the wound, he turned around, pretending to answer someone who had called his name.

"Sorry, lad," he said without so much as sparing a glance behind his shoulder. "Gotta go."

"It was a pleasure talking to you!" He could hear the excitement edging his tone, could hear the smile in his voice.

Yeah, whatever.

All he needed was a breath of fresh air.

Tonight was the last night he could afford to get drunk and make mistakes. It would be all over in a few days as soon as he had to go back to training. He couldn't allow himself to step over the line once the season started again. Therefore, tonight was the only opportunity he could grasp to be himself one last time.

The salty air enveloped his senses, the still-warm breeze of the summer night brushing strands of hair off his forehead as the yacht drifted further away from the port. He watched the lights glowing on the city of Monte Carlo taper off as he swam towards darkness, where he hoped the secrets of his evening would stay hidden with nightfall.

As he turned around to check if the man he had been talking to was still there and found the coast clear, he bumped into someone—or rather the opposite—making them lose their balance.

He instantly gripped the woman's upper arms to help her steady herself, releasing her and stepping back to give her some space.

"I'm so sorry," she said, her Geordie accent thick. "I wasn't watching where I was going."

Thiago was met with a blue-eyed blonde, quite petite despite her high heels. He had never seen her before, yet her face was somehow familiar. She had a phone in hand and it looked like she had been occupied taking pictures of the horizon—or perhaps of herself.

"Do I know you?" he demanded warily.

"No," she answered with a chuckle, grin wide and eyes filled with mirth.

He narrowed his gaze, a sense of self-preservation ready to cocoon him with an unbreakable shield. "Why are you on my boat?"

She shrugged her shoulders with blatant nonchalance. "I jumped on with my two friends. I'm a friend of Alex, though."

"Oh." Thiago nodded, recognition ever so slowly flashing in his eyes. Still holding his bottle of beer, he pointed his finger at her face—not in an impolite way. "That's why your face looks so familiar. You're Indy Bailey, motorsports influencer, right?"

Surprise drew itself on her face, but her smile didn't falter. It was evident that she knew who Thiago was, though she was keeping her composure and remained calm.

"You know who I am?" she asked, bemused.

Thiago emitted a soft chuckle and gave Indy a short nod, burying his free hand in the pocket of his jeans. "I've heard of you and your podcast. I'm all for women in the industry."

It was evident that Indy was struggling to keep her excitement at bay. Her eyes widened slightly and she tucked a strand of blonde hair behind an ear, her hand shaking in the process. Her cheeks turned rosy as she gaped up at him with complete admiration. "Could I maybe have you on the podcast someday?"

Thiago grinned. "I'd love to."

The corners of her eyes crinkled. "Really?"

"You look surprised."

"Mostly excited." Indy shrugged. "I've never had the guts to reach out to you. I mean, you're Thiago Valencia. You're, like, ruthless and untouchable, and"—she winced as if scared to admit the rest, her voice lowering into a murmur—"unapproachable."

Way to make me look like an arse.

"On the track," he corrected. "But I'm a decent human being when I'm not racing. I promise."

"Decent," she hummed, amused. "Alright. I guess I'll have to learn more about you when I interview you."

"Sure." He then glanced around, smiling at the sight of his friends already high on euphoria and dancing around to the loud music blasting from the stereos. "Do you just jump on the first boat you see without being invited? You're lucky you're one of Alex's friends, or he'd have thrown you out the moment you tried to sneak in."

Indy shrugged sheepishly. "My best friend and I are on a mission."

"A mission?" He arched an eyebrow and took a sip of his beer.

"We're trying to get our other best friend to loosen up a bit and to make her forget about her shitty ex-boyfriend."

"Ah," he said. "I see, and where are those friends of yours?"

Indy pivoted, her eyes searching the small crowd. Her pink-painted nail was now pointed towards two people standing in the cockpit. "That's Diana."

Copper hair flowed down her back as she had her hands planted on her hips. She was talking with a frown on her brows to Cal—Thiago's best friend—like she was scolding him. Cal had a hand on the wheel, looking at Diana whilst arguing with her and waving his other hand in the air aggressively.

"She has the tendency of picking unnecessary fights," Indy

commented. "She's a sweetheart, though. She's probably giving shit to your friend for a valid reason."

"Like?"

"Like, for drinking when he's supposed to pilot the boat?"

Thiago snorted softly as he watched Cal roll his eyes. "Wait until she realises it's just iced tea. Cal is as sober as a brick. He rarely drinks. Don't worry, we're safe. You won't die stranded in the middle of the Mediterranean Sea."

Indy lifted her shoulders in a shrug again. "At least I would have spent my last hours partying with Thiago Valencia."

"Right," he laughed. "And the other friend?"

The broken-hearted girl.

"I was actually looking for her. Knowing her she's probably hiding somewhere." Indy sauntered her gaze around, lifting herself on her tiptoes. "She's, like, this tall,"—she lifted her hand until it was levelled with Thiago's eyes—"dark brown hair, crazy green eyes."

"Shy?" he asked.

"Careful."

"Pretty?"

"Gorgeous." She cast a wary glance his way. "But not looking for anyone or anything."

"Hm," he mused, brows raised. "Sad?"

"Not right now."

"Thank God," he muttered behind the rim of his glass bottle. "I don't want a random girl crying on my boat."

"Oh, come on," Indy teased. "Have some sympathy."

"Sympathy for some girl and her friends who have snuck on my boat without permission? You wish."

Indy's eyes narrowed. "You're never going to let that go, are you?" But before Thiago could answer, Alex called for Indy from the other side of the boat with two glasses of liquor in hand. "Sorry." She grimaced, pointing her thumb behind. "I haven't seen Alex in so long..."

"It's fine," Thiago said. Not that he cared, anyway. "Can I just ask you one thing, though?"

The influencer nodded.

He motioned towards her hand with his chin. "Please don't use your phone on my boat. Whatever happens on the Pura Vida, stays on the Pura Vida."

"Consider it done." Putting her device into her purse, she turned around and squealed in delight as Alex approached.

The universe wasn't on his side tonight. Perhaps there was a reason why he had been fated to meet this next person, because the very moment he turned around, another woman came into collision with his chest, nearly knocking the oxygen out of his lungs.

It all happened so fast—one moment he was standing there, and the next he was being cursed at.

"Oh, you've got to be joking! That's shitty." A smoky, enticing voice filled the air. The stranger's voice was something like he had never heard before—both alluring and intriguing all at once.

Thiago's heart was hammering and he soon realised he was holding the woman's elbow to help her steady herself. It also kept him grounded, because he swore he felt his knees threatening to give up on him.

"Do you not watch where you go?" she snapped, and he had to blink to make sure she wasn't a figment of his imagination.

Because she was... No words could come to mind to find the right words to describe her. He was downright speechless. Starstruck. Enthralled.

Thiago stepped away, dropping his hand from her bare arm, and let a scoff escape the back of his throat. "Don't *you*?"

She had been occupied wiping the sticky droplets of her spilled drink off her little black dress, a deep crease evident between her brows. But when she finally heard the sound of his voice, she looked up, and the world felt like coming to a halt.

Thiago had never seen this woman before, but by the look of

her height, her dark hair, and her crazy green eyes, he knew she was the third rule-breaker. She was definitely one of the tallest women he had ever met and, without a shadow of a doubt, the most breathtaking person he'd set his eyes on.

Despite the scowl etched on her bronze, freckled face, her green eyes were observing and studying his face as though she had never seen beauty quite like his, either. The reddish glow of the light on the deck was looming over one side of her face, the silvery moonlight shining on the other, making her appear like the devil's wife and an angel all at once. He didn't know which one she was at this exact moment as a wildfire of anger started to blaze around the edges of her pupils, but he tried to convince himself she was a divine being.

Her plump lips parted, like she wanted to say something, but no sound escaped her mouth. Her brows knitted together, like she was trying to understand the turmoil clouding her mind as she stared back into his eyes. Like she had forgotten about her soaked dress and her surroundings.

Thiago was fascinated as well. He was tongue-tied. At a loss for words. And he hated that. He also hated the way she was glaring at him, evidently cursing him inside her mind for having ruined her outfit.

He wanted to apologise. Wanted to offer another drink or perhaps a towel to help her clean the mess but, instead, he found himself asking, "Do you want a picture of me, or something?"

She blinked, and a scoff of disbelief fled past her lips. She folded her arms across her chest, her eyes narrowing into slits. "Aren't you an arrogant little thing?"

"Little?" he repeated, bemused.

"Why would I want a picture of you?" she queried, ignoring his baffled question.

"You don't know who I am?"

She tilted her head. Her gaze left his face and, in the most excruciating and deliberate motion, started to saunter over his frame. "Should I?"

She sure knew how to hurt his ego. It felt like receiving a punch straight to the gut.

"Well," he started, mimicking her defensive motion by crossing his arms over his chest. "Considering you snuck onto my boat, I think the least you could do is know who's providing you that drink and welcoming you on board."

Surprise ever so slowly started to draw on her face, her shoulders sagging as she breathed. "Oh."

"Yeah," he snickered. "*Oh.*"

Time seemed to slow down as she scrutinised his face. Not a flicker of emotion was perceptible in her eyes. "Pity," she said quietly. "Such a gorgeous boat for such a conceited man."

He had been expecting a lot of reactions, but not this one.

"You don't even know me!" he retorted, throwing his hands in the air.

Resentment flared in her pupils. "I know enough about men like you."

"What's that supposed to mean?"

The stranger only lifted her shoulders in a shrug.

"And who are you?" He took her in with a once-over that made a chill skitter down his spine. God, she was something else. "If you think you can just sneak onto my boat without facing the consequences, then you're wrong."

Despite the caramel tone of her skin, evidently sun-kissed by the summery sunlight, she managed to pale at the sound of his remark. She straightened herself, her throat bobbing as she swallowed hard.

She didn't want to get in trouble.

If anything, he almost thought she didn't *want* to be *here*.

Thiago smirked, contemplating whether to taunt her or let her go.

"Well," she retorted, her voice wavering despite the cool act she was putting on. "You should have had better security."

He couldn't help but snicker as a smirk spread across his lips. "Really?"

"Yes."

"What do you think security will say when we get back to Monaco and the police are waiting for you and your two—"

"Are you aware you're also breaking a rule?"

"Really?" He scoffed. "Please, entertain me."

"I watched a documentary—"

"Who watches fucking documentaries?"

"I do," she snapped. "And it was about yachts. Yours cannot welcome more than twelve guests, plus your crew, and I think there are over twenty-five people on here."

He blinked. She was good. "I bet you're going to have the time of your life reporting me to the police, aren't you?"

She raised a hand, a trembling one at that. He could see right through her: a tough façade that concealed fears and incertitudes. "Here's a deal. I'll stay out of your way if you stay out of mine. I'll spend the rest of the evening hidden somewhere, so we can ignore each other and forget about this whole misunderstanding."

His brows shot up in disbelief as he repeated, slowly, "A misunderstanding? Is this what it is?"

"Yes," she breathed frustratingly. "A mistake."

His gaze narrowed on her. "I might agree with you on that. Don't ruin my night, and I won't ruin yours."

She gestured to her dress whilst turning on her heel, the roll of her eyes decipherable. "It's already ruined."

Good God, this night was going to be a long one.

CHAPTER THREE

📍 *MONTE CARLO, MONACO*

K AMARI WAS GOING to get in trouble.

She knew it.

She could feel it deep inside her bones. Could feel the ever-growing bubble of uneasiness inside the pit of her stomach taking over her senses.

Indy and Diana instantly disappeared through the cramped yacht, the both of them searching for someone or something, intent on making this night the best one of their lives.

"Thanks for nothing, you guys," she muttered under her breath when she was pushed by a person, a faint apology echoing through the loud music.

The hills of Monaco were now distant—too far away to plunge back. Kamari grunted frustratingly. She could feel the liquor she had drunk earlier losing its effect as she felt the fresh yet warm air brush her arms. The sounds surrounding her were clear. Her vision wasn't hazy anymore, like she had instantly sobered up the moment she stepped foot on this magnificent, luxurious boat.

She had never been on a yacht before, but *God,* did she love it even if she tried to appear like she despised having her feet on the deck.

That was one thing she could cross off her bucket list.

Wait, scratch that. She could cross off a good number of things from that list: travel to Monaco with her best friends, drink a cocktail that had cost over twenty euros, go uninvited to a party filled with rich people—and probably famous ones—and jump onto a random boat.

As she pushed past a small group of people gathered on the deck, she internally cursed Indy and Diana for dragging her into their wild chaos. She could still hear Indy's dulcet voice encouraging her to get out of her comfort zone. Could hear Diana's tone of exasperation as she pushed her to be young, wild, and free.

Kamari was snapped out of her thoughts when a man came to stand before her eyes. She first saw his black shirt, mostly unbuttoned which revealed a pale yet muscular torso. Then, her gaze collided with warm, kind eyes smiling back at her. With his blonde, tousled hair, and a lazy grin etched on his face, she instantly recognised him as Indy's friend—the one who had invited them to the party.

"You look lost," he stated, his grin never faltering as he studied her hardened features and defensive demeanour. She let out a breath as she realised her arms were folded across her chest, letting them fall to her sides. "You're one of Indy's friends, right?"

She nodded, forcing her lips into a tight smile. "Kamari."

"Kamari," he purred, brows raising as he extended a hand her way. "Gorgeous name."

She shook his hand, finding herself surprised by the delicacy of his touch. "You can call me Kam."

His grin widened and he released his gentle grip. "It's nice to finally meet you, Kam. I'm Alex. Can I get you anything to drink?"

Kamari chewed the inside of her cheek, contemplating his offer for a flickering heartbeat. She knew her friends were already having fun. Regardless of the fact she hated being in this position, Kamari wasn't one to do things halfway, so she only shrugged. If she were to be on this boat, she was to have a memorable evening. She deserved to have fun too.

"Sure," she said. "What do you have?"

With a nudge of his head, he motioned her to follow him inside. She was astonished by the grandeur and simplistic beauty of the yacht. Alex led her towards an area where a leather sofa surrounded a square table that was occupied by two men and two women playing poker, a few bottles of beer scattered around their cards.

"Guys," Alex said. "This is Kamari."

They greeted her with "hi's" and "hello's", waving and smiling, and she mirrored the kind gestures.

A drink cooler was sitting in the corner of the room. Alex opened it, then glanced at Kamari. "You're not a beer gal, are you?"

She blinked. "Do I look like one?"

"Feisty," he mumbled, but chuckled, nonetheless. "Wine?"

She shook her head. "Had too many glasses during dinner."

He winced. "You don't want a wine hangover."

She shuddered. "They're the worst."

"They are," Alex agreed, then suggested with a small smile, "A gin and tonic?"

"Sure." She wiped her hands on the sides of her thighs, that feeling of discomfort never faltering despite the ambiance of the place. People didn't seem to care about her presence. Stereos were blasting loud music, and most of the guests were dancing or chatting joyfully with one another. "Indy gave me too many drinks already. What's one more?"

Alex laughed as he moved towards the bar on the other side

of the room to make her cocktail. "Is it your first time in Monaco?"

She nodded, following him and leaning her arms over the countertop as she watched him open a bottle of tonic. "I don't travel much."

He gaped at her. "You're the friend who owns a business in London? The one who wants to expand her brand over the country?"

"Yes." Her shoulders released the tension they'd been holding for so long. "Did Indy tell you that?"

Alex answered with a nod. "She told me about you when we met in Miami a few months ago."

"Oh."

Sliding a tall glass towards her, he winked. "Enjoy your drink."

"Thanks," she replied, stirring the beverage with the stainless-steel straw. "Have you seen Indy and Diana?"

Alex pointed behind him. "The redhead is over there."

Diana was standing in the cockpit, talking with a tall man with dark skin and only wearing loose pants. By the aggravated look on her face, it was evident something was bothering her as she gestured around aggressively. Kamari twisted her mouth into a grimace before taking a small sip of her drink.

"I'm sorry about her," Kamari said. "She's..."

"Got an attitude?" Alex chuckled.

She lifted her brows. "You could say that."

Kamari finally spotted Indy's blonde hair on the other side of the deck. She was talking to someone with a big smile plastered on her lips, but Kamari couldn't see the other person.

"There's Indy."

Alex had been busy making two other cocktails—one for himself and the other for Indigo. He nodded, as if giving his approval for Kamari to join her friend.

She turned on her heel, then glanced at Alex whilst lifting her glass in the air. "Thank you for that."

"No worries," he replied with a wink. "Cheers."

Kamari could feel eyes upon her, studying her steady steps, the sway of her hips, the motion of her long curls swaying down her bare back as she walked. She felt out of place and the centre of attention all at once.

Kamari just needed one last drink with her friend before letting go fully of all her worries. Just needed one last moment of reassurance.

But Alex beat Kamari as he came from the other side, shouting Indigo's name through the loud bass of the music. The blonde turned around with a grin, then talked quietly to her interlocutor—whose back was turned to Kamari—before running towards Alex.

Kamari kept her gaze on her red-painted toenails as she walked, set on finding a quiet spot to drink her gin in peace.

The universe, though, was intent on making her night everything but peaceful. Air got knocked out of her lungs the moment someone collided forcefully with her, making the contents of her drink spill over her chest. Cold liquid ran down the valley of her breasts, soaking the fabric of her dress, and instant molten rage started running through her veins.

Once her stance was steady, she glanced down at herself and huffed a frustrated breath at the sight of her damaged dress. It was only when she started cursing that she realised a large, warm hand was holding her elbow.

Kamari felt his presence—punishing, corrupting. He was so close to her. She blinked, kept wiping her clothed chest, and refused to look up. The intoxicating scent of musk swirled in the air, somehow overpowering the smells of sea salt and alcohol.

She decided to say something before he could. "Do you not watch where you go?"

His hand fell from her arm, and she suddenly felt cold, but she instantly convinced herself it was because she was standing outside, on a moving boat, during nightfall.

She heard a scoff fly past his lips. *"Don't you?"*

The gruffness in his voice sounded like rough velvet, causing chills to arise on her spine. She shivered. Blinked. Still, she refused to show how much she was being affected by this proximity and by the sound of his coarse timbre. She lifted her gaze and met with the most striking, ridiculous, and hypnotising eyes she had ever seen. She had never seen irises of such colour; grey, almost silver. Her drunken thoughts made her believe that, in the sunlight, flecks of amber and gold and blue would be perceptible around his pupils.

She couldn't speak. Couldn't move. The stranger's skin glowed beneath the moonlight, his sharp and enticing features making her believe he had been carved from marble—or by the Gods themselves. His dark hair curled around his ears and waved atop his head, and the barest line had formed between his brows as he stared back at her.

She was in trouble. Such deep, calamitous trouble.

THE STARS HAD BECOME a hazy mass of golden splatters shimmering in the night sky.

Kamari's dress was still slightly damp, and she had managed to find a bathroom to clean her outfit without attracting any attention. The intriguing encounter with the owner of the yacht had caused her heart to race and batter in an unpleasant rhythm.

Arsehole. What a conceited prick.

Even now, as she was lying atop the roof and stargazing, she couldn't help but let her mind drift towards the man with grey eyes and a foul mouth.

No. No. No. Don't think about him. He doesn't deserve a second of your time, let alone invade a fragment of your thoughts.

Quite frankly, she had been just as rude, but it was her self-preservation that had shielded her from the raging storm this man evidently was.

Kamari had to submerge her intrusive thoughts. Had to

forget about them. She didn't know where Indy and Diana were. The music sounded louder than before, and the yacht had come to a halt somewhere in the sea. Despite the loud cheers and laughter and chatter reverberating from all around, Kamari felt serene.

She'd gotten a refill—since the ever-so-humble owner of this boat had knocked her previous drink all over her—and had chatted with a few people. It was no surprise to her that most guests were acquaintances with Indy. Indy was a motorsports influencer, and her audience grew daily—it was only natural for her to befriend every person she came across.

Lifting her glass up, she emitted a soft grunt when she noticed it was already empty. Just as she sat up, gathering her loose curls over a shoulder, a silhouette emerged from the shadows and stole her breath away.

The yacht's owner—whose name was still a mystery—walked onto the roof, phone in one hand and beer in the other.

But the very moment his gaze landed on her, he stilled. At first, surprise appeared on his chiselled face, but he let his features harden as he huffed loudly.

"Not you again."

Her brows rose and she pursed her lips in disdain. "I'm glad I'm sharing the exact same sentiment towards you."

He stepped forward and she felt so petite under the intensity of his scrutiny. Tucking a strand of hair behind an ear, she didn't falter and watched his every move as he approached the mat she'd been lying on.

"What are you doing here?" he asked, tone chilly and rough on the edges.

"What does it look like I'm doing? Sunbathing?" Sarcasm dripped off her tongue like sweet poison and it made him narrow his stone-cold gaze on her.

"Obviously," he responded, sardonically.

He turned his gaze towards the horizon where the harbour of Monaco was perceptible from where they were stranded. She observed as he tucked one hand in the front pocket of his jeans whilst lifting his beverage to his mouth.

Kamari needed to leave. Had to get away from this man who had promised her trouble as soon as they'd get back to land. But she couldn't bring herself to move. Couldn't even look away from the unnerving yet alluring stranger standing metres away.

His linen shirt was unbuttoned at the top, revealing a silver chain sitting between his collarbones. She wasn't sure if she had dreamt it, but she had perhaps, glimpsed an earring on his left ear—the one she couldn't see.

"I can feel you staring at me," he stated bluntly, though he didn't meet her gaze.

"Not like I'll be remembering this exact moment," Kamari mumbled. "You're kind of blurry."

Her vision wasn't all *that* hazy. It was like the alcohol consuming her system had vanished the moment he stepped into her line of vision. Like he had an uncanny power over her. She hated that. She hated *him*.

He snorted, as if he could see right through her. "Right."

"Are you..." She moved to sit on the edge of the large sun-lounger, crossing one leg over the other as she studied his allure. "Are you hiding from your own party?"

"Yes, and?"

"That's sad."

Silver met green. "Not sadder than a girl like you avoiding socialising."

She lifted her shoulders in a shrug. "I'm just trying to stay out of trouble."

"By inviting yourself to a private party?"

Kamari didn't respond as her lips pressed into a thin line. A smirk played on the corner of his mouth, causing her to roll her eyes in blatant annoyance.

He gestured to the empty spot next to Kamari, and she shrugged lightly. He took a seat, but a great distance was still separating them. Leaning his elbows atop his thighs, he gripped his beverage in both hands before turning his head to look at her. That was her cue to divert her gaze towards the dark ocean.

"Why aren't you partying with the others?"

She could feel his scrutiny scorch the side of her face, but she refused to give him the satisfaction of meeting his curious gaze.

She rolled her shoulders, making her hair fall down her back. "Probably for the same reason you're finding shelter up here."

"You mean avoiding general conversation?"

Incredulity etched on her face, and she finally shifted to look into his eyes. "You host a party, and you avoid your guests? That's a bit weird."

"Weird?" he scoffed. "You know what's even weirder? The fact that you're not getting drunk like Indy and that other friend—"

"Diana."

"Whatever." He paused to take a sip of his beer.

Kamari placed her empty glass on the table to her right. "Someone has to get them back to the hotel safely."

He stayed silent for a heartbeat, allowing the sound of music to fill the void. "Something tells me you're always the one to look after your friends."

She swallowed, hard. "Are you judging me?"

"Yes."

"Why?"

"Because you're depriving yourself of having fun for your friends' sake."

She kept her chin high as she maintained his gaze. "You know nothing about me."

"Just like you don't know anything about me," he argued. "We're even."

His mere presence heightened all her senses, even if she was supposed to be stumbling into an abyss of haziness. Chills skittered down her spine as he kept his gaze fixed on her as though he was trying to see beyond her façade.

The man shifted until he was lying down, distance still

hanging between them like the heavy silence that had fallen. With one hand braced behind his head, the other lay atop his stomach with the half-full bottle of beer in his grip whilst he let his stare meander over the starry sky.

Kamari couldn't bear staring at him for too long. There was something about him that she both loathed and admired at the same time: his infuriating attitude and effortless beauty. She wasn't certain if she was nervous or annoyed to be sitting next to him. Perhaps both, but surely more of the latter.

She turned her head to look at the water lapping peacefully around the boat, noticing the notes of musk whiffing towards her when the breeze caressed her skin.

"Do you want me to go?" she asked quietly.

A beat passed. "What?"

"I asked—"

"I heard you," he said. "But why do you ask?"

She turned to look at him, only to find him already staring at her. A dry chuckle escaped the back of her throat. "I'm intruding on your party *and* personal space. You're entitled to be annoyed with my presence."

"I didn't say that," he drawled. "I mean, we didn't start off on the right foot, but that doesn't mean your company is annoying. As long as you stay silent, we're fine."

"Charming," she retorted before looking away.

"You really don't know who I am?" he asked after a while of complete silence. Bewilderment laced his tone, but she could also hear a faint hint of hurt and curiosity.

Who the hell is this pompous guy?

She pinned him with a glare. "What happened to staying silent?" He only responded with a shrug. "I know something about you: you have an ego the size of Monaco."

He laughed. Not a snicker, not a mocking chuckle. He laughed—a heartfelt and genuine sound—whilst tipping his head back against the mat as he exposed the strong column of his throat.

"Damn," he muttered after regaining composure. With a hand above his heart, he turned his face just to stare back into her eyes. "I don't know if you're trying to flatter or hurt me."

"Are you finding this funny?" she gritted.

He nodded, smirking. "You're the greatest entertainment I've had in years."

"Oh, right." She rolled her eyes. "Now you're trying to flatter me."

"Is it working?"

"You wish."

She cleared her throat, twisting her upper body so she was turned to properly face him. She leaned a hand on the mat, her head tilting sideways as she studied his striking features. He was ruggedly handsome, and she hated him even more for that. Hopefully, though, she'd forget all about him in the morning. "This is your boat, right?"

He nodded. "Yes."

She gestured around them. "I'm not an expert in yachts, but I'm assuming this one cost hundreds of thousands—"

"Millions," he corrected with a smug grin.

A small scoff of disbelief erupted from her throat, and she rolled her eyes. "Okay, then. So, you're a millionaire."

The corner of his lips tipped upwards. "Whatever you say, love."

"Don't call me that," she bit out, distaste lacing her tone. "Are you famous, or something?"

"Maybe." He shrugged lazily before twisting his body until he propped himself on an elbow, fully facing Kamari. "Do you really want to know?"

She blinked. "Actually, no. I don't want to know who you are."

He nodded as if dismissing that foreign feeling of rejection, but she could still detect that flash of vexation in his eyes.

Truth be told, Kamari didn't care about who this guy was.

Something deep inside her gut told her it was better to shelter herself from the truth.

He studied her features for a moment, for an eternity. Though she had expected to feel uncomfortable or judged under the intensity of his stare, she felt anything but. She held his gaze, as if they had entered a staring contest, but all she could think about was how ridiculous and otherworldly the colour of his eyes was.

"Are you planning on hiding the rest of the night?" he then asked quietly. She blinked, and her mind was back to spiralling.

"Are you?" she shot back. "Aren't you supposed to be socialising with those people invading your boat?"

"You know," he breathed, passing ring-coated fingers through his dark hair. "Sometimes I just need to be alone for a few minutes before having to be someone I'm not around other people."

A minuscule, sympathetic smile ghosted Kamari's lips, making his gaze drop to her mouth. A shiver rolled down her spine, but she was certain it was because of the cold air. She straightened herself and watched the horizon. "At least we agree on something. I'm going to leave now."

She heard some shuffling around. "What? No. You can stay."

"An hour ago you were ready to throw me into the water to get rid of me—"

"Hey," he cut in dryly. "I'm a gentleman."

"That's debatable."

Another beat passed. "You don't have to go," he said almost in a whisper.

A small line appeared between her brows as she met silver moons staring intently at her. He had moved, now sitting up and somehow closer to her. She wasn't sure why she wasn't backing away. "I don't want to be a burden. I've caused enough problems by inviting myself to your party. I'm sorry about that, by the way. Can I just ask you not to say anything to the authorities when we get back to Monaco? I have a reputation to uphold—a perfect one—and it can't be tainted by the mistake my friends made. I promise you won't ever hear from us again—"

"Do you ever shut up?" he drawled.

"What?"

Kamari swallowed hard when the stranger inched closer. "Do you ramble all the time?"

Had his voice dropped to a lower octave?

She wanted to look away, to hide, but she couldn't. "Only when I'm nervous."

Grey eyes fell on her mouth, and she swore she was witnessing his pupils expand until his gaze became onyx—hypnotic. "Do I make you nervous?"

"In your wildest dreams."

Though she wanted to laugh at his question, she couldn't deny the way her heart started to thunder because of their proximity. The way her breath nearly caught in the back of her throat when he lifted his hand to grab a wild strand of her curls.

"What are you doing?" she whispered. Up close, he was magnificent. Like the sea of stars swirling above their heads. Like the silver moonlight glowing upon his high cheekbones, leaving the faintest trail of starlight like he was made of angelic stardust. Kamari knew he was no angel, though.

"What are *you* doing?" he murmured, his tone like gravel. She frowned, not understanding his question. "Why aren't you moving?"

"I don't know." She was paralysed, starstruck; just like when she had collided with him earlier.

His gaze was fixated on her lips as though he didn't want to look away. "Are you drunk?"

She shook her head. "Not really. Are you?"

"Not really."

His warm hand cradled the side of her neck and suddenly, her surroundings became a blur. Sounds ceased to exist. The world stopped spinning. She could feel her skin burning up beneath his touch—like he had the power to set her ablaze.

Whilst she would usually run away when another person's skin came in contact with hers, there was this bizarre sensation flooding her veins as she allowed herself to feel the callouses marring his palm and stay in his patronising hold.

And for some foreign, uncanny reason, she didn't mind being touched by this stranger.

She forgot where she was. Who she was. She needed to go. She couldn't make a mistake. Couldn't kiss him—because it was obvious, he wanted this. But she was mesmerised by every single inch of him.

His lips gaped, and she allowed her stare to drop to them. Then, he smiled.

God, he was so, so charming with that lopsided grin and that dishevelled hair, lazy strands falling over his brows. She couldn't exactly ignore the way she reacted to his touch: staggered breaths, pounding heart, pebbled skin as he ran his thumb over the curve of her jawline. He caressed her delicately, carefully, as though he was afraid to destroy her. He was tender—a stark contrast to the man she had met less than an hour ago.

"What are you doing?" she asked again, her voice barely audible.

His eyes momentarily flickered back to hers as he leaned closer, and closer, and closer, until she could feel the warmth of his breath disappear atop her lips. "I'm going to kiss you."

Oh, God, she couldn't even think straight. "Why?"

"Do you overthink everything?"

"Yes."

"Don't ask questions," he murmured. His nose brushed hers, and she sucked in a breath. "Can I kiss you?"

She didn't think twice. "Yes."

His lips fell on hers. Tentatively, softly at first. Kamari instantly lost herself in the kiss as she put her hands on his shoulders—like she was urged by the universe to touch him. If she had been standing, she knew her knees would have given up on her.

He cradled the back of her neck, pulling her closer as their lips parted in synchronisation, their tongues brushing and discovering each other's mouths. Her whole body was numb yet alive all at once, sending her mind into overdrive.

She wasn't sure when the kiss had turned into this passionate, feverish battle of tangled breaths, but she almost laughed when she heard his bottle hit the ground as he came to grab her face with his other hand. He moaned in the back of his throat, repeatedly so, causing her to deepen the kiss because those sounds were as addictive as his lips.

She wanted to pull herself closer to him. Wanted more. But she couldn't. Not here, not now, not ever.

She pulled away, breathless, but he didn't allow her to put much distance between their blood-rushed lips.

"Do you want me to stop?" he asked, panting, too.

Her chest rose and fell, and she didn't dare open her eyes. She felt the tip of his nose graze hers, and she heard herself respond, "Keep going."

He kissed her with such passion, like this was the last time he could touch someone. He kissed her with such intensity, domineering her whilst he slowed his pace, tilting her head to kiss her deeply. The leisure strokes of his tongue against hers caused a small whimper of need to escape the back of her throat, and she felt him smile against her mouth.

She felt him everywhere: hands on her hips, her bare back, her neck, her face—corrupting all her senses.

Teeth clashed, tongues danced, breaths entwined.

Kamari had been kissed before, but she had never been kissed like *this*. She had never felt so grounded, yet so high in adoration all at once. Had never felt so ablaze and alive yet frightened because her heart kept threatening to come to a complete stop.

It was just a kiss—a meaningless one. She'd never see that man again, but why was she craving more?

CHAPTER FOUR

♀ *MONTE CARLO, MONACO*

I T WASN'T THE bright morning sun's rays nor the sound
of an alarm clock ringing that had awoken Kamari, but
Indy's chants.

Indigo's voice sounded distant, yet so close and loud at the
same time. "Kamari," she kept saying. At first, it felt like an angel
had been repeating her name in a dream, but she soon realised it
was only reality striking. At that moment, Indigo Bailey was
everything but an angel.

Kamari released a small grunt as her body slowly came back
to life—or rather was forced to, because Indy kept shaking her
arm. Burying her face in the soft pillow, she sighed, then
suppressed a whine of agony as she could feel her pulse throb
against her temple in a painful, scorching rhythm. Fatigue overtook her senses as she kept her eyes shut, not wanting to face the
aftermath of last night's events.

It took a few heartbeats for her to realise she was back at the
hotel.

"Kamari," Indy said again, pulling the covers off her body.

"What?" Kamari grunted, blindly searching for the duvet to tug it over her body again. She turned her back to her friend, silently telling her she wasn't in the mood to chat right now. She needed to wake up first. She couldn't even remember how she and her friends had gotten back to their hotel. Quite frankly, she couldn't remember much from the second part of the night.

She recalled being dragged to a party by Diana and Indy. Remembered stumbling onto a luxurious boat, then colliding with its owner. Memories started to flood her mind, and when she remembered the feeling of soft, demanding, addictive lips on her, she opened her eyes. Like she refused to acknowledge what had truly happened last night. Like she wanted it to be a mere dream.

But her pounding migraine was proof nothing had been a figment of her imagination.

She had kissed a handsome man whose face was now a blur. That wasn't like Kamari. She didn't sneak into random parties; let alone kiss people she didn't know. But even now, as souvenirs felt like a fever dream, she understood she had been drawn towards him, albeit against her will. He'd been able to charm her, and damn her for falling into his trap.

She didn't know for how long they had kissed, but she remembered staring into his eyes, breathless and speechless, his touch lingering on every inch of her skin. Then, his name had been called out. "*I'll find you again,*" he had promised before leaving her alone.

She didn't see him for the remainder of the night. Diana had found her, and they took shots together until everything became hazy again.

"Kamari," Indy pressed louder.

She rubbed her temples. All she wanted was to sleep for a few more hours. "Can whatever you have to tell me wait?"

"No." Her tone was urgent, and when Indy started to bounce excitedly on the mattress, Kamari grabbed a pillow and threw it her friend's way. "Seriously, Kam, wake up. You're going to freak out."

The sound of the door opening resonated, then Diana's voice could be heard. "Did she see it yet?"

"She won't wake up," Indy told Diana.

"Kamari," Diana said firmly. "You're going to want to see this."

Kamari sighed heavily, the sheets rustling as she tossed and turned in the bed. When she opened her eyes, she had to blink several times for her vision to adjust to the bright rays of sunshine peeking through the curtains. She met Indy's wide eyes and Diana's stone-cold face.

"What do you guys want?" she snapped. "Why aren't you guys hungover?"

"Oh, trust me," Diana mumbled. "We are."

"What's so important then?"

Diana gestured to Indy. "I'm letting Miss Sunshine announce the wonderful news."

Kamari didn't know if Indy was on the cusp of breaking into a fit of tears or grinning like today was the happiest day of her life.

"Just get it over with, Indigo." Kamari yawned, waving a hand in the air. "I hate it when you beat around the bush."

Diana slumped down in the armchair in the corner of the room, sipping on her coffee as she, too, waited for Indy to break the news.

Indy arched a brow up. "I didn't know you were into athletes, Kam."

"I'm not."

"So why didn't you tell me you made out with Thiago Valencia last night?"

She felt her heart skip a beat. "Who?"

Indy waved her pointer finger at Kamari's face before having it batted away. "Don't act like you don't know who I'm talking about."

Oh, she knew exactly who she was referring to. Kamari didn't know his name until now.

Kamari was aware she couldn't lie to her best friends. A small crease made its appearance between her brows as she held Indy's gaze. "How do you know?"

Indy and Diana shared a glance that spoke thousands of words. The blonde tapped on her phone before turning the screen towards Kamari.

Kamari felt her world coming to a halt. She ceased to breathe. She couldn't blink. Couldn't muster a single word.

Finally, after what felt like an excruciating eternity, she felt more than awake as jolts of awareness seeped through her veins, so blazingly that she felt like she might combust and then crumble to ashes. Eyes widening, her lips gaped as her hands trembled when she reached for the phone.

"It's a joke, right?" Unable to disconnect her gaze from the screen, she scrolled through the hundreds of pictures displayed before her eyes.

"It's not," Diana replied, sympathy laced in her tone.

No. No. No.

Pictures of her and Thiago shamelessly kissing on the rooftop of his yacht were flooding the internet.

CHAPTER FIVE

📍 *MONTE CARLO, MONACO*

THIAGO WASN'T SURE he wanted to pick his phone up, knowing what kind of storm was about to unwind, ready to strike him with the most hurtful truth and blatant reality.

He watched Leo's name flash across the screen, passing a hand through his hair and tugging at the roots. He knew what was coming his way, and to be fair, he had every right to find an excuse for ignoring all those calls. Thiago didn't want to face the consequences of his actions. Not right now.

"Answer that damned phone," Cal muttered harshly as he entered the living room, dressed in nothing but boxer briefs, his gaze fixated on his own phone.

A beat passed as Thiago watched the device vibrate on the glass table. "I don't want to."

Cal's head snapped, and a scowl instantly drew on his sharp features. "What are you, five? Answer it before I do it myself."

Thiago couldn't help but roll his eyes. "You're *such* a delight, Callahan. Especially in the morning."

Cal only narrowed his eyes into thinner slits, a small grumble of protest rumbling in his throat. He continued to pin Thiago with a glare that urged him to pick up the call. It was evident that his patience was hanging by a very, very thin thread.

Thiago released a huff, grabbed his phone, and hit the green button. "Leo, hey."

"Put me on video," his agent demanded, his tone as chilly as the crisp morning air. "Right. Now."

"Ah, shit," Cal said, finding a seat on the armchair opposite Thiago. Propping his feet atop the coffee table and lacing his fingers behind his head, he smirked at his best friend—as if witnessing his downfall was his greatest entertainment. "Someone's in trouble."

"Fuck off," Thiago mouthed to Cal before clicking on the video call button.

Leo's face appeared on the screen, his gaze hard and striking Thiago with unyielding anger. He was sitting at his bureau, elbows propped atop the expensive oak as his hand rubbed his tense jaw.

"What's up, man?" Thiago tried to appear cool and collected as he leaned back into his sofa, pulling the hood of his jumper atop his tousled curls.

"You know exactly *what is up*," the man answered, using his fingers as quotation marks for the last three words he spat out. "Do you take everything I advise you as a joke?"

Thiago's lips pressed into a thin line. "No."

A scoff escaped Leo's mouth. "Really? Because it looks like you're fucking with my head right now and, Thiago, I'm this"—he shoved his hand in front of the camera, pinching his forefinger and thumb together, leaving a millimetre between his digits—"close to quitting my job."

"Oh, don't be so melodramatic," Thiago drawled. "It's not that bad."

Leo inhaled, then exhaled whilst pinching the bridge of his nose. "Do you take your job as a Formula 1 driver as a joke, too?"

That question triggered the growth of a bubble of fury deep in the pit of his stomach. "Of course not," he replied through gritted teeth.

His agent let a few heartbeats pass by, obviously trying to calm his nerves down. His tongue rolled over the interior of his cheek, his nostrils flaring with anger. He was everything but serene, and Thiago deserved every bit of Leo's wrath after everything he'd put the man through over the past five years.

Leo cracked his knuckles, leaning back into his leather chaise. "You were supposed to put this summer break to use, to get back on track. You know your contract with Primavera Racing is hanging by a loose thread. They don't want to renew your contract, and no other team is interested in you."

"Please," Thiago scoffed, rapidly glancing at Cal to watch the latter shrug nonchalantly. "You know damn well they will renew my contract before the end of the season. I'm the only one who can score points during races."

"You're fifth in the drivers' ranking right now."

Thiago blinked. "I'm aware. Isn't that good enough? I've been struggling with the car, you know that."

"It's not enough," Leo bit out, reaching out to grab a pen to keep his hand occupied. If they had been meeting in real life, Thiago would already have been in the palms of his agent's hands, being shaken to his senses. "Do you even see what they say about you?"

They, as in the media. As in motorsports experts, reporters, influencers, fans.

Thiago answered with a lazy shrug.

"Do you think your reputation does you any justice?" Leo continued bitterly, yet his eyes held some kind of raw emotion— sorrow, pity. "The fuckboy who parties every night, who's seen with a different girl every other week, who doesn't care if he's late to press conferences, or ends the race in tenth place, isn't the Thiago I know."

The athlete clenched his jaw, feeling a lump starting to grow inside his throat. "Yeah, well, that's how the fans love me. They prefer it when I act careless."

"That's what you think?" A disappointed shake of the agent's head was perceptible. "They think you don't care about racing. About your future. They want to see you win another championship, want to see you at the top again, but how could you when you're being photographed making out with some random girl instead of training and focusing on your career?"

"Cut me some fucking slack, man." Thiago rubbed his temple. Thankfully, he had managed to control his hangover way before Leo called. A migraine started to bloom regardless. "It's my last week of summer break. Can't I enjoy a good time with my buddies?"

"Sure you can. But what about all those nights out during the season? God damn it, Thiago. Your career could come to an end, and a talent like yours cannot go to waste. You've been acting like this for over a year, and it has to stop."

A small scoff fled past his lips as he darted his gaze to the ceiling. He let his head fall against the sofa, wanting nothing but to be hit by the coldest shower. He knew Leo was right, but even with the harsh truth, he still couldn't care less.

Thiago was a well-respected and appreciated driver. He was known as ruthless, untouchable, and heartless—mostly when he was behind the wheel of his Formula 1 car. He was aware the first half of the season wasn't his best, though. He knew he could do better. Be better. All he wanted was to be on the first step of the podium after every race again.

"My car is shit," Thiago said then.

Cal snickered from where he sat, smirking behind his cup of coffee, because seeing his friend's despair was thoroughly amusing.

Leo sighed softly. "I know that the car is different from last season, but you should spend your free time working with your car mechanics, trying to solve the problem instead of being the problem. And the issue here isn't only your performance during races, it's the way you act daily."

Thiago frowned, glancing back to the phone, only to find his agent looking at him with deceit. "I care about F1," he said, voice cracking. "You know I do. It's the only thing I love."

"Act like it, then." Leo leaned forward, lips pressed in a thin line as he thought, carefully, about the next words he'd say. "Stop being late to press conferences. Stop moving from girl to girl like they're stupid pairs of socks. You're ruthless and heartless on the track, so you better start acting like this with your women and sort out your priorities. You have the privilege to be one of the twenty Formula 1 drivers—one of the best racing drivers in the world—and you cannot afford to lose your seat. Prove them wrong, Thiago. I know you have it in you to win other championships."

Thiago didn't know what to say. Instead of protesting, instead of saying he was thinking his youth was going to waste away if he didn't party as much as his friends, he stayed silent.

"Listen, man," Leo continued quietly. "I'm sorry for being so harsh with you, but I've known you since you were, like, sixteen. I know the man you pretend to be on camera isn't the guy who was crowned World Champion two years ago. I don't know what goes through your head most of the time since you always keep your pain to yourself—"

"He's right," Cal interjected.

"—but," he paused, then frowned. "Hey, Callahan."

"Hello," Cal said, coyly. Thiago narrowed his gaze on his friend, and the latter flipped him off, a shit-eating grin spreading across his mouth.

Imbecile.

Leo cleared his throat. "But I just wanted to let you know that my job is to keep you on track, to help and guide you towards the right path, and you and I both know that you're stumbling down the wrong way. You might ignore everything they say about you in the press, but I see everything, and it hurts me, too. I'm your friend above all, and I just want to help."

"I know." God, was it difficult to speak through the ball of anger and sadness stuck in his throat. His heart was heavy, and Thiago understood it was time to let go of that pent-up stress.

"Good."

Absentmindedly staring at his coffee cup on the table, memories from last night started to spiral back into his mind. His heart made a somersault, thundered wildly, making him wonder if the sound of his pounding heartbeat was audible to his two friends. The girl, the one who had snuck in with her friends, was the first person on his mind. He breathed in and out, trying to forget about the way her lips had felt against his own, and how she'd been able to make him forget about the world.

His head took over, controlling his every thought. And before he could stop himself, he said quietly, "She was no random girl."

Leo's brows drew together. "Sorry?"

He met his agent's gaze. "The girl from the photo," he clarified. "She wasn't a nobody."

"Okay? I'm not sure why you're telling me this."

Perhaps if Thiago was committed to a relationship, people would start taking him seriously. If settling solely for one woman could guarantee him a future in Formula 1, then taking the risk was worth it.

"She's my girlfriend."

———

ALEX'S FACE was woven with shock. He didn't blink. Didn't breathe. Didn't say a word.

And then, he burst into a fit of laughter, like the news he had just been told was the funniest thing he'd heard. He held his stomach, tears welling in his eyes as he tried to catch his breath, curled in a ball on the armchair by Cal's side.

"Wait." Alex laughed again, waving a hand in the air as he planted his feet on the floor before leaning both elbows on his thighs. "You're fucking with me, aren't you?"

"No," Thiago answered, tone clipped. "I messed up."

"You were convincing, though," Cal added coyly. "You were blushing and all. Leo believed you."

"I was definitely *not* blushing, and I'm sure Leo can see right through me and my white lies."

"That's why he wants to meet your girlfriend at the next race," Alex realised. Silence, then laughter again. Thiago couldn't help but throw a pillow into his friend's face. Alex caught it, swiftly so, before releasing a breath to calm himself down. "Your girlfriend who isn't even aware you're her boyfriend."

"I panicked, okay?" He started pacing back and forth in his living room. Raking his hands through his hair, he could feel his friends' gazes upon him, following each one of his movements. "I don't know what to do."

Cal raised his hand. "I have a suggestion."

Thiago gestured towards his friend, defeated. "I'm sure your idea is brilliant. Please share."

"How about you text your girl and explain the mess you've put her in?"

"I don't even know her name," Thiago admitted, running a hand over his flushed face whilst groaning. "I am so stupid."

"So very fucking stupid," Alex confirmed.

"I know, Myers. Don't remind me." He let his forehead fall against the wall, his eyes shutting close as he thought about a way to fix his mess. "Help me out, guys. I promised Leo she'd be there in Spa. I can't just hire some random girl to pretend to be my girlfriend because the girl's face from the party is all over the internet."

"She's probably freaking out," Alex said, his mouth twisted in a grimace. "I know I would be."

"How do you know?" Cal asked.

"I know her through Indy and—"

"Indy!" Thiago exclaimed, fingers snapping as he turned around to face his baffled friends. "That's it."

"Uh," Alex started, scratching the back of his head. "Are you aware Indy is blonde and your girl has black hair?"

Thiago glared at his friend. "I know that, you arsehole."

Grabbing his phone, he decided to block out the insult Alex threw his way and opened his Instagram account. He thoroughly ignored all his notifications, instantly finding Indigo Bailey in his direct messages.

What else did he have to lose, anyway?

@THIAGOVALENCIA

Hey, Indy. I need your help.

CHAPTER SIX

📍 *LONDON, ENGLAND*

T HE BELL ABOVE the door chimed, and even though Kamari had been so intensely focused on her laptop, she couldn't help but glance at the new incoming customer who had managed to distract her.

The sun had already set, and the café would be closing soon. Kamari had been caught up in so many taxes and numbers that she hadn't noticed nightfall embracing the universe with a warm welcome, golden filaments swimming through a sea of navy and orange before allowing the moon to take over the sky.

"Hi, Charlotte. Late night?" She was a regular customer, who usually came in before catching the underground.

The younger teenage girl lifted her hand in apology. "Can I buy something real quick before you guys close?"

Kamari nodded, letting a small smile spread across her lips. "Take whatever you'd like. It's on the house."

"Thank you, Kamari." She walked to the counter where Kieran was busy cleaning the oakwood. "You're the best."

"She knows," Kieran drawled. Kamari couldn't see her brother, but she took a guess he was rolling his eyes. "Don't feed her ego too much or else she'll become even more unbearable than she already is. Anyway, what can I get my favourite customer?"

Kamari blocked out the sounds surrounding her, the tip of her pen grazing at her lips as she stared at her empty café. Plants hanging from the ceiling, vinyl's decorating a whole wall made of bricks, the farthest corner of the room transformed into a bookshop; it felt like home.

When her phone vibrated in the palm of her hand, she jumped with a start, not expecting anyone to text her. And when she peered at the device, she swore she could feel her heartbeat stop before going back to beating, now hastily.

Breath caught inside her throat, she blinked. Once. Twice. Three times until she was sure she wasn't dreaming—or perhaps, having a nightmare.

@thiagovalencia wants to send you a message.

Oh, God. How did he find her?

It must have been because of Indy.

Not to be dramatic, but Kamari had burst into a fit of tears the moment Indy had told her about the leaked photos. Overwhelmed with both fatigue and stress, she hadn't been able to control the tears streaming down her cheeks.

She had been so reckless. The consequences of that kiss were so disastrous and unexpected that she didn't know how to handle her emotions.

Diana had reassured her—countless times—that nobody knew who she was, and no one would discover her identity. Kamari was her own boss, so she wouldn't have to own up to her faults with anyone at work.

On the internet, hundreds and hundreds of pictures of her and Thiago could be found. All from the same angle though, meaning there had been one paparazzi lurking around Thiago's yacht that night.

Kamari wasn't one to care about others' opinions. But she hadn't been able to stop herself from reading what the media had said about her.

"Thiago Valencia having fun before the end of summer break."

"Mystery girl all over famous racing driver, Thiago Valencia."

"Thiago Valencia spending his evening in great company with a mystery girl, kissing and smiling. Is love in the air?"

There weren't any negative comments aimed at her, per se. Only pure curiosity coming from his fans.

Indy, too, had told her that neither her name nor her profile had been found. She was safe.

At least she thought she was.

Kamari grunted and opened the message Thiago had sent, albeit reluctantly. Her heart was pounding, and she wasn't sure what to expect.

@THIAGOVALENCIA

I found you.

@KAMARI.MONROE

Who are you?

She couldn't help but gnaw on her lower lip as she clicked on his profile—a bad habit she tended to show when anxious or, like at this exact moment, concerned, nervous, and annoyed. She wasn't quite sure why she was so nervous to be interacting with this man. She had kissed him, for fuck's sake.

Her eyes widened in bewilderment at the number of followers he had; over 11 million. She had to admit she had been scared to face reality, and that was why she hadn't dared to look at his profile before tonight. She knew he was famous, rich even, but she wasn't aware he was loved by so many people around the world. She wasn't aware he was a high-performance athlete either.

Her heart threatened to leap out of her chest again when his name appeared on her screen as he replied to her message. She had been so mesmerised by his pictures that she hadn't noticed a full five minutes had gone by since she had answered him.

@THIAGOVALENCIA

No need to pretend, love.

I know you remember me.

@KAMARI.MONROE

Sorry. I don't.

@THIAGOVALENCIA

You're a liar

Drop the act.

Kamari couldn't act as though she didn't remember him. As much as she tried to, she couldn't. She despised him for ingraining himself into her mind when she was supposed to forget everything about that night. Up until now, she had done an effective job at keeping her thoughts busy, until he stumbled back like a whirlwind into her life. Only now, she knew he was forcing himself to come to her, unlike the other night in Monaco when it was the universe's fault for introducing him.

@KAMARI.MONROE

What do you want?

He was so rapid at responding. Was he also waiting behind his screen, pulse drumming and palms of the hands damp?

Kamari didn't pay attention to Charlotte exiting the café and surely didn't hear the question her brother had asked. She could only hear and feel the deafening thrum of her pulse.

@THIAGOVALENCIA

Can we meet?

@KAMARI.MONROE

Already missing me? Cute.

Not in Monaco anymore.

Whatever you have to say to me can be said here.

@THIAGOVALENCIA

And you said I was the conceited one.

Actually, it can't. I need to see you in person ASAP!

It's super urgent.

I'm in London.

I need to talk to you.

@KAMARI.MONROE

I'm busy.

Unlike some people, I don't have a yacht and spend my free time basking in the sun.

I have work and a life that doesn't revolve around you.

This better be important.

Perhaps she was being too harsh with him, but she didn't want to appear like she was interested in this man. She didn't care for him. He was a one-time thing, and if he thought it could happen again, she had to make sure he was misreading the whole situation.

@THIAGOVALENCIA

Here I was thinking you had an attitude only when tipsy… Guess I was wrong.

It is important!!

You know what it's about.

@KAMARI.MONROE

I don't.

@THIAGOVALENCIA

Please?

@KAMARI.MONROE

I didn't take you for someone who likes to beg.

@THIAGOVALENCIA

You haven't seen anything yet.

Wait until you bring me to my knees.

God, was she blushing? How pathetic of her. How foolish.

@KAMARI.MONROE

How about you settle down and have a bit of self-preservation?

@THIAGOVALENCIA

You're feisty

Having a bad day?

@KAMARI.MONROE

You haven't seen anything yet.

It was decent until you messaged me.

@THIAGOVALENCIA

Like I'd believe you. I'm the best part of your day!

Kamari, please.

All I need is ten minutes of your time. I'll buy you lunch.

@KAMARI.MONROE

I guess I can fit you in between meetings tomorrow.

Lunch in Notting Hill @ noon.

I'm only accepting because you're paying.

@THIAGOVALENCIA

Oooooh romantic! Send me the address, love

Can't wait to see you.

Kamari didn't answer the message. All she could do was glance at the clock hanging on the wall behind her brother, watching the minutes pass by as time came closer and closer to meeting with the bane of her existence.

CHAPTER SEVEN

📍 *LONDON, ENGLAND*

A SHADOW APPEARED in a slow motion like dark, brooding clouds ready to submerge the world in an apocalyptic tempest, yet warmth still managed to be cast upon Kamari's frame.

When she looked up at the silhouette blocking the sun's rays from procuring her serotonin, she scowled.

She ignored the uncanny thud inside her chest, like her vital organ had tried to flip upside down at the sight of grey eyes staring down at her. A broad grin was etched on Thiago's lips, a dimple evident on his sun-kissed cheek.

"Hi."

Kamari blinked. Didn't smile. "You're late," she said, shifting to face the empty chair opposite her.

"You're just early." He took a seat right in front of her. "Wow, hide your joy. You look so thrilled to see me," he deadpanned.

His cologne whiffed in the air, and the smell of it was surprisingly pleasant—citrus mixed with a hint of cedar—and already so, so addictive. Kamari observed him settle down as he put his sunglasses atop the bridge of his nose, his beige cap hiding the curls that lay beneath.

Kamari had asked for the farthest, most private table on the terrace. The table for two was in a quiet corner, near a tree, but the sunshine was still shining upon the pair.

"I'm not early." She was. Fifteen minutes early, even. She just fucking hated being late, even to a rendezvous she wasn't willing to go to. A small line made its appearance between her eyebrows as she leaned back in her chair, placing one thigh above the other. "What's with the cap and sunglasses?"

"Trying to go unnoticed," he explained. "Why? Do you want me to take off my glasses so you can look at my gorgeous eyes?"

She rolled her eyes. "I'm all right. Thanks for offering."

He flashed a wide smile. "You're welcome, love."

His grin made it extremely difficult for Kamari to keep her cold façade. She wanted to graze her fingertips over his dimple, wanted to feel the way his lips curved against her own as they—

"Don't call me that." Her tone was clipped as she narrowed her gaze on him.

Kamari took her time to seize him up—just like he was shamelessly looking at her, too. Wearing loose jeans and a plain white t-shirt, he still managed to be effortlessly handsome. She made sure not to linger her stare on his broad neck and strong biceps when he crossed his arms over his sculpted torso.

He was unnervingly beautiful—his face was aristocratic with regal cheekbones and a straight nose. The rest of his features were just as ruggedly handsome, and his dark hair curled right above his ears where a silver hoop was decipherable on one of them; the left one.

He had that kind of corrupting regard—lethal and hypnotising and absolutely mesmerising—that would leave any woman speechless, that would become the object of one's daydreams. Silver eyes, cold as ice, but gleaming with starlight whenever he let his armour down. Thiago Valencia was devastatingly beautiful in every way, and that was why he was the epitome of trouble.

He smirked then, catching the way her gaze had been sauntering over his frame. He looked around as he made himself comfortable in his chair, a small flicker of awe drawing upon his face. "Sweet place," he murmured. "Quiet and private. Smart woman, that you are."

She looked away because the magnolia tree was obviously more interesting than the racing driver facing her.

"How have you been?" His voice was gravel-like, rough, and hoarse. She only had vague memories of the encounter on the yacht, and she definitely didn't recall his voice to be as enthralling as its owner.

Kamari loosened her breath, grabbing the pair of sunglasses resting next to her purse to shield her eyes from the sunlight—and from Thiago.

"Get straight to the point," she demanded, firmly. "What do you want?"

"Relax, Kamari," he murmured lazily, a wicked grin on the corner of his lips. The sound of her name on the tip of his tongue caused shivers to skitter down her spine. "We're having lunch, and I intend on taking all my sweet time to talk to you."

She blinked. "You're paying."

He chuckled and stared at her amusedly, as if her frustration was the only thing that could entertain him. "I know that."

Resting her elbows on the armrests, she started to fidget with the golden ring on her forefinger. "Why are you even in London? Were you that desperate to see me again?"

"*Jesus*," he muttered, leaning back in his seat. "The world doesn't revolve around you."

"That didn't answer my question."

He opened his mouth but didn't get the chance to emit a word as the waiter came to stand next to their table. "Hello. Can

I get you two something to drink as you decide on your main course?"

Kamari exchanged a glance with Thiago. The latter shrugged and jutted his chin towards the menu. "Get whatever you want."

She looked back at the waiter who tried his hardest to display a smile. "I'll have a glass of white."

"Sauvignon Blanc?" he asked, hands clasped behind his back. She nodded. "Perfect."

"Make that two," Thiago said, and the waiter answered with a curt nod before disappearing.

Kamari opened the menu and swiftly roamed her gaze over the suggestions. She often came here with her brother, so she knew every item on the card. Still, she liked to pretend to read it even if she knew what she was going to eat.

Thiago interrupted the silence. "I have a house here."

She looked at him, only to find him deeply focused on the menu, a small line noticeable between his brows. "In Notting Hill?"

"Kensington."

"Oh. So, you live here?"

He gaped at her. "Sometimes."

She scoffed. "What is that supposed to mean?"

He closed the menu and leaned back in his seat. The waiter placed a glass of fresh wine in front of Kamari and gave Thiago the other one. They placed their orders and waited to be alone to carry on the conversation.

Thiago grabbed his wine glass and lifted it up, mischief drawing itself onto his expression. "To new friends."

Kamari rolled her eyes and didn't clink her glass to his. He feigned hurt by putting a hand above his heart.

He took a sip of his beverage, a pleasured hum vibrating in his throat. "I mostly live in Monaco."

With her fingertips, she twisted the small vase that lay between them, so it was perfectly centred on the table. "Why the house here? Apart from the obvious fact you're a Brit, too."

"Aren't you a curious little thing? Well, because I work here."
She blinked, and he continued, voice quieter, softer. "Primavera
Racing's headquarters are based right outside of London."

"Primavera Racing," she echoed in a murmur.

"The team I race for," he explained. The glow of the sun had
a wonderful effect on his skin: golden, ethereal, which made him
look even more enthralling than he already was. "Assuming you
know what I do for a living."

"I know," she said, lifting her glass up to her lips. Despite the
sunglasses hiding his eyes, she could feel the intensity of his scrutiny following each one of her movements, the heat of his gaze as
warm as the sun's.

The corner of his lips tipped upwards. "You did your
research on me, didn't you?"

"I did not." Not really, anyway. Indy had vaguely told her
who he was, and Kamari had scanned his Instagram profile.
"The world doesn't revolve around you."

He chuckled as she parroted his expression then nodded.
Silence fell, but not the kind of uncomfortable one that made
her writhe with uneasiness. The kind of serene silence that made
her realise his company was enjoyable, and that she could spend
minutes—or even hours—just listening to the sounds
surrounding her without having to say a word to Thiago. His
perusal, though, could make her combust into flames.

She hated the power he held over her.

"What about you? You live around here?" he inquired
between two sips.

She shook her head, ignoring the flutter inside her stomach
as he was genuinely trying to make conversation. "I don't give
personal information to strangers."

His mouth curled into another smirk. "I'm no longer a
stranger to you, love. I'm trying to get to know you."

She exhaled a long, irritated sigh. "Are we seriously doing
this?"

"Doing what?"

"Making small talk," she noted coldly. "Just tell me why you wanted to meet and let's get this over with."

He opened his mouth then closed it, as if he had forgotten what he was about to say—or as if he was unsure of his words.

"Listen," he said then, leaning forward. As he grabbed his glass, she couldn't help but stare at the rings adorning his fingers. "I'm sorry about the pictures."

A beat passed, and she swallowed thickly. At this moment, she wished she were able to see the grey of his eyes, just to see how sincere he truly was. But the softness of his tone, the barest crease between his brows, the way he held her gaze despite the shield between their stares, proved how much he meant his words.

"It wasn't your fault." She kept her tone clipped, cold. "Unless you hired paparazzi to—"

"I did not."

And she knew that. From the reaction she had witnessed when she and her friends had snuck into the party, it was evident he didn't want any strangers to interfere with his private life.

"Okay," she murmured quietly. Drumming her red-painted nails atop the table, she kept her glance on her cold drink, watching the condensation fog up the glass. "Are you going to ask to take those pictures down?"

"Is that what you want?"

She replied with a shrug. She had gotten used to the fact her face was now all over the internet and she knew that despite all the effort he'd be making to get everything taken down, archives would remain somewhere.

"Kamari," he said. The way her name rolled on the tip of his tongue made her skin pebble as if a cool breeze had brushed her arm. "Look at me."

She looked up, only to find herself thoroughly disappointed at the sight of his still-shielded eyes.

His chest rose and fell as his hand found the back of his neck to rub the sun-kissed skin. "Do you want those pictures taken down? My agent can do it."

"I don't know," she replied truthfully. She paused before taking a breath. "Yes. People think I'm your girlfriend or something."

His mouth was now twisted in a grimace. "You've seen the things they said about you?"

"How could I not?" she scoffed. Though the comments were made out of curiosity, she hadn't gotten nor seen any negative remark about her appearance. "You can't exactly ignore what people say about you when you've been photographed"—she lowered her voice even though no one could listen to their conversation—"kissing some famous dude."

"Some famous dude," he echoed with a soft snort. "Right."

Kamari cleared her throat and took a gulp of her drink. "Look, Thiago. I don't know what you want from me. If you're here because you think I'm some groupie—or whatever you call it for motorsports—or because I want something from you, then trust me, I am not. I don't even know who you are. So, please, just get straight to the point because I have a schedule to follow—"

"A schedule?" he asked incredulously as if it was the only information he had retained. As if he wasn't fazed by her anger. "It's Saturday."

"Yes, well, some of us have lives outside of work."

A scoff erupted from the back of his throat. "Are you saying I don't have a life outside of racing?"

"I don't know," she retorted, shrugging. "Do you?"

"Of course I do. As a matter of fact, I'm here with you."

Kamari huffed. "Stop beating around the bush. What are you here for?"

The waiter appeared with two steaming plates in hand. His smile was absent, but he gaped at Thiago like he had recognised him. His hands started shaking and he hurried to deposit the meals onto the table before scurrying off.

"Did he recognise you?" Kamari asked Thiago as she draped her napkin on her lap.

Thiago shrugged. "Probably. Sunglasses and a stupid cap aren't enough to go unnoticed."

Kamari's brows raised. "You think?"

A smile spread across his lips, and his expression softened. Grabbing his fork, he jutted his chin towards Kamari's plate. "Eat before we get down to business."

CHAPTER EIGHT

📍 *LONDON, ENGLAND*

T HIAGO WASN'T USED to this. To be in the company of a gorgeous woman who had blatantly told him she didn't know who he was and had admitted she wanted nothing to do with him.

He'd be lying if he said she hadn't hurt his ego.

Kamari had been scowling at him every time he tried to make conversation. Her answers were short and cold, but that only intrigued him even more. He wanted to understand her hesitation in opening up.

As she lifted her nearly empty wine glass up to her lips, her gaze following an elderly couple walking along the road, Thiago couldn't help but observe the way the sunbeam glowed upon her caramel skin. He knew she was a pretty woman, but he hadn't remembered her being so devastatingly beautiful. And infuriating. And enchanting.

He was an observant person, and he had noticed how careful she was being as she ate—how she always made sure to gently deposit her cutlery before wiping the corners of her mouth before answering him, albeit coldly. How she discreetly checked the time on her small watch. How she made sure to always maintain eye contact when he spoke to her even if it was evident she was annoyed to be here.

Still, Thiago didn't mind her company and that feeling of comfort was utterly foreign.

"Why are you looking at me like that?" she asked, a small frown etched between her brows as she placed the napkin back onto her lap.

She was wearing a simple sundress, yet she looked like the most elegant, exquisite creature he'd ever laid eyes on. When he'd arrived, her long curls were floating down her shoulders, but the moment they began eating, she tied those locks into a neat chignon at the nape of her neck.

He cleared his throat, the stem of his glass in between his fingers. "Most girls I take out to lunch or dinner usually settle for a salad."

A cold, hollow laugh erupted from the back of Kamari's throat. "Are you seriously comparing me to the girls you hook up with?"

"You're definitely not like them."

"Is that supposed to be a compliment?"

"Yes."

Thiago didn't know what fascinated him the most: the fact she was aware of how popular he was but wasn't acting on it, or that she showed absolutely no interest in him.

She put her fork and knife on her empty plate, then took her sunglasses off. Thiago swore he ceased to breathe at the sight of her unique, mesmerising green eyes. Her gaze though, was anything but warm. It held a tint of malice, a flicker of frustration that only threatened to spread wider along the edges of her irises.

"Now that I've eaten, will you tell me what all of this is about?"

He tilted his head to the side. "No dessert? I'll get you dessert."

"Oh, right," she chuckled dryly. "What? You'll get one chocolate lava cake for the both of us with two spoons so we can share like a cute little couple?"

The laugh that escaped his throat was out of his control. He shook his head, baffled. "You're so feisty. Do you want to share a lava cake with me, Kamari?"

"No, I don't."

He snorted softly. "That's what I thought. Would you perhaps like another glass of wine?"

"Why?" She peered at her empty glass, an eyebrow arched. "Are you suggesting I might need it to get through whatever you have to say to me?"

"Yes," he replied without missing a beat.

"Should I be scared?" She politely lifted her hand to call the waiter, and when the latter arrived, she kindly asked for a refill.

He shook his head. "Maybe?"

Her gaze narrowed on him. "You don't sound convinced."

"Listen." He paused as he allowed the waiter to refill their glasses, continuously holding her stare. His voice dropped to a quieter tone when they were left alone. "Remember those comments saying you and I are dating?"

Kamari blinked. "Yes."

A few heartbeats passed and, as Kamari watched Thiago with wary eyes, he rubbed the back of his warm neck before loosening a breath.

"Are you nervous?" she asked in a scoff, like she couldn't believe someone like him could be nervous around someone like her. "Don't tell me you're about to ask me on a date."

"I'm not," he grumbled. *Here goes nothing.* He inhaled and spoke as fast as he could, as if by doing so this nightmare would be over as rapidly. "I, uh, kind of told someone you were my girlfriend."

She blinked. Straightened herself. Frowned. Parted her lips in

FALLING OFF THE CLIFF

confusion. Then, she laughed, a hand on her chest. Though genuine mirth didn't glint around her pupils, her laughter was soft and heartfelt yet mocking in a way that made his chest clench with anger. "Oh, that's a good one."

"Don't laugh," he bit out, albeit more aggressively than intended, and leaned forward, palms pressed onto the warm surface of the table.

Her laughter ceased when she noticed his serious expression, her features drooping as well as her hand. "Tell me it's a joke."

A subtle shake of his head, a small tug of his lips into a grimace. "I'm not a pathological liar."

"Yes, you are," she retorted, bewildered. She kept her anger at bay, taking a deep breath in. He could almost hear the questions rattling inside her mind as she scrutinised his face. "Why did you just randomly say I was your girlfriend? Are you insane? Who does that? If you wanted to date me, you could've asked—"

His brows were high with both amusement and curiosity. "Would you have accepted?"

"No. Just—Fix your mess. I don't want to be part of it."

He rubbed his jaw. "It was an accident."

"An accident?" she bellowed, eyes wide, pupils flaring with molten wrath. She then lowered her voice, also leaning forward as her gaze flickered back and forth between his. "An accident? How did that even happen?"

"It was in a moment of panic," he explained with a small shrug.

She threw her hands in the air. Melodramatic, she was. "How?"

"Please, listen to me," he murmured. The people surrounding them were wrapped in their bubbles, but he made sure to keep his tone low yet gentle. "I need your help."

The crease between her brows deepened. "Why?"

Thiago sighed heavily and took his sunglasses off. A flicker of surprise lit her eyes, but he didn't know what caused that surge of astonishment. He scooted closer to the table and took a long, much-needed sip of cold wine. "My future in F1 is hanging by a very, very loose thread, and—"

"And I care because..."

He suppressed a grunt, closed his eyes, and inhaled. "Will you let me speak?"

"Fine." She took her glass in hand and absently waved it in the air. "As you were."

"So sweet," he muttered sardonically. "My future in F1 is compromised. I have a terrible reputation, and all I need is to renew a contract with Primavera. I can win another championship but not with the car I currently have."

Instead of walking away, she took interest in his problem. "What did you do?"

"People think I don't take my career seriously. I'm always seen out partying—"

"Bringing different girls home every night?"

"I'm not like that," he countered. "I swear. But, yes. I'm photographed with girls in my arms. I'm seen in pubs and clubs. My results and performance during the first half of the season have been shitty, but I refuse to give up on my dream. The media thinks I don't care about the championship."

"Well," she said promptly, head tilted sideways. "Do you?"

"Do I what?"

"Do you care about winning another title?"

"Of course, I do."

"You're seeking redemption," she noted quietly. Not a question but rather a statement.

He dipped his chin in a curt nod. "Smart woman."

Kamari nodded and sipped on her beverage. Her features were no longer stricken with anger, now replaced with simple curiosity. "What does this have to do with me?"

"Look." He adjusted his cap and folded his arms over the edge of the table, causing her gaze to drop to his forearms. "They're threatening to give my seat to some rookie. I can't afford to lose my seat. Not now, not ever."

She arched a brow. Pure arrogance. Absolute disdain. "I don't see how that's my problem."

He ignored her remark, holding her gaze with equal defiance. God, he could get lost in those forest green eyes even if they were dark with indifference. "I've been seen kissing girls before and, every single time, I've been criticised because of who those women are. I usually hang out with models, influencers—basically girls who are anything but private. But ever since those pictures of you and me dropped, I've seen nothing but encouraging comments. Have you seen those?" She replied with a shake of her head, as if she were unable to use her voice. "Nobody knows who you are. No one has ever seen you around."

She scoffed softly. "I can't tell if that's supposed to be a compliment."

His tone softened, and he nearly reached out to catch her hand but refrained from doing so. He simply curled his fingers into fists. "Can you do me a favour?"

She blinked, her fingers tensing around the stem of her glass. "What kind of favour?"

"Can you pretend to be my girlfriend for a few weeks? You'd only have to attend a few races, maybe an event or two to be seen with me. Until my agent and everyone around me realise I'm serious about keeping my seat, and that I'm a man who can commit to a relationship. A few weeks is all I need to sign on for at least another season with Primavera."

Kamari's lips parted. "I—"

"I'll even pay you."

She raised an eyebrow. "Do I look like I need money?"

"Jesus," he muttered. "No, you don't. I'm just saying that you don't have to do it freely."

She didn't say a word. Didn't move. Didn't blink. An excruciating moment passed, feeling like an eternity of agony. The drum of his heartbeat was deafening, the sounds of chirping birds a distant melody.

Say something. Say something. Say something.

He knew he was a fool for even asking Kamari to meet him. Alex had told him the plan wouldn't work out, and Cal had only shaken his head in disbelief.

There was no way Thiago could pull this off, and he'd be losing his seat with Primavera Racing. All his dreams would crash into dust because of his reckless decisions. He'd been warned, but he hadn't listened.

After what felt like an endless moment of heavy silence, Kamari only shook her head. He knew what was coming his way. He was ready to face the tornado. "I'm sorry, Thiago. I'm not the person you're looking for here. I can't help you. This is a mess I cannot fix."

Thiago didn't know what to say as shock skittered down his spine, making him tremble with deceit. Deep down, he had wished for Kamari to play along, but he had also expected to be rejected.

She stood up and made sure to leave a fifty-pound bill next to her half-full glass.

"I'm paying," he said, bemused, extending his palm to place it over the back of her hand.

She startled at the touch but didn't retreat at first. Gingerly, she pulled her hand away to tuck a strand of hair behind an ear. He slouched into the back of his seat, not knowing how to process the way his life had become so chaotic in the span of a week.

"It's fine," she replied softly. Grabbing her purse in her hand, she pushed her chair until it was neatly tucked under the table. She then walked towards Thiago, and he couldn't do anything except look up into her eyes. "I don't know you, Thiago. I have no idea who you are, and which version is the real you. But if I can give you a piece of advice, don't ever let others crush your dreams. I think you know your worth, so don't let it be tarnished by other people's expectations. Get a grip and, please, do not contact me again."

CHAPTER NINE

📍 *LONDON, ENGLAND*

RAIN SPLATTERED HEAVILY against the windows, engulfing the world in its darkness, the calamitous clouds rumbling with sizzling, dangerous electricity they desperately ached to release.

Kamari stared absentmindedly at two droplets of water racing against each other as they cascaded down the glass, her chin placed in the palm of her hand.

"Kam," said Kieran as he plopped down on the chair opposite her, a bowl of pasta in hand. It was past eight and they had closed the café an hour ago. "What's that look on your face? Do you think you're in a movie or something?"

She kicked his shin under the table as she met his mocking gaze. Kieran had piercing blue eyes while Kamari's were green, but the resemblance in their features was so strikingly similar that they were frequently mistaken as twins. "What are you on about?"

"You look fucking nostalgic," he mustered between bites. He

tried to mirror her previous actions by putting his chin in the palm of his hand, lowering his brows, and fluttering his lashes as he stared out the window.

Kamari scowled and closed her laptop, abandoning the pen she had been holding on the table, aggressively. "Just lost in my thoughts."

"Oh, whatever, you over-thinker." He rubbed his face, lazily eating his late dinner. "Man, I'm exhausted. Today was hectic. That lady threw a fit at Mila because apparently, she didn't put enough ice in her iced coffee. So, Mila, as kindly and sweetly as ever, made another drink, and that time she had put *too* much ice."

Kamari rolled her eyes. "Some customers can be such arseholes."

"Tell me about it," he muttered. A small line appeared between his brows as he studied his sister's expression. "Where were you today by the way?"

Kamari lifted her glasses to rest them atop her head. "Had a meeting."

"Where?"

"Notting Hill."

"With whom?"

"What are you?" she asked, eyes narrowed. "My father?"

"Your brother," he deadpanned. "So?"

"None of your business."

"Oh," he scoffed, offended. "You're keeping secrets from me now?"

Kamari winced. *You'd freak out if I told you I had lunch with one of your idols.*

Kieran was a big fan of motorsports—Formula 1, Moto GP, Indy Car, Formula E, Porsche GT Cup, Karting, NASCAR, World Endurance; you named it and he'd watched it all. Followed it closely. She was surprised he hadn't stumbled upon a photograph of her and Thiago. He would have mentioned it, would've tormented her for being so reckless, then would've begged for more information about *the* prodigious Thiago Valencia.

The mere thought of him made her skin prickle with irritation.

"It wasn't anything important," she ended up saying.

No matter how hard she tried to keep her mind busy, she couldn't control the way Thiago's face kept flashing inside her head. Those sharp, enticing features stricken with downright deception when she had rejected his offer. That spark of hope that had been alighting his eyes ever so slowly vanishing into stardust.

Kamari wasn't one to linger on the past, let alone be consumed by regrets. She didn't care about Thiago, didn't care if he had a tarnished reputation he needed to polish. But she couldn't exactly ignore the overwhelming feeling that gripped tightly at her chest when she thought about the way she had dismissed his demand. She hadn't been mean, had she? She had every right and every reason to refuse. So, why was she feeling guilty?

She hated that sentiment of culpability.

A loud, disturbing knock brought her back to reality. She jumped with a start, glanced at her brother who was gaping down at his phone, unbothered by the disturbance, then turned towards the front door of the café.

Kamari's heart somersaulted only to end up shattered like a droplet of rain that had crashed against the concrete. The sight of him made her vital organ bleed, and she loathed that feeling. She didn't want to feel that pain today.

He knocked again. Drenched in water, his blonde locks were sticking to his forehead and his clothes were as ruined as the rest of his body.

Another knock.

A grunt rising from the back of Kieran's throat echoed. "Are you not going to open the door for the arsehole?"

Kamari looked at her brother. "No. He can catch pneumonia for all I care."

Kieran wasn't fazed by his sister's words. He peered at the door, lifted his middle finger at James, and let a faux smile spread across his lips. "What is he even doing here?"

"I don't know," Kamari said. "I don't care."

Another pattern of incessant knocks.

Kieran huffed loudly. Standing, he cradled his bowl to his chest like a precious object. "Go talk to him or else I'll open the door and unleash the beast on his face. I'm famished so I'm getting seconds."

"Thanks for nothing," she muttered, which only earned a mumble of incoherent words in response as Kieran disappeared into the back kitchen.

A defeated sigh fled past her lips. Kamari wrapped her cardigan around herself and padded towards the front door, not bothering to turn the main lights on. James' face was contorted with sorrow, but when he saw Kamari approach, his eyes lit up as he allowed a smile to take over his features.

Begrudgingly, she turned the keys, though she debated whirling around and leaving her ex-boyfriend to his misery.

A swirl of cold air, summer rain, and pain rushed towards her as she opened the door, only letting it ajar.

"What do you want?"

James' shoulders slumped as he exhaled. He was looking up at Kamari with such sorrowful eyes that she was impressed by his act. He blinked, letting a drop of water fall from his lashes onto his cheek, then pushed his wet strands of hair away from his forehead.

"Hey," he said, breathless.

Kamari stood one step higher, and she enjoyed that overpowering sensation she finally had over him. "Don't 'hey' me," she sneered coldly. "What do you want?"

James flickered his gaze behind her head. "Let me in."

"No."

"But it's raining," he noted. "I'm drenched."

Kamari suppressed the urge to roll her eyes. "Oh, cry me a river."

"Okay then." He cleared his throat. "Can I talk to you?"

"Depends," she said, tilting her head to the side. "What are you going to say? The same thing over and over again? This is getting old, James."

He clenched his jaw at the sound of her condescending tone. "You haven't been answering my texts."

"And?"

"Nor my calls."

"I blocked your number."

James tugged at his hair, his head ever so slightly shaking. "I fucked up, Kam. I miss you."

Her chest tightened. She wanted to look away. To turn around. But she held his gaze, hoping he could see the fire burning in her eyes. "You don't."

"I made a huge mistake," he murmured, pained. "We can fix this."

Her grip around the doorknob tightened as she frowned. "First of all, there is no 'we' anymore. You made that same mistake over five times, if not even more. I don't think you can call that a fucking mistake."

A hollow chuckle rose from the back of his throat. The rain kept pouring down, thunderbolts cracking overhead as they matched Kamari's burning anger. He gestured towards her. "Come on, Kam. You're nothing without me. You still love me. I know you do. Let me in so we can talk and fix everything. We were so good together. We had such a bright future ahead of us."

She gritted her teeth, thinking it'd be painful to say those next words, but it felt more relieving than anything. "I don't love you, James. I stopped loving you when I caught you with your co-worker the first time. I stopped loving you when I realised you were playing me as you continued to cheat on me. I stopped loving you when you threw our five-year relationship to waste for some younger girl."

James swallowed thickly. He took one step forward, and she nearly closed the door in his face. "It's over between Lina and me. No one is like you, Kamari."

"I don't care," she snapped harshly. "You deserve to be alone, you scumbag. You don't get to come here, act like everything's okay, and try to emotionally manipulate me again! I won't fall into your trap. Leave." Her voice cracked and she hated how vulnerable she was becoming. He didn't deserve her tears, her pain, let alone her time. "Don't make me ask you again."

He took another step forward, his hand swiftly catching her wrist. His fingers were cold, his touch sending shivers down her spine. "I miss you. I'm miserable without you. I'm nothing without you."

She tried to retreat her hand from his grip, but was unsuccessful. She glanced at his slender fingers encircling her wrist, a surge of abhorrence washing over her. "Let me go."

He tightened his grasp. "Not until you hear me out."

"Don't touch me," she spat, wriggling her arm. Though she stayed calm and collected, her insides were everything but. She could feel the fury rushing through her system. Could feel the bile rising as those filthy hands touched her like he hadn't laid a hand on another woman before coming here. "Let me go. Now."

A cruel, vicious smirk played on the corner of his wet lips. "You're as feisty as I remember. I love that about—"

And then, she swore she stopped breathing when she heard a deep, hoarse voice rumble through the loud anger of the heavens. "She told you to step away."

His silhouette cast a dark, dangerous shadow over James' frame. Kamari used the momentum of surprise to step away from the punishing grip.

Thiago stepped out of the darkness like the devil emerging from the depths of Hell, but she couldn't help but think he was a divine being at this very instant. He grabbed James by the shoulder, forcing the latter to take a step backwards, his dark gaze strained on Kamari's face. "You're in my way, buddy."

Everything happened so fast; one moment James was gaping incredulously at Thiago, ready to raise his voice at whoever had decided to interrupt him. The next moment, Thiago was standing next to Kamari, draping an arm around her shoulders and pulling her close to his side.

"Hey, baby," he murmured gruffly against her temple, loud enough for James to hear. "Sorry, I'm late. You know how my mother is when I visit."

Kamari blinked, peering up at Thiago. She wasn't sure if she was breathing. Wasn't sure how her knees hadn't given up on her yet. He pressed her with a look, and within the shades of grey present in his eyes, she could read what he wanted to tell her: *play along.*

She then leaned into his side, suppressing the urge to shiver, and threw him a tight-lipped smile. "It's okay. We were waiting for you."

Thiago nudged his chin towards James' chest, tracing a route of detestation over his face with a lethal glare. "This guy bothering you?"

"He was just leaving," Kamari muttered. Her shoulders were tense, her body shaking with unyielding wrath. Thiago felt her despair and, ever so softly, rubbed the pad of his thumb over her shoulder blade—light-feather, nearly nonexistent.

James parted his lips in confusion, but no sound escaped. He looked at Kamari, then at Thiago, and back at Kamari. Thiago pulled her nearer to his side, letting her soak his warmth in.

"I'm not done with you," James said at last. She noticed how he had curled his hands into fists. How hurt and betrayal were etched on his face. He deserved to feel every shred of pain because that was how he had made her feel for endless, excruciating months—years, even.

A scoff of disbelief fled past her lips. "You should be, because I'm completely done with you."

Grabbing Thiago's wrist, she pulled him inside, locked the door, and tugged the blinds down. Her heart battered in inconsistent, wild beats as she walked further inside until she was out of sight. When she turned around, she observed Thiago watch James get into his car. He didn't move, didn't yield. It was only when James' car was long gone that he allowed himself to pivot, locking his stormy grey eyes with Kamari's.

"Don't tell me you used to date that prick," he gritted, tone clipped, as he gestured at the door.

She rolled her eyes. "Fine. I won't tell you."

Thiago opened his mouth then closed it, as if the words that were coating the tip of his tongue suddenly disappeared. "Did he hurt you?"

"What?"

He took long, furious strides towards her. She couldn't look away from him. Couldn't do anything except observe his sharp features hardening with some kind of emotion she couldn't quite decipher. Standing right in front of her, his eyes were molten with anger. But his fury didn't look like it was directed towards her.

His gaze flickered down, and that was when she realised she had been absentmindedly rubbing at her wrist—the one James had held so tightly that it could have cut her blood's circulation.

She released her grip to bury her hands in the pockets of her cardigan, but Thiago didn't allow her to do so. Instead, he caught her hand and brought it up at eye level. She ignored the tingly sensation spreading from the tips of her fingers towards the rest of her body. Though he was holding it, his touch was careful and delicate—like he was scared to shatter her.

She couldn't fathom why his caress was coaxing. Why she didn't retreat her hand.

His jaw clenched as he gaped down at her wrist. His voice dropped an octave, and she swore the thunder rustling amongst the cataclysmic clouds was in perfect sync with his wrath. "Did. He. Hurt. You."

Kamari swallowed. Fury laced his tone like lethal poison, causing shivers to race down her spine, and his touch was as feather-light as ever, yet punishing with a delicacy she didn't deserve. "Why do you care?"

"Just answer the damned question." He still didn't meet her eyes, a deep frown now settled on his eyebrows. "Yes or no, Kamari?"

"Yes," she admitted quietly. "But I'll be fine. It was nothing."

"That wasn't nothing," he bit out frustratingly, his brows knitted together, and he studied her skin under the dim light of the café.

"Thiago," she sighed tremulously. The sound of her voice forced him to look into her eyes, and his shoulders released the tiniest bit of tension. "I'm alright. I can stand up for myself."

Finally, he let go of her hand and she suddenly felt cold. The corner of his lips curved into a smirk. "Yeah, I saw that."

In the distance, she could hear loud music emerging from the kitchen, indicating Kieran was lost in his own world. She took a step back, making Thiago frown but he didn't comment on it.

"What are you doing here?"

His smirk only grew. "Came to rescue my lady in distress, of course."

Her expression was blank. "Wrong answer. Try again."

"Alright." He reached into the pocket of his hoodie. "You forgot this when you left."

He handed her pair of sunglasses, gently. A bit too aggressively, she took hold of it, crossing her arms over her chest, as if doing so would shield herself from the whirlwind that was Thiago Valencia.

She bit the interior of her cheek and counted three heartbeats. "You could have kept them."

A soft chuckle rose from his throat. "Thank you, but they're not my style."

Kamari's eyes narrowed whilst she took in his demeanour:

dishevelled hair tousled by the stormy weather, wet jumper as if he had walked under the rain before arriving at the café, flushed cheeks but she didn't know the cause of this sudden crimson colour coating his cheekbones.

"You came here just to give these back to me?" An eyebrow was arched, curiosity laced to her tone.

He shrugged. "Yep."

"How'd you find me?"

He pressed his lips in a thin line, and she understood. "Indigo," they said in unison.

"She's impossible," she muttered to herself with a shake of her head.

Thiago slipped his hands into the pockets of his jeans, taunting her with a vicious smile. "This is the moment you usually thank me."

A huff escaped her mouth. "I was getting there."

"No need."

A low whistle reverberated as he scanned the room, walking towards the counter with his gaze settled on the plants hanging from the high ceiling. After having encountered her ex-boyfriend, all Kamari wanted was to be alone and perhaps let the tears that had been threatening to break free cascade down her cheeks. But instead, she found herself stuck with this man and in no control of her emotions.

"So, you're the owner of Dawn's Café?" He was in awe, his eyes glinting beneath the dim light. "Indy told me you've dedicated most of your life savings for this place."

She leaned her hip against the closest table. "How much did Indy tell you about me?"

He peered at her from his shoulder, an idle finger running over the vintage jukebox stationed in the far-left corner of the room. "Don't worry, she didn't reveal any of your deepest and darkest secrets. I wish she had, though."

"Trust me, there's nothing interesting about me."

Whilst most people would certainly freak out to be in Thiago's company, she was thoroughly unfazed by his presence. Still, she couldn't ignore the way her body reacted to him when he glanced at her, his perusal feeling like sparks upon her skin. So, she took a seat, glancing outside only to notice the downpour had ceased.

She stared at her pair of sunglasses, a frown drawing on her eyebrows. "Is there something you want from me, Thiago? I thought I had made my decision clear."

His voice was low, deep—a hum of power caressing the shell of her ear. "It was crystal clear."

When she peered up at him, she felt her breath catch in the back of her throat. His back was turned to her as he tugged behind his neck at the collar of his jumper, pulling the wet piece of clothing off his torso. The shirt he'd been wearing beneath rose, exposing lean, strong, and hard back muscles, contracting and flexing with each one of his motions.

As though he could feel the intensity of her scrutiny over his silhouette, he pivoted. She darted her gaze away, her cheeks unmistakably heated up. She knew he'd caught her red-handed because she could see his stupid, smug smirk from the corner of her eye.

"Do you mind?" She brought her attention back to him as he gingerly draped his hoodie atop the back of a chair.

She waved her hand. "Not at all. Make yourself at home."

Her tone was sardonic, but it made his grin widen. Then, he seated himself directly opposite her, strong arms folded across his broad chest, shadows lurking around him. "Sweet. Is someone else here?"

She nodded, a subtle jut of her chin towards the kitchen. "My older brother. He works with me. He's probably busy cleaning around."

As he pushed dark, wet strands of hair away from his forehead, a singular, rebellious one toppled over his brow. She forced herself not to gape at his displayed biceps, holding that gaze that had cleared from the previous storm she had glimpsed at. She had never seen eyes so raw with emotions, so easy to read within the unique colour. "Do you have any other siblings?"

Was this man genuinely interested in her? "I'm not playing 21 questions with you."

He leaned forward, putting an elbow atop the table and resting his chin in the palm of his hand. "How about 31 questions?"

"No."

"Okay." He clicked his tongue on the roof of his mouth. "Are you not going to offer me something to drink? What's your specialty? Is everything homemade?"

She rubbed her temple, feeling a migraine starting to bloom like undesirable weeds. "Tell me, Valencia. What's the other reason you showed up here tonight?"

A soft scoff rose from the back of his throat. "Is it so hard to believe I have no other intentions besides returning your pair of Bottega Veneta sunglasses? Surely a woman like you can't simply leave an accessory that costs over three hundred pounds behind."

She blinked. He was right, but she hadn't even noticed she'd forgotten them. She had left lunch with a hazy cloud of turmoil enveloping her, and when she had arrived at the café, her team was in desperate need of her help. There was no room for distractions.

"Actually," she said, "yes."

A heavy sigh fled past his lips. "Okay, fine." He scratched the back of his neck. "Look, I don't do this—ever, but I really wanted to apologise for the way I came onto you with my situation. I didn't mean to make you uncomfortable. We barely know each other, and I understand how weird it must have been from your point of view. All I want is a second chance."

"A second chance?"

"To start over with you. We started on the wrong foot— more than once I believe."

"Just that?" she asked. "Nothing else?"

He shook his head in response.

"You're not going to ask me *again* to pretend to be your girlfriend?"

A beat passed, then he smirked. "Unless you want me to ask you again?"

She rolled her eyes. "Please don't."

Thiago lifted his hands in semi-surrender. "I'm just saying—just in case—that the offer still stands."

She brought her lips in a pout. "Haven't found someone who could fill in for me?"

"Obviously not," he deadpanned. "You're incomparable."

"You're lying. There are hundreds of girls out there who'd love to date you."

"But they're not you," he supplied with a smirk.

She arched a brow. "You don't even know me."

"I want to."

"Don't try," she said. "I'm not interested."

"I'm serious, though." His voice sounded like spun sugar, honey—warm and setting her skin ablaze with the soft echo of his words.

"Now you're just being nice to me and hoping I'll help you."

He shook his head, his eyes flickering over her face as if he was trying to ingrain a photograph of her features into the back of his mind—like it was the last time he'd see her. "I'm just telling the truth."

She couldn't help but drop her gaze to the small plant placed in the centre of the table because she didn't want him to see the dismay glinting in her eyes. Absentmindedly, she rubbed the hem of her sleeve between her thumb and forefinger, focusing on her surroundings instead of the man who was watching her with tender, curious eyes.

She heard Kieran sing loudly, and she sucked in a breath as realisation hit her like a lightning bolt.

"Thiago," she murmured, not recognising how soft her tone had become.

"Yeah?" he replied with equal softness.

He looked absolutely mesmerising hidden in the shadows of her café—like he belonged there. She couldn't believe she was about to ask this. Couldn't even control her own body as the words slipped out of her mouth.

"Kamari?" he called out when she didn't speak.

The loud thumping of her heart was deafening. Good. She wouldn't hear herself as she asked, "If we do this, can you do me a favour?"

CHAPTER TEN

⚲ *SPA-FRANCORCHAMPS, BELGIUM*

T HE SMELL OF burnt rubber whiffed through his nostrils, despite the balaclava and helmet covering his face, and the heat coming off the circuit followed him like an invisible cloud of speed. Gloved hands were tightly gripping the steering wheel, his foot pressing down onto the throttle as he raced through Kemmel before decreasing his pace as he turned into Les Combes. His vision was entirely focused on his route, his surroundings and almost-full grandstands a colourful blur. He knew the circuit and its shape by heart. He could drive through the track of Spa-Francorchamps blindfolded.

"How does the car feel?" The race engineer's voice rang through Thiago's earphones.

"Feels okay so far," Thiago answered Luke in a breath as he passed through Malmedy's corner.

"Just okay?"

It was rather unusual to see the sun shining in Spa. Thiago

was used to coming back from summer break to a cloudy, rainy track, usually preparing himself for a wet and chaotic race.

"I feel like I can't reach top speed like I want to," he replied just as he passed his teammate who had just driven out of the pit lane. "Agility feels perfect, though."

"That's good." A rustling sound was followed by a few incoherent mumbles between Luke and another engineer. "Box on the next lap. We'll go out for a sprint after looking at the stats if we still have time."

"Copy."

The second half of the season was Thiago's personal favourite because he would race on some of his most-liked circuits: Spa where he won his first race his rookie year—the year he'd been identified as ruthless and heartless by multiple sports journalists; Monza where he'd won a race the day after his father's death; and Abu Dhabi where he'd brandished his trophy high in the air, claiming his World Champion title just two years ago.

And that was this year's main focus: secure his second championship. Get back on top. He was aware it was going to be a hard play, knew he had to push his limits to reach his goals. Surrounded by other ruthless and talented drivers, driving a car that had been struggling with the new regulations since the beginning of the season, Thiago wasn't sure if he could brandish the trophy in a few months. He had hope though, and he wouldn't yield just like that.

The second half of the season was like a fresh start. He had had four weeks to breathe, party, and disconnect. But now that there were only nine races left before the end of the season, he couldn't take the risk of failing. Couldn't lose the only thing he'd ever loved.

He drove through the pit lane slowly, the sun's rays blocked by the visor of his helmet. The moment he stopped in front of his garage where four mechanics dressed in red suits were waiting for him to shut the engine off, he loosened his breath.

There was nothing like driving a Formula 1 car. Nothing like the thrill of the speed, the feeling of the heat coming off the circuit, the exhilaration and frissons jolting through his body as the world blurred around him. There was nothing like the universe of Formula 1. It was his life, and he'd make sure it would remain his future.

Once Thiago got out of the car, he received a few pats of encouragement on his back. He walked towards Luke, taking his helmet and balaclava off. Luke was furiously typing on his keyboard, a frown on his face, and didn't so much as glance at the driver when he approached.

"Just tell me the bad news now," Thiago demanded coldly.

Cal was now standing beside him. Gently, he grabbed the helmet from Thiago's hands but stayed by his side.

Luke pivoted and slid his red headphones off his head to put around his neck. He wasn't one to beat around the bush and said, "We might need to change the power unit."

"Again?" Cal asked, baffled.

Thiago only nodded, jaw clenching for a flickering heartbeat. "That is going to cost me a penalty grid."

Luke held his gaze. "Yes, but it's better to change it now rather than later during the season. We still have the third session of free practice tomorrow morning, so we'll wait to see the car's performance and make the change then."

He pushed a strand of hair away from his forehead. "Right before quali?"

"Yep. On a lighter and happier note"—Thiago scowled at the sound of Luke's too-forced, joyous voice—"you made the fastest lap during this practice session. Now you need to be on pole so you won't have to start too behind because of the penalty. The worst that can happen is that you'll start sixth. Actually, now's the moment to get your shit together if you want to win this championship."

A surge of anger seeped through Thiago's veins. He took a step forward, the roars of racing cars being tested by other drivers on the track zipping in the background. The loud noise of engines speeding wasn't as deafening as his thrumming, angry heartbeat. "This is a team work, Luke. You want me to win? Then get to fucking work and build me a perfect car. We spent the last week testing on the simulator and we know what's wrong with the car. Get me a perfect balance between agility and top speed, and I'll get you that championship medal. Work overnight if you fucking have to, but don't tell me what *I* have to do."

Luke's features flickered drastically—from a faux smile to a sneer. "Don't be such a dick, Thiago. You're on TV."

"I'm well aware," he said, all indifference and nonchalance. "Get to work."

Luke dipped his chin in a small nod, though he held Thiago's angry gaze. "There's still fifteen minutes left before the free practice session ends. Don't you want to go out for another few laps?"

He turned on his heel, accidentally bumping into Cal's shoulder. "No."

Thiago ignored the mumble Luke muttered under his breath as he walked towards the exit in the back of the garage that led to the paddock, where Primavera Racing's motorhome was. Some fans were walking around the paddock, their VIP passes hanging loosely around their necks. Some were photographing Thiago as he passed by them, others were begging for his attention and demanding pictures. He ignored them, rushing hastily towards shelter.

Cal caught up to him, a firm hand grasping his shoulder before applying pressure on his tense muscles. The paddock was flooded with sports reporters, mechanics, workers, and engineers from all ten teams. The atmosphere during a race weekend was incomparable, sizzling.

"I know you're known as the ruthless, heartless, untouchable driver, but you need to be nicer to your team."

Thiago glared at Cal, wriggling himself out of his punishing grip. "How is that going to make them work harder?"

"They're human beings just like you," Cal spat. "You know you have to do better if you want to keep your seat."

Thiago rolled his eyes as they stepped inside the motorhome. "They're just bluffing. All of them. I'll keep my seat. They'd be insane to let me go."

"They will let you go if you don't focus, Tito." Cal lowered his voice and handed Thiago his helmet. "I might be your physiotherapist, but I'm also your best friend, and it's killing me to see you so indifferent about the way everyone talks shit about you. We're thirteen races into the season and I don't think you're realising the clock is ticking."

Thiago's breathing became shallow because he knew Cal was right. Truth was, he was scared to make another mistake. "Whatever. Let's go on a run around the circuit when the sun is setting down."

THIAGO WASN'T SURE if this was a good idea.

Saturday had come, queues of Formula 1 lovers forming lines of different hues as they wore their favourite team's colours whilst waiting to enter the circuit. Saturday was the most anticipated day of the weekend—after Sunday, of course. It was qualifying day, meaning all twenty drivers would race, trying to make the fastest lap time to determine their position on the starting grid for Sunday's race.

Thiago had to drive the fastest lap to be on pole position. But even if he made it, he'd start the race further down the line because of the changes his team had made to the car. Every driver was allowed to change their power unit three times during the season, but making such changes meant receiving penalties. That was one of the many rules of Formula 1.

Phone in hand, his knee bounced up and down as he kept his

gaze focused on the screen, waiting for it to light up and indicate he'd received the so-anticipated response he'd been waiting for.

"Did she bail on you?"

Leo settled on the chair opposite Thiago, a cup of freshly brewed coffee in hand. They were sitting in the motorhome, sounds of chatter and laughter echoing in the background. Qualifying would start at four p.m., so Thiago had over three hours to sit and relax, talk with his strategist, and socialise with guests and other people who worked for Primavera Racing.

Thiago shook his head, leaning back in his chair. "She's arriving with Ava." Well, at least he thought she was. "She's been busy with work and couldn't come until now."

Leo lifted an eyebrow, doubtful. "Can't wait to meet her."

"She's the best," he said with a forced smile. *She's the devil.* It was a Herculean effort not to let bitterness weave into his tone. "You'll love her."

Leo's grin was nothing but a vicious display of pearly-white teeth. He adjusted the collar of his linen shirt with his free hand, gaze narrowing on Thiago's face. "I'm sure I will. You have the tendency of seeing women with, how should I say, particular styles." Models. Influencers. Singers. Actresses. All of them being the exact, stark opposite of *her.*

Thiago's jaw clenched. "She's nothing like them. I assure you."

Leo shrugged. "If you say so."

Cal took a seat next to Leo and clapped him on the back with a force that made the hot liquid in the agent's cup rattle like tidal waves. "What are we gossiping about?"

Leo gaped at Cal who was wearing his red Primavera polo. "Have you met Thiago's girl?"

It was evident Cal was refraining from bursting out in laughter, but he only let his lips curl into a polite smile. "Yep. Lovely girl. In fact, Alex told me she was here with Indy."

Thiago's heart started to hammer erratically, and he hated

FALLING OFF THE CLIFF

how vulnerable he could become by the simple thought of Kamari Monroe.

He didn't know if he could pull this off.

He didn't know why he thought this was a great idea to begin with.

All he needed to focus on was winning a championship, on securing another multiple-year contract with Primavera Racing, and now he was allowing himself to be distracted by a girl who had zero interest in him.

His phone vibrated in the palm of his hand, and some kind of wave of relief coursed through his veins when he saw her name.

@KAMARI.MONROE

I hate you so much.

His grin was all mischief and confidence—a king's smile, triumphant, on the right path to redemption.

"She's here."

CHAPTER ELEVEN

📍 *LONDON, ENGLAND*

"WHAT DO YOU wear for a Grand Prix?"

Slowly, Indigo turned around. Her blue eyes were wide, her mouth nearly falling agape at the sound of Kamari's question.

The door slammed behind Kamari as she walked further into Indy's flat, the smell of Italian aromas swivelling in the small kitchen. She instantly reached for the bottle of wine placed atop the island and poured herself a much-needed glass.

"Why?" Indy asked slowly, narrowing her gaze on Kamari.

Kamari sipped on the Pinot Noir whilst keeping her gaze on the table where her friend had set up three plates, noticing the scented candle wasn't placed in the exact centre. A heartbeat later, the door to Indy's flat opened then shut.

Diana's voice boomed, making Kamari pivot. "Who called an emergency dinner on a Sunday?"

Kamari rolled her eyes. "It was me, grumpy. Not like you were busy doing something today, anyway."

Diana shrugged, soon finding a seat on the sofa after kicking her shoes off. "Look, Sundays are meant to stay at home, in a set of silk PJs, hair and face masks on, and Gilmore Girls playing in the background."

"Wow," Kamari deadpanned. "I see where your priorities stand. Don't worry, I'll make this quick so you can cross the road and put your silk PJs back on."

Indy interrupted, her dulcet voice coaxing and full of mirth. "I'm happy to cook for my besties. But yes, Kam, why the emergency SOS?"

With a heavy sigh, she sunk into the velvet sofa beside the redhead, ignoring the glance her two friends exchanged. She thought gingerly about how she'd announce the news to them all the while trying to haze her mind by taking another sip of her beverage.

"I made a mistake," she said quietly.

Silence.

Indigo took the lasagna out of the oven.

Diana shifted to face Kamari.

"Pardon me?" Diana asked, baffled. "You're Kamari Monroe. You don't make mistakes."

"But I did," she whined. Nearly sobbed. "I'm so stupid."

"What did you do?" Indy was concerned, her brows furrowed and her eyes searching for some sort of answer on Kamari's face. She sat on the armchair opposite from the pair, bottle of red in hand just in case she'd have to refill Kam's glass.

"You guys are going to take me for a mad woman," she mumbled, staring at the vibrant sunflowers blooming in the vase set on the coffee table.

Diana rolled her eyes, dramatically so. "Don't be silly. I bet you did something *crazy* like, I don't know, forgetting to water your plants for a week."

"Di," Indy warned. "Don't be mean."

"What?" Diana exclaimed, lifting her shoulders in a small shrug. "Kam isn't offended. She knows I'm right."

Kamari wasn't sure how to tell her friends she had made a bargain with the devil. She could still picture that sparkle of hope in his eyes that had transformed into a fire when she had asked for a favour in return. They hadn't had the chance to elaborate on the plan though, because Kieran had stumbled into the café, eyes wide and mouth agape at the sight of Thiago Valencia chatting with his sister. Thiago had stayed for over an hour, and all Kamari had done was listen to him and Kieran exchange about Formula 1.

When he had left, all he had said to Kamari was, "*I'll text you.*"

She had been ignoring her brother's questions ever since.

And Thiago hadn't texted her yet. She wasn't waiting for his message, anyway.

"Okay." She crossed one leg over the other, setting her wine glass down. "I had lunch with Thiago Valencia."

Both their faces were stricken with shock, their eyes round and wide. "What?" they exclaimed in perfect harmony.

"When?" Indy asked, sitting on the edge of her seat and nearly bouncing with excitement.

"Seriously?" Diana whispered as if she couldn't believe it.

She started from the moment Thiago had messaged her, to their meeting in Notting Hill and the particular deal he wanted to seal with her. She talked about her encounter with her ex-boyfriend, and how Thiago had magically appeared and rescued her like a knight in shining armour.

By the time she finished her monologue, Indy had poured herself and Diana a glass of wine, the both of them now staring at Kamari with parted lips, bewildered.

Kamari fell against the back of the sofa and hid her face in her hands, shaking her head in exasperation. She had to focus on work, on opening another café, and she was allowing herself to be distracted by some F1 driver. At what cost?

Diana was the first one to move. She placed the back of her hand on Kamari's forehead, concerned eyes searching her face. "Do you have a fever?"

"No," Kamari huffed, batting her friend's hand away.

"Are you okay?"

"Yes." She rolled her eyes, crossed her arms over her chest. "I know it's unusual behaviour of me—"

"That's bat shit crazy, even!" Diana exclaimed. "You don't even go on dates with guys who ask for your phone number."

"It wasn't a date. I'm not interested in him."

"Liar," Indy said with a giggle. "You totally did not kiss him in Monaco."

"We were drunk," Kamari declared, reaching over to grab her glass.

"And were you drunk when you agreed to date him for PR?" Diana inquired mockingly.

Kamari exhaled. "We agreed on going to three events together: next weekend's Grand Prix, a charity event organised by the F1 committee—"

"The FIA," Indy corrected.

"Yeah, that. And my brother's birthday party."

Diana's mouth twisted in a small grimace. "James is going to be there as well, isn't he?"

Kamari nodded. "Probably with his new girlfriend."

"What a dick," Diana muttered.

Her two best friends weren't fond of James. Never had been. What saddened Kamari the most was that it took her multiple years to realise he had been playing her all along.

She couldn't care less about him now, though.

"Okay, but I have to ask," said Indy. "Are you doing this because of James?"

Kamari shrugged coyly. "I know I don't have to prove anything to anyone because I'm happy without him. But yes, I just want to show him I can love and be loved after ending things with him. I want him to leave me alone."

She turned to Indy, ignoring how excited and happy she looked at this exact moment. She didn't know what thrilled her friend most; Kamari getting out of her comfort zone or Kamari about to make the biggest mistake of her life by fake dating Thiago Valencia. "So? What do you wear for a Grand Prix?"

Indy stood up. "You've come to the right place, babe."

🏁 SPA-FRANCORCHAMPS, BELGIUM

"Are you nervous?"

Kamari cast a glare in Indy's direction. "You wish."

A chauffeur had picked them both up at the airport, and they were now stuck in traffic. The queue of cars that led towards the racing circuit felt endless, and Kamari couldn't help but bounce her knee as the faint melody of a Taylor Swift song echoed in the background.

Indy was tapping on her phone, most likely texting Alex Myers to update him on their whereabouts. "It's okay if you are."

"I'm not."

Indy's gaze collided with hers and she arched an eyebrow up. "I've known you my whole life, Kamari. I know when you're lying."

She rolled her window down, letting the warm breeze caress her face. Cars further down the line honked—as if being impatient would solve every problem in the world. "What if they don't like me?"

"Who's 'they'?"

Kamari shrugged. "Valencia's agent. His team principal. His fans."

A small snort fled past Indy's nose. "First things first, everyone likes you, Kam. Just smile and it'll be fine. Secondly, I think Thiago's a big boy and can make his own decisions. Who he hangs out with shouldn't be anyone else's business but his."

Kamari nodded and dug into her purse to retrieve a tube of gloss. "You're right."

She scoffed. "Of course, I'm right. I'm Indigo Bailey." She then clapped her hands, a beam drawing itself on her lips. "I'm so excited. I can't believe we missed all three free practices, though."

"Sorry for scheduling meetings with the bank," Kamari drawled. "Next time I'll try to be free during all events of the weekend and not work during free practices."

Indy scowled at her best friend. "No need to be all sarcastic and grumpy today."

"Sorry," Kamari murmured, putting the gloss back into her bag. "I'm kind of nervous."

"I know. Have you heard from him?"

"Nope. He's the worst boyfriend ever." She felt the chauffeur's gaze on her from the rear-view mirror, and she looked at him. "Don't tell him I said that."

Rick—as he had introduced himself when he picked them up—chuckled. "My lips are sealed, miss."

She couldn't help but glance at her phone, her heartbeat speeding up when she saw three messages from the devil himself.

Indy's perusal was burning her physique, but all she could think about was the loud and deafening drum of her vital organ. "Shit, Kam. If Thiago doesn't fall in love with you..."

She pursed her lips with distaste. "He can stay where he is, which is far, far away from me."

"Seriously?" Her friend was bewildered. "Who says no to a fling with a sexy driver? Oh, right, you."

@THIAGOVALENCIA

Where are you?

Don't tell me you bailed on me

> My PR officer is waiting for you at the
> parking entrance with your and Indy's
> paddock passes.

Kamari didn't answer as the car finally moved. Rick made a left turn towards a VIP parking where security guards stood. Some fans were waiting near the barriers, probably wanting to see some of their favourite drivers, even if they were already supposed to be inside the track. Some were peering inside the car, some of them recognising Indy. The latter waved and blew kisses, her smile so bright and big that it could outshine the sun itself.

> @KAMARI.MONROE
>
> I hate you so much.

She could see Thiago's vicious smile. Could hear his low snicker. She was already infuriated before even seeing him.

When Rick parked the car, Indy unbuckled herself with so much enthusiasm that Kamari nearly wanted to hide in the trunk until the end of the day.

"Oh, there's Ava!" Indy got out of the car and strode towards a woman wearing a red Primavera Racing polo with black trousers. They shared a hug, and Kamari wished she had Indy's ability to socialise.

Rick turned towards Kamari, a gentle smile displayed on his lips. "You'll have fun," he assured. "Race weekends are filled with exciting moments. Is this your first one?"

Kamari nodded.

"Good luck." He winked. "Your secret's safe with me."

Kamari was greeted by Ava when she got out of the car.

Black hair, dark brown eyes, and tan skin, she had a warm smile that managed to soothe all of Kamari's anxiety. "Kamari? I'm Avery, but please call me Ava. I'm Thiago's PR officer." She extended her two VIP passes—a neon pink one for the paddock, the other red one marking her as a Primavera guest, both featuring the picture she had provided Thiago. "Keep those on you at all times. They allow you access to pretty much everywhere in the paddock."

She grabbed the passes and pulled them over her head. Indy was occupied taking pictures of her and she scowled in return.

"Stop it."

Indy extended her arms, like she wanted to embrace her friend, her smile still on display. "But it's your first Grand Prix weekend!"

All she did was glare at the blonde. In all honesty, Kamari had hoped for Indy and Diana to convince her this whole scheme was a bad idea. She hadn't expected them to encourage her.

Ava smiled up at Kamari. "Ready? Thiago's waiting for you by the gates."

Was she ready at all? No.

Was she ready to pretend? Also no.

"Let's go," she suggested with a tight smile.

Photographers were lined up near the gates, some of them photographing Indigo and Kamari walking side by side. Kamari kept her chin high, and when Indy nudged her elbow, she let a smile spread across her lips—a forced and faux one at that.

But the moment she passed the gates leading to the paddock, she felt her heart momentarily stop. Thiago was standing there, looking all handsome and devilish, chatting quietly with a couple of fans. Silver met green, and the world stopped spinning. He was wearing his red racing suit, its upper part unzipped and hanging at his waist, his toned and muscular chest hugged by a white, long-sleeved fireproof shirt with Primavera's sponsors embroidered on his pectorals.

He excused himself to the people surrounding him without so much as disconnecting his gaze from Kamari's and walked towards her, all confidence and power.

All eyes were on them.

All cameras turned towards them.

There was no turning back, unless she wanted to make a fool of herself. But Kamari wasn't one to lose, to back out of a challenge.

Thiago's intoxicating scent enveloped her senses when he pulled her to his chest, his hand cradling the nape of her neck. His touch was punishing, his tone patronising when his lips found the shell of her ear.

"Smile, baby," he murmured. She could hear the wicked smile in his tone. Could feel the warmth of his hand on her skin. "All eyes are on you."

CHAPTER TWELVE

⚑ *SPA-FRANCORCHAMPS, BELGIUM*

UNDER NORMAL CIRCUMSTANCES, Thiago would have loathed being as tall as a woman. But with Kamari Monroe by his side, he couldn't help but feel powerful, seen, and admired for being someone other than a famous, skilled F1 racing driver. A stark contrast to the reputation that preceded him: compassionate, lovable, and, perhaps, loving.

Whispers echoed, longing and curious stares were thrown their way, clicks of cameras stuttering in sync with their hasty footfalls as they rushed towards Primavera's motorhome.

All his life, he'd been used to being the centre of attention, to being under the spotlight. He wasn't certain Kamari felt as comfortable, though. But a woman like her—bold, cunning, beautiful—couldn't fear anything, right?

"Everyone is staring at us," she noted quietly.

The corner of his lips tipped upwards. "That's because we look so good together."

Thiago placed his hand on the small of Kamari's back as they walked, and he felt her tense beneath his light-feather touch.

"Don't touch me," she bit out through gritted teeth.

She was looking at the ground whilst he kept his chin high. Her eyes were hidden behind a pair of dark sunglasses, and he couldn't help but glance at her sharp profile—devastatingly beautiful and intimidating all at once.

His breath had caught inside his throat when she had stepped inside the paddock. Kamari could've taken this whole deal as a joke, could've tried to ruin him by showing up looking homeless and out of style, but she was everything he had ever dreamed of. Wearing a white jumpsuit, she had rolled the sleeves to her elbows, the hem of the pants up past her ankles, and high heels at her feet that showed off her red-painted nails. The first few buttons were unfastened, revealing a red bralette that only attracted his regard.

God, she was something else.

"Did you wear red for me?" he asked smugly, ignoring her demand as he kept his hand on her back. He could feel a zip of electricity skittering down his spine, and he wondered if she could feel the sparks on the tips of his fingers. He hadn't anticipated that feeling and wasn't sure he enjoyed it.

Kamari glared at him, and he wanted to laugh out loud. An angelic face like hers shouldn't be made of ice. "In your wildest dreams, Thiago. It was Indy's suggestion to wear red."

"Yeah, because she knows it's my team's colour." He turned to Indy who was strolling behind them with Ava. Their gazes met, and he winked. "Thank you for your service."

Indy wasn't certain why he was thanking her. Nevertheless, she shrugged and smiled. "You're welcome?"

He could feel Kamari's gaze on his face, so he turned to her. He wished she wasn't wearing those sunglasses because he yearned to see the unique green of her eyes, the coldness swirling along the edges of her irises.

"I know you're shooting daggers at me," he taunted, though he tipped his lips up, thoroughly amused by the whole situation. "But you're going to thank me someday."

"Thank you?" she asked in an outraged scoff. "For what? If there's one person who should be grateful, it's you. I'm basically saving your life."

He grinned, making her halt in her tracks, like she'd been stunned by his bright smile. Then, he put a hand above his heart, his grin never faltering. "You're right. You have my *eternal* gratitude."

"You're so annoying."

"Am I, though?" Crossing his arms over his chest, he stepped aside to let Indy and Ava walk inside, the latter showing him the time on her phone. He nodded before turning his attention back to the object of his nightmares—or daydreams, he didn't know yet. "Is this why you agreed to do this with me?"

Kamari pressed her full lips into a thin line, then parted her mouth, then closed it again, as if she'd forgotten what she wanted to say—or as if she was carefully thinking about the next words she'd use.

"Whatever," she ended up saying. "I need to talk to you in private."

He arched a brow. "Now?"

"Yes."

He gaped at her, all curious and intrigued. "Okay."

Silently, he led her towards the entrance of the motorhome, hand placed between her shoulder blades. The moment they stepped inside, she slid her sunglasses off, putting them atop her head.

All eyes turned to them.

Silence.

Kamari's body was taut with discomfort, rigid with fear.

Sensing the shift in her demeanour, he gently rubbed the pad of his thumb over the nape of her neck. She didn't move. Didn't breathe. Eventually, she peered at him, seeking comfort in the grey of his eyes.

He winked, thinking she'd roll her eyes in annoyance, but she only held composure over her hatred for him. He turned to the people scattered all around the sitting area in the motorhome. "Everyone, this is Kamari." He smirked. "My girlfriend."

Delighted "hi's" and "welcome's" echoed, and Kamari waved timidly, though a sweet smile plastered her face.

From the corner of his eye, he could see Cal and Alex whisper to each other, mocking smirks on the corners of their mouths whilst they gaped at the athlete. Right next to them was Leo, leaning on a wall, busy with a phone call. His gaze was strained on Kamari, curiosity alighting his eyes.

"Be nice to her or you're all fired." Thiago knew he didn't have the power to fire anyone, didn't have any right to come to her defence like this. But he felt a sudden urge to protect Kamari, and he didn't know why.

A few chuckles rose from all corners of the room, other mumbles of comprehension reverberating off the walls.

Thiago leaned towards Kamari's ear, her perfume already corrupting him. She smelt divine yet she radiated with such coldness that it was evident she wanted him to step away instead of feeling drawn. Soft notes of green tea, sage, and citrus enveloped his senses, and it took everything in his power not to lean in to kiss her neck.

"Come with me."

Gently, he led them into a small and private room with his name on the door. He closed the door and watched Kamari walk further into the confined space, running an idle finger on the small table placed in the right corner.

"Don't be looking for dust," he drawled. "My space is always clean."

She hummed, now grazing her finger on a jacket hung over the back of a chair. "What's this room for?"

Not much was in there apart from a small sofa that could barely fit two people, a table and its matching chairs, a few pictures hung on the wall, and a few clothes scattered here and there.

"It's where I come to escape reality in between interviews, meetings with the engineers and strategists, to take a quick nap or rest. You know, it's just my room."

"Oh," she said. "I thought you'd say something like it's where you take your girls and fuck them."

He gaped at her, shocked, then threw his head back and laughed. "Sweet, naive Kamari." He shook his head, folding his arms over his torso, making her gaze drop to his chest for a flickering heartbeat. "We don't just allow anyone into the motorhome, and even less into my room. No one comes in here."

She didn't show a flicker of emotion—no relief, no questioning. Instead, she nodded and drifted her gaze around. "There's not much in here."

"Gee," he breathed. "It's not my bedroom at Mum's house, either. What? Do you want to hang a picture of yourself on the wall? Have it printed poster size?"

"Sure," she droned, all the sarcasm laced in her tone frustrating him for no reason. "I'd love that."

He smirked. "Send me your best picture then."

She pulled a face, mirroring his actions by folding her arms across her chest. He made the biggest effort not to stare at the swell of her breasts and the rest of her pristine physique. "I'm not sending you nudes."

"Never said anything about nudes, love. But if you're suggesting..."

"Ugh," she huffed, shaking her head. "I've no clue how we landed on this topic, but whatever."

He gestured towards the small sofa but she refused to sit, only glaring at him. Stubborn. Beautiful. Bold. To summarise, the bane of his entire existence. "Okay, then. What did you want to talk to me about?" He glanced at his watch. "I have to warm up before quali, so be quick."

Kamari reached into the small purse that she had set atop the bureau and retrieved a piece of paper that she had neatly folded. Carefully, she opened it out and extended it to him.

"What is it?"

"Take a look." She rolled her eyes when he didn't budge as he kept looking at the paper like it was poison. "It's just a sheet, Thiago. Just take it."

Okay, so maybe all of this was a bad idea. Had he made a mistake by pursuing her? Her open disdain and icy façade made Thiago believe she had ulterior motives than what they had settled for. Perhaps she'd use him and hurt him. Perhaps she'd truly ruin him. Perhaps she wouldn't help him salvage himself. She was so cold. So guarded. So detached.

If she wanted to keep a certain distance, then maybe he could, too. *Better be safe than sorry.*

Begrudgingly, he grasped the note between his fingers, keeping his gaze narrowed on the infuriating woman. Curious by whatever she had to offer, he leaned his shoulder against the wall and finally looked down.

Thiago smirked, rolled his tongue over the interior of his cheek, and scoffed softly.

"I can't tell if you're amused or irritated," he heard Kamari say.

He met green eyes from across the room and lifted the sheet of paper up. "A fucking contract, Kamari? Rules? Are we in secondary school or something?"

Kamari lifted her shoulders in a coy shrug like she had anticipated this reaction. "You never know."

"You never know," he echoed, puzzled. Quite frankly, he

didn't care about her rules, so he crumpled the so-called contract and threw it in the bin. "This is stupid, Kam."

"It's Kamari to you."

His jaw tightened. "Okay, witch."

"Witch? You're such an arse."

"Brat."

"Bellend."

He tried to conceal his growing smile by huffing and clearing his throat. "*Kamari,* we don't need rules. We do what we have to do, and if you stay out of my way, I'll stay out of yours."

"Already backing out? You were ready to beg on your knees to have me help you. Just say the word, and I'll walk out and let you deal with your mess on your own."

Fuck, no. He couldn't do it without her. It took great effort to persuade her to do this, so he couldn't let her go.

"That's the Kamari I know," he smirked. "All high and mighty, so tough and unbreakable."

She took one step forward, and he pushed himself off the wall. "I'm doing this—pretending to be your girlfriend—on *my* terms. You don't want to read the contract? Fine. Let me say the rules out loud."

Sounds of heels clicking on the floor resonated as she marched confidently towards him. He wanted to survey her moves, the sway of her hips, the mannequin demeanour of hers. The power she emanated demanded for him to succumb and bow, but he wouldn't yield.

"First rule," she started, voice not so much as wavering as she held his ruthless regard. "No kissing."

"No kissing? Sorry to break it to you, love, but couples usually kiss to show their affection towards one another. Did your stupid ex never kiss you in public as a display of adoration? Arsehole."

Her gaze flickered down to his mouth, then back up to his eyes. "This isn't about my past."

"What is it, then? Scared to fall for me if you taste my lips?" He laughed when she grimaced. "Look, this rule is as stupid as your contract because we'll have to kiss. I'm not asking for tongue, groping, and grinding. Just a sweet peck if I get on the podium because you'll most likely be attending races and be on TV."

"There's no place for *ifs*," she snarled. She poked his chest, though she wasn't able to feel his thundering heart. "You *will* be on the podium and you *will* win races. You'll focus, win that fucking championship, and sign another multi-year contract with Primavera. I haven't agreed to do this for your sole entertainment and for you to enjoy walking around with a woman like me on your arm."

His smirk never once broke from his lips. "Aren't you a little thing full of yourself? Cute." *And sexy.* "Whatever. That's not for you to decide if I win or not."

"No, but you're a smart man, Thiago." The intensity of her scrutiny could set him ablaze, yet he made no move to shield himself. "You know how to win."

"I do," he murmured, feeling determination flow through his veins. "Moving on. Kissing?"

She bit the inside of her cheek, then gave in with a defeated sigh. "Just a peck on camera to congratulate you."

He grinned. She scowled. "Fine by me."

"Second rule: I will attend three events with you. This weekend, the gala in late September, and my brother's birthday party where my ex is going to be."

"Wait." He scratched his jaw and frowned. "You have to come to every race. Or most of them, at least. My reputation precedes me. I can't get rid of everything that tarnishes the way I'm seen if you're not here."

She smirked, giving him a once-over that made heat creep up the back of his neck. "Desperation doesn't look good on you."

"Brat," he bit out. "Seriously. We didn't think this through the first time we talked about it. You can't just come this weekend, never show up again for another month, then disappear. It'll never be convincing or realistic."

"Listen," she said firmly. She didn't have to raise her chin to stare into his eyes, didn't have to crane her neck. At eye level with her, he could decipher the flecks of amber swirling around the edges of her pupils. "I have a job, Thiago. I have a life. I'm about to open a second café and I can't just leave everything behind to be the girl who walks behind you, holds your hand, and smiles at the camera. I have shit to do, to take care of, and I won't make your misery my priority."

"I hear you." Strangely, her features relaxed, and his shoulders sagged in relief when the hard line that had made its appearance between her brows disappeared. "First things first"—he reached out to her to brush lint off her jumpsuit—"I will never let you walk behind me like a lost puppy. You'll always be by my side, like my partner, my equal. I know you think I'm a shitty fuckboy, but I will never treat you badly. You have a job you're dedicated to, and that's fine. But I need you to consider this and make some time to come to other races. Think of your end of the deal, too. James won't believe you're happy without him if you don't pretend you are."

A few heartbeats passed. Muffled voices could be heard as people walked by Thiago's room. Kamari shook her head at last, darting her gaze away. "Fine. I'll see what I can do but I can't promise to be there every single weekend."

"Thank you," he breathed, nearly lifting his arms to tuck her into his chest. Seeing the glower on her face, he made no move and rubbed the back of his neck instead. "Any more rules, boss? As much as I enjoy your delightful company, I need to go warm up. You can stay in the garage with Indy and Alex during quali. Ava will give you a set of headphones so you can hear whatever is being said on the radio between Luke and me."

"Yes, there are a few other rules—"

He rolled his eyes. "Like what? No sex?"

"Obviously. We'll stay out of each other's way behind closed doors."

He scoffed then. "What else? No falling in love?" His tone was taunting and mocking, but when she only shrugged, his grin drooped. "Are you being serious, Kamari? We're two grown-ups, not teenagers."

Her eyes rolled in annoyance. "I didn't write it, but I think it's pretty obvious we can't cross that line."

"Don't worry, darling," he droned, stepping forward and leaning close to her. "I won't fall for you, if you don't fall for me."

"Consider it done." For a heartbeat, for a moment, her gaze fell on his lips. "Do we have ourselves a deal?"

He extended his hand and she let her palm collide with his, albeit reluctantly. "What a pleasure doing business with you, Kamari Monroe."

"I wish I could say the same."

He huffed a laugh then lifted their hands to his mouth, planting a soft, lingering kiss on the back of hers. Heat emanated from her fingers, and he was certain he could see the hairs on her arm rise at the contact of his lips on her warm skin.

"Stop this," she snapped, retreating her hand. "Go qualify and finish first—"

"You mean get pole position."

"Whatever," she dismissed, an annoyed roll of her eyes perceptible. "You do that and win, Thiago. It's time for redemption."

Stepping backwards, he didn't look away from the green eyes staring back at him. He grinned widely, shaking his head in slight amusement. "God, there's so much I need to teach you and I'll have so much fun doing so. I'm getting my kiss tomorrow."

Kamari's stare trailed on his physique. With her hands in the pockets of her jumpsuit and her gaze filled with defiance, she said, "I know you're a man of word. Don't deceive me."

He'd never met a woman ready to take on every challenge he

threw her way, as though she was accepting a lethal flame in the palm of her hand only to give it back to him, ignited like hellfire. Brave. Fierce. Fearless. That was who she was.

For a fragment of a second, he was hoping to finally teeter between redemption and salvation, but there wasn't a shadow of a doubt Kamari Monroe would be the very reason for his ruination.

CHAPTER THIRTEEN

⚲ *SPA-FRANCORCHAMPS, BELGIUM*

THERE WAS SOMETHING strangely enticing about Thiago Valencia. Something that managed to distract Kamari to the point of forgetting about her surroundings. She was on the cusp of losing sense of time, sense of herself.

And she hated this feeling.

She detested the way she couldn't stop looking his way whilst he didn't so much as spare her a glance.

She loathed everything about this ordeal.

Kamari wasn't sure if it was the cold mask he had put on the instant he stepped out of his room, or the way his allure radiated determination and power and devastation. Regardless of the undeniable resentment she felt for this man, she couldn't help the way she was lured towards him, as though an invisible string was tying them together despite their efforts to stay away from one another behind closed doors.

Leaning against a wall, phone in hand with the message she

had been typing to her brother completely forgotten, she kept her gaze on Thiago. He'd been busy pulling the fly of his suit up, a frown etched on his face as he listened to Cal talk, occasionally nodding in understanding. Then, his personal trainer handed him a white balaclava he pulled over his head. Strands of hair peeked out from the thin fabric, and smoothly, he adjusted his rebel locks. He put his helmet on, secured it, then fist-bumped Cal.

"Kam." A voice pulled her out of her daydream with a simple whisper.

"What?"

"Amazing arse, right?"

Kamari blindly smacked Indy's arm a moment before slipping her gaze away from the driver who was stepping inside his racing car.

She glared at her friend who obviously couldn't contain her mocking smile. "He's whatever."

"You're so full of shit." Indy laughed softly, then energetically waved her hand in the air when Alex approached, a digital camera in front of his face, a click echoing when he snapped a photograph of the two women. "Kam, you remember Alex, right?"

Kamari put her phone in her bag as she nodded. "I do."

He looked exactly like the last time she had seen him, except now large glasses were framing his face, and two cameras were hanging around his neck.

His grin was all mischief and sabotage as he took her appearance in. "Kamari," he purred. "Tito's girlfriend."

"Aren't they the cutest couple?" Indy teased, playing along with her friend's game.

Alex grinned. "The sweetest."

"I'm *so* envious!" Indy sighed, a longing gleam shining in her regard. "I want a love like yours."

Kamari pushed herself off the wall, her gaze narrowed on Alex. Dragging his glasses back up the bridge of his nose, his smirk fell when she came to stand before him, tugging Indy by her elbow. "Listen to me, the two of you. I know you find this all amusing and entertaining, but I need you to keep your mouths shut. Got it?"

Alex blinked then scoffed in amazement. "Shit. Got it, boss. My lips are sealed."

Indy's arm draped across Alex's shoulders. Her tone was quiet as she spoke to her friend, though she kept her gaze on Kamari. "She can be a bit scary, but I promise she's the kindest person."

"I can see that," Alex snorted. "Indy, do you also want to bet with Cal and I?"

"About what?"

"I put money on the fact Thiago's going to fall first, but Cal bet it'll be Kam."

Indy's gaze was malicious, and before she could say anything, Kamari grunted, "I hate you two."

Feeling an intense perusal burn the side of her face, she turned towards the source of the flame only to find Thiago looking at her from the cockpit of his car. Their gazes collided, and he winked before going back to focusing.

"Tito gave me a mission, actually," said Alex as he came to stand on Kamari's other side. The qualifying session would be starting in a few minutes, and from where they stood, Kamari could feel the excitement emanating from her entourage. "I need to stay close to you and prevent any interaction between you and Leo."

She rolled her eyes. "I don't need a bodyguard."

"You do," Alex teased, nudging her elbow with his. When he received a glare in return, he lifted his hands up in surrender.

"What's wrong with his agent?"

"Nothing. Leo's a great guy, but Tito told me you two still need to talk about your whole arrangement or whatever stunt you're pulling. He just told me to keep you away from Leo until tonight's dinner."

She frowned, peering at the tall blond beside her. "What dinner?"

Alex's eyes bore into hers, amusement sparkling in his cerulean irises. "Does Thiago ever tell you anything?"

"Obviously not."

He exchanged a look with Indy. "This is the best thing I've witnessed to this day."

Indy chuckled. "And this is the most exciting thing that's ever happened in your life, Kam."

She frowned. "It's not. My life is plenty of fun and unexpected events."

Indy burst out in laughter. "Not really, no. I wish Diana was here to hear the bullshit coming out of your mouth."

"I despise you," Kamari bit out, pivoting to face Alex. She ignored the side hug Indy gave her and Alex's mirth-filled stare. "Who's Leo talking to?"

On the other side of the garage, Leo was vividly talking with a man wearing a Primavera jacket with a set of headphones hanging around the back of his neck.

"That's Primavera's team principal, Simon Romano. And over there"—he motioned towards a tall girl with curly brown hair and bright blue eyes, talking with someone else—"is his daughter, Aïda."

Kamari kept her gaze on the man, studying his demeanour and the way he stared at Thiago whilst waiting for the qualifying session to begin. Whispers were being exchanged, looks filled with deep secrets were thrown at the racing driver.

Something flared inside Kamari's chest. She didn't like the way Romano looked at Thiago. Didn't appreciate how he was blatantly talking behind his back whilst he was just there.

She frowned, unmoving. If she could, she would step in and ask these grown men to be nicer to Thiago. "He's the one who gets to decide if Thiago gets to race with them again next season?"

"Smart woman," Alex praised. "I know Simon still sees

Tito's talent, but he believes his spark is gone. Deep down, he's just hurting to see the championship slip away so easily. Simon's not the best at communicating with his drivers, so the only way he manages to speak with Thiago is by pressuring him and threatening him to give his seat to an F2 driver. See, though, Primavera is nothing without Thiago. Sure, Rowan—his teammate—is also a great driver, but everyone associates Primavera with Tito."

Alex had piqued her curiosity. "How come?"

He cleared his throat as he ran his fingers through his dishevelled locks. "Tito's dad, Evan, he's...was a Formula 1 icon. For most of his career, he raced with Primavera and won seven championships with them. Tito is carrying Evan's legacy by racing for this team."

"Oh." Uneasiness settled in the pit of her stomach. "Is his dad..."

"Yeah." The sound of an engine revved, and Kamari diverted her attention to the F1 car parked in the middle of the garage. Out in the grandstands, cheers and claps echoed, evaporating into the canopies surrounding the circuit. "Listen, I know you're not fond of him, and I'm not sure how he feels about you. But if I can give you some advice, do some research on him before you end up alone again with him. You don't want to say the wrong thing to him. He can be heartless."

A small line drew itself between her brows. "What are you saying? That I'm not careful with my words?"

"Hey," he coaxed. "No need to get defensive with me. I'm just saying you two have fierce personalities, so I'm just preventing chaos from unravelling."

Perhaps all she had to do was be the match that would set Thiago ablaze, and all their combined frustration and anger would blast into a hellfire. Alex was just looking out for his best friend, she supposed.

"Come on, mate."

Cal had come to stand beside Alex a moment after greeting Kamari with a warm hug that she felt entitled to return, albeit begrudgingly. Though she had assumed it correctly, Alex confirmed Callahan was Thiago's childhood friend and personal trainer.

Wherever Thiago was, Cal was too.

Tension was palpable in the room as silence reigned, save for the few words engineers were exchanging as they analysed the driver's performance through their computers. All eyes were turned towards the several TV screens hung on the wall opposite where Kamari stood as they watched the beginning of the qualifying session.

Apart from the car mechanics, engineers, two or three members from the marketing team and the guests, the rest of Primavera's team was watching the event in the motorhome.

"Okay, so." Indy leaned towards Kamari. "You know how quali works?"

Kamari shook her head. Discomfort seeped through her veins because she had agreed to enter Thiago's world without knowing and understanding a single thing about it. She had had a week to do her research and didn't make the effort to do so. Too caught up in her own life, she hadn't realised how bad it would look for Thiago to have a girlfriend who didn't know a thing about Formula 1 nor care about his job—his passion.

"Isn't Kieran a big F1 fan?"

Kamari nodded. "And?"

"You never watched it with him?"

Kamari had vague souvenirs of sitting next to Kieran and their father on Sundays. Whilst they were watching Formula 1, cursing or cheering, she'd read books. Submerged in her own universe, she never felt the need nor the want to take an interest in her brother's passion

"Not really."

Still, Kamari was always open to learning and experiencing new things.

The whole place was roaring with the racing cars exiting their respective garages, and the more time passed by, the more excitement and anxiety lingered in the air.

"Okay." Indy's gaze was focused on a screen that showed a black car bolting through the track. "Qualifying is divided into three parts: Q1, Q2, and Q3. Q1 runs for eighteen minutes, and during that time, all twenty drivers go out to run the fastest lap. The five slowest drivers get disqualified. Still following me?"

Kamari nodded. When claps and cheers of encouragement resonated, she saw Thiago on the screen. Formula 1 cars were impressive. Large. Imposing. Fast.

"Starts Q2 then, with the fifteen remaining drivers. The session lasts for fifteen minutes. Same thing: they try to secure the fastest lap—"

"Are they allowed to drive multiple times or only once?"

A small smile spread across Indy's lips at the sound of Kamari's genuine curiosity.

"They can do as many laps as they want during that set time," Alex said. "Again, the five slowest drivers are disqualified."

"Okay."

Indy continued, softly. "Then, it's time for Q3, which is the most important for the remaining ten drivers. Their position after the qualifying determines their starting position for tomorrow's race."

"Unless there are grid penalties," added Alex.

"Right." Indy nodded and glanced at Alex. "Which Thiago is going to have because he has changed his power unit, right?"

"Yep," the photographer said. "He'll get a five-place grid penalty."

Kamari kept her gaze on the screen. She could hear the roars of the engines from afar, but Thiago was all she could see. He was skilled, talented, brilliant. She wasn't an expert in the racing domain, but from the way he handled the car and the speed, it was evident he was carrying years of experience on his shoulders.

She had been told the track was seven kilometres long, and Thiago managed to race through it in under a minute and forty-five seconds. She was completely impressed and in awe.

"For the last twelve minutes, the ten drivers are going to secure the fastest lap time to put themselves as highly as possible on the starting grid. Tito's aiming for pole position—the first place. Frankly, they all want to be on pole."

"He looks fast," Kamari mumbled.

"He is," Indy agreed cheerfully. "His teammate is currently the fastest, but Thiago's only second. He'll get through Q1 and Q2 easily."

Kamari gaped at Alex, whose gaze was intensely focused on the TV screen. "Let's assume he gets pole position but starts sixth tomorrow... Can he win the race if he starts back there?"

"For sure," he replied, nodding. "His strategist better not fuck his race up, though. A podium is totally possible, but a win would be so fucking great."

Kamari tilted her head. "Has he won a race so far this season?"

Alex shook his head, a sad gloom misting over his pale blue eyes. "He was on the podium once or twice where he finished third." He leaned back against the wall; his shoulders falling in sync with the heavy exhale that fled past his lips. "I don't know, man, I just want him to win again. He can't afford to lose his seat. F1 is his life. There's nothing that makes him feel more alive than this sport."

All Kamari could do was nod as an unwanted lump formed inside her throat.

IN THE HAZE of utter happiness, strong arms came to wrap around her shoulders, pulling her into a sweat-clad, toned and hard chest.

Loud cheers were flying around, though the only sound she could hear was the rapid thrum of her heart and his bated breaths fanning across the shell of her ear.

Kamari wrapped her arms around Thiago's waist, gently rubbing his back as she saw a camera following the athlete who had just secured pole position.

Time stopped for a moment, for an eternity, as Thiago's hand came to cradle the back of Kamari's head. He slipped his hand lower, gently squeezing her nape and moved on to Cal, who was standing next to her.

The moment the black and white flag was brandished, Thiago had claimed pole position with the fastest lap time of a minute and forty-four seconds. His teammate, Rowan, finished second, so Kamari knew it was a great day for Primavera Racing. Car mechanics were lined up behind barriers, congratulating their drivers after they had gotten out of their cars, pride and happiness etched on all their faces.

Kamari's heart thundered against her ribcage because she knew, at this moment, as photographers snapped shots of her, and as the camera caught hers and Thiago's interaction, that there was no turning back.

When Thiago took his helmet and balaclava off, followed by his earplugs, Kamari wasn't certain how to react at the sight of his wide, genuine smile. He looked so happy. So beautiful, even with the droplets of sweat falling down his temple like rivulets, his face flushed and his chest heaving.

A sports journalist came up to him, a microphone in hand and a cameraman in tow behind her.

"The top three qualifiers get interviewed," Indy murmured in her ear.

His gaze collided with hers, and all she could see was the

mischief sparkling along the edges of his irises. He winked at her, his smile promising utter devastation.

———

"WAIT. WHAT? IS THIS A JOKE?" Kamari searched Indy's eyes for a clear answer, and all she earned in response was a shrug.

"Is everything okay?" Ava asked, complete confusion brimming her dark eyes. "Do you want me to ask Thiago—"

"No, no, it's fine." Kamari rubbed her temple, as though the motion would clear her head from the clouds of turmoil. "I didn't know the arrangements had changed. Can I have a word with Indy for a sec, please?"

Thiago's PR officer nodded. "So sorry for this mess."

Though Kamari could feel the anger flow through her veins, she sighed and pinned Ava with a look filled with sympathy and kindness. "No need to apologise, darling. It's not your fault."

Indy's brows were lifted in both surprise and curiosity when Kamari turned to her. They had left the circuit to go to the hotel which was right down the road. Standing in the lobby, they were waiting to get a hold of their room's key, but Ava had appeared to hand Kamari a keycard, saying, "*Thiago sent me to give you this.*" It was the key to their room; hers and Thiago's.

"Weren't *we* supposed to share a room?" Kamari hissed, flickering her pointer finger between her chest and her best friend's.

Indy lifted her shoulders in a coy shrug. "That's what I thought but it appears like your boyfriend had different plans."

"This can't be happening," she muttered under her breath.

Indy's mouth twisted in a grimace. "He's coming this way. Good luck."

Kamari glared at her friend. "You're seriously leaving me?"

Her friend smiled sheepishly. "Gotta go and get ready. I'll see you in a bit."

"Bitch," she mumbled.

"Are you trying to cause a scene?" A low, deep voice rang in her ears, making unwanted chills rush down her spine.

She turned around and was faced with grey eyes, not expecting Thiago to be standing this close. He had changed out of his racing suit, now dressed in jeans and a Primavera shirt that did wonders to put his toned chest in evidence.

"What is wrong with you?" she snapped, keeping her voice as quiet as possible.

People were entering and exiting the lobby, but most of them were part of Primavera's team.

He lifted a brow, bemused. "Is this how you congratulate me for being on pole? That's a tad rude, sweetheart."

When her gaze narrowed on him, he tipped the corner of his mouth into an amused smirk. "We're not sharing a room, Thiago. I was supposed to share one with Indy."

He rolled his eyes, hands finding shelter in the pockets of his jeans. "Oh, don't be daft. You and I both know Indy will find her way into one of my mechanics' beds tonight." The once-over he gave Kamari caused her cheeks to flush, though he was too enthralled by her long legs to notice her crimson face. "I don't know how to break the news to you, *witch,* but couples share a room and a bed nowadays."

"Well, *arsehole,* I don't want to share a room with you."

He scoffed. "What are you, twelve? You're being ridiculous."

Arms folding across her chest, she scowled. "No, I'm not."

"Kamari."

"Thiago."

He sighed heavily, throwing his hands in the air before looking around to make sure they weren't attracting any unwanted attention. His voice became a whisper, though he was anything but sweet in the way he spoke. "How are we supposed to make this convincing if you sleep in one room and me in another? This hotel is flooded with members of the racing team, fans, and another racing team. It's just for one night, Kamari. Grow the fuck up."

She didn't want to cause a scene. Didn't want to show weakness or fear. Holding his gaze, she wanted to scream how much she hated being in this position, scared to fall into a trap. She needed to put a barrier between her and this devastatingly handsome man, and sharing a bed with him was not the solution.

"Listen to me," he muttered, the sliver of distance between their chests ever so slowly disappearing as he stepped closer and closer and closer until his intoxicating scent enveloped her senses with a spellbinding breeze. She could feel his warm breath on her lips. Could feel her heartbeat pick its pace up at their proximity.

The calluses scarring the tip of his forefinger came into contact with her cheek. As he brushed a strand of hair away from her face, pinning her with that lethal glare of his, she couldn't understand how Thiago was such a paradox—rough and soft all at once.

She held his gaze. Never faltered. She trembled beneath his light-feather touch, and he smirked. Like he knew how much power he had over her.

His murmur was hoarse, coercing her with the mere whisper of his words. "You hate this as much as I do, and I get it. But if you so much as try to sabotage me with that attitude of yours, I promise I won't be gentle with you, Kamari. I need you to take this seriously."

She hadn't realised he was gripping her elbow so tightly, as though he wanted to keep her close. "Sharing a bed with you is my worst nightmare."

Thiago chuckled, amused. "Yeah? Well, you're a goddamned nightmare and total menace. Guess we're even now, love."

CHAPTER FOURTEEN

⚲ *SPA-FRANCORCHAMPS, BELGIUM*

S HE WAS CERTAIN Thiago was busy plotting her disappearance from the other side of the door as she stared at her reflection.

Would they manage to pull this off? She wasn't sure.

Did they have enough chemistry to appear like a serious and committed couple? She wasn't sure about that, either.

The physical attraction was obviously mutual and undeniable. But was their emotional connection established enough? Of course, it wasn't. She barely knew the bloke. And he knew nothing about her.

Busy applying a coat of gloss over her full lips, Kamari was lost in her thoughts. Her mind was racing with hundreds of unfathomable questions, and her heart was threatening to leap out of her chest with the rapid and uneven beat of the muscle.

A knock on the door brought her back to reality, causing her to drop the tube of gloss in the sink.

"Kamari," Thiago said, voice muffled. She could hear the irritation woven into his already deep timbre. "Don't make me come in and drag you out by force. We're going to be late."

He started pounding on the door, which made frustration rattle inside her. He wanted to get a reaction out of her, and testing her patience was the way to do so. Tipping her chin up, she pivoted to face the door. Gingerly, she twisted the doorknob and faced a Thiago Valencia thoroughly annoyed by her lack of response.

Leaning against the doorway, fist up in mid-air as he was getting ready to knock again, he abruptly stopped and dropped his hand. Silver was intensely staring into green, but when he lowered his gaze to scrutinise her face followed by her body, Kamari suddenly felt like burning under the intensity of it all. His mouth opened then closed, like he had forgotten what he wanted to say. Like she had managed to render him speechless.

Kamari planted her hands on her hips, frowning up at the tall man. She hadn't put her heels on just yet, but he seemed so much taller than she remembered.

"Are you done knocking like a maniac?"

He stared back into her eyes, and she made the greatest effort not to notice the flicker of surprise around his pupils. "It was either that or coming in to see if you were still breathing."

"I'm grand," she bit out. Gesturing to herself, she asked, "Is this okay?"

Grey eyes roamed over her figure, not sure where to settle. "More than okay," he murmured hoarsely. "Do *you* like it?"

"Yes." She didn't miss a beat, catching a glimpse of herself in the mirror behind Thiago. The black fabric clung to her body like a second skin, its strapless and heart-shaped neckline putting the swells of her breasts in evidence. The dress descended to stop below her knees, a slit visible along the outside of her right thigh.

"So you don't need anyone else's opinion." His tongue made a brief appearance to wet his lips. "It's just team dinner, though."

"I know."

Kamari pushed past the athlete to face the mirror, shrugging with nonchalance and satisfied with her appearance.

She met Thiago's eyes through the reflection, and she wasn't sure if she was still breathing properly. He had told her it was a simple dinner with his team like it wasn't of any importance, yet he still sported the most devastating look: black trousers and an Italian black shirt, the matching blazer to complete the look hanging on the hook to her left.

"Thiago," she said firmly.

He swallowed thickly. "Yeah?"

"Be a sweetheart and grab the necklace on the counter, please."

He didn't think. Didn't retort. He simply turned on his heel, searched for the piece of jewellery with his eyes for a fraction of a second, then grabbed it.

Kamari couldn't move. She wasn't certain what she was trying to do, but the anticipation coiling in the pit of her stomach was almost thrilling.

"Are you going to ask me to put it on you?" He was already smirking. Under normal circumstances, she wouldn't have thought of the possibility of asking someone else that. Had she gone mad?

"Sounds to me like you're ready to do it, so I think there's no need for me to ask."

He scoffed, shaking his head. Still, he closed the distance between them until he stood right behind her. "Brat."

"Arsehole."

Disoriented by the delicacy of his touch, Kamari ceased to breathe. Ever so carefully, he brushed her hair away from her neck, gathering it over her shoulder. His fingertips grazed at her bare skin, leaving a trail of shivers in their wake along the route of this short yet powerful caress.

She was ready to move away, to writhe with discomfort, but the confusion never came.

His gaze was hypnotised by his own movements. By the feel

of her skin beneath his callouses. By the rise and fall of her upper body, so close to his own chest.

Feeling his warm breath fade atop her skin, she resisted the urge to close her eyes and lose herself in the moment. He was so close. So careful. So gentle. Reaching around, he draped the golden necklace around her neck before swiftly securing it.

Delicately pushing her hair away from her shoulder to let it fall down her back, she could hear how unsteady his breathing had become despite his greatest efforts to stay indifferent.

Silver met green through the mirror, and nothing else seemed to matter. "I'm going to be all over you tonight," he murmured gruffly. "I like physical touch."

Kamari's chest rose and fell. She swallowed then, unsure of how to react to this. "Do you?"

"Yes." He tipped the corner of his lips into a wry smirk, his dimple making an appearance. She hadn't noticed he was standing even closer now, the heat radiating off his body cocooning her into an unbreakable bubble. Musk. Power. Devastation. That was all she could feel from the energy he emanated. "But I won't touch you without your permission. You're going to tell me if this is okay."

Feeling like her breath had been caught in her throat, she barely managed to make her question audible. "What?"

Her hands were limp at her sides, as though she couldn't move. She was immobile. Helpless. She couldn't detach her gaze from his face, from the concentration etched on it as a small crease drew itself between his dark brows. When his fingers gently wrapped around her hands, a wave of chills skittered down her spinal column and, by the minuscule twitch of his lips, she knew he had felt the effect he was having on her.

Running the pads of his thumbs over the back of her hands, Thiago kept his gaze focused on Kamari's face. Cataloguing every single inch of her features, surveying her reaction, studying how her body responded to him.

She didn't appreciate being touched, but why was his touch so different?

"Hands?" His murmur caressed the shell of her ear. She had lost sense of herself—she couldn't think. Couldn't find a way to unwrap herself from that spell he had put on her. Couldn't do anything except be compelled. "Can I touch them? Hold them?"

"Sure." She found herself surprised by the steadiness of her tone, of the clarity of her voice. "But hold them only when necessary. I hate holding hands."

His brows slightly rose at the sound of the revolt laced in her tone. "Okay. Good."

Coldness took over her senses when Thiago let go of her hands. Grazing his fingertips up her arms, she could feel flames resting on his punishing digits as they touched the goosebumps forming on her skin. Her body was blatantly betraying her, and she hated that. Hated not having control. Hated how, deep down, she didn't mind those light touches, that heady gaze of his —almost salacious in its negligence, almost like a lover's stare.

"Arms?" His tone was still low, quiet. He was tracing a route with his middle fingers on both her arms, his gaze following his lazy movement.

Oxygen suddenly got caught in the back of her throat. "Whatever."

Large hands found her shoulders, thumbs slightly digging into her skin, ready to soothe out the tension lingering in her muscles. His rings felt cold—a stark contrast to the way he was burning up. "Shoulders?"

Despite being tall, she had never felt so tiny, so vulnerable.

Kamari observed how he leaned closer, ever so slightly turning to face her side profile. For an unknown reason, his jaw clenched. He ran his palms over her bare shoulders, and it took everything in her willpower not to shiver at the feeling of his rough callouses.

Her lashes fluttered. What was he doing to her? "Fine by me."

Thiago exhaled tremulously. The next moment, Kamari felt her breath hitch when, without any sign of warning, his hands found the curve of her waist.

"What about there?" he whispered, rapidly glancing at their reflection.

She wasn't sure if it was a trick of her imagination, but she thought seeing silver eyes turning into a shade of molten grey— like a storm brewing itself along the edges of his irises.

Kamari narrowed her eyes. "You're enjoying this way too much."

A smirk played on the corner of his lips. "You're not complaining."

Cocky bastard.

Pivoting, she faced this devastatingly handsome man who was evidently hellbent on ruining her. His gaze promised devastation. Ruination. Damnation. Still, she wouldn't yield. She never would.

"Listen to me, Thiago Valencia." She wasn't affected by their proximity. Wasn't distressed by his fiery gaze observing her face. Reaching out, she grabbed the collar of his shirt to adjust it, neatly and carefully. If she hadn't been so enthralled by the colour of his eyes, she would've heard the sharp intake of breath he had taken. "You get to touch my hands, shoulders, and hips only if it's necessary. But, behind closed doors, you stay as far away from me as possible. Got it?"

"Like this far way?" Flickering his gaze down, he silently referred to the sliver of distance separating their chests from colliding.

A roll of her eyes. A huff flew past her lips. A push at his broad chest, making him stumble backwards whilst he laughed loudly. "I despise you."

Kamari's frustration seemed to be his favourite kind of entertainment. Smirking and smoothing out his shirt, he winked. "Sure you do, love."

Focused on hiding the flush that had made its unwanted

appearance on her cheekbones, she turned to make a beeline for her luggage. She had unpacked the moment they entered the room whilst he went to isolate himself on the balcony, busy doing whatever he had to do. Retreating a pair of high heels, she strapped them on, grabbed her purse and faced Thiago who was lazily shrugging his jacket on.

She didn't know if he liked the fact she was as tall as him, or if it irritated him to the point of having eyes as ashen as a thundering sky.

"Let's go," she said firmly, brushing past him. "We're going to be late."

"Can we hold hands?"

"Do you want to skip whilst we're at it? Idiot."

"Fuck," he chuckled as he followed her out of the room, thorough amusement drawn on his face when she didn't hold the door for him. "You're going to ruin me, aren't you, Kamari?"

He had no idea.

What she had yet to understand, though, was that he'd ruin her all the same, if not even more.

"WE HAVE EXACTLY LESS than a minute to get to know each other."

Standing in the empty corridor, waiting for the lifts to reach the eleventh floor, Kamari turned to Thiago with a frown on her face.

"Excuse me? I don't want to make small talk with you."

"God," he muttered. "You're impossible."

When the doors to the lifts opened, he gestured for her to step inside first. "M'lady."

"Such a gentleman," she teased as she watched him press the first floor's button.

Thiago was standing next to her, purposely brushing his shoulder to hers as though the space was confined when it was anything but. Keeping her chin high, she stared absently at the doors.

"What's your favourite colour?"

Kamari almost laughed. Turning to look at him, she asked, baffled, "How is knowing what my favourite colour relevant to our relationship?"

He had tucked his hands in the pockets of his trousers, his brown locks falling over his forehead in a dishevelled manner. "Everyone knows their partner's favourite colour."

"This is stupid."

"Well?" he pressed, his eyebrows lifting in slight impatience.

She looked back at the doors, watching the red numbers above them as they kept descending. "Black."

"Why am I not surprised?" he deadpanned. "Mine's red."

"I didn't ask." A beat passed. "I'm not surprised either."

From the corner of her eye, she could perceive the coy shrug of his shoulders. "What's your middle name?"

"What the hell, Thiago? There's no way in hell you're going to call me by my middle name in front of your boss. Just ask relevant questions."

"Jesus," he muttered. "I'm just trying to get to know you."

"Well, try harder."

"Okay," he trailed, turning to face her and leaning against the wall. Jerking his chin towards her, he asked, "What makes you passionate?"

Taken aback by this sudden question, Kamari blinked up at him. He sounded sincere and looked rightfully curious. The sound of the lifts stopping and the bell ringing saved her from this wave of surprise.

"Time's up," she said, brushing past him to walk out into the hallway.

Several people she had seen earlier walking around the paddock and garage were also headed towards the terrace where dinner awaited the whole team of Primavera Racing and their guests.

She could feel a familiar ball of anxiety roll in the pit of her stomach, and she inhaled deeply whilst no one paid attention to her.

"Wait." Thiago caught her elbow, gently, and made her spin around. "What if they ask questions? Like where we met? Stuff like that?"

"Well, I don't know, hotshot," she replied grimly. "Perhaps you should have thought about those details before begging me to pretend to be your girlfriend."

For a flickering heartbeat, he looked around to see if anyone was listening. The coast was clear, and he let go of his grasp on her elbow. "Well, sorry! I didn't have time to think this through. You're the organised one, not me."

She eyed him warily. "What's that supposed to mean? Was I supposed to come here with our backstory written like a fucking novel?"

He sighed. "Means you've got everything sorted out whilst I'm a hot mess."

Kamari rolled her eyes. "You've fed me a ton of bullshit ever since we met, and this might have been the biggest lie. It's fine, Thiago. We'll just improvise, okay? I'll follow your lead."

The moment he rubbed his jaw, appearing lost in his thoughts, she couldn't help but follow his motions with her gaze, completely mystified by his hands and fingers and silver rings. "We don't have much of a choice, do we?"

Kamari didn't reply as Cal and Alex came out of the lifts, both also wearing tailor-made suits. Alex clapped his best friend on the shoulder and winked at Kamari, the smile drawn on his lips nothing but a mocking, vicious thing of beauty.

Thiago turned to Kamari. "Ready?"

"No."

"Want me to hold your hand?" he mocked. "Might help with the stress."

She scowled and pivoted, pushing her hair away from her shoulder. "Don't touch me."

"Brat," he hissed under his breath. Still, he followed her like he was tethered to her by an invisible thread. "There's still time to hold hands and skip, you know."

She peered at the man who was blatantly watching the steady rhythm of her footfalls, the sway of her hips. "You're going to make my life a misery, aren't you?"

"Oh, yeah." He grinned and rushed to walk by her side. "This is only the beginning of your nightmare, darling."

"KAM, THIS IS LEO, MY AGENT."

Graciously offering the man before her a warm smile, she placed her palm in his and accepted his handshake. Leo McConnell didn't appear much older than Thiago—perhaps two or three years older at most.

Whilst she greeted the man, she almost narrowed her gaze when he surveyed her allure, like he was ready to give Thiago his approval.

"It's nice to finally meet you," he said as he released her hand before rounding the table to take a seat.

Tables were scattered around the terrace where everyone had found their seat with friends and colleagues. Kamari had noticed a few fans, who were staying at the hotel, ogling at Thiago and his teammate with admiring gazes, but made the respectful choice not to bother them during this moment.

A few lanterns were hung overhead, glowing beneath the sunset's canvas.

Thiago pulled a chair out for Kamari, winking when she gaped at him like he had suddenly grown a second head. She thanked him, quietly, and took a seat directly across from Leo, albeit with noticeable reluctance.

"He won't bite," Thiago murmured, his lips awfully close to her ear, as he sat down beside her.

Their table was the largest with multiple people sitting

around it. Kamari noticed Indy at the far opposite end, sitting between Alex and Cal and energetically talking to them.

"I'll bite harder," she stated calmly, offering a tight-lipped smile to Leo when he nodded curtly at her.

Earning a chuckle from Thiago, she peered at him just as he popped the buttons of his vest open. "I know that."

"So, Kamari," Leo started as he leaned in the back of his seat. "Is this your first time in Spa?"

Digging into her purse to retrieve an elastic band, she nodded. Securing her long, dark locks into a bun at her nape, she let her gaze roam around the cramped space. Sounds of laughter and chatter resonated, making all the stress clamping at her chest vanish. "Yes. It is absolutely breathtaking."

Leo agreed. "You should take a walk around the circuit with lover boy here when the sun is rising."

Kamari and Thiago exchanged glances. He grinned. She narrowed her eyes.

"You'd love that," Thiago said, amused by the annoyance she knew he could see flaming in her eyes.

"Sure." *I'd love to knock some sense into you.* "It's a plan, then."

"Sweet." Draping his arm over the back of her seat, he opened his menu, noticing she didn't have one laid in front of her. He then pushed the booklet towards her. "What do you want to drink?"

Leo had gone into a conversation with Ava who was sitting to his right, so Kamari took the opportunity to kick Thiago's foot. He huffed a laugh, shaking his head. "So violent."

"You had it coming."

"True." He shrugged. "Drink?"

The frown taking over her features was out of her own control. When she dated James, he always chose her drinks. Most of the time, she was allowed one glass of wine whilst he took whiskey after whiskey.

Kamari blinked and nodded. "A glass of wine is fine. Are you allowed to drink before a race?"

Thiago shook his head. "No. And I have to be careful with what I eat as well. Did you know we can lose up to five kilos during a race? We sweat a lot whilst driving."

She met with silver eyes, intently watching her. "Really?"

Thiago smiled softly. "Yeah."

Oh, hell no. He didn't get to be all sweet and pretty when she knew he was the devil himself. A dimpled smile would never make her succumb.

"Does your weight before the race have an impact on your performance?"

If he was surprised by her genuine intrigue, he didn't show it. "No. We all have the same car—well, they all weigh the same. Engines, chassis, and aerodynamics are different, though."

"Interesting."

"Don't worry about me, darling. I'll still enjoy my dinner. I'm in the great company of a beautiful, charming, sweet, funny—"

"Shut up," she gritted, which made him laugh out loud.

The sound of his delight attracted curious eyes, caused quiet whispers to erupt around the tables. Indy, Alex and Cal were watching them with mirth-filled gazes, and Kamari resisted the urge to shout at her best friend how much she hated her for leaving her in this mess alone. Alex, always in the company of his camera, snapped a picture of the couple. Cal only smirked, purely amused by the situation, and Indy shaped a heart with the help of her hands.

Then came Leo's long-awaited question: "Where'd you two meet?"

Thiago nudged Kamari's thigh, the fabric brushing at the exposed part of her leg. He made no move to shift away, and even pulled his chair closer to hers, letting the warmth of his body envelop her senses, mixing with the intoxicating odour of his cologne.

"A party," he said.

"On a boat," she said at the same time.

"At a party on a boat," Thiago clarified, his strong, muscular thigh still pressed against hers.

"When?"

Leo had every right to be suspicious about this new relationship Thiago was putting on full display, like he had won a trophy and wanted to show it to the world. Still, Kamari wasn't sure if the agent's questions were crafted from genuine curiosity or aiming to see through their little white lies.

When Thiago didn't reply as he pretended to read the menu, Kamari lifted her chin. She could feel her heart batter as he was giving her full permission to build their story from her imagination.

Kamari hated comparing whatever this was with Thiago to her ancient relationship, but she couldn't help but notice it; James always talked for her, barely gave her time or space to express herself.

"About a year ago," she admitted.

Leo flickered his gaze to Thiago. "And you've been dating for..."

She lifted her shoulders in a shrug, all nonchalance and indifference. "A few months or something, but who's counting?"

Hurt and betrayal flashed across Leo's features. Finding the athlete's gaze, he frowned. "How come you've never introduced her? Does she know about all the girls you've been pictured with during those months of *unconditional love*?"

For a moment, for a heartbeat too long, she lost control of her emotions. Fury and pain came spiralling through her mind in a whirlwind, threatening to spread throughout her body to put every particle of her being through that affliction she knew all too well. The accidental nudge of Thiago's thigh against hers forced her to come back to reality, and she had never been more grateful for his unsolicited presence.

Looking over to her right, she saw the subtle clench of Thiago's jaw, the discreet thrum of his fingers atop his thigh. Perhaps they should have talked their scheme through before entering the lion's den.

"I've seen the photos," Kamari explained quietly. "Though there were never allegations of cheating."

Thiago found her gaze. Searched her face. Dipped his chin in gratitude. "I'd never cheat on you, you know that."

"I know." She patted his leg, then instantly retreated her hand before she could feel the firmness of his muscles. "Besides, Leo, I was at most of those parties."

"Were you?" he asked, suspiciously.

"She was," Thiago confirmed. "But Kam is a very busy woman. She owns a café in London and is planning on opening another one soon. She's also a private person, and I've always respected her choice of not wanting to attend races."

"But I'm your agent," Leo retorted, voice thick with emotion. "You could've told me."

Kamari was quick to jump in. "I'm here now, aren't I? Look, I'm not going to apologise for wanting to keep my relationship with Thiago a secret. Dating a celebrity can be overwhelming for a simple person like me. Let's not fret about the past and just enjoy tonight's dinner, yes?"

Leo couldn't manage to answer verbally. He simply nodded and eyed the couple, warily. Kamari knew that flicker of resentment in his eyes, and she knew he wasn't fond of her. Or maybe he was simply apprehensive.

The moment Thiago's hand cradled the back of her neck, she stilled. "Is this okay with you?" he whispered.

Thankfully, Leo was now busy reading the menu, though she was sure he was observing the couple from the corner of his eye. The athlete ran his thumb between her shoulder blades, able to feel how tense her body was. She was supposed to be hating the feeling of his hands on her, to not enjoy the way he managed to coax her through the wave of anger and turmoil. Still, she didn't move and let him caress her flesh for a few heartbeats too long.

She needed to say no, though she replied, softly, "Yes."

Because she thought she was almost enjoying the sensation of his skin on hers.

She peered at him, and he was busy looking elsewhere—at the sky. She nearly found herself enthralled by the gleam in his eyes when it lit up the moment he found what he was looking for. Almost let her gaze linger on every inch of his face.

Finally, Thiago leaned towards her ear and whispered something only she could hear. "Thank you. I owe you."

Kamari shook her head as if saying, "*Don't worry about it.*"

When a waiter passed by their table, Thiago called the young man over. "Can my girl get a glass of white, please?"

CHAPTER FIFTEEN

⚲ *SPA-FRANCORCHAMPS, BELGIUM*

SUBTLE NOTES OF sage and green tea embraced him in a cocoon of pure solace, tethering him to that invisible bubble that procured an intense sense of serenity.

The feeling was foreign, though Thiago didn't want to wake up. It took a few heartbeats to comprehend he wasn't stuck in a dream but collapsing into a reality that felt as heavenly as this moment, soul-shattering in an oddly good way.

Body and mind in perfect synchronisation, Thiago awoke slowly. He could feel a warm body pressed against his front as his arm was wrapped around the person's waist. Feeling the steady rise and fall of their chest, he allowed his breathing to match the soft rhythm of the other person's inhales and exhales.

Slowly opening his eyes, he watched the early morning sun's rays slip through the curtains, a soft yet bright white light lurking upon the walls of a room he'd never seen before. He didn't want to move. Wanted to stay there, with his arm wrapped around—

His heart nearly made a full stop when he realised where he was. Who he was with.

The haze of fatigue instantly dissipated, awareness replacing the clouds of euphoria in his head. He stilled. Ceased to breathe. Blinked and faced a mop of dark brown curls.

Kamari Monroe was in his arms.

He had been snuggling with Kamari Monroe.

Fuck. Fuck. Fuck.

Did anything happen last night? No, certainly not. That woman would've not wanted his hands on her body.

He inhaled calmness. Exhaled anxiety. Fearing to wake Kamari up, he didn't move his arm away. Barely breathed, scared that his warm puffs of breath would disturb her peaceful sleep. His heart, though, started beating erratically, and he knew she would be able to feel his distress pounding against her back. After all, he wasn't wearing anything. Only the flimsy piece of clothing sticking to her torso separated them and, if she wanted, she could simply turn around, take hold of his heart and crush it into dust.

Repressing a small grunt, he let the souvenirs of last night's events flood his mind. Leo had asked questions, though he looked proud of Thiago for finally settling for someone. Still, Thiago knew his agent wasn't wholly convinced by their act. He'd stayed by Kamari's side all evening long, occasionally talking to her but mostly listening to her talk to the people around them. He remembered thinking, "*God, she's mesmerising. Is this just an act or is this really who she is?*" He recalled touching, caressing her back and shoulders, sometimes grabbing her hand before she kicked his foot to let go. He recalled her stiffening beneath his touch a moment before relaxing when she understood that his strokes were nothing but genuine tenderness.

He remembered hating and loving the skin-on-skin contact. Remembered how she allowed him to have a certain power over her when it was evident she loathed every moment of it. Remembered it all: how natural and easy it felt despite their lack of communication.

Perhaps his initial plan of putting distance between them would never work. He wasn't certain he could hate her, even if he tried.

They had gone back to their room after dinner, and Kamari hadn't said a word to him as she went to hide in the bathroom to get ready for the night. He'd been busy scrolling through his phone when she emerged in the room, not particularly paying attention to the woman who would be sharing the bed with him. With the use of spare pillows, she had built a wall between them and told him to stay on his side. He had laughed, and she had scowled. Regardless, he had made no move to disrespect her and made sure not to lay a finger on her for the remainder of the night.

Before he'd been able to make small talk with her, exhaustion had overpowered him and pushed him to plummet into a deep, dreamless sleep.

So, where had the wall of pillows gone? How had they managed to end up in each other's arms?

All of this was so bizarre to him—he never cuddled. Never allowed his one-night stands to stay over. But this had been, without a shadow of a doubt, the best night of sleep he'd gotten in a while.

"Valencia?"

The sound of Kamari's harsh whisper made his heart stop beating once again. He swallowed, stiffened. He could feel how her body had gone rigid against his.

"Morning, sunshine," he rasped in the crook of her neck. He was taking risks—he was aware but basking in her scent had never felt so relaxing.

A beat passed. He understood she was trying to remain calm, cool, and collected. "Why is your arm around me?"

Her smoky voice was laced with sleep, hoarse on its edges, making it all even more enticing to him.

"Maybe because you came crawling into my arms," he teased.

Silence. "Did we..."

"No," he was quick to say. "But we could."

"You have exactly two seconds to move away before I kick you."

He chuckled. "So violent."

"Seriously, Valencia. Get away from me."

"Why aren't *you* moving? Seems to me you enjoy being in my arms." Annoying her had become his favourite hobby. He pulled himself even closer, tightening his hold over her frame. "Come on, Kam. Isn't this nice?"

"It's not," she bit out, still not moving.

"But friends cuddle," he whined. He enjoyed her warmth, the soft press of the fabric of her nightgown beneath his hand, the way she fitted in the palm of his hand as though she had been made for him.

"We're not friends, Thiago." Grabbing his wrist to push him away, she stilled. "Is that your dick pressed to my bum?"

A loud laugh escaped his mouth and, finally, he loosened his hold to roll onto his back. Running a hand over his flushed face, he couldn't contain the chuckles erupting from the back of his throat. He then draped his forearm over his eyes to shield his vision from the sun's rays, the ball of anger Kamari was, and the reality of it all. "Sorry, love, but morning woods are just a natural thing for us men."

He felt the bed shift as she crawled away, taking the warmth of her body with her along the way. "Keep your dick away from me. In fact, just stay away from me. I told you not to touch me in private."

"For fuck's sake," he grumbled. "Maybe you're so touch-deprived that *you* came onto me. Stop putting the blame on me when it's obvious you like me."

"Keep dreaming," she muttered.

The moment she threw a pillow on his stomach, he laughed again. "So violent."

Finally, his eyes landed on her. Back turned to him, Kamari was busy pulling her untamed curls into a rapid chignon. He couldn't help but saunter his gaze over her physique—how could he not when she was sitting there, looking like *that?* Sighing heavily, she pushed herself off the bed, carefully sliding her feet into her slippers.

"Nice legs," he told her.

She locked her gaze with his, yet this time genuine annoyance gleamed along the edges of her irises. Flickering her perusal over his exposed torso, she held control over her emotions by not showing how much this situation was truly affecting her. The duvet was covering him from the waist down, and the intensity of her scrutiny set him ablaze. There was an undeniable flash of exhilarating heat expanding her pupils, an unfathomable vehemence in her reaction that made him want to catch her wrist and pull her towards him.

"I detest you."

He grinned. His voice had turned hoarse, husky. "I know."

"I'm using the bathroom first."

It was at this exact moment that he knew this plan would be impossible to execute. Staying professional with Kamari would be as complicated as redeeming himself.

"ARE YOU SURE you don't want to eat anything?"

The faint melody of a *Queen* song was resonating softly in the background whilst the late August, summer breeze caressed the outline of his jaw. Drumming his fingers to the rhythm of the music on the steering wheel, Thiago glanced at Kamari who was sitting in the passenger's seat. With his elbow resting atop the panel of the car, he passed his fingers through his hair whilst waiting for her green eyes to collide with his.

"I'm sure," she replied steadfastly, putting her sunglasses atop her head.

The roar of his Ferrari Roma echoed loudly when he pressed the throttle. Thiago wasn't paying attention to the fans walking along the road towards the circuit of Spa-Francorchamps, snapping pictures of his car. His attention was solely on Kamari who had been oddly quiet since the moment they had woken up. A small squeal of surprise fled past her lips when he accelerated once more.

"You only had a coffee," he stated quietly.

Her brows slightly rose in surprise. "You noticed?"

Yes, he had spent the majority of breakfast ignoring Kamari and had only spoken to his two best friends. And, yes, he hadn't so much as spared a glance her way, but nothing this woman did went unnoticed by him. "I'm very observant."

"I'm not usually hungry this early in the morning," she explained.

He smiled softly. "Well, we have great catering service in the motorhome. Feel free to ask for anything if you want to eat at some point during the day."

Kamari nodded before turning her attention towards the screen. Her dark hair fell over her face like a curtain, and she tucked a strand behind a pierced ear. No matter how hard he tried to focus, he couldn't keep his wild eyes on the road—not when she was there to distract him.

Thankfully, the journey from the hotel to the circuit was thoroughly short. It was only protocol for the drivers to arrive at the track in their cars.

"Is this your car?" She ran an idle finger over the yellow logo on her seatbelt.

"No, though I have a Ferrari in Monaco."

He couldn't see it, but he knew she was rolling her eyes. "Of course, you do."

He glanced her way. "Primavera and Ferrari are partners.

Every country we go to for races, they lend a car to Rowan and me to use over the weekend."

"That's cool."

He shrugged and smirked smugly. "Being an F1 driver has its perks."

Passing through security with fans lined up behind barriers, Thiago waved his hand through the open window. Cheers erupted, blending with overjoyed screams.

"This is insane," Kamari mumbled, pulling her sunglasses back to the bridge of her nose.

"I know."

He lifted a hand to thank a security guard before pulling into the private parking lot. Turning the engine off, he unbuckled his seatbelt and turned to face Kamari. She mirrored his actions, and for some odd reason, their surroundings seemed to blur for a moment. Photographers and reporters were waiting around his car for them to come out, but Thiago had no intention of putting an end to this moment.

"Are you nervous?" he asked.

She scoffed. "No."

"It's okay if you are," he assured softly.

Digging into her purse, she retrieved a small tube of gloss. "Are you?"

"Obviously." Loosening a breath, he watched her apply her makeup expertly. He was hypnotised by the fullness of her lips. By the way she tried, albeit unintentionally, to lure him closer and closer, like a siren with lethal intentions. "I can't fuck up anymore."

A small line drew itself between her brows. All he wanted was to make her sunglasses disappear because he needed to see forest green. Needed to get lost yet feel grounded at the same time. "Look, Thiago. I think you love racing, and I think you have it in you to win. But you're going to need to do more than say empty words to reach your goals. Actions matter. Results matter. I've no clue what your agent, team principal, or media have been saying about you and me, and quite frankly I don't want to know, but I hope you're not solely relying on me to clean your reputation."

She was right. He wasn't sure if he enjoyed that; that sense of realisation, the uncertainty of it all despite thinking he had a firm grip over his future.

"You're a pawn in my game," he murmured fiercely. He watched her chest rise then fall when she realised his timbre had dropped to a lower octave. "And a king doesn't win without his queen."

When her lips curled into the smallest smile, Thiago felt a wave of relief wash over him. The rare moment crumbled to dust when she let a soft scoff fly past her lips. "Evermore the poet, Thiago Valencia."

He grinned, wondering if her gaze had dropped to his dimples behind her dark glasses. "You haven't heard any of it yet." Ever so carefully, ever so slowly, he lifted a hand up, delicately cupping her jaw. The pad of his thumb ran over the corner of her lips, where he collected the barely noticeable stain of gloss on her skin. When he heard her breath hitch, he realised that he, too, had stopped breathing. "I'm going to be on that podium, Kam. I'm going to win."

She placed her hand on top of his and, for a fragment of a second, he thought she was ready to lean into his touch. Instead, she pulled his hand away, though she applied a minuscule pressure around his fingers; a touch of encouragement, a touch of reassurance.

"Do it for you, Thiago. Not for anyone else."

THE RUSH OF adrenaline was incomparable, irreplaceable, unique.

His staggered breaths could be heard, his heart thundering so wildly that it was nearly foreign to be living through this sensation of raw, unrestrained thrill.

"Full push," Luke said through the radio. "Two laps left. You're currently P2. I repeat, P2."

Second place.

Finally.

After an exhausting race in the rare heat of Belgium, with a strategy that had required countless minutes of negotiations, an outstanding performance from his mechanics who had managed to make his pit stops impressively rapid—under two seconds and a half—Thiago would finally stand on the podium.

"Where's Rowan?" Thiago asked his engineer as he decreased his pace in Stavelot's corner.

"P3."

So that would make a double podium for Primavera Racing.

"Come on, man," Luke said. In the background, Thiago could hear cheers of encouragement, he could feel the anticipation through his engineer's voice.

He focused on pushing at full throttle towards the finish line, his gloved hands gripping tightly his steering wheel. Vibrations jolted through his body; frissons covered every inch of his clothed skin.

Afar, in the distance, the chequered flag was brandished in the air, waved as a token of peace after the forty-four-lap race.

Accelerating one last time after taking the last turn, racing through the last straight line at nearly two hundred kilometres per hour, Thiago lifted his fist in the air when he passed that line —a symbol of triumph and pride and delight.

"We did it, baby!"

All he could hear was the deafening drum of his heartbeat. All screams of excitement were now distant, his surroundings a hazy blur of colours, but he was smiling under his helmet.

He'd done it.

The cool-down lap was a whole blur of red—a sea of fans and supporters jumping in the grandstands. Rowan drove by

Thiago, offering him a thumbs-up, creating a feeling of joy to grip his chest.

Thiago parked his car, and he took a moment to reflect on what he had accomplished over the weekend. To breathe. To sink that feeling in. It had been too long since he had felt so elated and proud of himself.

Lifting the visor of his helmet up, he pressed his fingers against his closed eyes, to prevent threatening tears from falling.

He swallowed thickly. Breathed heavily. Tipped his head back against his seat whilst waiting for his heartbeat to come back at a steady rhythm, but he knew it wouldn't stop. Not today, at least.

Cutting the engine off, he looked up at Rowan who had come out of his own car. They exchanged a fist bump, and by the sight of shimmering stars in his teammate's eyes, he knew Rowan was equally blissful to finally share a podium.

Thiago unfastened his seatbelt, unlocked his helmet, and took the steering wheel out of his car to put it on the hood.

The moment he jumped out of the cockpit, the loudest whistles and claps and applause filled his ears. He made a beeline towards his team who had been waiting behind the barriers and jumped into his car mechanics' arms.

They patted him on the back, the bum, the top of his helmet. They screamed and cheered and cursed in over-excitement.

And standing in the back with Indy, Kamari caught his attention. She had her arms folded across her chest, a small smile illuminating her features when her friend elbowed her side.

Thiago took his helmet and balaclava off, absentmindedly handing them to Cal before threading his fingers through his damp hair.

He winked at Kamari, and she dipped her chin in a subtle motion.

He thought his world was collapsing at this very moment. Thought his surroundings came crashing down to dust, and he didn't know why he was feeling this way—so helpless, and powerless. He could feel the hammer of his heart battering ferociously like rising tidal waves—uncontrollable and wild. Her smile was precious, unique, and rare, and the sight of it sent him plummeting into an abyss of devastation.

And for a moment, for an eternity, time didn't seem to matter anymore because that secret smile of adoration and that longing stare of sincere respect almost meant more than standing on the highest step of the podium.

He'd managed to break one of her walls, to catch a glimpse of her true self behind that tough façade she'd been showing ever since they met. If scoring points, standing on the podium, and brandishing a trophy in the air meant gaining Kamari's validation—and the world's—then he would fight.

Just as Indy pushed her towards him, he gestured for her to come closer. Begrudgingly, she made her way through the crowd, and there she was. Standing before him, putting on that act he had begged her to wear. But she was there, looking radiant, smiling, and putting her trust in him.

"I'm on the podium," he murmured through a broad smile as he held the railing.

She winked playfully, and it was a Herculean effort not to let surprise draw upon his face. They were on camera, on TV, and couldn't afford to make a mistake. "I knew you could do it."

"I couldn't have done it without you and your unconditional support," he teased.

She took a step forward, and he thought he saw a glimpse of her lips tipping upwards. "Shut up."

"I'm going to kiss you, Kamari."

"Do it before you make a fool of yourself for simply looking at me like that."

He cupped her cheek then. Leaned forward. Put his lips on hers.

The kiss was chaste and brief and rapid, yet it felt freeing. Kamari had the power of disentangling the knots of nerves restraining his mind, his heart, and the soft contact of her lips made him feel alive. Thiago kissed her, smiled, and pulled away to go back to reality.

"Thank you," he whispered.

She caressed his upper arm, delicately. "Thank me when you win that championship, pretty boy."

It was a foreign feeling, a wild sensation of the unknown, to find a purpose that drove him towards success and redemption, and to do it for someone else other than him.

CHAPTER SIXTEEN

📍 *SPA-FRANCORCHAMPS, BELGIUM*

T HE SOUND OF a door closing was followed by footsteps that she somehow managed to recognise.

"Are you going somewhere?"

Kamari neatly folded her dress before placing it on top of the clothes that she had already packed inside her luggage. She had overpacked—of course, she had—but panic had overpowered all her senses the moment she knew she had to attend a weekend in Spa. She had to make an appearance in front of important people in the motorsports universe; had to impress Thiago's agent and team principal, and Thiago himself.

"Yes," she said. "Home."

"Home?" Thiago echoed. She could hear the confusion in his voice, could imagine the frown on his face. "With Indy?"

She didn't glance at him from where she knelt on the floor. "Yes. Have you seen her by the way?"

She felt his shadow brushing past her, then he came to sit in the armchair by her suitcase. Kamari couldn't help but look up at him—completely magnetised, spellbound. Grey eyes shone like a pool of starlight, a crimson tinge flushing his sun-kissed cheeks. He was still coming down from his high after securing that podium, and the ecstasy etched on his face suited him.

He had changed out of his racing suit after being sprayed with champagne, into casual jeans paired with a white t-shirt. Leaning back in the chair, legs spread out and elbows resting on both armrests, he peered down at Kamari with curious eyes.

Kamari could still feel the vibrations of the aftermath of the race on her body; the screams of joy, the sprays of champagne falling like rivulets of rain, the happiness unravelling around as she stood with Indy, Cal, Alex, and the Primavera Racing team, looking up at the podium where Thiago claimed the second place and Rowan the third.

She had realised that there was nothing like Formula 1.

During the race, she had managed to control herself from asking too many questions, but she had made a mental note to self-teach when she would be back in London. Quite frankly, all of it had felt like an enigma, and she had stood in the garage for almost two hours, not comprehending a thing, solely smiling and pretending to care for Thiago.

"Sorry to disappoint," he started, not sounding apologetic at all, "but Indigo is getting shit-faced with Cal downstairs at the bar."

"Seriously?"

He chuckled. "Okay, I might've been a little overdramatic here, but she's just having a drink with the guys. What time is your flight?"

Searching around for her phone and giving up after a few heartbeats as she remembered she had left it on the bathroom counter, Kamari reached out and grabbed Thiago's wrist.

A small chuckle erupted from the back of his throat. "You could have just asked for the time, you know."

She released his hand. "Thanks. We have to be at the airport at ten."

"Ten?" he repeated, slightly outraged. "That's, like, in three hours."

Kamari shrugged. "And? It's common knowledge that we should arrive two hours in advance at the airport because we have to check in, go through security, find our terminal—"

"Do you ever stop?"

Kamari blinked. Stared up at him, letting her gaze follow his moves when he leaned forward. "What?"

"Do you ever stop overthinking?"

"Nope." Standing to her feet, she made sure her glare was chilling enough. When he raised his hands in surrender, leaning back in the chaise, she rolled her eyes and took a seat on the edge of the bed.

A sudden flash of unwanted memories started spiralling inside her mind—strong arms, hard chest, warm breaths. She blinked the corrupting memories from this morning's misunderstanding away and asked, "Why aren't you celebrating?"

He pointed to his luggage which he hadn't even unpacked. "Just came to grab a hoodie and a cap." A beat passed, and the way he spoke softly whilst asking the next question was surprising. "Do you want to come with me? I'm going to take a small walk around the circuit."

Something uncanny, foreign, gripped at her chest before slowly releasing until her organ started ricocheting. She hadn't expected this offer, let alone to be included in his late evening activities. "That didn't answer my question."

"About celebrating?" She nodded. He shrugged. "I'm only leaving tomorrow. There's all the time to get drunk later. Come on now, you haven't walked around the track at all this weekend."

Kamari wasn't certain how to react to this—to everything he had noticed about her.

She watched him walk to his suitcase to retrieve a Ralph Lauren cap he placed atop his curls, then grabbed a jumper. He then stood in front of Kamari's bags and took out a light cardigan without disturbing the set up of her clothes.

"Seriously," he said, staring at her. "The more you sit there and watch me with those eyes of yours, the more time will pass by, and you'll be missing this huge opportunity of watching the sun set on a racing circuit. I know I'm pretty to look at, but—"

"You're so full of yourself," she bit out, pushing herself onto her feet. "Fine. Only because I'm not in the mood for socialising and drinking before taking a flight."

Opening the door, he tipped his lips into a roguish smirk. "Just admit that you want to spend some time with me."

"You wish," she drawled, purposely bumping into his shoulder as she exited their bedroom. "No, but seriously, I can't miss the flight, okay? I have to get back to work in the morning, and Indy is working as well. The café opens at seven, but I have to be there at six to help the bakers and—"

"Hey, hey." Catching her elbow, he forced her to stop in her tracks. Flickering her eyes between his, she could perceive that soft glint of concern shimmering around his pupils. "Breathe. Relax, yeah? We'll get back on time and my chauffeur will drop you at the airport. Do you want me to call your parents and tell them I'll have you home by midnight?"

She wriggled out of his grip, scoffing loudly. "You're so annoying."

He grinned, and she couldn't help but rapidly glance at his prominent dimples. "You love me."

"I really don't."

In the lifts, Kamari texted Indy to let her know where she was headed. "No stupid questions to ask?" she demanded, eyes fixated on her message thread with her best friend.

INDY

Be careful babe. Kiss that man for me. Shag him too. PLEASE.

She could see from the corner of her eye that Thiago was

leaning against the panel, watching her with amused eyes. He had draped his jumper over one shoulder, holding Kamari's cardigan in one hand despite her insisting she could carry it herself. "No, unless you want me to play 21 questions."

"Please don't. Your silence is great."

He snickered. "That's what I thought."

Passing by the lounge room that was filled with people celebrating Primavera's double podium, Kamari tried to find a mop of blonde hair certainly tangled in other men's arms. Thiago urged her outside though, a hand on the small of her back.

When he didn't walk towards the parking lot where he had parked his gorgeous Ferrari, she frowned. "Are we walking?"

"No. We'll take the bikes."

"Bikes?" she echoed. "Seriously? I'm not cycling around the circuit. That place is steep, and I haven't worked out this week."

He was thoroughly amused by her burning annoyance. "We're biking to there, not on there."

"Oh."

"You know how to ride a bicycle, don't you?"

"Do I look like I can't? I'm offended."

"That's not what I said."

"Well, yes, I can ride one."

He smirked. "Ride what? Are we talking about a bike or my—"

"God," she grunted, slamming the palm of her hand on his mouth. He laughed, his delight sending vibrations through her digits, tingling towards her arm and the rest of her body. "Why did I agree to do this with you? You're the absolute worst piece of shit."

"You're so easy to annoy," he teased, after batting her hand away.

"Because you're absolutely infuriating."

The smug smirk on the corner of his lips nearly made her temper spark. He leaned closer, and only now did she realise he was gripping her wrist. "Yeah? Is this why you've agreed to do this with me?"

"Go on a track walk?" She scoffed. "I just need to get some air."

A shallow chuckle broke free. "You know I'm talking about dating me, love."

Kamari took one step forward, and the tip of her nose nearly brushed his. "Fake dating," she clarified dryly.

Silver moons dropped to her lips whilst he glided his hand up her forearm, excruciatingly so, feeling the way chills had risen up beneath the scarred palm of his hand. Again, she couldn't find the strength to move. "Don't make a scene now. We have some company and eyes on us—on everything we do."

Glancing sideways, she noticed Leo sitting on the highest step in front of the hotel's entrance, a cigarette hanging loosely between his lips. He dipped his chin in acknowledgement when Kamari met his gaze, and she waved.

Through gritted teeth, she demanded, "Okay, can we go now?"

Thiago smiled widely, then wrapped his arm around her shoulders to pull her to his side. "Look who's eager to leave now. And before you push me away and be all like '*Ew, don't touch me—*"

"I don't sound like that." She was outraged by the voice he had used as she cast a lethal glare she knew would burn his sharp, perfect jawline.

"—please just act like you love being in my arms because McConnell is still looking at us," he continued, ignoring her protest.

"Fine," she muttered with disdain. "I think he hates me."

"Leo?" He led her towards a small shed where the hotel's bikes were kept.

"Yes."

"Impossible." He peered behind his shoulder to watch his

agent. "He asked me a bunch of questions about you this morning when I was warming up for the race."

"What kind of questions? What did you say?"

The shoulder brushing hers got lifted into a small shrug. "I fed him a bunch of bullshit. He wanted to know what you do for a living, and I said you're a model."

A small yelp erupted from her throat. "What?"

His cheek curved inwards to let place to a dimple. "I'm kidding. But you could be one."

"Yeah, you're just trying to flatter me."

"I'm serious," he breathed. "I think you're a beautiful woman, Kamari. You're a bitch, though."

She scoffed, feeling her cheeks tingle as heat spread across her cheekbones. Absentmindedly, she started fidgeting with her ring, keeping her gaze fixed ahead. "Did he say something specific?"

She had been careful about the way she spoke, the way she acted.

"He said you were pretty down to earth. Said you were the most interesting girl I've introduced him to."

"Is that supposed to be a compliment?" A small frown settled between her brows. "Because I didn't talk *that* much."

"You're not the usual obnoxious, attention-seeking gal who knows nothing about F1—"

"Well, I'm a bit uneducated on that."

He shrugged, as if he didn't care about that, as if he would find pleasure in teaching her everything there was to know about his passion. "Leo's just a bit curious about your intentions. He thinks you're looking for fame, thinks you need someone to buy you bags and shoes. He thinks you're using me, but he doesn't know I'm using you all the same."

Kamari scoffed softly. "Oh, please. I don't need anyone to buy me anything."

His stare dropped to the small purse hooked under her arm. "I can see that." A beat passed. "He's just looking out for me.

He's my friend before anything else. Being my agent is his job—it's what I pay him for."

The crease between her eyebrows deepened, and she gaped at him, flickering her gaze over the stubble dusting over his jawline. "Why don't you tell him the truth then?"

"Because he's like the others. He doesn't think I'm capable of loving, of being loved. He thinks I'm just an arse who likes to get my dick wet every night, who'd rather party than race. He doesn't think I can settle down and be serious for once in my life."

Kamari knew she shouldn't care. But there was this subtle pang in her chest that made her heart ache at the sound of the pain laced in his voice. Thiago Valencia was all nonchalance and indifference, accepting the way his fate was written upon the stars, but beneath that radiant smile and golden attitude, lain a broken heart and tarnished soul looking for daylight.

They were now out of sight, and he released her, putting distance between them. She faced the athlete, tipped her chin up, hoping he'd mirror her—an act of confidence, power. "Prove him wrong."

Slowly, he nodded as his eyes sparked with determination. "I will, Kamari. I swear I will."

KAMARI HAD NEVER WITNESSED a scene so unique and mesmerising. From where she stood, she could see an expanse of endless pine trees where the sun was finding shelter behind the canopies. On the other side, she could see a part of the circuit. Yellow and red lines delimited the routes which were free from racing cars, grandstands scattered along the track now empty—a full contrast to when they were filled with motorsports lovers just a few hours ago.

"This is Eau Rouge and the Raidillon," Thiago had said as

they walked up the steep road. "*Two of the most famous and dangerous turns in the motorsports universe.*"

He was now lying down on the warm concrete, his jumper bundled into a makeshift pillow beneath his head as he stared at the sky.

The moon was still hiding behind clouds, and she wasn't sure what Thiago was looking for as he watched the heavens. But the look on his face was something of raw beauty, slow acceptance of the serene silence between them.

They had been sitting there for a moment, and it was the strangest sensation to be in the company of someone whose silence felt like solace.

"Did you have a good day?"

Kamari was taken aback by his sudden question. Sitting beside him with her knees pulled to her chest, her chin resting atop one of them, she glanced at him. The sky's reflection was golden and flaming upon his face.

"Sorry?" That simple word was strangled in her throat.

"I asked if you had a good day."

She furrowed her brows. "Why?"

"Because I want to know."

"Because you want to know," she parroted as if she couldn't believe his interest was genuine. It was, though, because he waited for her to answer.

"A yes or no is enough," he said. "You look surprised."

Wrapping her cardigan around her torso, she settled in the wool's warmth and the late evening sunlight. She didn't know why she was opening up to him as she confessed, "I'm not used to people asking me that."

"Why?"

She shrugged. "Because I'm always the one who asks this question without receiving equal interest in return."

Thiago rose from his position, wiping the concrete's dust off his shirt. He bent his legs at the knees, twisted his cap until it lay backwards on his head, then laced his fingers together. He scoffed loudly, in both outrage and incredulity. "What kind of people do you hang out with, Kam?"

"Kamari," she corrected coldly.

"Really? We're still on a first name basis after that extraordinary kiss we shared at my podium? After cuddling this morning? I thought we were friends."

She didn't blink. "We're not friends."

He tried to suppress his smile, but she managed to glimpse the small twitch of his lips. "Sure, love. You're different, you know. You're not as rude as you try to appear."

Yes, because she'd been so used to putting different versions of herself out to people: the ambitious, selfless, kind entrepreneur and owner of Dawn's Café; the cold-hearted woman who was concealing the deepest, painful wounds; the woman who preferred pushing people away when they got too close because she'd rather be alone than getting hurt over and over again.

But for some uncanny, annoying reason, he had managed to see through her armour.

"Don't let this moment fool you, Valencia. I think I owe you a bit of kindness after all."

"Would it hurt to be nice all the time?"

"Yes," she said. "Because people take advantage of my kindness and take it for granted."

"I'm not most people, Kamari."

She looked away. "Whatever you're trying to do, please stop."

"You mean trying to be your friend? What's the harm in that?"

She would just end up pushing him away, too. "This is strictly professional. We can't cross any line, okay?"

His jaw ticked. Even though it was evident he wanted to fight her, he didn't push her.

A few heartbeats passed by. "You're the people pleaser. The mum of the group. The one who cares too much about others, so that's why you prefer being closed off and putting on that cold façade so you don't get any more hurt than you already are."

Her well-known sense of self-preservation kicked in. "You know nothing about me, Thiago."

"I know," he said quietly, the intensity of his scrutiny burning the side of her face. "But I still stand by what I've already told you: I want to know you."

It was after a moment that she shook her head and whispered, "You're wasting your time."

He thoroughly ignored her remark. "You still didn't tell me how your day went. For me, it went great. Finally scored a podium. It was a sunny race. Feels like I'm on the right path, but it feels a bit too good to be true."

"Well." She paused to peer at him. "Hard work pays off."

It was evident, by the small motion of his lips parting then closing, that he wanted to reply. But not a sound escaped his mouth as he waited for her to speak.

Finally, Kamari sighed. "I had a good day."

There was this eerie feeling of tenderness swirling around them in an invisible yet warm caress—like the summer breeze. She understood she didn't have to pretend around him. Understood she could be honest and blunt and herself.

He tipped the corner of his lips into a small smile. "Did Ava take care of you?"

She shook her head. "I don't need anyone to take care of me, Thiago."

"Who takes care of you then?"

She hated how his features instantly softened the second their gazes collided. How he watched her without a hint of judgement.

She kept her chin high. "I do."

She was not superhuman, she didn't possess magical powers, though she wished she did. She was aware of the way her eyes had misted over—it always occurred when she pretended to be strong, but her eyes always betrayed her.

Thiago released a small breath, a tremulous one. His fingers twitched, like he wanted to reach out to her, but he refrained himself from doing so by rubbing the back of his neck.

"Kamari," he started gruffly.

"What?" she snapped.

He swallowed, and she could almost hear the thoughts ricocheting against the corners of his mind. He bit the inside of his cheek, forcing himself not to ruin the moment. "Nothing. What'd you do today, then?"

She hadn't seen Thiago all day. When they arrived at the circuit, he had a few PR activities to do with Rowan. He then had a meeting with his engineers, and soon came the driver's parade. That activity consisted of all twenty drivers, each sitting in the passenger's seat of a vintage car as they went around the whole circuit, waving to their fans.

She had watched the race by Cal's side in Primavera's garage, an immense bubble of anxiety stirring in the pit of her stomach. Despite it all, the atmosphere was indescribable. From the mutters of encouragement from every single person standing in the room to the vibrations jolting through her body whenever Thiago managed to overtake another driver, to the euphoric screams and excitement when he'd nearly passed in front of Miles Huxley, the winner of the Grand Prix.

Kamari had never witnessed, had never felt such intense oscillations rocketing through the entirety of her body.

"I was mostly with Ava and Indy," Kamari said after letting out a breath. "We ate in Primavera's motorhome and, by the way, your catering service is excellent."

Thiago grinned. She forced herself not to stare at his bewitching smile and landed her gaze upon the small, silver hoop earring on his ear. "I know."

"We walked around the paddock. Talked. Took some pictures."

"And how did you like watching the race?"

She allowed herself to smile, albeit faintly. "I loved it,

although there were a few things like terms, the way strategies work that I didn't understand."

His smile didn't waver, and disappointment did not shine in his stare. "It's okay."

Kamari tilted her head, frowning. "Don't you hate it? The fact I'm not part of your world. That I know nothing of F1 or motorsports."

He scratched his jaw and shrugged with such nonchalance that it almost made her laugh. "I should hate it. It should frustrate me, but no. I think I like it. Makes me look forward to the amount of time I'll be spending with you, teaching you everything there is to know. I'm going to make you love F1 and after that, you won't ever want to leave my world."

She didn't know how to act when he looked at her like that. Particular intentions, unspoken promises were shimmering along the edges of his starlit pupils, and that scrutiny was intense enough to make shivers roll down her spine.

"You'll come to another race, right?"

A soft sigh could be heard through the distant chants of birds and chatter coming from the paddock and garages where workers were packing everything away. "I don't know, Thiago."

He tried to coerce her with a dimpled smile and, as the last sun's ray shone upon his face in a golden streak, she thought the heavens were on his side, too. "Please. I won't be coming back to London this week but if you want to go over your rules again some other time, just invite me for a coffee and I'll sign whatever you put on the table."

"Desperate much?" She arched a brow. "Is this your way of asking me on a date?"

He scoffed. Still, he had tipped his mouth into an amused smirk. "You wish."

Rising to his feet after grabbing his jumper, he extended his hand. He rolled his eyes when Kamari glared at him as though he was plagued with poison. "Come on, Kamari, I'm not your enemy here. Take my hand."

Palm against palm, electricity coursed from one hand to another, setting the rest of her body on fire. She was ready to let go, utterly confused by the way her body had reacted, but he tightened his fingers around hers. Like he didn't want her to go. Like he wouldn't allow her to walk away.

Thiago pulled her up, effortlessly. Grinning at her, he released her hand to nudge her chin with his knuckles. A rapid, light-feather touch, enough to make the walls shielding her heart rattle.

"Let's get you on that plane," he said. "You sure you don't want to stay? Your flight is pretty late. You can skip a day at work."

Kamari shook her head. "It doesn't work like that, pretty boy. I can't leave my business in my brother's hands."

"Okay." As they walked down the road, she noticed the moon had made its appearance in the pink sky. He nudged her with his elbow. "Thank you, pretty girl. For having faith in me when even I can't find that glint of hope."

CHAPTER SEVENTEEN

⚲ *LONDON, ENGLAND*

S HE DID EVERYTHING in her power to stay occupied, to not be distracted by the notification that had lit the screen of her phone up. From cleaning the countertop, to organising the coffee syrups by colour, to rearranging the way she had set her homemade pastries in the fridge; she didn't want to stop and needed to keep her mind busy.

It was a gloomy afternoon, customers were rushing in and out of Dawn's Café whilst others were getting seated to enjoy a drink and a pastry, alone or in the company of friends.

Kamari deposited a cappuccino followed by a cinnamon roll in front of a woman sitting in the furthest corner, right by the large bookshelf, offering a kind smile her way.

"Enjoy," she said sweetly before pivoting, tucking the empty tray under her arm.

A blossoming migraine was growing like poisonous vines, making her pulse thrum against her temple. Setting the tray down on the counter, she glanced around, noticing there wasn't a single table empty.

"Kam," Kieran said, his back turned to her as he cleaned the espresso machine. "I need a favour."

"No," she instantly replied dryly, rounding the counter to grab a glass of water to soothe her headache.

"Please," her brother pleaded, facing her. He set the teacups where they belonged, offering a coy smile to Kamari.

She shook her head. "No. I already know what you're going to ask."

He leaned his hip against the countertop, folding his arms across his chest. His locks fell over his brows in a dishevelled manner when he contorted his face into a glower. "You owe me one after you hid the fact you're"— he lowered his voice, leaning forward—"dating an F1 driver."

The roll of her eyes was nearly automatic. "God, Kieran. You're never going to let that go, are you?"

Kamari had never told the truth behind the deal with Thiago to her brother. Why? Because she didn't trust him. Kieran and James were childhood friends, and there wasn't a shadow of a doubt that Kieran would tell her ex-boyfriend everything was a scheme of pretence—a faux story meant to deceit and break more hearts.

Embarrassment would flood her if the truth got out of her inner circle.

Kieran threw his hands in the air. "I love F1. I love Thiago Valencia. All I want is a paddock pass and a picture with the bloke."

"You talked with him the other night," she pointed out. "Isn't a private moment like that better than race tickets?"

"No! Well, yes, but still." A deep frown settled between his brows as he pushed his hair back. "How did you even meet him?"

"I already told you." She untied the knot of her short, black apron, shook the material aimed to protect her trousers, then tied it back around her waist. "At a party through Indy."

Kieran had been asking her the same question every day since she came back from Belgium three days ago.

"Will he come to my birthday party?" he asked after a moment of silence.

She took another sip of water. "Yes."

"Is he coming by any time soon?"

She lifted her shoulders in a small shrug, controlling the annoyance threatening to fester into a burning fire. "I don't know. He's in the Netherlands right now."

She was aware her brother already knew about that. "I know," he said, eyes illuminating with a small spark of hope. "Can I ask him for paddock passes when he comes by?"

The small bell above the door chimed, diverting her attention to the incoming customer. Relief surged through her when Diana strolled inside, shopping bags in hands. "Sure."

The redhead found the empty stool in front of the counter. Dropping her bags on the floor, she sat down as a sigh escaped her mouth. "I'm broke," she announced, leaning her chin in the palm of her hand.

"You wouldn't be if you hadn't spent all your money on unnecessary clothes," Kieran commented quietly.

"Clothes are always necessary," Diana snapped.

"Tired of studying?" Kamari asked, slightly amused by the scowl on her friend's face.

"Criminal law can kiss my bum," Diana mustered, reaching over to grab a homemade cookie from the tray. "I can't believe I'm still in uni whilst you're all thriving with adult life."

Kamari couldn't help but snort. "Adult life isn't *fun*, Di. It's all bills and anxiety."

Diana flickered her gaze over Kamari's physique, her brows slightly rising. "If bills and stress look like *you*, then I can't wait to graduate."

Kieran interjected as he made Diana a tall glass of iced

caramel coffee. "Weren't you supposed to be graduating the same year as Kam?"

"Yes," Diana drawled. "But I took a gap year when she was in her first year, remember? What the hell, Ki? We see each other every day. How did you forget about that?"

"Gee, Diana, I don't know. Cut me some slack, will ya?"

Kamari ignored them when her phone resting next to the register chimed. She made the fatal error of glancing at the notification, only to feel her heart momentarily stop before going back to beating erratically.

@THIAGOVALENCIA

Kamariiiii

Heyyyy

She thought about not answering him, but she knew the voice in the back of her mind would not stop bothering her if she left his message unread. She hadn't heard from him since Sunday night. After walking her back to the hotel, he had hung out in the room as she packed the last few items into her luggage whilst rambling about a time he had broken his elbow during a karting race when he was six years old. He had walked her and Indy to the car where Rick waited patiently, then charmingly kissed her cheek before murmuring another whisper of gratitude in her ear.

Kamari wasn't sure what he had been up to. His social media activity had been quiet for the past three days, but she knew he had left for the Netherlands for the upcoming race.

The only thing she had been fearing was to stumble upon photographs of him partying or with another woman on his arm. She had seen neither of those, only a few videos from Alex when they grabbed a few beers at the hotel's bar.

@KAMARI.MONROE

What do you want?

@THIAGOVALENCIA

Ever the sweetest person I know

How are you?

@KAMARI.MONROE

Miss me much?

@THIAGOVALENCIA

Yes, and?

@KAMARI.MONROE

You've got no sense of self-preservation.

@THIAGOVALENCIA

As if you didn't know that by now.

What are you up to?

@KAMARI.MONROE

Working

It's busy today

@THIAGOVALENCIA

Did you manage to get some rest after your
late flight?

@KAMARI.MONROE

No

We're short on staff this week

@THIAGOVALENCIA

I'm sorry 😔

Take a nice bath tonight, yeah?

@KAMARI.MONROE

A bath sounds so good right now

@THIAGOVALENCIA

Send me a pic

@KAMARI.MONROE

No

Why are you even texting me? What do you want?

@THIAGOVALENCIA

Do you want to get away for the weekend and come to the race?

I can ask Ava to send you the passes and arrange for Rick to pick you up

@KAMARI.MONROE

Can't.

@THIAGOVALENCIA

Oh

Can you at least pretend you'll be watching?

@KAMARI.MONROE

How?

@THIAGOVALENCIA

Just put a story of you watching the GP

Tag me and I'll repost

Feel free to put lots of hearts

And a caption like "good luck to the love of my life"

@KAMARI.MONROE

You're insufferable.

@THIAGOVALENCIA

I know

@KAMARI.MONROE

I guess I can do that. But I'm leaving my account on private.

@THIAGOVALENCIA

Accept my follow request then

You've left me pending for DAYS

I'm dying to access your personal world

Wait WTF!

How come Alex is following you

And CALLAHAN ffs?!!?

What about ME!! Your BOYFRIEND

@KAMARI.MONROE

Stop being dramatic. I'll accept the request now.

@THIAGOVALENCIA

I'm the happiest man alive <3

People will have to get through me before talking shit about or to you.

@KAMARI.MONROE

I can defend myself just fine.

@THIAGOVALENCIA

I know

Don't you think it's time you let someone take care of you though?

CHAPTER EIGHTEEN

⚲ *LONDON, ENGLAND*

S HE HADN'T PLANNED on watching the F1 qualifying, but Indy had insisted on putting the sports channel on the moment she had entered the café.

Kamari was busy working, though. So, in between brewing coffee and tea, making plates filled with pastries, registering customers' orders, and running left and right, she was barely able to glimpse at the television that had been stealing most of her customers' attention.

"Ah, that sucks," Indy mumbled to herself in between bites of cheesecake.

Kamari passed by her with an empty tray, lifting her brows at the sight of her friend's lips twisted into a wince. "What?"

"Rowan didn't make it through Q1. First time in the season a Primavera is out so quickly."

Looking up at the screen, she watched the cameraman follow Rowan Emerson walking back to the garage, tearing his balaclava off. He looked absolutely furious as he talked in quiet murmurs with his physiotherapist. Kamari hadn't spoken to him, nor had she seen that much of him when she was in Spa, but she'd heard he could be as ruthless and heartless as Thiago if he didn't get what he wanted.

She frowned slightly. "How? He has the best car."

"Engine failure," Indy explained. "That cheesecake is marvellous, Kam. Did you change the recipe?"

Kamari shook her head and grabbed the fork Indy tended to her. Taking a small bite, she approved of the sweet taste with a small nod. "I used biscoffs—or as they call them in Belgium, speculoos—instead of the usual digestive biscuits."

Indy emitted a delighted sigh when she bit into the pastry, pointing at the cake with her fork. "So good."

Kamari smiled. "Thank you."

Indigo patted the empty stool next to her. "Sit down for a second. You're overworking again."

Begrudgingly, Kamari sat down, knowing her best friend would be capable of manhandling her into a chair if she didn't take a break. "You know how I am."

"Why don't you hire someone else? You could work morning shifts and use your afternoons to pay bills, go over legal stuff and all, instead of doing paperwork at night."

Propping an elbow atop the counter, Kamari leaned her chin in the palm of her hand. "It's not financially possible as of right now."

Indy's eyes misted over with a sorrowful gloom. She placed her fork atop the midnight blue plate, sighing softly. "Can I maybe help you? I could take a shift or two if you'd like, and I'm sure Diana would love to help—"

"No," Kamari answered. "You two are sweet but I don't need help."

Indy didn't try to fight Kamari, because she knew she shouldn't be wasting her time arguing. Instead, she only dismissed her friend's remark with a shrug, lifting her gaze back up to the television. "Oh, here's your man."

Resentment surged through her, but mostly at her own self because she was rapid at reacting. Straightening herself and tipping her chin up, she brought her undivided attention to the screen.

Thiago was driving out of the pit lane, ready to make his first lap.

Kamari reached over the counter to find her water bottle, distracting herself from the battering rhythm of her vital organ. "He asked if I wanted to go to the race the other day."

Surprise edged Indy's tone. "He texted you?"

"Yeah."

"Why didn't you say yes?"

Kamari waved a hand around. "Can't you see the business I'm trying to run?"

Indy rolled her eyes in slight annoyance. "Your brother and employees can take care of Dawn just fine, Kam."

Kamari didn't respond, and she could feel the worry in her friend's perusal burn the side of her face.

"Anyway." Noticing the lack of response from Kamari, Indy changed the subject. "You never told me how it was to share a bed with him."

She had tried her hardest to push last weekend's events in the very back of her mind, not wanting to recall how it felt to be in his arms. Lifting her gaze back to the screen, she announced, frankly, "There's nothing to say because nothing happened. We crashed as soon as we got into bed."

"Bullshit," her friend replied loudly with a snort before slapping a hand over her mouth at her loud outburst. "Like two individuals like you have managed to keep your hands off each other."

Kamari glared Indy's way. "We didn't even look at each other."

Blue eyes glimmered with sparkles of amusement. "Liar. Does he sleep naked?"

A beat passed. Kamari bit the inside of her cheek. "Just shirtless."

Kamari almost thought Indy was about to faint. With a soft squeal flying past her lips and her pupils dilating, the blonde asked, "And?"

A rosy tinge started to bloom on her cheekbones as she tried to bring back the memories of his hard ridges to the surface. She'd been enveloped in a haze of fatigue, slight anxiety, turmoil, and unfathomable comfort when she had woken up. Nevertheless, it was quite difficult not to remember sun-kissed skin, a muscular chest, a toned abdomen, strong arms and biceps.

"I don't remember." She shrugged, indifferent. "Didn't even look at him."

"Oh, seriously?" Indy grunted in defeat, then grabbed her best friend's upper arms. "Give me something, girl. Not even a kiss? You didn't get handsy?"

"No."

"That's insane." A pout formed on Indy's lips. "Well, you're stronger than me because I don't know if I would've been able to keep my hands to myself with Thiago Valencia sleeping in the same bed as me."

Kamari snorted, though she wasn't amused. The back of her throat burned as she said, "Get with him, Indigo. He's all yours."

"No, thank you. Besides, Thiago would never accept that."

"Why not?"

Indy's eyes shined. "Because the way he looks at you, Kam... You're like a gold medal, something as beautiful as a World Champion title."

"I don't care about him, and he only sees me as a pawn in his game. Don't be delusional, Indy. Nothing will *ever* happen between us."

Sᴜɴᴅᴀʏ ᴄᴀᴍᴇ ʙʏ in the blink of an eye, and all Kamari could think about was the way Thiago had celebrated the ending of yesterday's qualifying.

Having managed to make the third fastest lap, he had been more than delighted to participate in the post-interview reserved for the top three qualifiers.

Kamari had been busy cleaning up a table when the chequered flag was brandished at the end of Q3, putting Thiago third overall. She hadn't been able to ignore the small spark of happiness surging through her veins when she had seen the camera pointed at him, focusing on his gleaming eyes—like actual stars had been shining in them.

She had found herself utterly mesmerised by the way he ran his fingers through his dark locks, the way crimson coated his cheekbones. He'd stood in front of the presenter quite happy with his results, his lips tipped into a dimpled smile that was meant to destroy Kamari's heart.

She was now sitting in between Indy and Diana on her sofa, a few snacks scattered on the coffee table whilst they were enveloped in blankets. The weather had shifted drastically; the sky was dark with brooding clouds all the while misty rain fell all over town in fine lines.

"Race predictions?" Indy asked in between mouthfuls of popcorn.

"I don't care," Diana grumbled, her eyes fixated on the book opened on her lap.

Kamari shrugged, silently hoping Thiago would be on the podium.

She had done what he had asked. Under the amused gaze of Indy, Kamari had taken over ten pictures, trying to find the perfect one, before putting on her story a photo of her television displaying the starting grid with all twenty drivers sitting in their cars, waiting for the lights to go out after driving around the track for the formation lap to warm up their tyres.

She had tagged Thiago, followed by a fingers-crossed emoji.

A few of her acquaintances had reacted to the story, wondering when she'd become an F1 fan, but she blatantly ignored everyone.

Holding her breath, she cradled a pillow to her chest and watched as the five red lights hanging horizontally above the drivers' heads went out.

"It's lights out and away we go," Indy said at the same time as the commentator, seamlessly clapping in her hands as she sat on the edge of the sofa.

Kamari watched as Thiago pushed on the throttle, whilst all the cars started in perfect sync. She could barely breathe when he overtook Miles Huxley, who was starting on the front row in second position, their front wings mere centimetres away from touching as they took the first turn.

"Ah, fuck," Indy mumbled, grabbing Kamari's upper arm as though it would help her ease her nerves. "I'm so stressed out."

Pushing Indy's hand away, she focused on the red car with the number seven on it. She watched Thiago and Miles drive wheel to wheel, though never touching. Set in the Netherlands, this particular circuit was short, winding and sinuous, yet tricky. Indy had told her it was difficult to overtake on that track—but not as arduous as overtaking in Monaco.

Diana wasn't paying attention at all. She had come to *'emotionally support her friends'* and get away from her housemates who had partied all night long.

Thiago managed to overtake Huxley, earning a loud cheer of encouragement from Indy, and a small sigh of relief from Kamari.

Suddenly, Huxley passed by him, followed by another car, and another one, until Kamari realised he was slowing down and losing power.

"What's going on?" she asked quietly, frowning.

"Shhh," Indy hushed, turning the volume up until the zipping roar of engines was replaced by the diffusion of Thiago and his engineer's exchange through the radio.

"I'm losing power," Thiago announced, raw anger thickening his voice. His wrath could be poisonous, lethal—everyone knew that. *"Fuck. This cannot be happening!"*

"I'm sorry," his race engineer replied.

"Idiot," Indigo mustered.

"Sorry? Is sorry going to fix the engine? You fucking—" The radio cut before he could express his anger on live TV.

A yellow flag was brandished in the air, indicating to all remaining nineteen drivers to slow their pace down as they were forbidden to overtake. Thiago could barely pull to the side as he stopped in the middle of the track.

The camera's angle showed him from the side as he repeatedly slammed his gloved palm upon the steering wheel. Lifting the visor of his helmet, he pressed his fingers to his eyes—forcing himself not to break down in front of millions of spectators.

Kamari's heart ached as she watched the torment of his nightmares unravel before her eyes.

"Fuck!" he shouted again. Then, his voice grew angrier, raspier. *"No. No. No!"*

Finally, he took his steering wheel out to pull himself out of the cockpit. Stewards dressed in vibrant orange were circling him and the car, trying to guide him towards an exit to keep him safe whilst others waved at a tractor to come to extract the car out of the way.

"This could take some time," Indy explained. "The safety car is out."

A burgundy Mercedes AMG was leading the queue of F1 cars that had slowed down.

Kamari couldn't muster a single word as she watched Thiago kick a tyre before walking hastily towards an exit. Passing through protective barriers, ignoring the stewards running after him, shrugging the hands daring to comfort him, his own hands were curled into fists, his demeanour a mix of burning wrath and defeat.

"Well, looks like it's a bad weekend for Primavera Racing," Diana said.

Failure would destroy Thiago.

Kamari didn't care about him. She barely understood how the regulations and everything else worked in the F1 universe.

Nevertheless, she wanted to reach out to him, let her guard down for a fraction of a second, and coax him through that undeniable pain.

CHAPTER NINETEEN

⚲ *ZANDVOORT, THE NETHERLANDS*

T WAS THE startling buzz of steady vibrations in the front pocket of his jeans that brought him back to reality.

A long puff of breath escaped his mouth, evaporating into the salty air surrounding him. Glancing at the unknown number flashing on his screen, Thiago debated not to answer. Perhaps his number had been leaked—it had happened before—and it was some fan trying to get a hold of him after he went into hiding after today's disaster. Or maybe it was one of his one-night stands whose number hadn't been registered in his contacts, calling him to meet up. The temptation was there, but he wasn't in the mood to distract himself like that and, besides, he still had a reputation to clean. Allegedly, he was dating someone too, and he wouldn't betray Kamari.

He stared at the number, waiting for the caller to hang up, which they eventually did after thirty seconds. Regardless, the bizarre sensation stirring in the pit of his stomach almost made him think he should've picked up. His screen flashed again, but the caller didn't insist.

About to pocket his phone, the incoming text message illuminating his screen made his heart do a somersault.

@KAMARI.MONROE

How about you answer my phone call?

An involuntary smile spread across his lips. Leaning against the bricks behind him, he let the cool breeze brush his cheekbones—a tender caress despite the chilling temperatures.

He knew Kamari had been a caring woman her entire life— he had watched and seen the way she acted with Indigo and her entourage—and that was why she had called. Because she cared. Because she felt. And no matter how hard she tried to appear cold and bitter, no amount of flaring annoyance could truly shield her heart.

@THIAGOVALENCIA

I'd love it if you begged to hear my voice

@KAMARI.MONROE

Keep dreaming.

A scoff fled past his lips when he brought the phone to his ear, waiting for Kamari to pick up the call. She let it ring, again and again, evidently taunting him by testing his patience.

"Hello?" she said, as if she didn't know who was calling, incredulity blended into her tone.

"I didn't take you for a resentful person," he stated calmly despite his heart hammering at the sound of her smoky, enticing voice.

"I'm not," she retorted, coldly. "I forgive easily, but I never forget."

He chuckled. "You're such a loser."

"I'm not sure you're in the right position to call *me* a loser after DNFing your race, Valencia."

"Ouch." He even rubbed his chest, but his smile was obvious in his tone. "I had it coming."

"Yep."

Tipping his head against the wall, he closed his eyes, loosening a long, heavy breath. He absorbed the peaceful sounds of waves colliding with each other, listening to a rustling sound on the other side of the line. "Hey, brat," he murmured.

"Hey, pretty boy," Kamari whispered back.

His shoulders slumped as though a huge torrent of relief came crashing over him. This was foreign—finding comfort in someone's voice, wanting to hear more of it as though it would keep him anchored, grounded.

"Where are you?" she asked.

She could probably hear the whirring sound of the wind blowing and the distant cacophony of the ocean's chant. Many people surrounded him, but still, he wanted to be lost in a world alone.

He pulled the hood of his jumper over his dishevelled hair. "At the beach."

"Wow," she mused. "And here I am, under rainy London."

He shrugged, then remembered Kamari couldn't see him. "You could've been here with me if you had accepted my offer."

"Maybe another time."

He smirked. "Maybe?"

"Maybe," she echoed, emphasising this word that had managed to alight some spark of hope inside him.

He allowed a smile to stay on his lips. "Why are you calling, Kamari? I'm going to start thinking you care about me."

There was an excruciating moment of silence, then a rustling sound as if Kamari was moving around. Her voice grew distant, and he understood she had put the speaker on. "I don't know," she murmured. He could hear the turmoil in her tone, the hesitancy in her words. "I'm going to hang up, okay? I didn't mean to force you to call me back—"

"Don't," he interrupted quietly. "Stay on the phone. Talk to me, Kam."

"Kamari," she corrected dryly. "I'm going to start thinking you miss me."

There she is.

"Don't be delusional," he teased. "Actually, hearing your voice is not that much of a nightmare."

"Charming." Another beat passed, and then, as softly as ever, she asked, "Are you okay?"

This moment was rare—a moment where Kamari allowed Thiago to glimpse the big heart she always kept hidden behind an ice façade. She was only meant to help him redeem himself, but finding solace in forest green eyes wouldn't harm him, right?

His jaw unconsciously tightened. "What do you think?"

He imagined her sitting on her windowsill, watching the raindrops crash on her window. "What happened?"

He ran a hand over his face, trying to rub the frustration and fatigue off. He could feel the coldness on the tip of his nose as the cold wind crashed over him. "Did you watch the race?"

"Yes," she admitted quietly, as if she had suddenly become timid. "I posted the story like you asked."

"I know." He smiled, revelling in the view of the tidal waves reflecting the burning sky's colours. He didn't know for how long he had been sitting here, but he assumed it had been hours. "You could've put a heart or something, but I guess tagging me was already a tremendous effort for you."

She scoffed. "I've been avoiding my account like the plague."

"Why?"

"I keep receiving hundreds of follow requests."

He exhaled. "I'm sorry."

"Don't be," she assured. "I guess people are just curious to see who your mystery girl is."

His pulse started thrumming in sync with the wildness of the sea. "Well, I kind of want my mystery girl to stay my secret."

"Your way of flirting doesn't work with me."

"What does then?"

"Nothing."

"Yeah, sure," he scoffed playfully. "I bet you're all flushed and nervous right now."

"You wish," she bit out, her voice not wavering. "I called to hear about your disastrous day, not to hear your conceited jokes."

"You are as lovely as ever, Kamari." When she didn't reply, he released a long sigh, tremulous and filled with chagrin. "I think it was my fault."

"What was?"

"The engine failure."

Thiago could almost see the frown on her face as she said, "I might not know much about F1 and cars, but I don't think it's something you can control, Thiago. It was in no way your fault. You can bounce back next weekend, right?"

He swallowed, thickly. "I don't have much of a choice. The title is slipping through my fingers."

"What happens if you don't win the championship?"

"Then it might be over." His voice cracked, and he didn't want to think of the possibility of his dream coming to an end. "The team's going to see me as a fucking failure, and no other team would want to sign me. I don't want to drive for another team. I don't want to be done with F1; my career's only starting."

Another rustling sound. A soft sigh escaping her mouth. "You don't see it, do you? The way people root for you. The way they still believe in you despite the mistakes that have been done. I'm not saying you won't win this season, but what if you only focus on gaining your agent's, your team's trust, before anything else?"

Clenching his jaw, he tried to make the lump inside his throat disappear. "I don't know."

"As I said, I'm not really familiar with your universe, but I think great sportsmanship comes with showing the real human behind that racing suit and helmet. I don't know what you said to your engineers and car mechanics when you left the circuit, and whilst I know each driver only cares about themselves, it's also a team sport, isn't it? You can be angry at yourself and at the whole world, but your anger shouldn't destroy your dreams. Tomorrow, you're going to walk into the garage and sit around a table to work with your mechanics so you can win next weekend's race, okay?"

He wasn't certain how he was still breathing after hearing those words coming out of Kamari's mouth. She'd been so intent on not showing her true colours, thinking she was dressed in black and white, but he was convinced she was golden—she simply didn't know it just yet.

"What are you going to do if I don't win?"

"I'm walking away from you."

He rubbed the back of his neck, ever so slightly shaking his head. "Oh, no," he started sardonically, "how will I ever survive without my incredible girlfriend?"

"You won't," she simply answered.

The crescent moon had made its appearance from behind the clouds, waning overhead and casting its silvery glow on the ocean. Even kilometres away, Kamari managed to find a way to make her presence noticeable.

"How many races are there left?" she then asked. He liked it when her curiosity was genuine.

"Seven."

"You've got this." He heard a soft swishing sound, then her voice became louder and clearer as she held the phone to her ear. "My Nana used to tell me that everything was possible if we poured all of our will and desire into our dreams."

He couldn't help but smile softly. "I think your Nana might've been right."

Kamari hummed. "She was always right."

"What are you doing?" He looked at the time on his watch, noticing it was nearing nine o'clock.

"Aren't you a curious little thing?" she parroted the words he'd used on her once, making his smile grow wide. "I'm making myself a snack."

"That's nice." He dipped his chin in a nod when an elderly couple passed by him. "Tell me about your day."

"Why? My life's not as interesting as yours."

"It is to me."

"Trust me, it's not. My life consists of work, work, and more work."

"I admire your resilience."

Silence.

"Kam?"

"Yeah?" she breathed.

"Did I say something wrong?"

"No," she whispered. Her voice was strangled in her throat, and she wasn't able to hide her vulnerability. "No one has ever told me that before."

"Fuck, Kam," he said. "What kind of people have you dated before?"

"Arseholes, it appears."

Now it was his time to be silent. Hands curling into fists, he could feel molten anger seep through his veins.

"I'm sorry—"

"Can we not talk about that?"

He rubbed his eyes. "Yeah, I'm sorry."

"Stop saying you're sorry."

"I'm sorry."

"Thiago."

He pressed his lips into a thin line, then forced himself to let out a heavy breath. "I like the sound of your voice."

The sound of a cabinet door closing behind her could be heard. "Thiago," she started. "We need to keep this professional. I'm going to hang up, and you're going to stop flirting with me."

He bit the interior of his cheek. "You know you're making it impossible for me, right?"

Her voice was graced with a teasing tone. "I know."

"Don't push me away," he asked, tone low and quiet, as though he'd been terrified of murmuring those words that had uncontrollably slipped out.

"I can't promise you that," she said after a few heartbeats.

"Kam... I am not your enemy."

She sighed. "I know. I'll try."

Thiago didn't know how a stranger had found so much faith in him. Perhaps she'd been able to see something that lay deep beneath his heart that even himself couldn't find despite his greatest efforts.

Kamari made it harder for him to see her as a mere pawn in his strategy.

"I've got to go," she said at last, after what felt like an eternity of peaceful silence.

"Yeah," he breathed. "Okay. Thank you, Kam."

"Of course. Good night, Thiago."

"Good night, love."

And even when the line went dead, he kept his phone to his ear, hoping she'd call again, wishing she'd let her armour down. He watched the moon, longing for that sensation of completeness, wanting nothing but for the void around his soul to finally fill itself.

CHAPTER TWENTY

⚲ *LONDON, ENGLAND*

"WHAT ARE YOU doing here, Valencia?"

Kamari wanted to wipe that smirk playing on the corner of his mouth. Wanted to erase that gleam of satisfaction swirling along the edges of his pupils when he noticed the frustration emanating from her demeanour.

Leaning against the doorframe, Thiago stood with his arms folded across his chest, amused by Kamari's deadly glare. "Is this a way to greet me, Monroe? That's not very nice." He shook his head, then lowered his brows, blinking. "You're breaking my heart into millions of pieces."

"My heart is bleeding," she noted, impassively. She took him in with an excruciating once-over, causing him to smirk smugly. "How'd you find my flat?"

He arched a brow. "Doesn't take a genius to know you live above the café you own."

Kamari narrowed her gaze on him. "And how did you manage to get through the door without the passcode?"

She already knew the answer.

"Indigo," he replied, unfazed.

"I hate her," she muttered under her breath.

He lifted his shoulders in a small shrug. "Well, you weren't answering your phone so I had to do something about it."

Gripping the doorknob, she held Thiago's magnetising stare, controlling herself to stay cool and calm and collected when it was everything but easy not to shift under the intensity of his scrutiny.

She hadn't seen him since Spa, which was over a week ago. She hadn't heard from him since their call on Sunday night, which was two days ago.

"As you can see,"—she gestured behind herself, forcing him to look at where she was pointing—"I am super busy and have no time to reply to your messages."

He pushed himself off the doorjamb, and his sudden presence was punishing—his height, his chiselled features, his cologne that left trails of musk in its wake. "Don't tell me you're spending your evening doing paperwork."

Kamari lifted her shoulders in a sheepish shrug. "Welcome to the life of an entrepreneur."

"Overachieving, overworking, overthinking entrepreneur," he corrected.

She crossed her arms over her chest. "You're saying this like it's a bad thing."

Expression softening, he offered her a sweet smile and shook his head. "It's not. I think it's admirable, but maybe you should take a step back tonight."

A small line drew itself between her brows. "Why would I do that?"

"Because it's your birthday."

Everything stopped—the time, her heart, her racing thoughts. "How do you know that?"

He grinned, and it was impossible not to stare at his handsome features brightening like he'd been exposed to the brightest ray of sunshine. "I watched Indy's story."

She suppressed a grunt. "Of course you did."

"Why aren't you celebrating?" he asked, slightly tilting his head to the side before letting his perusal travel down her physique. Chills skittered down her spine, though she felt hot all of a sudden.

Kamari shrugged, flickering her stare to the white wall behind him. "I hate my birthday."

"Oh."

"You're supposed to be in Italy to prepare for this weekend's race. Why are you here?"

He rubbed the back of his neck. "If you think I came back to London to take you out for your birthday, you're absolutely wrong. The world does not revolve around you. But since I was here for testing and sim sessions at the factory, I thought I'd stop by."

Heart somersaulting, pulse thrumming against every inch of her skin, Kamari needed to hold some semblance of control through this storm of wild emotions. "How considerate of you." She was ready to close the door. "Thanks for that. Bye now."

"Wait." He caught her wrist, gently. "One hour of your time. That's all I'm asking."

She dropped her stare to where his large hand enveloped her wrist, wondering if he could feel the jolt of electricity coursing down her arm. "For what?"

A coy smile spread across his lips. "Can't tell you. Come on, it's a nice evening and people are out. Might be a good opportunity to be spotted by some fans."

Hesitantly, Kamari released a soft sigh, observing the tenderness glinting in his grey moons. She couldn't keep lying to herself and pretend she was having fun filling in all of those administrative papers. Still, she didn't need to be saved by this man who had the tendency of showing up during her worst moments of dismay.

"You're getting one hour max," she said firmly, giving in.

Thiago released her wrist and lifted his hands in surrender, acquiescing her demand with a vigorous nod. "Yes, ma'am."

Kamari took a step to the side and invited him to enter her flat. She wasn't sure how to act with Thiago Valencia walking around her living room. With anxiety coiling deep inside her gut, she collected books scattered on her coffee table, picked up the empty teacup laying next to her laptop.

"Don't mind the—"

"If you say your place is a mess," he started, voice low, chilling, and gravel-like, "I swear I'm going to laugh at you."

She wasn't expecting him to be standing so close when she pivoted. Breath hitching, she lifted her gaze to look into his eyes, cradling her novels to her chest, one hand tightly gripping her mug as though it would keep her grounded.

"Your place is immaculate," he whispered whilst his eyes were roaming over her face—analysing, observing, remembering.

"Thanks."

His mouth curled into a devastating smile. He took one step forward, and she made no move to back away, like she had been struck immobile. "Do I make you nervous, Kamari?"

She tipped her chin up. "No."

Lies.

Her heartbeat had been thundering wildly, ferociously, ever since he had knocked on her door, and she knew he would have been able to hear the rhythm of her dismay if the distance between them had been smaller. She watched as his pupils dilated, turning his eyes into a riveting shade of molten grey.

"Sure," he droned, gaze settling on her lips. Giving her space by taking a step back, he raked his fingers through his hair, ever so slightly shaking his head as though he was battling with his inner thoughts.

"I'm going to go and get changed," she stated, impressed that her voice didn't quiver.

"Yeah," he rasped, now rubbing the back of his neck, looking at the picture frame hung above her television. "You do that."

Placing the items she had been holding on the kitchen's island, she peered at him from her shoulder. He was now sitting on her sofa. "Yeah, sure, make yourself at home."

"Thanks," he grinned, evidently taunting her. "I thought you'd never give me permission."

She couldn't help but roll her eyes. "Should I wear anything specific?"

She thought he took his phone out to force himself not to stare at her. "Whatever you're comfortable in. And wear something warm. Preferably a few layers."

"Warm? Layers?" She looked out the window, remembering it had been a rather sunny day. "Why?"

"You'll see."

TIME SEEMED TO come to a halt the moment she stepped out of her bedroom. Thiago had lifted his gaze from his phone to gape at her silhouette, only to keep his burning regard on her, brows lifting in pleasant surprise and lips curving into a smile that managed to make shivers crawl down her spine.

Kamari looked down at herself, frowning. "What? Is this too much? Or not enough?"

Thiago leaned back on the sofa, legs spread out. He lifted both his hands to tangle his fingers through his tousled hair, making his jumper rise. She tried—she really did—to hold his stare, but she couldn't help but gape at the displayed bronze skin, glimpsing at the sliver of prominent abdominals he showed.

"No," he said gruffly, forcing her to find silver eyes already looking at her. He stood up, and she suddenly felt so small. "You're always fucking pristine wherever you go, Kam."

She didn't want to blush. Didn't want to show how much he was starting to affect her. Didn't want him to be nice and sweet and attentive.

She almost told him it was because she cared about other people's judgment, but she decided to keep this secret to herself.

Kamari lifted her shoulders in a shrug as she walked towards the closet by the entrance to retrieve a pair of shoes. "I could die tonight, so I'd rather die in fashion."

His laugh was loud, almost contagious. "That's the spirit."

After tying her shoelaces, she scowled at Thiago when he looked at her with a grin on his lips, the top of his cheekbones slightly tinted in crimson. "Don't be a weirdo. Let's go now."

He followed her out of the flat, excitement emanating from his allure. She could feel the heat his body radiated on hers as they descended the narrow staircase leading to the café, and suddenly, all of that open space before her felt like a ravine of darkness.

"How long have you been living here?" he asked, unaware of the way his existence affected her.

"About three years."

"And the café? When did you open it?"

"A year or so ago. It used to be a bakery before, but they had to close for personal reasons."

"That's impressive, you know. Starting a business at such a young age. Wait, how old are you?"

She stopped in her tracks, turning. He abruptly came to a halt, holding on to the railing to keep himself from falling. He stood on a higher step, forcing her to crane her neck to stare into his eyes. "How old do you think I am, Thiago?"

He shrugged.

"Turning 24 today," she said, pivoting to stride down the stairs.

"Oh." His footfalls came in behind her, his shadow following. "I'm 25."

"I didn't ask."

"My birthday's in July."

"You're a cancer?"

A soft grunt was audible, blending with their loud footsteps. "Don't tell me you're into that astrology shit."

"Fine," she said, finally reaching the bottom. "I won't tell you."

They exited the dimly lit corridor which didn't require the passcode to leave, landing on the sidewalk. The cool breeze hit her like a gentle caress, the fresh air reminding her she was alive.

Unable to avoid Dawn's Café, she stepped away from Thiago and peered into the place. She saw Kieran and Mila chatting quietly as they cleaned the tables.

Just as she was about to wave, Thiago came behind her and grabbed her shoulders firmly, making her spin in the opposite direction. "Yeah, no. You're not worrying about that today."

Kamari wriggled out of his touch, just because she couldn't bear how he managed to set her ablaze with a mere contact of their skins. "What's with you and the girls forcing me to stay away from *my* café today?"

"I don't know, maybe because it's your birthday and you always work like a mad woman?" Sarcasm dripped off his tongue like sweet poison ivy.

She didn't say anything because he was right—they all were, but she didn't want to give them the satisfaction of admitting her own faults.

"Whatever. Where are you taking me?" She tapped her wrist as if to show the non-existent watch adorning her arm. "Clock's ticking, pretty boy."

They stopped in front of a motorbike parked near the sidewalk, and Kamari furrowed her brows.

"Why are we stopping?" she inquired, gaping at the tall

athlete who had come to stand beside her, hands tucked in the front pockets of his jeans.

His smile was made of vicious thoughts and mischievous plans. "That's how we're getting to our destination."

Her eyes widened. "You're joking. Please tell me you're joking." Taking hold of his upper arms, she pressed him with a glare that urged him to tell her he was simply messing with her. He only laughed, though. "We're driving, right? I don't care if it's not a Ferrari or a Porsche or whatever, that cute little VW over there is fine."

"Holy shit, Kamari Monroe," he chuckled, gently grabbing her hands to pull them away from his arms. She hadn't noticed she had dug her nails into his jumper. "You're scared. Ladies and gentlemen, that is a rare sight right here."

Straightening herself, she shook her head. Still, terror was decipherable in her eyes, and she knew Thiago could see it—like he always saw her.

"Nope." She shut her eyes when her voice pitched higher than usual. "It's a racing motorcycle, Thiago. They're not made for two people."

A soft chuckle fled past his lips. "We're not going far. We'll be fine."

"And what if we get in trouble?"

Nudging her chin with his knuckles, he winked playfully. "That smart mouth of yours could get us into more trouble than riding a bike."

She felt as though standing beneath a spotlight, its sole purpose to put the crimson blush blooming on her face in evidence. "You're so annoying."

"We won't get in trouble," he said, ignoring the insult thrown his way.

She arched an eyebrow. "And how are you so sure of yourself? Do you do it often?"

"Yes."

"Right," she scoffed. "With your groupies or whatever you call them in F1."

Thiago narrowed his gaze. "No, you're the first and only one who has the privilege of riding this beauty."

Kamari wasn't certain on how to react. Thank him? Run away? There was an undeniable, heavy gravity pulling her towards him, and she knew this could either end in burning flames or paradise. Still, she didn't turn around. Didn't walk away.

"Hey, it's okay," he murmured softly when he noticed she had let herself be consumed by her fears.

Thiago grabbed one of the helmets he had dared to leave on both handgrips, then turned to face Kamari.

"Do you trust me?" he asked.

Kamari nodded without thinking.

He emitted a soft *tsk*. "Words, baby."

"I trust you," she said at last, albeit quietly because of her frustration.

"Good." He jutted his chin towards her hands. "Now grab that hair tie of yours and pull those pretty locks in a bun, yeah?"

Whilst her heart skipped a beat, she frowned. "You know I always carry a hair tie on me?"

He winked. "I know a lot more about you than you think."

Being noticed for the smallest things was not a concept she was familiar with, despite her being the most observant person to exist. She wasn't used to being the centre of someone's attention. Especially someone who wasn't supposed to care for her.

When her hair was finally tied, Thiago took one step forward. His gaze was wild, running over every inch of her facial features, a small smile plastered on the corner of his lips. When he brought the helmet above her head, she ceased to breathe.

"Fuck," he mustered, jaw clenching. "Don't look at me like that."

She feigned innocence, completely aware of the kind of emotion that shone around her pupils. "Like what?"

"Like you're scared. It makes me want to hug you and protect you, and I know you'll just push me away."

She hadn't intended to appear cold and unapproachable, but she didn't know how to take her armour down. She wore her sense of self-preservation akin to a second skin, needing to protect herself from all the damage she had endured in the past.

"Right," she strangled out. "Don't touch me."

"Can I at least put the helmet on you?"

Kamari rolled her eyes. "Sure. I don't want to hurt your ego more than I've already done today by telling you I'd rather do everything on my own."

He chuckled, lowering the helmet on her head. "I know that. But I'm not letting the birthday girl do anything tonight."

"How sweet of you," she deadpanned. "I can't wait for tomorrow to go back to normal life."

"You're insufferable." Securing the helmet by clasping the retention system, he found her gaze. "I won't let anything happen to you."

She flickered her eyes between his, searching for the lie, but she didn't find it. All she could see was reassurance, glinting promises, and minuscule golden stars shimmering amongst a pool of silver.

"I know."

HER GLOVED HANDS were resting on his ribs, and she could feel the firmness of his torso through the few layers he was wearing. She was slowly starting to accept the fact she was okay with touching him—invisibly binding herself to him. She just didn't know why everything felt so natural with Thiago because, in the very back of her mind, he was still a stranger.

They had been riding across town, witnessing the sun's farewell to the day, and he hadn't gone over the speed limit just yet.

"Hold onto me," he asked as he revved the engine.

Kamari had realised her fears started to dissipate the moment she wrapped her arms around his waist, her chest pressed to his toned back.

They had stopped at a red light and she knew exactly what lay beyond the traffic light: roads, upon roads, upon roads where he could speed at one hundred kilometres an hour.

Thiago Valencia wasn't scared of anything, but he would never put someone else's life at risk for his own pleasure. Oddly, Kamari trusted him. She didn't want to admit it, but she'd found some kind of comforting promise in his starlit eyes.

"Relax," she heard him say.

He was unexpected, unpredictable, and astonishing in every possible way.

Delicately brushing her knee with a gloved hand, he tried to coax Kamari through the wave of fright coursing through her veins, maintaining his gaze on the lights on the cusp of turning green. What surprised her the most was that she didn't retreat from his touch, almost enjoying how tender he was being with her.

"Ready?" he asked, slightly craning his neck to make his voice audible. The rise and fall of his chest was steady beneath her fingertips—even and reassuring.

"Not at all."

The engine roared one moment, and the next one they were nearly flying on the road. She felt her heart momentarily stop before dropping inside her stomach as she wrapped her arms around his waist, tightly.

"Holy shit," she screamed, resulting in hearing a heartfelt laugh in response.

"You're safe with me, Kam," he promised.

She had shut her eyes the moment they accelerated, but she was now looking at the hazy streetlights glowing in yellow and golden. Everything was a blur, nothing existed except them.

Fear instantly got replaced by a rush of adrenaline, a feeling of exhilaration and thrill she had never experienced until now. She could feel her senses heightening by the second, in perfect sync with Thiago's speed: her heartbeat increased; her blood pressure rose; her breathing started to stagger.

Kamari and Thiago's gazes collided through the mirror, and she knew he was smiling behind that helmet by the sight of wrinkles appearing on the corners of his eyes, by the gleam of raw happiness swirling around his pupils.

She slipped her gaze to the blurry horizon, and finally set herself free.

———

"IT WASN'T SO BAD, was it?"

Kamari could feel her body vibrate with frissons, adrenaline still rushing through her veins as though the hormone never wanted to leave her body.

"Okay," she admitted, nodding her head, her voice still muffled by the helmet. "It was pretty awesome."

Thiago had taken his helmet off, his hair tousled because of the amount of time he'd passed his fingers through it. He looked like a whole different person in this very instant—carefree, young—as opposed to the man wearing a ruthless façade and a racing suit whenever he was behind the wheel.

He stood before her, then lifted his hands up to her helmet. He clapped her shielded head on either side, grinning foolishly. "You're adorable."

Kamari scowled, which made him laugh out loud. "I'm not."

She unclasped the helmet on her own, batting his hand away when he tried to do it. She released her hair, letting it fall down her back. Thiago was enthralled by her motions, by everything she did, and his perusal caused the tremors skittering down her body to blend with arising chills.

"Have you eaten yet?" he asked as she glanced at her reflection in the bike's mirror.

She shook her head. "Only had brunch with the girls."

"Brunch?" he repeated, bemused. "That was ages ago."

Kamari raised her shoulders in a shrug. "What are we doing at Primrose Hill?"

He hadn't lied: they didn't go far, though he had taken the long way to reach the destination, only for her to experience the thrill of the speed.

"You'll see," he said. His hand then found the small of her back. "Let's go grab a bite first."

———

"Do you want my pickles?" Thiago inquired.

Sitting on a bench beneath a tree, they had reached the highest part of the hill to rest amongst other nature lovers who were also watching the unique canvas colouring the sky, which was now fading into a more sombre shade of blue. *"You've never seen a view quite like this one,"* he had told her as he was leading her towards the spot he enjoyed going to, to seek comfort.

Kamari shifted to face him and nodded. She watched how he took the four round slices of pickles out of his cheeseburger, his nose slightly scrunched with distaste.

"Not a big fan?" she demanded as she opened her burger to let him put the pickles on top of the patty.

He responded with a slight shake of his head from left to right. Somehow, his musky fragrance managed to overpower the scent of their food. Unconsciously, she dropped her gaze to his neck, catching a glimpse of the silver chain he always wore. "I hate them."

Kamari shrugged. "Thanks."

He met her gaze and winked. "You're welcome."

In the corner of a busy street lay a local business which was Thiago's favourite place to eat. He had gotten both his favourite items from the menu, then suggested eating outdoors.

Basking in the soft glow of the sky, Kamari could feel Thiago's gaze observing her profile, its intensity as blazing as a wildfire's flames. She watched the expanse of trees and buildings hiding behind the canopies on the horizon, the city lights shining in yellow hues as she found herself incapable of looking into his eyes.

"Do you really hate your birthday?" His voice was quiet, soft, careful, as though he'd been afraid to ask.

Kamari felt her shoulders tense in a heartbeat, and she hoped he hadn't noticed the shift in her demeanour. She tried making herself more comfortable with her back leaning against the wooden bench, one thigh placed atop the other. Her foot started swinging absently, and she settled her gaze on the helmets they had put on the grass, on top of Thiago's jumper.

"I just don't care about it," she explained. "It doesn't feel like it's a special day to me."

She could hear the smile in his voice, the tenderness laced to it. "It *is* special because you've made it to another year on this wonderful planet Earth."

She threw him an amused glance before reaching out to the packet of chips laying between them. "Evermore the poet." She took a small bite of her burger whilst she debated opening up to him, a sudden wave of comfort surging over her just by sitting in a serene silence with him. "Actually, I think it's because my parents never made a big deal out of it. I never had birthday parties as a kid, barely received presents. Most of the time, my parents forgot about it until Kieran had to remind them."

A frown had drawn itself between his brows. "You're not close to your parents?"

Kamari shook her head, depositing her foam container on the bench to wipe the corner of her mouth. "Not really."

Genuine curiosity flashed in his eyes. "Do you see them often?"

Her stare dropped to his mouth when he bit into a chip. "They moved abroad."

His brows shot up. "Really? Where?"

"Cambodia," she said. "Mum's Cambodian from her mother's side, and half British and half Filipina from her father—"

"Wow," he interrupted with a whistle, his gaze meandering her features—soft, like a lover's gaze. His chest expanded with the deep breath he took, his face softening. She could see it all—the admiration, the adoration she didn't want yet still received like a warm embrace.

"I know, and my dad's British. He's a surgeon and works in a hospital over there in Cambodia."

He responded with an understanding nod. "Do you miss them?"

Kamari shrugged. "Not really. They used to care more about Kieran than me. It took me a while to realise they would never treat me equally to my older sibling. The moment I understood it, I just went and did everything on my own. It wasn't easy to tell my sixteen-year-old self 'you're on your own, kid' after fighting and begging for my parents' attention for years, but now I guess I'm okay with it. Indy's parents have been more present for me than my own."

He had set his container down, and swallowed, a deep frown settling between his eyebrows. "I'm so sorry, Kamari."

A breath escaped her mouth. "You've got nothing to be sorry for. You've got to bleed in order to grow. And everything you lose is just a step you take."

Thiago breathed, unable to take his eyes off of hers. Time seemed to slow down for a fraction of a second, and she wondered how she managed not to blush under that tender gaze of his. Dipping a chip into ketchup, he asked, "And why aren't you celebrating? In a club or a pub with your friends? You'd steal the spotlight as soon as you'd walk into the place."

She rolled her eyes, playfully so. "I'm blushing! Stop flattering me." She reached out for a chip at the same time as him, causing their fingers to brush. "I don't know. I'm not really in the mood to party today. I had brunch with Indy and Diana earlier, but I know Indy will drag me out of my sofa on Friday to go clubbing. Besides, I'm not interested in random hookups."

I'm not interested in anyone, in committing, in getting my heart broken again after what happened with my ex.

Kamari wasn't certain why she was talking so much, why she was opening up to him so easily. Talking to Thiago felt like the most natural thing she'd had to experience because she didn't feel that flame of judgement she'd been so used to seeing in other people's eyes.

A small grin spread across his lips, trying to conceal the slight concern that had washed over his expression. "Yeah, 'cause you're supposedly dating me, Thiago Valencia, the most handsome, fun, amazing man you've ever—"

She batted his hand away when he tried to grab her burger, making him laugh rather loudly. It sounded like a sweet melody, a soft serenade meant to melt her barriers. "Whatever. I'm not sure people would recognise me, but I'm not taking the risk of being seen with someone else."

Thiago's features hardened, and she didn't know why. Jaw ticking, he averted his gaze towards the sky. Despite having his eyes settled on something else, she perceived a flash of recognition, of affection, when he found what he had been looking for in the dark heavens.

"Do you want to?" he asked, his tone clipped. "To see someone else?"

"No," she replied without an ounce of hesitation because she didn't want to see anyone—whether it was real or pretence. "Do you?"

His gaze collided with hers. "No."

Kamari shrugged. "We never talked further about the rules, so you do you, Thiago. As long as you're being careful—"

"Will you stop?" He wiped the grease off his fingers, a frustrated huff escaping his mouth. "I'm here with you, aren't I? I made this deal with *you* for a reason. I'm not just going to stab you in the back by going and finding someone else. I'm not that man, Kamari."

Not once had he disconnected his intense regard from hers, causing unwanted shivers to rush down her spine. Ignoring the sped-up rhythm of her heartbeat, she grabbed her water bottle, and lifted her shoulders in a shrug, acting as though his promise hadn't affected her in the slightest.

"Good."

Thiago chuckled softly. He draped his arm over the back of the bench then, his fingers almost brushing her shoulder blades. She didn't move. Sucking in a breath, she waited for his digits to graze her clothed skin, already expecting a trail of sparks to linger beneath his touch. The caress never came, as though he was being careful not to touch her—because they were by themselves, and they didn't need to put their act on. "Talk to me about your project—the second café."

She couldn't contain her bewilderment. "Really?"

The grin plastering his face made him more handsome than ever. His whole attention was on her—nothing else mattered to Thiago. He responded with a nod. "Yeah. Tell me everything about it."

CHAPTER TWENTY-ONE

📍 *LONDON, ENGLAND*

T HIAGO SAT THERE, unequivocally mesmerised by the woman talking to him.

There was a rare light in her eyes—something that shone brighter than the stars, that was more enthralling than the galaxy itself. Something he hadn't seen until now and wished would never fade away. Though he knew this moment was temporary, he focused his attention on her, and only her.

Their food had been left forgotten, still laid between them. With his arm draped over the back of the bench, he was almost touching her—he wanted to touch her. Wanted to twirl his forefinger around that rogue lock that fell out of her bun. Wanted to caress her shoulder in silent encouragement to keep talking.

"I want to open the shop in Soho," Kamari explained. Hands placed on her lap, she looked graceful and elegant and beautiful, and somehow younger as her features weren't as cold and tight as he'd been used to seeing. The soft glow of the moon started shining on her face, just as if she was meant to be part of the satellite's magic.

"Why there?" His voice had turned hoarse, like he hadn't spoken in hours when it was only minutes. That was Kamari's powers affecting him; rendering him speechless.

"It'll be the same concept as Dawn's: a coffee shop with a bookstore, but I want to add a twist to the new place, which is going to be a bar. I thought Soho was the perfect neighbourhood for it."

His brows raised with admiration. "A café slash library slash pub? Sorry, but you might never be able to get rid of me. I'll be living there from now on."

She pivoted and faced him, making her shoulder bump into his forearm. Neither of them moved. "Yeah, because you read?"

He scoffed, offended, letting his mouth fall agape dramatically. "Because I'm a high-performance athlete means I can't read? That's rude."

She let her stare roam over his face, and its feverishness made heat creep up the back of his neck. "Entertain me, then. What kind of books do you read?"

He grinned, jutting his chin towards her. "The same ones you do."

Her smile was as radiant as the sun's rays, and he wished Kamari would show that side of herself more often. She shook her head, and he swore she snorted softly. "You're so full of shit, Valencia. I know you don't read."

Thiago lifted his hands in slight surrender. "Fine, I don't read as much as I should, but if you give me some recommendations I will totally devour them in my free time."

"You would?"

"Of course," he said earnestly. "Did you always want to open your own coffee shop?"

Kamari nodded. "I think so. I studied business in uni. I love coffee, tea, pastries, books—"

"Cocktails?"

A soft chuckle fled past her lips, making him drop his gaze to her full, enticing mouth. "Sure. Cocktails, too. When I moved into the building and the bakery downstairs was closing, I jumped on the opportunity to rent the place myself, then created my business with Kieran's help."

He admired this woman, he truly did. She wasn't aware of her bravery and resilience, he supposed. "So, you're currently renting Dawn's?"

Kamari nodded. "Yes. The plan is to buy the place along with my flat above, and the second café—eventually. But financially speaking, it's sadly out of my reach at the moment."

"But you won't give up."

A line drew itself between her brows. "Of course not. Have you seen me? I fight until the end."

"Yeah," he breathed. "I see you, Kamari."

Time stood still as green and silver collided into a tangle of secret pining, wordless exchanges that only their eyes could reflect.

"Enough about me," she said then, breaking that heavy silence that only coerced him to gravitate more and more towards the moonbeam she was. "What about you? What do you think you would've done if you weren't a racing driver?"

"That's a good question." He frowned, letting his stare slip away for a fragment of a second, only to catch a glimpse of a group of teenagers sitting a few metres away from them, busy recording and taking pictures of the pair. "Shit. I'm sorry, Kam."

"What?" She followed the route of his perusal. "Oh."

"I'm sorry," he repeated. "I didn't think anyone would spot us."

Thiago was aware Kamari wasn't comfortable with the whole situation. She didn't like being the centre of attention, didn't like having cameras pointed at her. Still, she had been doing an outstanding job at keeping cool the times she had to walk by his side whilst numerous cameras were directed at them.

"It's fine," she said, her voice somehow strangled in her

throat. He wanted to believe that she, too, was disappointed that their bubble of solace had been burst open by reality. "You can go over and take pictures with them if you want to."

He frowned slightly. "Are you sure?"

The corner of her lips was curled into a small smile. "Positive."

Standing up, he grabbed Kamari's hand and planted a soft kiss on the back of it, never letting his gaze falter from her face, from the slight annoyance blended with surprise flashing in her eyes. "Don't miss me too much. I'll be back very soon."

As he strode towards the group of fans, he heard Kamari muster, "*Idiot*", and his grin only widened.

WHEN HE CAME BACK to the bench, he noticed their food was gone.

"Were you *that* hungry?" he asked, bemused.

Kamari looked up from her phone and scowled. "Yes," she deadpanned, "I was famished. No, actually I went and gave the leftovers to that homeless man sitting by the tree down there."

He followed her gaze, slipping his hands into the front pockets of his jeans. Some kind of foreign warmth started to bloom inside his chest at the sight of the man thoroughly enjoying his meal, and when he looked back at Kamari, she was already looking at him with a flicker of tenderness he hadn't seen before.

"That's sweet of you," he said gruffly.

She shrugged. "I have my moments."

Thiago bit the inside of his cheek—to stop himself from blurting out what had been going through his mind for the past hour.

Do you want to grab an ice cream?

Do you want to hang out?

What would you like to do? I'll take you anywhere.

"Come on," he said at last. "Let's get you back home."

If Kamari was disappointed, she didn't show it, but she grabbed her bag with slight hesitation and stood up. "Sure. Time's up anyway."

Thiago picked up their helmets and his extra jumper, following her down the hill. She was oddly silent, and he thought he had messed up somewhere along the line.

"Wait, Kam." He caught her elbow, forcing her to spin around. Her addictive fragrance started corrupting his senses, nearly bringing him to his knees when her wide, green eyes found his gaze. "I didn't bring you out there to be seen by people, to have a picture of us going around the internet in the morning. I meant it when I said I wanted to get to know you, and I'll spend all my free time running after you. Tonight was not a PR stunt. You know that, right?"

Kamari tipped her lips into a smirk—all vicious and condescending. "You're going to run after me? What happened to self-preservation, Thiago?"

He huffed, handing her a helmet. "Looks like I have none when you're around."

HER SMALL HANDS were holding his hips, and he wondered if she could feel the way his skin blazed under his clothes.

He glanced at her in the mirror, seeing her eyes wandering around the starry sky whilst they waited for the light to turn green. He was intrigued, drawn to this woman he knew so little of. He could stare at her for a lifetime if he could, trying to read past her cold façade.

Thiago revved the throttle, making the engine roar. He felt Kamari push herself closer, wrapping her arms around his waist. Her hands were laid flat against his abdomen, and clothes were preventing their skins from touching. Even then, chills had made their appearance on every inch of his flesh and, if she trailed her hands upwards, she would be able to feel the hammer of his heart.

"Valencia," she murmured.

The thrum of his heartbeat was rapid and loud. Unsteady. Uncontrollable. "Yes?"

"You managed to make my birthday decent for once. Thank you."

Silver found green through the mirror and, even though she couldn't see his smile because of his helmet, he knew she could glimpse at the stars in his pupils.

His hand found her knee, brushing then squeezing delicately. "Anything for you, Kam."

And he meant it; he'd get down on his knees just to see more of this side of Kamari.

HIS CHEST ROSE and fell as he watched Kamari let her nearly black hair loose. She looked like an enchantress ready to put a spell on him, and he was completely at her mercy. Her cheekbones were tinted with a faint coat of blush, her eyes wide and full of life.

God, she was breathtaking.

They were standing in front of Dawn's Café. The lights were all switched off, but she stood under the streetlamp that shone upon her like a ray of sunlight pushing through dark clouds.

"Thank you again," she said, handing him the helmet she had worn.

He nodded. Swallowed. When he spoke, his tone was hoarse. "No problem."

He couldn't look away. Didn't want to.

Rubbing the back of his neck, he nearly jolted at the feeling of his warm skin, like he had been set on fire.

Invite me in, Kam.

Tell me to stay.

Kamari studied his face, softly, slowly, carefully—as if trying to ingrain this exact moment in the back of her mind. She then released a tremulous breath, a small line appearing between her brows as though she had just realised something she didn't quite enjoy.

"I'll see you later," she finally murmured, turning on her heel and creating an immense distance between them.

Wait.

Wait.

Wait.

The word never came out, stuck inside his throat, clinging to his chest like a lethal, poisonous vine.

"I'll text you," he said. Because he had to say something. Had to make this moment last. He didn't care if he kept making a fool out of himself.

She peered at him from her shoulder as she retrieved her key from her purse. "Don't."

He smiled. "I will."

"I won't answer."

"You will."

She disappeared, and Thiago was left alone in the empty street, standing under the glow of the streetlamp that seemed meaningless if Kamari Monroe wasn't beneath it.

He made a beeline for his motorcycle, knowing all too well he'd make a mistake if he stayed there, waiting for her to open the door and tell him to come in.

There was a very thin thread between staying professional and crossing the line, and Thiago knew he couldn't break that string, even if he wanted to.

"Kamari," he echoed in a whisper that evaporated into the night sky, the souvenir of green eyes and the smile of a devastating angel ingrained like an everlasting memory in the back of his mind.

Kamari.

Kamari.

Kamari.

She was a burning star shooting in the night sky. She was a shimmer of starlight on a moonlit sea. She was an entire galaxy, most beautiful in darkness, and she didn't know it. He wanted to embrace her like the night wrapped its arms around the moon, but she was the embodiment of the very moon—unattainable, untouchable, unbreakable. Therefore, he could never have her.

CHAPTER TWENTY-TWO

⚲ *LONDON, ENGLAND*

THE SMELL OF creamy butter whiffed in the air as Kamari took freshly baked, golden croissants out of the oven. Kieran's voice blended with the music blasting from the stereo as he arranged the bookshelves, a watering can in one hand whilst the door of Dawn's Café was wide open, allowing the fresh and cool breeze to swivel inside the place. The Monroe siblings were setting up the coffee shop, waiting for the first customer to show up and order his usual latte macchiato with a pain au chocolat.

"You never told me what you went to do with your boyfriend on Tuesday night," Kieran said out of the blue, his back still turned to her.

She ignored the way her heartbeat picked up at the mention of Thiago, who wasn't even her boyfriend, let alone a friend. She wasn't sure where they stood, but she knew she had crossed the line of hatred with him. Still, that didn't mean his existence didn't annoy her to the point of feeling irritation flare inside her chest whenever she thought of him.

"We went to grab a bite in Primrose Hill," she told her brother, taking her oven mitts off.

Kieran turned, his brows raised in slight puzzlement. "Really? You rarely go out on your birthday."

Kamari shrugged. "I know."

Something gleamed around her brother's pupils—an emotion she couldn't place a word upon, but still managed to make her chest warm. She'd been so used to seeing Kieran pity her after her breakup with James, and even though her brother never said it out loud, she knew he was devastated for her. Perhaps he was happy to see Kamari get out of her shell. What he didn't know, though, was that she refused to let her walls down.

The relationship she had built with Thiago was just a publicity stunt, and nothing more. She didn't want attachment, didn't want friendship, didn't want heartbreak.

He put the watering can down by a bookcase, huffing when he noticed two books weren't perfectly aligned. Then, he shook his head, and said, "I still can't believe you're dating my idol."

Kamari rolled her eyes. "That's exactly why I didn't tell you. You'd be capable of leaving Tillie for Thiago."

"True." He didn't even deny it. "Have you seen him? Anyone would leave their significant other for that bloke."

She tried not to think about pearly, silvery eyes. About a devastating smile. Dimples. Dark locks that looked so smooth that she wondered how they'd feel beneath her fingertips. "I'm telling Tillie you said that."

She didn't hear Kieran's complaint because of the sound of her phone ringing.

She frowned; she was slightly dazed and confused. Who would call her on an early Friday morning?

Alex Myers' name flashed on her screen, along with a selfie he had taken in Primavera Racing's garage at Spa-Francorchamps.

"Hello?" She pressed the phone between her ear and

shoulder as she grabbed a cup to brew herself some coffee, grabbing the portafilter in the other hand.

"Hey, Kam," Alex said. She stilled at the hesitancy lacing his tone, rapidly glancing at Kieran only to see him still busy rearranging the bookshelf. "So sorry for calling this early. Am I interrupting something?"

She frowned. Sounds of chatter lingered on the other side of the line. "No, you're fine. Is everything okay?"

Kamari put the portafilter down, and took hold of her phone, leaning her hip against the counter.

There was a pause, an oddly long one at that. "Yeah," Alex replied gruffly. "I mean, ah, this is weird."

"You're being weird."

"Yeah, sorry." He cleared his throat, and she imagined him scratching his moustache. "What are you doing today?"

"Why?" she asked coldly. "You're not trying to steal me from your best friend, are you?"

"I'd never break bro code," he retorted.

She lifted her brows, slight annoyance starting to bloom, but she found herself being concerned, albeit against her will. "Just get to the point, please."

"It's Thiago."

For some unknown reason, her heart ceased to function for a fragment of a second that felt like an eternity of anguish.

"What happened?" Everything felt stuck: her voice inside her throat, her heartbeat confined in her chest, her thoughts inside her clouded mind.

She couldn't help but imagine the worst—a car crash, an accident on the track. She knew, though, that free practices wouldn't start until later, so what could've happened?

"I just—" She heard Alex sigh then swallow. "I know it's not cool to ask now, but do you think you could fly down here for the weekend?"

Her eyes widened as she straightened herself. "Where?"

"Monza."

"Alex—"

"He needs you, Kam. Please."

He needs you, he'd said. Not, *'he wants you to walk around the paddock with him.'*

She found Kieran's gaze from across the room. He watched her with slight incredulity, striding slowly towards her. She observed one of their loyal customers cross the road, then glanced around the pristine place ready to welcome regular and new patrons.

Kamari didn't care about Thiago. She really didn't, and she didn't know why she felt her pulse drum hastily when she pressed her eyes closed. Disquietude was overpowering her exasperation, worry consumed her senses, and she hated it.

She sighed heavily. "You two better not be wasting my time."

"Is that a yes?"

She shook her head, annoyedly. "Sure."

"Good. Ava is going to send you your plane ticket and I'll pick you up at the airport. Thank you so, so much, Kam."

CHAPTER TWENTY-THREE

📍 *MONZA, ITALY*

K AMARI FELT LIKE drowning the moment her gaze settled on Thiago. Her breath caught inside her throat; her lungs were craving oxygen; and her mind started to race.

He had just gotten out of his car after running a few laps, busy unstrapping his helmet. There were a dozen people walking around, but her whole attention was on him. Kamari was a whole anxious mess, especially since Alex had called earlier this morning. She had told Kieran she had an emergency and had to fly to Italy.

"Is everything okay?" Kieran asked as she untied the apron attached to her waist.

"I'm not sure," she replied, frowning. She turned to the espresso machine and finally brewed herself the caffeine she desperately needed to consume. "I'm going to have to leave you for the weekend. I'm sorry, Ki, I'm the worst manager ever—"

"*Breathe, Kam.*" *Kieran walked around the counter and grabbed a small bag, putting a blueberry scone in it.* "*It's fine. I've got this. Stay over there as long as you need to.*"

"*But—*"

"*There are no buts, Kamari,*" *he snapped, giving her the paper bag.* "*It's your boyfriend, and I'm sure he'd drop everything to run to you if you called, too.*" *A small frown drew itself upon his brows, yet his eyes shone tenderly.* "*I've never seen you leave your life behind for a man before.*"

Kamari swallowed, and the urge to stay here became more and more overwhelming. "*Is this a bad thing?*"

"*No.*" *He grabbed the full cup of steaming black coffee from his sister's grip, setting it on the counter before gently gripping her upper arms to stare into her eyes.* "*It means you genuinely care about him to the point of rethinking your priorities. This love is good for you, Kam. I don't know if you can see it, but I do.*"

But did Kamari care about Thiago, or did she care about his reputation? About what he could accomplish if he was seen as who he truly was?

Kamari was someone who liked to grasp all the time she had in the palm of her hand to pack and organise for a trip, even if this one was supposed to last for a few days. But when she had received Ava's email with her plane ticket details, she had felt as though her heart started racing whilst anxiety coiled in her gut. She had rushed upstairs, making a mental list of everything she'd be needing to go to Italy.

Kieran had called a taxi for her, and when she had emerged downstairs wearing a totally different outfit, face woven with panic, she gratefully accepted the extra coffee he had made for her.

"*Can you bring me some merch?*" *Kieran pleaded.* "*You can do that for your amazing brother who lets you travel here and there whilst he's being the best barista in town, yes?*"

Kamari's nerves hadn't settled down yet. Even when she had seen Alex's delighted smile at the airport. Even when Ava had given her the paddock passes.

By the time she made it to the track—the Autodromo Nazionale Monza—the second session of free practice was about to end.

"What's going on?" Kamari asked Alex who was standing beside her in the garage. Though Thiago hadn't seen her arrive just yet, the few car mechanics and engineers roaming around the space greeted her nicely.

Alex had been avoiding telling her what all of this was about, which only piqued her curiosity.

"I'm not sure," Alex answered, his gaze also strained on Thiago.

She made herself small in a corner of the garage whilst she studied the way Thiago radiated both power and destruction all at once. He had taken his helmet off and had given it to Cal, who was standing behind the driver. As he tore his balaclava off, he raked his fingers through his hair, pushing the wild locks away from his brows, yet there was still a rebel strand that kept falling over his forehead.

Sharp, chiselled, enticing side profile turned to her, Kamari glimpsed the twitch of his jaw's muscle when it tightened. He was standing close to his engineer, looking at the screen which showed statistics and his car's performance during the free practice session.

"He's, like, another person when he's racing, huh?" Alex's voice snapped her out of her daydream, and she straightened herself.

She folded her arms across her chest, shrugging. "I guess so."

She had seen him race before, and even if she didn't know much about racing, she had been able to recognise the determination in his driving style.

Ruthless. Heartless. Untouchable.

"Do you think he can win the championship?" she asked the blond. "Honest."

She watched Alex swallow, and finally came a subtle nod of his head. "He can. But mathematically speaking, he has to win all remaining races in order to get as many points as he can to be at the top of the drivers' ranking. His car isn't the best this season, and it sucks. His team is working really hard to help him get back on top. Besides, there is also a championship for the constructors, and Primavera wants to win—just like the other nine teams —but the struggle is obvious on both ends."

Kamari could only manage to nod, comprehensively.

Thiago was wrapped in his own bubble as he tried to fix an apparent issue with his engineer.

"Come on," Alex whispered, nudging her elbow with his. "Let's go wait for him in the motorhome. This could take a while."

A SHADOW APPEARED OVERHEAD, then disappeared as quickly as it came into sight. When Kamari lifted her gaze from her phone, she collided with hazel eyes glinting with mirth. Rowan Emerson had taken a seat opposite her in the hospitality room of the motorhome, a cup of steaming tea in one hand.

"Hello, love," he said, a smirk dancing at the corner of his lips, as he leaned back in his seat. "I'm Rowan."

Kamari blinked. "I know who you are."

"Really?" Surprise was etched on his face as he took a small sip of his beverage. A set of killer dimples appeared on his cheeks when he grinned broadly. "I bet Thiago loves talking about me."

"He never mentioned you once," she countered bluntly.

"Shocking," Rowan deadpanned, brows lifting. "He's my biggest fan."

Rowan's arrogance appeared akin to a second skin as he let his smile grow. Putting his mug on top of the table, he placed his hands behind his head as he took Kamari in with a once-over that was supposed to affect her, though she only narrowed her eyes. A sleeve of tattoos was peeking beneath his layer of fireproof shirt, the continuity of the art branded onto his skin curling at the base of his throat.

"You're his girlfriend?" he asked, though it was evident he already knew the answer.

"Yes."

It was at that moment that she wondered if her acting had always been so natural.

"How come I've never seen you before?"

"You saw me in Belgium."

"And before that?"

"What are you?" she scoffed. "The police?"

Rowan lifted his shoulders in a small shrug. "I'm just trying to get to know my teammate's girl."

She pursed her lips. "I'm not certain this is the way to do it."

"Well, what do you want me to ask? Your favourite colour?"

Alex was sitting beside her, editing pictures he had taken today. A soft snort erupted from his nose, though he didn't intervene in this exchange that seemed to entertain him.

"What's with you, F1 drivers, and asking us about our favourite colour?"

"Dunno," Rowan mumbled. "We didn't get the chance to chat at the team dinner in Spa, so I'm seizing the opportunity now. So, how long have you and Tito been together?"

"Rowan," Ava interrupted as she stopped in front of their table. She was holding two phones in one hand and a portable recorder in the other. "Stop bothering everyone. We've got interviews to get to."

"Now?" he asked, gaping at the raven-haired girl. "But I was having *so much fun* with Kameron."

"Kamari," Alex corrected, amusedly.

"No, you weren't," Kamari said at the same time.

With a loud, dramatic sigh, Rowan let his hands fall to his sides. He stood up, grinned at Kamari and Alex, then followed Ava out of the motorhome without so much as saying another word to the pair.

"Avery," he called out, "can we get ice cream afterwards?"

"Not if you keep calling me Avery," Ava bit out, holding the door open for him.

"It's your name," Rowan retorted as he exited the room. "Why can't I call you by your name?"

"Well, that was Rowan," Alex announced, an amused smile on his lips.

Kamari scooted closer to Alex, and whilst leaning her elbow atop the table and placing her chin in the palm of her hand, she pretended to be interested in his work. "Are he and Thiago friends?"

Alex shook his head, his voice quiet when he said, "You're not really great friends with other drivers on the grid. Sure, you get along with some guys more than others, but rivalry will always stand between all of you. Thiago and Rowan do get along on their best days, and they do PR activities together without complaining, but they barely talk to each other outside of that."

"Oh."

Kamari saw Leo McConnell walk inside the motorhome, phone pressed to his ear as always. When he met Kamari's gaze, he lowered the device and waved at her.

"Kamari," he acknowledged with a nod. "Thank you for coming. I know it's not easy, but Thiago really needs you. So, thanks for being here."

She barely had the time to blink that he rushed towards another room, bringing his phone back to his ear. Kamari was confused by the sorrow in Leo's tone, so she turned to Alex, whose lips were pressed into a thin line, like he was forcing himself not to talk.

"What was that about?"

Alex lifted his hands in surrender. "I told you it wasn't my place to tell you what this was about."

"Does Thiago even know I'm here?" Kamari asked, a small line drawn between her brows.

"Nope."

"Are you serious?" she hissed in a whisper.

Alex smiled under his moustache. "I bet he'll be very happy to see you."

"Alexander Francis," she mustered, "if—"

"How do you even know my middle name?"

"My best friend is fuelled by gossip. Anyway, if you don't tell me what's going on, I will steal your camera for the whole weekend."

He laughed loudly, throwing his head back. "Is that a threat?"

"It's a promise, Myers."

He chuckled, shaking his head. "You don't scare me. You look all tough and mean but—"

"Kamari?"

Thiago's deep baritone caused chills to rush down her spine, making her whole world halt at the sound of that coarse voice.

His face was stricken with raw surprise, but the moment green met silver, his features broke into illumination as he smiled handsomely.

Sounds clattered when she blinked whilst he took rapid steps towards her.

"What are you doing here?" His chest rose and fell steadily whilst his gaze started searching her face as though trying to understand if she was real or a figment of his imagination.

She wanted to say she didn't know. That an uncanny sensation inside her gut had pushed her to accept Alex's plea.

"Surprise," she said, enthusiastically, as she stood up to face the tall athlete.

"Kam," he breathed whilst pushing his hair away from his forehead. "Come here."

No time was given as he nearly fell onto her, his strong arms wrapping around her waist. She ceased to breathe, though her heart was hammering violently.

"Hug me back," he ordered in a whisper.

"I don't like you."

She could feel a smile growing on his face as he had buried it in the crook of her neck, his warm breaths fanning across her skin in steady sequences that set her whole body to flames. "Happy to see you, too, Monroe."

She wasted no time enveloping him in an embrace with equal affection, arms curled around his neck as their chests pressed together.

Kamari couldn't help but close her eyes—she was either enjoying the moment or fighting the tears of fear, she didn't know just yet. Being in Thiago's arms felt so easy and natural and safe, that she had to force herself to remember it was all an act.

"Fuck," he whispered. "You're really here?"

"Yes." Pulling away, she cupped either side of his neck, feeling the warmth of his skin and the drum of his rapid pulse beneath the palms of her hands. "Are you okay?"

Thiago swallowed, thickly, and his eyes started misting over. She had never seen him so vulnerable, so out of control of himself. "I'm fine. Just surprised to see you here. I thought you were busy."

She shrugged and stepped back. "Change of plans."

His touch lingered on her hips even when he brought his hands to his sides. Rapidly, he flickered his gaze over her face then crooked a small smile whilst a sigh of relief escaped his mouth.

"Come with me," he then said, sensing her discomfort as numerous eyes were on them.

Thiago grabbed her hand and pulled her towards the exit. She could feel the slight tremor on his fingers, the way he held her hand so tightly as though he didn't want to let go.

"Where are we going?" They passed by Cal, and he gaped at the couple with wide eyes. "Hey, Cal."

"What are you doing here?" he asked, glancing at Thiago who was set on pulling her away from the crowd.

Kamari shrugged. "You tell me."

Cal shook his head, but his features softened. He winked at Kamari, then entered the motorhome without saying a word.

Thiago ignored her stare when she glanced at him, silent questions burning in her eyes. Fingers tightly wrapped around hers, he walked by her side through the paddock.

Kamari couldn't help but lower her gaze to the ground when she saw a horde of photographers follow them, clicks and shutters of cameras audible.

He squeezed her hand. "You look beautiful. Do you always dress so...perfectly?"

Kamari's eyes found his grey moons. She responded with a small shrug. "I try to, but I make sure what I wear exceeds your expectations."

"My—" He stopped and faced her, the crease between his brows hard and deep. "What does that mean?"

She shook her head. She couldn't think properly through the turmoil creating a haze inside her mind, through the deafening sound of her erratic pulse. "Means I don't do things halfway. You want to be seen with someone perfect? Well, I'm trying my best."

"Where is this coming from, Kamari?" He scoffed softly, eyes flickering back and forth between hers. "You could wear basic jeans and a simple t-shirt and the whole paddock's attention would still be on you. I would never force you to be someone you're not. Wear whatever pleases *you*, not me."

Glancing down, she lingered her gaze on the numerous logos branded on his fireproof shirt, ignoring how the thin piece of clothing clung to his torso.

"I know," she muttered. "I'm dressing like this for myself."

"That's what I thought." Then, ever so gently, ever so softly, he brought his fingers up to her face, brushing a strand of hair away from her cheekbone to tuck it behind her ear. "Who hurt you, Kam?"

Her chest rose and fell, and she shook her head, not wanting to jump into this topic that had the tendency of destroying her more than she cared to admit.

"Tell me," he murmured, using the side of his pointer finger to lift her chin up. "Was it that ex of yours?"

"Fifty points for Gryffindor," she mused.

A small smirk made its appearance on the corner of his mouth. "I'm a Slytherin."

"I'm not surprised."

"What house are you?" He titled his head, curious.

"Something between Gryffindor and Slytherin."

He smiled softly. "I'm not surprised either." Somehow, someway, he managed to make her forget about all the people surrounding them. "So, what did that arse do to you?"

Kamari sighed heavily. Confessing to him couldn't harm her. Biting the inside of her cheek, she swallowed the lump that had formed inside her throat. "For years he used me as some kind of object. I've always been my own person, you know, but he liked it when I looked pristine when we went out with his friends. My only purpose was to sit by his side and look pretty. I wasn't allowed to speak, and it took me over five years to realise I was just an object to him."

"Shit," he breathed, grabbing both her hands. His jaw was tight, taut with anger, and his eyes were starting to burn with unyielding wrath. "This isn't okay, Kamari. I would never treat you like that, you hear me? You might be the key to redeeming myself but that doesn't mean I'm going to disrespect you. I'm lucky as hell to have you by my side because have you seen yourself?"

Warmth blossomed inside her chest—as if the dead flowers had bloomed into lively, vibrant ones. Kamari couldn't contain the timid smile spreading across her lips, and she realised then she had given him a glimpse of her demons, willingly.

"I have," she replied, smugly.

Thiago's lips curved into a smile that managed to have the same corrupting effects as his words on her soul. He cradled her face, delicately, as though he was scared to shatter her. "Can I kiss you?"

She pursed her lips in disdain. "No."

He emitted a soft grunt. "Damn it. At least I would've tried."

And the moment he placed a gentle kiss on her forehead, she couldn't help but close her eyes to savour the feeling of his lips on her skin, to get lost in a world where perhaps she would let her armour down to make all of this real.

"Okay, pretty boy." She shoved him away playfully, trying to distract herself from the rosy tinge that had been heating her cheeks up. "Where were you about to take me?"

His grin was all delight and exhilaration. "Have you ever been in an F1 car before?"

AN IDLE FINGER grazed the halo serving as protection atop the cockpit whilst her eyes sauntered over the large car.

The sound of her heels echoed in the garage as she walked around the car, making sure her touch was delicate and feather-light, as though she was afraid to scratch the livery. The moment they had entered the garage, Thiago had asked his car mechanics to leave. The front door had already been closed to prevent fans sitting in the grandstands to see the mechanics working on the car, but he closed the small door leading to the paddock to give them as much privacy.

Kamari could sense Thiago's intense scrutiny following each one of her moves as he leaned against a table. With every second passing by, she was able to feel her heart pound ferociously, and perspiration clamming her hands.

She couldn't fathom why she felt so powerless because of his mere existence.

"Why number seven?" she asked, her voice slightly trembling. She desperately wished he couldn't see her distress.

From the corner of her eye, she saw him push himself off the table, slowly closing the distance between them. "My birthday's on the seventh."

"Of July, right?"

She could hear the smile in his voice, though she kept her gaze fixated on the yellow number on the hood of the car—a stark contrast to the burgundy livery. "You remember."

"Of course," she murmured, walking to the right side of the car—escaping Thiago.

"Yours is September seventh."

"You remember," she teased, rapidly glancing up at him to notice his silver eyes already on her.

"Well, yeah," he smiled. "It was three days ago."

Kamari nodded, rapidly darting her gaze away because she didn't want to show him how much it had meant that he had found the time to spend her birthday's evening with her. He didn't owe her anything, didn't need to pretend he cared, yet he kept breaking their rules, continuously so.

"Get in the car."

Her eyes widened. "Really?"

"Yeah," he replied gruffly, his features soft and enthralling as he looked at her. "Take your shoes off, the car's clean."

Kamari nearly lost her balance at the sound of his hoarse voice. She rounded the car to reach where he was standing, then unstrapped her heels, observing Thiago take a small stool from under his engineer's desk. He deposited the footboard next to her feet, grinning like a child on Christmas Day as excitement emanated from his allure.

"Step on here, m'lady," he murmured, gesturing to the stool.

"What a gentleman," she teased, accepting the hand he offered for support.

"Always," he answered. "Put your feet on the seat before sitting down. It'll be easier."

Her skirt rose up her thighs as she stepped into the car, and she released his hand when she planted both feet on the seat, tugging the fabric of her dress down. She rapidly glanced at the athlete to see his eyes strained on her bare legs and watched how his throat worked up and down before he looked away.

As she sat down, she understood this seat had been moulded to fit Thiago's physique. Despite her height, she felt so small in this imposing, fast car. He grabbed the steering wheel from Luke's desk and plugged it where it belonged.

"Wow," Kamari whispered. Her foot touched the throttle, though she didn't dare apply pressure. "This feels unreal."

Thiago had lowered himself into a crouch, elbows draped over the panel of the cockpit. "This car's speed can go up to three hundred and seventy kilometres per hour."

She started raising her hands to grab the wheel, but she halted before touching it. "Can I?"

"Yeah, Kam," he whispered. "You go ahead."

Fingers on either side of the rectangular-shaped steering wheel, she wasn't sure where to settle her gaze. Numerous buttons were adorning it, each one of a different colour.

"Do you learn the buttons' emplacements by heart?"

She saw him nod. "Yes."

She almost laughed when she realised she was nearly lying down. The space inside the cockpit was confined, yet still adapted to his long legs and broad build.

He shifted as closely as he could, pointing to a button on the top far left corner. "This is the radio button. I communicate with Luke by pressing on it."

Kamari nodded, grazing said button with the tip of her pointer finger. "What's this one for?" she demanded, showing a yellow button on the right side of the wheel.

"That one I have to press when I enter the pit lane—to reduce my pace to the speed limit. We can face penalties if we breach the limit whilst driving down there." He then pointed to two pedals on both sides. "These are the clutches to change gears. An F1 car has up to eight forward gears."

"Wow," she repeated. "You guys go fast."

"The fastest cars in the world."

She found his gaze, and there was a flash of tenderness, of adoration perceptible in his eyes.

Kamari dropped her hands on her lap, slightly shifting to face Thiago. "You do realise you're so lucky to be one of the 20 drivers who can be part of the sport, right?"

He furrowed his brows, leaning his chin atop his forearm. Absentmindedly, he studied the rings adorning her fingers, watched the way she toyed with a bracelet to keep her hands occupied. "I know. That's why I can't lose my seat."

"You've got this," she whispered, obliging him to collide his hooded gaze to her.

For a few heartbeats too long, he stayed silent whilst holding her gaze—as though the green of her eyes could keep him anchored.

"Yeah," he said at last, voice gravel-like, nodding. "Yeah, I do."

Unable to hold his stare without feeling like she might combust into a wildfire, she cleared her throat, tucking a strand of hair behind an ear. "So, are you going to help me out of this car or am I supposed to stay in here until tomorrow?"

Thiago chuckled and stood up. She swore she could see the blush ever so slowly coat the tops of his cheekbones in a crimson tinge. "Wait. Can I take a picture of you in the car?"

She scowled. "Seriously?"

"Yep." He took his phone out. "You're just so tiny in this car."

Rolling her eyes, she gave in. Rapidly adjusting her hair over her shoulders, she gave him a smile as he snapped a picture, before putting her cold façade back on.

Thiago sighed softly as he lowered his phone. The look in his eyes was enough to make her breath catch inside her throat. Swallowing, he ran a hand over his flushed face, then shook his head.

"Come on," he said then, extending both hands to help her get out.

She stepped onto the seat, holding his warm hands for support. But just as she was about to put a foot on the stool, he wrapped an arm around her waist and lifted her up.

She couldn't help but let out a squeal of surprise. "What are you doing?"

"Stop asking questions."

She pressed her hands on his shoulders as their chests collided. Everything happened so fast: one moment he lifted her up as though she weighed nothing, and the next moment he set her down onto the nose of the car.

"What's the matter with you?" she asked, her chest heaving.

"Relax."

He grabbed her heels from the ground, then knelt on the floor.

"Can I touch you or are you going to kick me in the face?" he asked, brows raised as he looked up at her.

"Why don't you try and see what happens next?"

He clicked his tongue on the roof of his mouth, head shaking slightly. His eyes sparkled as he chuckled, and God, did he look devastatingly handsome. "So violent."

Delicately, he took hold of her foot to put her shoe on. His warm fingers were burning her ankle, sending zips of electricity through her leg and all the way up to the rest of her body. Refusing to hold onto him, scared of what might happen if she touched this man, she kept her hands on her lap. She had debated leaning onto the car, but she didn't want to touch the vehicle. She was already uncomfortable as it was to be sitting on it. Still, it was evident Thiago didn't mind having her there.

Kamari watched how he expertly strapped her shoe on, then moved her perusal to his face, woven with concentration. His dark hair was slicked back. The bridge of his nose was dusted with faint freckles, and she wondered if they would be more prominent in the sunlight.

"Other foot, princess," he ordered huskily.

She quirked her brows in defiance. "Call me that again and watch where my foot lands."

His laugh was a sweet melody that she longed to hear more often. "You're such a violent little thing."

As he wrapped his hand around her other ankle, securing the shoe and strapping it, she counted the seconds, the unsteady heartbeats. Even after he'd put the heel on, his caress lingered on her skin. His calloused palm trailed up her shin, excruciatingly, slowly so. His gaze followed an invisible route up her bare legs, and she knew he was able to see the goosebumps making their appearance on her skin.

Kamari sucked in a breath at the sight of his eyes turned ashen. His perusal was nearly salacious in its carelessness as he was taking his time to ingrain the image of this moment in the fore point of his mind. The risqué scan over her physique was undeniably seductive, and he wasn't even trying to hide his blatant attraction.

"Thiago." She could hardly breathe. Hardly move.

"Yes?"

"Don't look at me like that." *Like you want me. Like this isn't a game to you.*

He clenched his jaw and dropped his head forward. After exhaling, he lifted his gaze again, strands of hair blocking his view. "Sorry," he apologised hoarsely.

They stood up in synchronisation, the distance between their chests and their noses and their lips infinitesimal. Minuscule. Barely existent. She wasn't certain how she was still breathing, even when his thumb came to graze the corner of her mouth.

His soft murmur caressed the seams of her lips. "You should smile more often. You're bloody gorgeous."

She couldn't help but look at his own lips—pink, full, pulling her thoughts towards him. "And you should stop flirting with me behind closed doors."

"Can't help myself."

Kamari was too well tangled in this chaos, and it was at that moment she realised she couldn't untangle herself from Thiago, no matter how hard she tried.

CHAPTER TWENTY-FOUR

📍 *MONZA, ITALY*

T HE SOUND OF the door sliding open, then closing shortly after distracted Thiago from his thoughts. He could feel that heavy, invisible thread urging him to gravitate towards the source of light that came to shine where he sat—a power that, someway, somehow along the route of playing wicked games became more and more familiar, and strong. But, even after wanting to look into green eyes, he kept his gaze on the horizon and the setting sun.

"Sorry." Kamari's smoky voice echoed, creating a trail of chills to skitter down his spine. "I was on the phone with Indy."

"Is she okay?" He rubbed the back of his neck, able to feel the knots full of tension that had formed after his long day.

"Yes, she's flying down here tomorrow."

From the corner of his eye, he could see the silhouette of a devastating angel entering his personal bubble to which he held its doors open, her sweet fragrance swirling after her shadow and leaving a trail of earthy, blossomed freshness in its wake.

"I was about to say," he started. "One's never seen without the—"

It was at that moment that he decided to look at Kamari, and thought he was teetering on the edge of an endless precipice with no safety net.

The chances of appearing like a fool were high as he felt his jaw go slack, his lips parting and his eyes wandering over her physique. She looked like an angel in disguise on the cusp of ruining him.

"I packed the wrong dress," she noted, unaware of the way she had managed to render him speechless.

"I think you packed the perfect one," he said gruffly after what felt like an eternity.

Kamari shook her head. "I was in such a rush whilst stuffing my luggage this morning."

As she walked towards the railing, Thiago couldn't do anything except stay seated and watch her. Her dress was red, and at that point, he was certain she was wearing this colour on purpose just to get to him. Vibrant red—like a burning flame shooting in the night sky—short, with a neckline that descended to the middle of her abdomen, putting in evidence the swell of her breasts and her sun-kissed skin. Her dress ebbed and flowed in perfect combina-tion with the woman who wore it: breathtaking, alluring, captivating.

He released a breath, completely aware of the power she held over him. Raking trembling fingers through his hair, he watched as she pivoted to face him.

"It's perfect," he said. *You're beautiful,* he wanted to say.

He thought he saw her blush. "Are you sure?"

"Certain."

Kamari leaned the small of her back against the railing, folding her arms across her stomach. A small line made its appearance between her eyebrows as she dropped her gaze to the floor. "You're oddly not yourself today."

Thiago's brows rose in surprise. He leaned back in the armchair and tilted his head to the side. "What do you mean?"

"You're very quiet," she observed. "Look, I know my arrival was unannounced and I completely understand if you don't want me here. I was thinking of getting a room for myself to give you space. I promise I'll be careful and—"

"Kamari," he interrupted quietly. "Relax."

She paused, her chest rising and falling. The soft glow of the sun was proof she wasn't as unattainable as she wanted to be, and he took the time to watch how mesmerising she was whilst standing under the fading sunlight.

"You're not switching rooms."

"I don't want to be a burden," she whispered. "I thought you knew I was coming but—"

"I'm just surprised," he breathed out.

"Bad or good surprise?"

His lips twitched into a small smile as he held her gaze. "Definitely good."

It was barely noticeable, but her shoulders slumped when she sighed in relief. She only nodded, diverting her gaze to the side to watch anything but him.

Seeing her sitting with Alex in the hospitality centre earlier had been a shock. He hadn't expected to hear from her, nor to see her in Italy, but warmth had flooded inside his chest when he'd realised she had dropped her personal plans to fly to him.

"Come sit next to me for a sec," he demanded softly.

"Aren't Cal and Alex going to wait for us?"

He chuckled. "They'll be fine. They can wait for us before we head to the pub."

Reluctantly, Kamari walked in his direction, causing his stare to drop to her long legs.

This woman would wreck him. And for her, he would ruin himself a million little times.

Earlier today, he had felt all sorts of bizarre sentiments whilst she had sat in his F1 car. And when she had allowed him to put her shoes back on, he had wanted to touch every inch of skin. Had wanted to kiss her—everywhere.

She was about to take a seat on the other armchair beside him, but he tugged her by the wrist to take a seat on the edge of the small coffee table, so she would be facing him. Her green eyes were glinting with curiosity and concern as she studied his features, carefully.

His legs were spread out on either side of her own, and he leaned forward whilst threading his fingers together—so he wouldn't touch her.

Kamari placed one thigh atop the other, making the fabric of her dress rise ever so slightly. He swallowed, slowly lifting his gaze to meet hers. She was watching him wearily, and she wasn't even aware she had let her walls down.

"You can talk to me," she began softly, "or not. But just know that I'm here."

He let a small taunting smirk draw upon his lips. "Who would've thought you're not always a bitch?"

She rolled her eyes, though she was amused. "Very funny."

Holding her stare, he dipped his chin in an appreciative nod. "Thank you. I just, ah, I don't talk about it very often."

"It's okay. Take your time."

Unwanted tremors started to corrupt his body, and he inhaled shakily. "Can I—" He paused to breathe, flickering his gaze between Kamari's eyes. "Can I touch you?"

She frowned slightly but nodded.

"Words, Kam," he demanded firmly when she didn't respond vocally.

He counted three heartbeats before she said, "Yes, Thiago."

Rapidly yet gingerly, his trembling hands found the outsides of her thighs, large porcelain palms displayed against caramel skin. The moment he felt her cold skin beneath his palms, he felt as though he could breathe again.

A stranger had become his anchor—how could it be possible?

"How come you're cold?" he asked, incredulously. "It's, like, 25 degrees."

"I'm always cold," she answered quietly, her stare focused on his veiny hands. "I'm fine, though."

He smirked, trying to distract himself from the turmoil clouding his senses. "I know a way to warm you—"

"Finish that sentence and I'm forcing you to sleep on the balcony tonight."

"That's rude," he scoffed, though mirth laced his voice.

She shrugged. "Yes, well, I'm apparently a bitch on my worst days."

Thiago smiled softly, letting his perusal meander over her features—remembering, memorising, studying. The burning sky was reflecting an amber glow on the side of her face, putting in evidence the dust of freckles on the bridge of her nose.

Delicately, his thumbs started to brush her soft skin, and he could hear the way her breath caught.

Thiago swallowed the lump constricting his throat. "Today marks my father's death anniversary."

"Oh, Thiago." Her voice was woven with a rare melancholy, expression softening. She placed a hand atop his to give him more reassurance. "I'm sorry. I didn't know."

"It's okay. Today marks two years without him and it's just hard, you know? The loss, the grief, everything still feels so fresh."

"That's normal." A small line had drawn itself between her eyebrows. "You lost your father, and I bet he was your hero. The world cannot expect you to be perfect every day."

"He was the best," Thiago whispered sorrowfully, looking at her small hand hovering over his. "He was ill; that's why he passed away."

"He used to be an F1 driver, too, right?"

He smiled, sadly. "Yeah, back in the day. He won seven

championships. He was such a legend, such a good man." Shaking his head, he dropped it forward, a few rogue strands of hair tumbling on his forehead with the motion. "Do you know how hard it is to live up to people's expectations? How hard it is to follow my father's steps, and see everyone thinking a talent like his runs through my veins as well? I used to believe in everything, and everyone believed in me, and that was beautiful but now... now I feel hopeless. Bearing all that heavy weight, all that pressure is getting too much today."

"You're only a human being, Thiago. Grieving isn't easy, and it doesn't fade away in the blink of an eye. You might feel helpless right now, but I know that the moment you put your racing suit and helmet on, you'll become that ruthless driver everyone loves. You're your father's son, yes, but you're also your own person. People love you—they worship you. I've seen it with my own eyes, and no one is losing faith in you despite the rough patches you've been going through."

Thiago had to blink, multiple times, to make the burning feeling in his eyes go away.

"I'm so sorry for your loss," she whispered, words blended with emotion. "I can't imagine how hard it must be to lose your hero, but you're allowed to be vulnerable, you know."

"I know," he answered in a murmur, blinking again. "Sometimes, I don't want the world to see me, because I don't think that people would understand. But I just—" He took the time to breathe, to open up his heart to this woman whose eyes reflected a sea of solace. "I just want you to know who I am. I want you to be able to trust me even if it's all a game. I want you to see me, Kam."

"I do see you. I really do." Her voice had cracked, and it was evident she hated the way she was allowing herself to be vulnerable, to feel. "I see a cunning man, persevering and ambitious. Strong-minded. Talented. Unbreakable, because you're hard on yourself."

He couldn't help but tip the corner of his mouth into a mocking smirk. "I know you're dying to insult me, so go ahead."

Kamari laughed, and God, wasn't it the most beautiful, melodious sound he'd ever heard. He wanted to hear that tune of delight every minute of the day until it became his favourite song he would replay over and over again.

"True," she chuckled, absentmindedly tightening her grip around his fingers. "You're conceited, arrogant, annoying—"

"Handsome."

"I'm not saying that."

"Please?"

"No."

"I'm really disappointed," he teased, rubbing the spot above his heart.

She shrugged—all indifference and nonchalance. "Get used to it."

He could feel his chest rise and fall, a heavy weight gripping it as he tried not to break down. Kamari was looking at him so tenderly, so fondly, so adoringly, and he could feel himself free falling into an abyss of ruination.

Unexpectedly, yet carefully, she lifted her hand. She cradled his face, coaxing him through that wild storm of sorrow and melancholy and anger, and he couldn't help but lean into her touch—anchoring himself to her, tethering his heart to hers in an unguarded way he wasn't used to doing. He closed his eyes; to linger in her caress, to make that moment last, knitting his brows together.

Then, he felt the pad of her thumb brush the top of his cheekbone. She'd gathered a teardrop which he hadn't known had escaped of its free will—had collected all his vulnerability in the palm of her hand.

Thiago threw her a sad smile, to which she responded with a radiant grin that managed to outshine the sun.

"He'd be so proud of you," Kamari whispered softly.

And it was at this exact moment that he understood Kamari Monroe was the moon—his moon. A source of light through darkness, an illumination within an abyss so dark and profound, an ignited star in a galaxy so bright where she managed to be the brightest of them all.

CHAPTER TWENTY-FIVE

⚲ *MONZA, ITALY*

"QUIT BEING STUBBORN, Kamari," Thiago groaned as he made haste to catch up with the woman trying to get as far away as possible from him.

"Quit being a gentleman," she countered as she grasped the doorknob. "I can open doors for myself."

"You're a total pain in the arse," he muttered, grabbing her by the hip to pull her backwards until her back collided with his chest. He heard her breath hitch, and she stilled for a fragment of a second. "I'll hold the door because that's how I was raised."

"Fine."

"Brat."

She threw a lethal glare his way. "Arsehole."

Thiago held the door open, releasing her. They walked into the hotel lobby, their footfalls stumbling in perfect rhythm. "You can't stand the idea of people doing things for you, can you?"

She glanced at him. "Maybe."

The rare moment that had occurred on the balcony hadn't lasted long. After she'd gathered his tears, she had watched him carefully, like she had been trying to ingrain this moment in the fore point of her mind before putting her ice façade back on. Thiago had wanted her to stay there with him, but for some reason, she needed to escape, and he'd found himself respecting her decision.

He furrowed his brows. "You're giving me the one-word answer treatment now?"

"Yes."

Before they could step outside of the hotel, Thiago grabbed her elbow and made her spin around. "What's wrong?"

Kamari diverted her gaze to his large hand holding her, exhaling softly. "It's fine."

"Don't lie to me, Kam."

"Okay, don't lie to me either." She held his stare, worry evident as it swirled along the edges of her irises. "Do I look like a slut? I feel like I do."

Thiago blinked, then parted his lips but no sound escaped. "Excuse you? Why would you say such a thing?"

"The dress," she hissed.

He flickered his gaze down her outfit, jaw ticking. "What about it?"

When she didn't respond, he wove their fingers together and pulled her towards the lifts and into an empty corridor that led towards the ladies' room. A large mirror was placed on the wall, and he obliged her to face her reflection as he came to stand behind her.

"Look at you, Kamari," he rasped out, tucking his hands in the front pockets of his trousers so he wouldn't touch her like his body urged him to do. "You're fucking gorgeous."

"You're flirting with me."

"No, I'm just telling the truth." And he wasn't afraid of telling her how he felt about her.

He observed as she stared at herself, unsure and small and

insecure, and seeing her so helpless made molten anger rush through his veins.

He couldn't help but ask, "Did your ex-boyfriend ever call you names when you dressed like this?"

Kamari nodded. "It happened a few times."

Thiago brought a hand up to push her hair away from her shoulder to let it cascade down her bare back, purposely lingering his touch upon her skin. "I'm not him, Kam." He met her eyes through the mirror's reflection. "You're stunning. And you are aware you don't need anyone to shine, right? You don't need Indy to pick outfits for you, you don't need to be under the spotlight to be seen."

She nodded once more, processing his words as she slipped her stare to his fingers tracing intricate patterns on her shoulder.

"Look at yourself and tell me if you like this dress on you. The only thing that matters is if you feel comfortable in it. The only opinion you should care about is yours."

With a sharp intake of air, she wandered her gaze over her physique, straightening her posture and lifting her chin—just like the Kamari he'd always known. "I like it."

Her eyes shone with that wit he admired, with that determination he envied, that self-confidence that made her a million times more attractive.

"Good," he said. "Now I'm going to snap a picture of us and show you to the world, because a beauty like you can't hide in the shadows of her past."

He wrapped his arm around her waist to place his hand on her stomach, pulling her against his torso. He could feel the steady rise and fall of her chest, though her breathing had become bated because of their sheer proximity. Whilst he took his phone out and opened the camera app, she twined her fingers with his, sending jolts of electricity through his skin.

Thiago rapidly snapped a picture, though he couldn't help but notice how perfectly fitted they were—as if they had been made for one another.

Feeling a surge of heat overtake him as they stood in front of the mirror, entwined and flushed together, he glanced at Kamari whose eyes were strained on him, like she was totally hypnotised. Then, he dragged their hands up, slowly so, until his palm was splayed on the middle of her abdomen, his thumb finding the sliver of skin below the valley of her breasts.

"I'm going to show them you're mine," he whispered in her ear.

She scoffed softly. "I'm not yours. Never have been, never will be."

He grazed his nose on the side of her face, lips tipping into a vicious smirk. "That's where you're wrong, love. In public, you're mine."

"You wish."

If only she knew.

KNOTS OF TENSION had formed on his taut shoulders, and he disliked that sensation.

After spending a few hours in a local pub in the centre of Monza with Kamari, Alex, and Cal, Thiago had asked to get back to the hotel, knowing what tomorrow had in store for him.

He had spent the evening either taking pictures with fans that had been flooding the pub or conversing with his friends.

He'd watched men glance at Kamari, witnessed some of them trying to flirt with her. She had been sitting by his side the whole time, only speaking when Alex and Cal addressed a question towards her, but she still laughed when the pair acted like fools. Thiago had draped his arm around her shoulders, and she hadn't moved at all.

Thiago wasn't certain what had caused the tightness in his muscles. It was either the fact he had touched Kamari all night long—her shoulders, her hips, her thighs—and exchanged secret glances with her, knowing all too well they'd be back to ignoring each other once back at the hotel, or the fact he'd been able to sense the jealousy flare inside his chest like poisonous, deathly vines whenever another man had dared to speak to her.

He was currently sitting on the balcony, basking in the crescent moon's light, the top buttons of his shirt undone and head tipped against the back of the armchair.

He heard Kamari slip outside, so quietly as though she was hiding in the shadows, her familiar scent of green tea and sage engulfing him into a bubble of comfort he couldn't fathom just yet.

He gaped at her, watching how her dark hair spilled on one shoulder as she was still wearing the dress that would certainly be the object of his dreams.

"Is everything okay?" he asked gruffly when he noticed her closed-off expression.

She took a seat on the other armchair next to him, leaning over to unstrap her high heels. She nodded without meeting his gaze. "Just stumbled on that gossip page on Instagram."

He instantly sat up, frowning. "What kind of bullshit were they saying about you?"

"Not about me, about you." She rolled her eyes. "There's this picture you took with a fan earlier at the pub going around. She was standing awfully close to you. People say you ditched me for her."

"Rumours start so stupidly," he grunted. When he noticed she was avoiding eye contact and biting the inside of her cheek, he smirked. "Careful, Kam, I'm going to start thinking you're jealous."

"Jealous of what?" she scoffed.

"I don't know. But I'm going to start thinking you care about me, and my reputation more than you care to admit."

She faced him, pushing her hair away from her shoulder. "I don't."

"You flew here to me," he noted. "That must mean you like me."

Her eyes gleamed with some kind of emotion he couldn't name, but it caused his heart to batter furiously. Ever so slightly, her full lips tipped into the smallest, rarest beam. "I tolerate you, that's different."

As she put her feet atop the coffee table, he nudged one of them with his own. "I guess I tolerate you back."

"Wow," she deadpanned, one brow rising. "Here I am, *totally* relieved. Thought my feelings for you were unrequited."

"You're insufferable," he said with a chuckle.

Her eyes found the exposed part of his chest, lingering on his silver chain before finding his gaze back again. He didn't want it, but he could feel that cord tightening around his heart, pulling him and forcing him to gravitate towards Kamari.

"Don't worry about me," he ended up saying. "Rumours are just here to destroy me. Do me a favour though, and don't look at those."

"I'm not afraid to step up and defend you, you know."

He grinned. "I know."

When a peaceful silence fell, he forced himself to look away. He found the starry sky, settling his stare on the luminous moon. In the distance, the noise coming from the city could be heard; voices of chatter, laughter coming from the pubs where people were flooding the terraces, sounds of cars fading away.

Placing his hands behind his head, he threaded his fingers together whilst letting out a long exhale.

"Kam," he murmured.

"Yes?" she whispered back. He could feel her stare on him; intense, lingering.

"Thank you." He didn't need to elaborate to express his gratitude. "I hope you know everything you do, everything you sacrifice for me, means a great deal."

"You're welcome."

"Seriously, though," he continued softly. "You're an incredible woman. All those people who've hurt you, who've left you, aren't aware of how much you were willing to do for them. You probably think that going to great lengths for people you love is a bad thing, but I think it's the sexiest thing a woman like you"— *so intent on hiding the most beautiful parts of your soul—* "could do."

She didn't answer. She was surprised, overwhelmed, he supposed.

He didn't want to scare her away.

"You always look up at the sky," she noted then, voice thick with emotion. "Is there something beyond the stars you're looking for?"

"I'm looking at the moon."

A beat passed. A breath escaped. A soft caress of the clement breeze over the bridge of his nose when he felt her gaze upon his face, akin to a shower of starlight penetrating their cosmos of solace.

"Why?" she asked so quietly, so curiously without a hint of malice in her tone.

Silver met green, and a grin spread across his lips at the sight of her moonlit face. "It makes me think of you."

She frowned. Pivoted to face him. Paused. "It does?"

He didn't know how to tell her that, just like the moon, she had a side so cold and so dark that it only lured him towards the hidden, secretive parts of her soul. That, despite hiding in the shadows and waiting to be embraced by solitude, she managed to shine brighter than the stars. He understood she was afraid to show her own light, perhaps because someone had dared to extinguish her fire.

And, so, he asked, "Your name means moon, doesn't it?"

She smiled softly, and he was suddenly weak in the knees. "You did your research, didn't you?"

"Yeah," he murmured. "Pretty name—"

She narrowed her eyes, and there she was; the Kamari who had ruined him. "If you finish that sentence by saying that silly phrase, 'pretty name for a pretty girl', I swear I will end you."

He laughed, grinning up at the starry sky. Pushing his rebel locks away, he shook his head. "I'm going to start thinking you're immune to my flirting."

"Sorry to hurt your ego."

"Yeah, sure you are."

Silver and green clashed in a thunder of unspoken words where glances were more powerful than anything, where lingering in each other's regard was a certain form of serenity.

"Astraea," Kamari whispered softly, looking at him with that delicacy that made his stomach coil, like there was a bird trapped inside, trying to set itself free by batting its wings.

He frowned slightly. "What?"

She stood up after grabbing the heels she had taken off. "You once asked what my middle name is. It's Astraea."

"Kamari Astraea Monroe," he said in a whisper full of awe. *Please release my heart and give it back to me.* "It's nice to meet you."

A soft chuckle erupted from her mouth as she slid open the door leading to their room. "Nice to meet you too, pretty boy."

And he watched her disappear inside, tearing the zipper of her dress down before letting her silhouette fade through the bathroom door.

Thiago wasn't sure how he was supposed to go through long weeks of pretending she was a simple pawn in his game. The more she opened up her heart to him, the more he could feel himself falling off the cliff.

CHAPTER TWENTY-SIX

📍 *MONZA, ITALY*

K AMARI COULDN'T MANAGE to put her mind at peace. Couldn't fall asleep. Couldn't stop tossing and turning.

As she rolled onto her stomach, slipping her hands under the cold pillow, she kept her eyes closed but her mind was racing with millions of thoughts.

She huffed, a bit too loudly, blowing a strand of hair that had been bothering her away from her face. She then grew hot, so she slid her foot out of the duvet before tucking it back in, making the sheets rustle.

Her breath caught inside her throat when a pillow landed on her head, interrupting the racing thoughts skittering against every corner of her mind.

"Stop fucking moving, Monroe," a deep voice resonated.

How could she have forgotten about the man sharing the same bed as her?

Grabbing the pillow that had tousled her hair, she threw it back at him, resulting in hearing a grunt in response.

"Go to sleep," Thiago said, voice muffled.

"I'm trying."

She shifted to lie on her back, eyes opening to stare at the almost-black ceiling, barely lit by the silvery moonlight that managed to slip through the curtains.

She got her arms out of the comforter, but when the cold air collided with her skin, making it pebble, she made haste to bury herself into the warmth of the bed again.

This bed was bigger than the one she had slept in the last time in Belgium, but she felt as though the distance between her and Thiago was barely existent. She had built another wall made out of pillows under his amused stare, and he had riled her up by reaching over and ruffling her hair before whispering a good night.

She turned to her left side and tugged the duvet up to her chin.

"Stop moving," he groaned again.

"I can't sleep," she whispered, frustratingly.

"Well, that's because you're moving. Just settle down and stop thinking."

"Easier said than done, smart-pants," she bit out, tossing onto her right side, causing her to drag the comforter along with her.

"Brat," he hissed, pulling the blanket back towards him, and she gripped at it tightly so he wouldn't take all of it. "Can't you share?"

Kamari rolled her eyes. She was even more awake than she had been just a minute ago. "I didn't do it on purpose."

She couldn't help but lift herself up on her elbow and reach out towards the nightstand to grab her phone. The time indicated past eleven p.m., and she groaned with despair.

"Okay, what's wrong with you?" Thiago asked. When she

felt him move, she supposed he had rolled on his side to face her, even if her back was turned to him.

Why was he so concerned? Why couldn't he not care about her?

"Nothing."

"Liar."

"Mind your business," she spat, falling back onto her too-fluffy pillow.

A dry chuckle rose from his throat. "You know, you're in my bed, so I can't help but make *you* my business right now."

"Was that supposed to charm me or something?"

"No," he huffed, annoyed. "It's just pure concern, Kamari. Everything I say to you isn't a ruse to get you in bed, though you climbed into it of your free—"

A pillow landed on his face, cutting him mid-sentence. Kamari turned to glare at him even though he couldn't see her through the darkness.

"Witch," he laughed.

"Thanks."

"It wasn't a compliment."

"I know." She closed her eyes. "Good night now."

"Oh, right," he scoffed. "You're going to wake me up and act like a brat? That's not happening."

A loud, irritated huff fled past her lips, but she didn't move. She tried to calm her pounding heart, tried to collect her thoughts, but it seemed impossible as she felt Thiago shift around. One by one, the pillows in between them disappeared.

"Are you destroying my wall?" she asked, baffled, eyes still shut.

"Yes."

"Rude."

"You know it's unnecessary, right? Remember what happened last time?"

Flashes of his strong arms embracing her flooded her mind. "Nothing happened."

Thiago chuckled. "Keep telling yourself that, baby. Denial at its finest."

Moving to rest on her back, she exhaled through her nose, trying to ignore the wave of warmth inching towards her as Thiago shifted closer.

"What's going on inside that head of yours?" he murmured. She could feel his warm breath fan across her cheekbone.

She could sense the heat emanating from his body like sizzling embers, ready to set her ablaze.

"Nothing," she repeated. "I'm not tired."

"What are you thinking about?" he asked, blatantly ignoring her answer.

You.

"Nothing."

"Are you going to stop lying to me?"

"I'm not lying."

"Kamari," he droned.

"Thiago." She turned her head to look at him, but he was just a blur in the dark. "Go to sleep. I'm fine. I'll eventually fall asleep."

He groaned, loudly, evidently vexed by her lack of response.

What happened the next second made her heart stop beating, made her breath catch inside her throat, made the resting butterflies inside the pit of her stomach bat their wings wildly.

Thiago had moved so swiftly that she hadn't been able to anticipate his actions. Hovering over her, he caught her wrists, pinning them above her head, and settled in between her parted legs.

"You're so stubborn," he muttered harshly. His fingers were burning around her wrists, her chest rising and falling but never colliding with his.

She could make out the contour of his sharp face, of his toned upper body through the shadows of the night. She knew he was only wearing shorts as the fabric grazed her knees, and she couldn't help but wonder how the hard ridges of his abdomen would feel beneath her fingertips.

She was able to feel the intensity of his scrutiny on her face, even if he couldn't exactly see her either—like sparks igniting on her flesh.

"What's going to take me to make you fall asleep?" he asked in a murmur, voice raspy, tone chilling.

Every inch of her skin was covered in goosebumps, and she was certain he could feel the effect he was having on her beneath his fingertips.

"Sing you a lullaby?" he joked, letting a mischievous smirk be heard through his question.

She wanted to see him. Wanted to see his pupils expand so widely that his eyes would nearly become black. Wanted to watch how he would be utterly absorbed by her expression, focused on her breathing.

She let out a small scoff. "Really witty. Hilarious, even."

When she tried to wriggle out of his grip, he tightened his hold around her wrists, keeping them pinned to the pillow. "Stop. Always resisting me. Always fighting me. Stop it."

"Let go of me," she demanded in a firm whisper.

"Not until you settle down." His breaths had become ragged, but he was doing a phenomenal job at pretending he wasn't affected by their proximity. "Do you want me to tell you a story? Or maybe read out loud that book you left on your nightstand?"

She sucked in a breath, her mind wandering to quixotism where she imagined Thiago whispering the words inked in her favourite romance novel. "No."

Lowering himself, the tips of their noses brushed, his lips hovering centimetres away from hers. Kamari's eyes fluttered close, and she did everything in her power not to writhe under that punishing touch of his.

"How about we both stop pretending and succumb to our

desires? You want me just as much as I want you, Kam. Getting you off should be the perfect soporific."

Warmth flooded deep inside her core, a foreign yet powerful wave of lust corrupting all of her senses.

"You're wrong," she whispered bitterly. "I don't want you."

She saw the corner of his lips twitch upwards under the dim glow of the night sky. "You sure about that?" When he released one of her wrists, she didn't move. Couldn't move. He cradled her jaw, then slid his hand down to the side of her neck. "Your drumming pulse says otherwise, darling. The way you react to my touch... it drives me insane."

Steady breaths became uneven and heavy and ragged, and she shook her head. "I don't want you," she repeated.

"You're only saying that because you're afraid—terrified—to feel something. Because you know I make you feel, and you don't want it."

She gritted her teeth. "You know nothing, Valencia."

"Allow me to touch the rest of your body," he rasped. "I can prove you wrong. I can prove that mind of yours"—he tapped her temple—"that I'm all you need."

Her mind was clouded, and her heart was thundering like a furious thunderbolt in a calamitous sky. "I don't need you. I don't need anyone. You just want to use me to get it out of your system. You're annoying, pompous, vain, full of—"

Slanting his lips on hers, he inhaled the words leaving her mouth. She stilled. Ceased to breathe. Closed her eyes and returned his passionate pecks. He cupped her jaw, tipping her head back to have easier access to her mouth. His tongue found hers, instantly starting a battle for dominance. Kamari responded with equal fervour, her free hand tangling with his soft locks at his nape. The feeling of her digits on his scalp made him moan softly into her mouth, and Kamari pulled him closer.

As if reality suddenly hit him, he pulled away, lips millimetres apart, uneven breaths entwining with hers. "Shit," he whispered hoarsely. "I wasn't thinking. Is this okay? Do you want this?"

Kamari needed to push him away.

She needed to say no.

A nod of her head was her response, but he couldn't see her.

Thiago tucked a lock of hair behind her ear, lingering his scorching caress on her cheekbone. "I'm going to need you to use your words, baby."

"Yes," she breathed, without thinking of the consequences. "Yes, I want this."

She heard him swallow, thickly. "Good."

But she only arched her back, brushing her clothed chest to his bare one. A whimper fled past his lips, and she smirked. "Kiss me, Thiago. Kiss me and don't fucking stop."

"So demanding," he chuckled.

His lips found hers, softly at first, then rapidly shifted into a punishing kiss. He released her other wrist, finding her hip. Kamari wrapped both arms around his shoulders, able to feel his muscles contract and his soft, burning skin under her fingertips. She bent her legs at the knees, spreading them further apart to allow Thiago to settle comfortably in between.

He released a small grunt when his chest fell onto hers. The kiss turned headier—a rhapsodic melody of euphonious breaths, an intoxicating sensation as his tongue danced with her own, their ragged and heavy breaths entwining and becoming one.

His hand slipped beneath her camisole, caressing her ribs, fingertips digging into her flesh—claiming her.

"You're going to ruin me, Kam."

She only responded with a hint of a smirk, breaking the kiss. His lips trailed from her mouth to her jawline, up to a certain spot beneath her ear she knew would weaken her in the knees. Open-mouthed kisses were placed on her skin, but when he gently sucked on that particular spot, she couldn't control the sigh of pleasure that escaped.

He smiled against her skin before grazing his teeth there,

then trailing downwards to her collarbones. His hand had travelled upwards, thumb dancing on the side of her breast whilst she breathed heavily, her hands sauntering over his muscular back.

The moment their lips collided once more, she used his momentum of distraction to roll them over. Straddling his hips, she pulled herself as close as she could, fingers on either side of his large neck without so much as detaching their mouths. Moans erupted from the back of his throat—lots of them.

She felt his calloused hands touch her back, her ribs, her hips.

She wanted to feel his devastating lips everywhere on her.

She wanted to feel his powerful touch on every inch of her body.

She had a burning desire for him, and she couldn't deny it anymore. He was breaking her piece by piece.

He slid the strap of her camisole down her shoulder, lips following closely as he placed delicate kisses on her blazing flesh.

Kamari threw her head back and gave him access to her throat. He wrapped his hand around it, though he didn't apply pressure. His mouth found her pulse, and he grazed his teeth over the thundering point.

"Kam," he rasped out hoarsely, skimming his lips over hers. "What are you doing to me?"

He kissed her again. Stole each one of her breaths away, claiming them as his. It felt as though he was addicted to her lips, never wanting to tear himself away.

His fingers tangled in her hair whilst he nipped at her lower lip, soft groans catching in his throat.

God, had he kissed her like this on his boat a few weeks ago? Had he been able to make her feel like this?

Grabbing her waist, he pulled her further up onto his lap, rolling her hips over his already hard erection straining against the fabric of his shorts, his pelvis bucking upwards. To show her how she made him feel. To show her that he wanted her so badly, on the cusp of unravelling and being at her mercy.

She moaned softly, parting her lips to let a shaky exhale escape.

"Fuck," he breathed huskily. "I knew that bratty mouth of yours could make sweet sounds like that."

She couldn't recall the last time someone else—other than her own fingers—had been able to make her feel good. Actually, no one else had ever been able to send her into the pinnacle of pleasure.

Thiago was making her own bliss his priority, and it stirred an uncanny sensation inside her chest.

He guided her to rock her hips on his, meeting her halfway with leisure, torturous movements. He kissed her where her shoulder met her neck, whimpering when she rocked harder. Her breasts felt heavy, were aching, and she needed more friction. But before she could rub her hardened nipples against his naked chest, he pushed her away, torso rising and falling.

"Wait," he said, breathless, tone gruff. "We can't."

She inhaled. "Why?"

"Because." He cupped her face, kissing her softly to coax her through that new wave of turmoil. So softly that she felt her world crumbling down. So softly that she wondered who that man was, and what his intentions with her were. "Because I want you fully. With no layers between us, no darkness surrounding us. If you allow me to have you, you have to know that I might never be able to let you go afterwards. No matter what this is between us. I've got no idea what you're doing to me—I have never felt like this before. I never wanted to go this far with you, but now that I want you, I need you to think about it."

Dropping her forehead against his, she exhaled softly. Perhaps it was the fatigue overwhelming her, or his existence that had managed to consume her every thought, or his incredible tenderness and patience that caused a lump to form inside her throat.

"Thank you," she only whispered.

He pecked her lips. "Don't worry about it."

She emitted a quiet laugh. "Don't start making a habit of just kissing me behind closed doors, though."

"Come on," he grunted teasingly. "You're not cool."

"I know." She scrambled off his lap, adjusting her top and rubbing her flushed cheeks. She was thankful for the darkness, though she would've loved seeing him: his alluring physique, his hypnotising eyes, his handsome smile.

"Can we cuddle?" he asked when she was buried under the comforter. She was still burning, still heady with desire. "We're *waaaay* past the point of a pillow wall."

Kamari smiled. Still, she turned on her side—away from him. "In your wildest dreams, pretty boy."

She felt him shift closer. Then, he placed a delicate kiss on her shoulder blade. "There's my girl."

She couldn't help but bask in his devotion, closing her eyes and letting her mind wander to the *what ifs* and the dreams where she wasn't afraid of falling; in a world where she would finally bother with love because over there, it would last.

CHAPTER TWENTY-SEVEN

📍 *MONZA, ITALY*

S HE HAD AWOKEN in the middle of the night, limbs tangled with Thiago's like puzzle pieces that were meant to be. Barely awake, she hadn't been able to gather the courage to slip out of his hold, so she stayed and fell back asleep.

When she woke up several hours later, the spot beside her was empty and cold. Confusion had started blending with the haze of fatigue in her head, but she hadn't lingered on the fact Thiago was gone. He couldn't have been far, she'd told herself.

She took the opportunity of being alone to take a long, hot shower during which she reminisced about the events that had happened late at night, bracing herself for the moment she would have to face Thiago.

Their kisses had been full of desire and lust and passion—she'd never felt like that before, and she couldn't let him destroy her heart. Still, his burning touch lingered like tattooed kisses, every souvenir of his domineering lips, powerful caresses flashing inside her mind.

Once dressed and ready to head down to grab breakfast—
and rapidly calling her brother to check in, only for him to hang
up after saying everything was under control—she opened the
bathroom door and jumped up with a start, hand on her chest.

Thiago was standing in front of the door, fist raised in the air
as though he was ready to knock.

"Morning, sunshine," he grinned. "Woah, don't look so
scared. It's just me."

"You surprised me," she said quietly, dropping her hand to
her side, only to start fidgeting with her ring. "Don't sneak up on
me like that."

"Sorry," he murmured, his irises glinting with amusement.

Time slowed down whilst his silver eyes found hers in a
regard full of silent solace and delicate tenderness.

"Hi," he whispered.

Kamari furrowed her brows. "Hi?"

"Hi."

She stared gleefully at him. "You already said that."

"Yes, right." He rubbed the back of his neck, slipping his
gaze towards the ceiling as he chuckled softly. "You were sleeping
so peacefully. I didn't want to wake you up."

She wasn't certain what caused her cheeks to redden: the way
he was always so careful with her, or the way he brazenly lingered
his stare on every inch of her physique, making her feel exposed
despite the layers of clothes adorning her skin. "I appreciate
that."

Thiago maintained their steady eye contact, like he didn't
want to look away, and cleared his throat. Out of the blue, he
handed her a cup of steaming hot coffee.

Had he been holding onto it since the beginning of their
encounter? She'd been so enthralled by the man that she hadn't
paid attention to her surroundings.

"Black."

She blinked and grabbed the cup, their fingers brushing in
the process. "What?"

"Your coffee," he said. "You take it black, right?"

Kamari flickered her gaze from the hot beverage's steam evaporating into the air to Thiago's smile, and she nodded as though she had fallen speechless. "Yes."

He grinned, burying his hands in the pockets of his loose jeans. "I need to head out to the circuit now. I have a quick meeting with my race engineers, and then I've got to warm up with Cal, and get ready for FP3"—*free practice, session three*—"but feel free to take as much time as you need before coming to the track. Alex will take you there, and he'll spend the day with you."

"I don't need a bodyguard," she announced with a roll of her eyes that made him chuckle.

"I know. But I don't want you to be alone whilst I'm busy."

She lifted the mug up to her mouth to conceal the smile that was threatening to touch her lips. "Careful," she droned. "I might start thinking you care just a bit too much."

Silver eyes sparkled, like diamonds on a bed of crystal water as he smiled. "You wish."

She took a sip of her coffee, her brows ever so slightly raising in pleasant surprise. "That's good coffee. Rich and strong."

His smile didn't waver. "We're in Italy; of course, it's good shit."

As he turned on his heel to exit the room, Kamari felt the uncanny urge to hear his voice, to look into his eyes. She caught his elbow, and he stilled. "Wait."

His eyes lit up when he turned back around, and he took a step forward. "Yes?"

"Are you okay?" she asked softly.

"Yeah, why?" He frowned. "Because of last night? Don't worry, I'm used to you rejecting me."

She pinned him with a glare. "I barely rejected you, you drama queen. I'm talking about, you know... your father's death anniversary."

Thiago swallowed but nodded. Gently, he tucked a rogue strand of hair behind her ear. "I'll be okay."

"Promise?"

The corner of his mouth tipped into a smirk. "Careful," he whispered. "I'm going to start thinking you care about me."

"Never," she bit out. Regardless, she searched his gaze for the truth, her heart aching when she saw a sorrowful gleam swirl around his pupils.

He winked. "I'll see you later. I'll be that guy in the red racing suit pushing to get pole position."

"You'll be that guy making your dad proud," she whispered. "And I'll be that fake girlfriend of yours, secretly rooting for you."

He grabbed her hand and brushed his lips to her knuckles moments before planting a soft kiss on the back of it. His eyes shone with thousands of emotions, of unspoken words that he didn't want to say out loud because she knew that he didn't want to scare her off.

He exited the room, and Kamari suddenly realised silver had become her favourite colour.

"HERE," ALEX SAID whilst giving her a helmet. "Put that on."

"A Vespa?" Kamari chuckled. "Really?"

Winking, he clipped the strap of his beige helmet. "Gotta live the full Italian experience, love."

When Kamari was settled behind Alex, she held onto the hand grips on either side of her hips and waited for him to start the engine.

"Do you know how to drive that thing?"

"Nope," he answered, nonchalant. "Can't be *that* difficult, though. Besides, the circuit isn't too far away so there's a low risk for us to die."

"So reassuring," she mumbled when he drove off from the hotel's parking space. "I'll kill you if we die."

She saw his reflection in the mirror, his smile wide beneath his moustache. "Tito wasn't lying when he said you were a bit rough around the edges."

She frowned, keeping her gaze ahead of herself as he went through the streets. "He's giving you all the wrong impressions. I promise I'm not always a cold-hearted brat."

Alex's smile only widened. "He speaks so fondly of you, Kam. He never said a bad thing about you."

"Really?"

He hummed as he nodded. "I think he's just a bit scared of getting hurt, too. He's not sure what your intentions are with him."

Kamari's fingers tightened around the hand grips. "I don't want to hurt him. Don't plan on doing so. This is just a game between us, but it doesn't mean it has to end badly. He's a great guy."

"A game?" Alex repeated amusedly. "Anyway, you should say that to him, not me."

They drove past a group of fans, all dressed in red Primavera Racing merch. Alex honked, making them jump with a start but, as they realised who was sitting on the bike, they started cheering and waving.

"Hi, Kamari!" one of the girls exclaimed.

Kamari was startled but waved in response whilst Alex turned around the corner.

"People know me?"

Alex chuckled. "Of course. Tito's never brought a girl into the paddock before, so I think his fans are just very happy for him."

Her eyebrows jumped. "Guess we're doing a good job, then."

Alex threw her an amused glance. Again.

"So, did he ask you?" he inquired as he clutched the brake to come to a stop in front of a red light. His feet touched the ground as he waited for the light to switch to green.

She met his blue gaze in the rear-view mirror. "Ask me what? My hand in marriage? Never going to happen."

He snickered, shaking his head. "Nah. We're spending a few days at Lake Como after the race. He wanted to ask you to join us. Indy's coming."

A small line built itself between her brows. "She is? She didn't tell me."

"I called her this morning before she boarded her flight." Alex pressed onto the throttle's clutch and drove through the street, multiple signs indicating the direction towards the F1 circuit. "You should join us."

"I can't. And I think Thiago already knows my answer so that's why he won't ask."

"Bummer. Don't worry, I'll keep an eye on him. Make sure he doesn't invite random girls, doesn't sneak off with someone else."

She shook her head, but a bizarre sensation stirred inside her chest at the thought of Thiago with someone else. "You don't owe me anything, Alex."

"I do," he said firmly. "Because for some reason, you bring out the best in him, and I'm really thankful for that."

"EVERYTHING OKAY?" CAL asked as he took a seat next to Kamari.

She lifted her gaze from her phone, blinked and suddenly realised where she was. The sounds had disappeared for a fraction of a second whilst anger rushed through her veins, though that sudden wave of vexation only lasted for a heartbeat. Relaxing her face, she tried not to show how disoriented she was and nodded, offering a tight-lipped smile to Cal.

She directed her gaze away and watched Thiago as he sat in

his car, looking up at his race engineer whilst the latter showed him statistics on a tablet.

She could barely see his face hidden beneath his helmet because she was sitting in the back of the garage, but she could perceive the concentration and determination in his gaze.

He had made it through Q1 and Q2 without an ounce of struggle, always securing the fastest lap. He was confident today —it was obvious from the energy he had been emanating since the beginning of qualifying—and she was certain he could be on pole for Sunday's race.

Kamari studied his expression whilst he nodded as a response to Luke's inquiry. His grey eyes blazed with certainty, with a chilling tenacity she'd been able to glimpse a few times already. It was evident nothing could attain him when he was in the car— he was engulfed in his own world.

This person, behind the helmet, was someone else. He wasn't the flirty man who would go to great lengths to put a smile on her lips, wasn't the ray of sunshine capturing the room's attention when his obnoxious laugh reverberated. Whenever he put his armour on, his façade turned to ice and his determination was made of steel. He had one goal in mind, and it was to stand on the highest step of the podium and brandish the biggest trophy towards the heavens.

Nothing mattered to him. Nothing could distract him.

He was Thiago Valencia. Untouchable. Ruthless. Heartless.

The atmosphere was sizzling inside the garage whilst everyone waited for Q3 to start.

She snapped a picture of the red car with mechanics standing and walking around in their jumpsuits. She posted the photo on her Instagram story with a fingers-crossed emoji, then focused her attention back on Thiago when his engine roared. Drivers went out of their respective garages one by one, but Thiago didn't leave.

"Why isn't he leaving?" Kamari asked Cal.

The dark-skinned man leaned back in his chair, arms folded

across his chest. "The team's confident he'll secure pole position. They're probably waiting the last few remaining minutes of the session to send him out."

"Is it safe?" she inquired, incredulous. "I mean, like, what if he doesn't run the fastest lap?"

Cal shrugged and took down the pair of headphones circling the back of his neck to lay it down on his lap. "The car is doing well on this circuit, so I think he'd still end up in the top three. But we'll see. Doing crazy stuff like that is what makes the sport exciting."

Kamari nodded. She stared at the screen which showed Miles Huxley's black car, the garage falling silent as everyone was intensely focused on the qualifying session.

Indy, who had arrived earlier today, nudged Kamari in the ribs. "You look a bit pale."

"Gee," Kamari started sardonically, "thanks. No need to be so sweet to me."

"No, really, Kam." Her friend had leaned close to her ear as her voice had lowered to a whisper. "Is everything okay?"

Kamari swallowed the lump that had suddenly appeared in her throat. Unlocking her phone, she handed it to her best friend and showed her the cause of her distress.

UNKNOWN

Attention seeker.

That guy is using you.

"Do you think it's—"

"Yep," Kamari said, tone clipped and putting the device in the bottom of her purse. "There's only one douchebag walking on this planet Earth whose hobby is to hurt me."

"Don't pay attention to him," Indy whispered, leaning her head on her friend's shoulder.

Kamari shrugged. In all honesty, she didn't care about her ex-boyfriend, though she couldn't fathom why he would waste his time tormenting her. Especially when he was the one who wanted to leave by cheating on her, continuously so. She was better off without him, anyway—free, herself, teetering towards happiness.

"I'm not."

Strong arms came to engulf Kamari and Indigo in a bone-crushing embrace. "Why are we hugging?" Alex asked.

"*You*'re hugging us," Kamari mustered, wriggling out of his hold despite the nice feeling of being in his friendly cocoon.

"Rude woman," he bit out playfully before seating himself on Indy's other side. "Ah, there's Tito exiting the garage."

There were over two minutes left until the chequered flag would be brandished to indicate the end of qualifying.

Kamari's ears rang as the car sped out in the pit lane, but she maintained her gaze on the few screens hanging on the wall directly across from her. She felt Callahan's knee bop up and down, occasionally brushing hers whilst he rubbed his hands together. Indy, as dramatic as ever, was holding Alex's hand tightly all the while Kamari held her composure despite the thundering and wild rhythm of her heart.

"Come on, Tito," Cal murmured under his breath. "You can do it."

"He's purple on sector one," Indy cheered, which was followed by loud shouts and screams of encouragement echoing in the garage.

"Purple?" Kamari asked in a baffled whisper. "Sector one? Please speak English, thank you very much."

Alex peered at her with an amused glance. "Jeez, Kam. Keep up with the F1 slang, will ya?"

Indy elbowed Alex and turned to Kamari, though her gaze was still fixated on the television. "F1 tracks are divided into three sectors which are each one-third of the lap. We use three colours to determine how fast a driver goes through each sector: purple, green, and yellow. You can see here"—she pointed to the bottom of the screen where Thiago's name with the number seven was displayed, a follow-through of his lap time right below it—"that his sector one is purple which means he has set the fastest time through that segment of the lap."

"What does yellow and green mean, then?"

"Green means a driver has set a personal best lap time through that portion of the track. Yellow simply means a driver hasn't recorded a personal best."

"Oh." She nodded. "He's also the fastest in sector two?"

"Yes," Indy confirmed whilst Thiago hit the brake to take corner seven. "His car is impressive on this track, as well as Rowan's, as he's currently P2."

Kamari frowned. "How come a car doesn't work well on every track?"

"Well, every circuit is different, and each car is different," said Cal. "Some cars are made to be faster in long straights whilst others can be faster in corners. The goal though, is for the car to be fast in both, and to be rapid at reaccelerating."

"*Ohmygodness!*" Indy exclaimed as she jumped onto her feet, dragging Alex with her. "Go, go, go."

Thiago drove through the last long straight at full speed, and when Kamari looked at the drivers' ranking on the left side of the screen, his name jumped up to the first place as he secured the fastest lap in a minute and twenty-two seconds.

The chequered flag was brandished a few seconds later, and the whole room erupted in delighted shouts as pure ecstasy swamped the space.

Thiago Valencia was on pole position.

CHAPTER TWENTY-EIGHT

📍 *MONZA, ITALY*

"K AM," THIAGO WHISPERED. "Kamari? Kam? Moonbeam?"

"What?" she hissed through the obsidian light of the night. "Moonbeam?"

"Yeah," he murmured, a small smile gracing his lips. "You're the moon."

"Are you drunk?" Delight could be heard through her soft, yet fatigued tone.

"No. Just still high on today's quali results."

He watched as she turned to lie on her side, slipping her hands beneath her pillow. Her eyes were still closed, though he wished she'd open them just to witness how starlight would look on evergreen irises.

"Are you sleeping?" he asked.

"Does it look like I'm sleeping?"

The warm September breeze slipped through the crack of the open window, blowing the curtains slightly and brushing the outline of his cheekbone like a delicate caress.

Thiago watched as the sliver of moonlight fell directly upon Kamari's face, casting a silvery glow on her angelic face.

"Stop staring at me," she mumbled.

"Sorry."

"No, you're not."

"I'm not sorry at all," he replied with a grin she couldn't see.

Finally, she opened her eyes, though the lighting was too dark and dim to really perceive the glow around her irises. "What's going on inside that head of yours, Valencia?"

At first, he wanted to ask her if she was willing to talk about what had happened last night. If she was comfortable with sleeping next to him after those few kisses they had exchanged; if she was aware that she had admitted that she wanted him, too.

But he didn't want to ruin the moment.

Neither of them had brought the topic up since this morning, and he thought it would be best not to talk about it now.

And so, he said in a soft murmur, ready to expose the most hidden parts of his heart, "I'm really nervous."

She watched him with an intensity that made his senses heighten, but her voice was as soft as velvet. "About tomorrow's race?"

"Yeah."

"That's normal. So many people are expecting so much from you. I don't know how you deal with all that pressure."

He shrugged. "It's part of life."

"Are you feeling confident?"

"I think so."

A smile was perceptible in the dark. "Good, then. That's all you're going to need to get behind that steering wheel and go at full throttle to win the race."

He chuckled, rubbing his fatigue-stricken face with a hand too clammy for his own liking. He was so goddamned nervous around this woman, and he didn't like it. "Is that your pep talk?"

"I'm bad at it," she admitted with a grimace.

A full grin touched his lips. "I think it's cute."

She huffed. "I don't think *cute* and *Kamari* are two words that mix well together."

A laugh erupted from his throat. "You're right. You're a total menace."

"So sweet."

He traced the contour of her full lips with his regard, following the route of her nose until he found her eyes, wishing they'd be laying in full daylight.

There had been a time when he wasn't too fond of the idea of getting close to her, uncertain of her true intentions. But now, he wanted more; to get to know her, to be her friend, to hang on to that invisible string and pull her towards him until he could cage her in. He would take the risk.

"Thank you," he said after a long moment of silence. "For coming here. To support me."

"You think I came for you, huh?" she teased, nudging his foot with her own, resulting in him kicking her shin harder. "The world does not revolve around you."

He smiled softly. "Why are you here, then?"

"Because Alex called me."

"Are you saying you're here for Alexander?" He feigned hurt by putting a hand over his heart, outrage blending with his tone.

Her chuckle was a melodious song to his ears. "Maybe."

"Liar," he drawled. "You know why Alex called, right?"

"I know now."

He put his arm under his head and leaned his cheek on his bicep, threading his fingers through his curls. "I was busy watching Indy's story and you appeared in it, and I think Alex saw something on my face. He asked if he wanted me to call you, but I said no because I knew you wouldn't come. Didn't want to disturb you."

She was silent for a few heartbeats too long. He didn't know if she was vexed or pensive, but her voice echoed brusquely when she said, "Well, I'm here, aren't I?"

Thiago sighed softly. He didn't want her to shield herself. There were so many layers guarding her heart and he wasn't certain to know how to peel every surface with delicacy. "Can you let your armour down for one second and come here?"

He felt her go still even though he wasn't touching her. "Where?"

"Come here, Kam," he demanded, voice suddenly husky.

Begrudgingly, she scooted closer, and he didn't allow her to think. Didn't give her time to understand what he was about to do.

Then, he moved and tucked her into his chest, arms tightly secured around her frame.

She didn't move at first, as though she was scared to return the embrace. As though she couldn't believe he was hugging her. But after a moment, an eternity, her arms came to loop around his waist, and she eliminated the sliver of distance between them with a soft sigh.

"Thank you," he whispered against the crown of her head.

"For what?"

For helping me heal something you didn't break. For allowing me to see there's still something golden in a world painted in grey.

"For everything," he breathed out. "Don't shut me out, okay?"

"I won't," she promised, and he believed her.

CHAPTER TWENTY-NINE

📍 *MONZA, ITALY*

A TREMULOUS EXHALE escaped his mouth when he pushed his dark curls away from his forehead as his pulse pounded against his temple.

He inhaled. Exhaled. Repeated.

Trying to set his flaming nerves at ease, or at least trying to diminish the wildfire of anxiety into cracking embers, he continued to practise the breathing routine he would usually perform with Callahan before the race.

He had just gotten back to his private room after the driver's parade during which he had sat on the passenger's seat of an old Ferrari F40, absentmindedly waving at the crowd whilst his mind was flooded with unsettling thoughts.

He had changed into his fireproof underwear, had slipped his racing suit on, though he let the upper part hang around his hips.

Thiago pinched the bridge of his nose when he glanced at his watch. The race would be starting in an hour, and he needed to head out of his room in fifteen minutes to warm up with Cal.

He groaned, frustrated with himself for feeling so distressed and out of control over his emotions. He couldn't let his mood affect his race. Couldn't lose—especially not today.

Grabbing his phone, he texted the only person who seemed to be able to make him forget about the real world.

@THIAGOVALENCIA

Where are you?

@KAMARI.MONROE

Drinking champagne upstairs at the Paddock Club.

@THIAGOVALENCIA

Of course you are

Can you meet me in my room now?

Please

@KAMARI.MONROE

Since you asked so nicely

Omw

A pattern of soft knocks followed shortly after, and when he gave verbal permission for Kamari to enter, he felt the stress dissipate slowly from his veins as though she had the power of putting his whole mind at peace with her presence.

"You've asked for me, your Highness?" A small, amused smile graced her lips, which made him grin widely.

"You're doing wonderful things to my ego, Kam."

She rolled her eyes and closed the door behind her. "Enjoy it whilst you can because I'll go back to being mean tomorrow."

He chuckled as he took a seat on the small sofa placed against the wall. "I wasn't expecting anything less coming from you."

Trailing his regard over her physique, his jaw tightened at the sight of her long legs. As per usual, her outfit was elegant and pristine, and Thiago was starting to have a hard time realising other men and women were blatantly eyeing her, because she was not his and certainly would never be.

"Why the SOS message?" she asked, looking away from his scorching gaze to peer at a few Polaroids Alex had hung on the wall.

Thiago tipped his head back on the sofa, settling his stare on the blank ceiling. He breathed out and shook his head, exasperated with his own self for letting the detriment consume him.

"I don't know," he answered. "Just wanted you here."

She came to take a seat beside him, causing their thighs to press together. "Talk to me."

There was a softness, a euphony edging her tone he wasn't used to hearing. Her fragrance enveloped his senses, and he fought the urge to look at her.

"Thiago," she murmured when he didn't say anything. "I know it's a bit hypocritical for me to say this, but you don't have to keep everything bottled inside when you're with me. We can sit here in silence or we can talk about what's bothering you. But just know I'm here, okay?"

His hand found her knee, gently rubbing at it. "Aren't you sweet?"

He saw her lift her shoulders in a sheepish shrug from the corner of his eye. "It can happen sometimes."

Voice thick and slightly unsteady, he said, "I'm just anxious."

"That's okay," she told him kindly. There wasn't an ounce of judgement in her tone, and he appreciated that. "You just need to get back on track and focus."

"Yeah." He nodded, trying to escape all the spiralling thoughts clouding his mind. Leaning forward, he put his elbows atop his thighs and ran his fingers through the hair on his nape, letting his head fall between his shoulders. "Yeah, I've got it."

"Why don't you show this side of yourself to your fans?"

"Which one?"

"This one," she said softly. "The vulnerable driver, the one who's scared of failing, the one who cares about his future. You're nervous, and that's normal."

He shook his head, gaze settled on his white racing booties, absently tracing the contour of the suede shoe. "I think people like me best when I act like I don't care."

"I'm sure they'd love this Thiago who's sitting next to me just as much."

His knee started bouncing, and when she placed her hand on his thigh, every single little tremor racking his body vanished. "Vulnerability makes me weak."

"Is that what you think?" Vexation could be heard through her words. "Vulnerability is your greatest asset as a human being, Thiago. You don't have to offer a full glimpse of your fears, you don't have to put all your trepidation on a platter and serve it as it is to those who don't believe in you. You're a man who's chasing his dreams and who's scared of letting them slip away from his own grasp, and that's fine."

He felt like not being able to breathe for a few moments. His pulse was thrumming against his temple, and a lump had formed inside his throat. He had to blink, multiple times, to make the burning feeling prickling at his waterline to go away.

Kamari pivoted to face his profile, causing her knee to slightly dig into the side of his leg. Still, through the material of his racing suit, he could feel the heat emanating from her small hand that stayed on his thigh.

"Look at me," she asked, so sternly and so firmly that he couldn't do anything else but follow her command.

There was a slight crease between her brows, a gleam of concern shining in her gaze.

"Prove them wrong," she whispered quietly, yet fiercely.

"I will," he promised, words stuck in his throat. "I swear I will."

She brought her hand to her lap, and he desperately wished

he had the courage to grab it back, thread their fingers together and never let go. "That pain you're carrying—please don't keep it inside of you. Give it to me, Thiago. Give it to someone who knows what to do with it, so you don't have to bear that weight on your shoulders alone."

He swallowed. "Why are you doing this?"

"Because I wish someone would've said this to me every single time I was hurting. I wish someone would be brave enough to hold me whilst they, too, struggle."

"Kam," he murmured, flickering his gaze over her features. She was so beautiful to him—inside and out.

A minuscule smile brushed her lips. "This isn't about me."

As though he had fallen speechless, starstruck under that emerald gaze of hers, he could only manage to nod in response. Then, he wrapped his arms around her shoulders and pulled her into his chest.

She was immobile for a few heartbeats too long.

"Hug me back," he asked. "I need it."

"Don't get used to it," she said, yet her arms instantly looped around his middle as she returned the embrace.

He buried his face in the crook of her neck, nuzzling his nose to her soft skin. "But it feels nice."

It was only after a long moment that she confessed, "I suppose it's okay." Still, she didn't so much as loosen her grip.

To Thiago, Kamari was everything. The moon, his anchor, and a divine being that made him feel like floating above the clouds all at once.

They pulled away, and face solemn, she dropped her stare to his chest and the sponsors' logos branding his fireproof shirt— like she couldn't bear that look in his eyes. "I'm going to go and let you concentrate. I don't need to be a distraction."

That remark made irritation flare inside his chest. "You're not a distraction."

Never had been, never will be. He couldn't stand the way she thought of herself.

She rolled her eyes. "I am, Thiago."

His jaw tightened. "Stay until I need to warm up."

"But—"

Before she could react, before she could walk away, he slammed his lips on hers. A gasp of surprise erupted from the back of her throat, and when he cupped her face and kissed her with intense vehemence, she looped her arms around his neck again.

She had told him she had been consuming champagne before coming into the room, but her lips didn't taste like sparkling wine. He could only taste cherry—the flavour of her gloss—and that made him crave her more. He wanted to kiss her until his lips became numb, until the world was nothing but a blur, until he'd gasp for air.

"What are you doing?" she mumbled, nearly incoherently.

He chuckled, thumbs brushing her cheekbones. "Kissing you."

"Why?"

Because he could never think straight whenever she was near him.

Because he would always lose sense of time when he stared into forest-green eyes.

Because she was like a drug—the kind he couldn't stay away from, the intoxicating kind that would wreck him.

But he was addicted, and he wasn't certain he wanted to find a cure. He yearned and craved and longed for her touch—slowly resigning himself to the noxious power of ruination.

His lips moved to her jaw, peppering open-mouthed kisses. "Cause you look very kissable right now."

And fuckable.

"We agreed on not kissing in private."

He grunted softly. "No, Kam. You set the rules and I only followed."

She pushed him away, gently, chest heaving and eyes blazing with a gleam of desire he knew his own moons reflected. "This isn't a good idea," she said quietly, but she was looking at his mouth.

He leaned forward, staring at her already blood-rushed lips. "The worst possible idea ever. Did you actually have much to drink?"

Kamari shook her head, a slight frown on her brows. "No. Not even a sip yet."

His chest rose and fell, and he knew he needed to concentrate on his upcoming race. But the invisible string tying him to her was unwavering, unyielding, and obliging him to be drawn towards her in the most detrimental way. "Good."

He slanted his mouth on hers again, more demanding and punishing as he moved a hand to the back of her head, letting his fingers tangle with her silken locks. She parted her lips, allowing his tongue to brush with hers and start a salacious dance with it.

The kiss was messy, rushed, reckless. Nothing else mattered except this exact moment as he realised she had been able to lift the weight off his shoulders in such a short amount of time.

Kamari was breathing as heavily as he was whilst she tried to gain dominance over the kiss, and he smirked. Moving a hand down her neck, then her shoulder, then her ribs, he brushed her clothed side with his thumb before fully circling her waist with his arm.

"Thiago," she mumbled. "We—"

"We've got a few minutes."

Sounds of laughter echoed from the corridor followed by the sound of a door slamming, indicating Rowan had entered his room next door.

Thiago pulled Kamari on his lap and she straddled it without so much as breaking their heady kiss. When she ran her fingers through the hair at his nape, the sensation of her nails grazing at his scalp caused a throaty moan to escape.

His palms ran on the outsides of her thighs until they reached her backside and slipped lower. He kneaded at her flesh, eliciting a soft, pleasurable sigh past her lips.

Kamari's nails scraped the sides of his neck, slowly trailing down his chest, her light-feather yet powerful touch creating a trail of goosebumps in its wake.

Slowly, she started rolling her hips, and he could feel his erection grow more and more to the point of aching and throbbing with desire. Their chests were pressed together, the pounding of their heartbeats aligned like two metronomes in sync. Through the fabric of his fireproof shirt and the thin silk top she was wearing, he could feel her nipples—hard and taut with need. He wanted to see her naked, wanted to lie her down and fuck her senselessly. He wanted her—all of her.

He needed to get it out of his system or else he would combust.

She lifted herself onto her knees, fingers tugging at his hair to pull him away. He opened his eyes, and his breath caught inside his throat at the sight of her expanded pupils and the glint of desire swirling along their outlines.

Unexpectedly, she placed her hand on his hardened length, causing a strangled moan to echo inside the small room. As she applied the barest amount of pressure by dragging the heel of her palm against his cock, he bucked his hips forward, head tipped back and lips slightly parting.

There wasn't a note of hesitancy in her demeanour. There wasn't a flicker of uncertainty in her gaze. Still, he watched as her lips parted, like she couldn't believe she was doing this.

His breath caught somewhere in his lungs when he slipped his stare to her small hand covering him. "Feel how hard I am for you, Kam?"

She nodded in response.

"Do you want this?" she asked in a murmur.

"Yes," he responded, huskily, gaze searching her face, cataloguing her beauty. "I want you."

"We don't have much time."

She started rubbing his trapped erection, causing his breaths to stagger.

Her sinful lips trailed from his jawline to the side of his neck, grazing at the spot where his pulse was thrumming erratically. He felt her smirk against his skin, like she was aware of the power she had over him.

Dropping to her knees in between his spread-out legs, she held his gaze whilst a mischievous smirk graced her full lips.

She unzipped the rest of his racing suit, all confidence and unwavering boldness, a soft chuckle reverberating off the walls when she noticed the other layer of fireproof underwear beneath it.

Thiago smiled at the sight of a tiny dimple making its appearance next to her lips, softly caressing the indentation with the pad of his thumb.

Green eyes found his heady gaze. She palmed his hard erection through the last layer of clothes standing as a barrier between them, her perusal studying the way his brows knitted together when her thumb grazed the head of his shaft.

"Can you be a good boy and stay quiet, pretty boy?" she asked in a sultry whisper as her fingers moved to the hem of the underwear. "The walls are thin. We don't want Rowan hearing you, do we?"

He nearly gasped at the drastic change in her demeanour. He'd always known she was confident. Powerful. Enchanting.

But this woman right here was going to make him fall to pieces.

Thiago swallowed, thickly, and nodded as though he had fallen speechless at the sight of this enchantress on her knees for him.

"Words, Thiago," she demanded.

He smirked but shivered when her nails grazed the line of his v-muscle. "Yes, Kam. I'll be quiet for you."

"Good boy."

She tugged the underwear down, and her eyes slightly widened at the sheer size of him as she caressed his thighs.

Thiago leaned over, cupping her chin to oblige her to look

up into his eyes. He pecked her lips once. Twice. Three times until the kiss grew hot and messy. He whimpered into her mouth when she wrapped her hand around the base of his erection, gently pumping her fist up and down.

"You're a good girl," he murmured huskily. "You can take it."

He leaned back against the sofa, and he swore he could unravel right here, right now, at the sight of her fingers barely able to reach around his thick shaft. He gathered her long hair into a makeshift ponytail, gulping.

She then brought her mouth to the tip, licking the bead of pre-cum that had escaped whilst holding his gaze. Her nails grazed the sensitive underside of his hardened length, and she started stroking him. Slowly. Torturously.

"How do you like it?" she asked, her dulcet voice almost a purr. "Gentle?"

Her thumb brushed over the head, and Thiago dropped his head back, focusing on not letting a sound escape.

"Please," he breathed, bucking his pelvis upwards.

"Please, what?"

His jaw tightened. "Please, Kam." He looked back down at her, only to see her lips tipped into a malevolent smirk. "Don't tease me."

"Handsome when you beg." She wrapped her hand tighter, applying the perfect amount of pressure to make his legs tremble with need. "Hard?"

"F-Fuck," he breathed. "Just like that."

When her tongue slid across the reddened tip, the sensation made him whimper quietly.

She pinned him with a cold glare, and he swallowed in acquiescence.

Kamari wrapped her lips around the head, gathering every drop of moisture leaking out on her tongue, using her hand to pump at the base.

When she started sinking down lower, using the help of her

hand to pleasure him where she couldn't reach, Thiago whimpered again. Kamari huffed a laugh and licked a flat stripe from base to head.

He realised he was at her utter and complete mercy and brought a fist up to his mouth. Biting onto his knuckles, he tried to suppress the sounds threatening to escape his mouth. His grip around her hair tightened as he pulled at her locks, guiding her head up and down.

She started using both hands to pump his aching cock, her tongue working wonders by licking at the tip whilst her lips were fully sucking the head.

She took him deep, softly moaning when the tip hit the back of her throat. The vibrations sent jolts of electricity rushing throughout his bones, causing his hips to buck upwards.

She stroked him hard and fast, took him deep and sensually.

"Ahhh, f-fuck, Kam. I want to be inside you," he admitted as white stars started to blur his vision.

"Quiet."

A soft groan was audible. "I hate you."

Kamari huffed a laugh again, and the vibrations caused his head to tip back. Heavy breaths escaped his mouth whilst his brows were pinched in pleasure.

The tip of her tongue swirled around the slit, and the moment she took him deep again, he made the mistake of meeting her wide, green eyes, intensely watching him.

Unravelling, he couldn't help but whimper when her nails brushed the underside of his shaft. He came undone, hard, whilst stars whitened his vision.

He bucked his hips forward, and whilst maintaining her gaze, she swallowed every drop of his release before letting go of his semi-hard cock, a smirk of triumph on her lips. Wiping the corner of her mouth with her thumb, she caressed his thigh whilst he tried to recuperate his breath, ever so slowly coming down from his high.

"You're going to be the death of me, Kamari," he said, breathless.

"Good."

She stood up, fixed her hair, her outfit, and turned on her heel.

"Win that damned Grand Prix, Thiago."

SIMON ROMANO TAPPED the back of Thiago's helmet before throwing a thumbs up and disappearing through the crowd of mechanics flooding the starting grid.

"Don't fail me," he had asked as the driver was getting settled inside his car.

"I won't," Thiago had promised, though he had been able to glimpse the uncertainty glinting in his team principal's eyes.

Thiago's team of mechanics was surrounding his car as they waited for the Grand Prix to start. All twenty cars were lined up in their respective spots on the starting grid, Thiago being at the front row next to Miles Huxley who was starting P2.

Huxley was currently first in the drivers' standings with his team, Imperium Racing, but Thiago had managed to move up into fourth position with the results of the last two races, even with his previous DNF.

Thiago glanced at one of his mechanics who was intently checking the time on his wristwatch, then moved his gaze to Tim, who was kneeling before his left front wheel, holding the heating blanket atop the tyre to keep it warm.

Ten seconds before the start of the race, the mechanics took the blankets off the tyres, and scurried to the side of the track. A once packed circuit was now empty except for the twenty drivers who were ready to race the 2022 Italian Grand Prix.

Thiago dragged the visor of his helmet down, gloved hands gripping his steering wheel as his engine vibrated with anticipation. The signal was then given, and he pushed onto the throttle to lead the formation lap. This lap before the actual Grand Prix was meant to warm up the tyres, the brakes, the engine, and the oils—to make sure the car would perform well. His engineers would be checking on all statistics from the garage.

He warmed his tyres up by accelerating, braking, doing zigzags whilst he let the smell of burnt rubber envelop his senses.

Once the lap was done, he came back to wait at the front position on the starting grid, observing his rivals line up one by one behind him in his rear-view mirror.

Like before every race, his heart pounded furiously, on the brink of exploding. He kept his breaths even, steady, but his hands were already clammed with perspiration.

The five lights aligned horizontally above his head weren't lit up yet.

Time came to a halt.

Everything was quiet but for the sound of his engine needing to release its energy.

The first red light lit up.

Followed by the second one. And the third. The fourth. And the fifth.

All red lights froze—drivers never knew for how long they'd stop. It usually lasted between three and nine seconds. And for five excruciating heartbeats, time stood still, and the moment the red lights disappeared, Thiago pushed at full throttle.

Roars of excitement flooded the circuit, but Thiago couldn't hear anything apart from the loud noise of his car's power source.

Huxley had made a good start, too, now racing right next to Thiago as they drove down the long straight. They passed the first chicane wheel to wheel, causing the front wings of their cars to nearly collide.

Thiago was on the outside of the short turn, but he'd been able to pass before Miles on the inside afterwards, causing him to gain more space and put a distance with his rival. His car was rapid at reaccelerating, and Thiago flew away from Huxley by hitting the gas pedal, racing through the long straight line ahead of him.

The world was a mere blur, but his vision was solely focused on one thing: to claim the biggest trophy as his.

"You've got this," Luke said through the radio.

"Let me do my thing and don't talk to me unless it's something important."

"Copy."

"YELLOW FLAG IN SECTOR ONE," Luke said after the sixteenth lap. Thiago was still leading the race. "Safety car is out. Decrease your pace by 70 percent."

Thiago hit the brake and clicked on a few buttons on his steering wheel to set his pace at 80 kilometres per hour. He could feel the heat of the circuit emanating through his gear, blending with the sun's warmth, causing a bead of sweat to cascade down the bridge of his nose.

He frowned. "What happened?"

"Denver and Beaumont collided into each other in the first chicane."

"What a bunch of cunts," Thiago mustered. The safety car was now leading the queue of F1 cars that had slowed down on the track. "These rookies need to learn to stop causing those 'racing incidents' during every fucking race."

"Denver's not a rookie," Luke countered.

"Whatever."

"Box, box. We're going to put hard compounds on."

There were five types of tyre compounds: soft, medium, hard, inter, and wet. Thiago's tyres were currently medium ones, which meant they degraded faster than hard ones, but not as easily as softs.

He drove through the pit lane towards his garage, giving up

his position to Huxley. The pit stop's duration was set at two seconds and two-tenths.

Thiago smiled beneath his helmet at his team's efficiency but made haste to exit the pit lane whilst staying under the speed limit.

Usually, other cars would pass by him whilst he boxed. So, when he drove back onto the track, he fell into fifth place, right in front of Rowan who hadn't pitted yet, whilst other cars took the opportunity of going into the pit lane to change their tyres as well.

He needed to be at the front again, and he'd have to wait for the safety car to end to do so.

"WHAT'S THE GAP between me and Huxley?"

"He's two point three seconds behind you."

Thiago's car had a great pace on this circuit, and he couldn't be more delighted with his team's strategies. He had been able to overtake, easily, all four cars in front of him after the green flag was brandished.

He finally felt powerful. Like the heavens were on his side.

He knew a particular star had been looking down at him all weekend long.

"How many laps are there left?" Thiago asked.

"Nineteen," Luke said.

"Copy."

HE COULD SEE Huxley closing the distance between them, but Thiago always managed to get away from his rival, smoothly so, the dirty air following his car in an invisible cloud.

He drove through the last corner, frowning when Huxley's front wing nearly grazed his wheel.

"What the fuck is that bloke doing?" Thiago muttered, accelerating.

Taking as swiftly but rapidly the first chicane, he rushed through the straight line, driving on the right side of the track, wheels barely digging into the gravel but enough to spray some dirt behind him, causing some slight trouble with Huxley.

"You're racing dirty, Tito," Luke said. "Be careful."

He rolled his eyes. "Huxley can cry me a river."

"Last lap, I repeat, last lap."

The adrenaline rushing through his veins was burning. Thiago couldn't breathe. Couldn't think straight. His heartbeat was throbbing and pounding and ferocious.

Thiago was about to win the 2022 Italian Grand Prix, and he had to focus on making it to the finish line instead of trying to decipher the crowd's loud bellow through the noise of his engine's roar.

The chequered flag was so distant yet so close all at once, and seconds felt like an excruciating eternity.

He drove through the very last corner of the circuit, and in the distance, he could see all of Primavera's mechanics standing on the protective fences, clapping as they screamed for Thiago and Rowan to pass the finish line.

Thiago pumped his fist in the air as he flew past the chequered flag, claiming his first place.

The feeling of winning almost felt foreign, but it was exhilarating and electrifying.

He chuckled when the sound of cheers echoed through his earbuds. "The man that you are, Valencia! Mega race. Good job, mate."

He could feel a lump grow inside his throat as his pace started to decrease. He waved a hand in the air, his voice thick with emotion when he said, "Mega fucking race."

This one is for you, Dad. It's been a year since my last win. And it's for you.

He didn't want to break down whilst driving the car, but tears pricked at his eyes and he sniffed. It felt surreal to know he had won a race. Felt like a dream to realise his efforts hadn't gone to waste.

The cool down lap was a rollercoaster of emotions. Still euphoric from the past hour and a half, Thiago hadn't been able to control the drumming beat of his heart, the tremor in his hands, and the smile overtaking his features.

He parked his car where the podium lay overhead, stopping before the large panel with a large "1" drawn on it which was meant for the Grand Prix's winner. The moment he stopped his engine, he dropped his head forward and exhaled, tremulously. The pounding of his pulse was nearly as deafening as the screams of joy erupting from the whole circuit flooded with fans.

A tap on his back obliged him to look up, and he shook Huxley's hand when the latter winked.

Thiago got out of his car, planted both feet on the halo and raised his fists skywards. From afar, his team had lined up before the barriers, and all men and women were cheering and clapping in their hands.

He hopped off the red car, and one moment later, Rowan came to engulf his teammate in a bone-crushing embrace.

"Look at us," Rowan grinned. His face was flushed, rivulets of sweat shining on his temples as he had taken his helmet and balaclava off. "Sharing a podium together again."

Thiago chuckled. "Good job, man."

"You too." Rowan pushed Thiago's shoulder, a smirk evident on his lips. "Bet your sweet alone time with Kameron helped."

"It's Kamari," he retorted with a grunt whilst unbuckling his helmet. "And I don't know what you're talking about."

Rowan winked before making a beeline towards his own

team of mechanics, and Thiago followed shortly after, forgetting about taking his helmet off.

Thiago jumped into Cal's arms, then embraced Simon Romano. Witnessing that gleam of relief, of pride, in his team principal's eyes was as thrilling as winning for himself.

Alex and a few other car mechanics tapped on his back and bum, all wide grins etched on their faces.

Thiago moved on to Kamari who stood next to Indy. Kamari was silent, but the smile on her face made him forget about all his surroundings. He grabbed her face, and she chuckled before pressing a small kiss on his helmet. He threw a wink her way, and he thought he saw a faint coat of crimson paint the tops of her cheekbones.

HANDS BEHIND HIS BACK, head tipped backwards, eyes closed as the sun's rays shone upon his delighted face, Thiago exhaled a long sigh as he listened to the British national anthem ring through the expanse of trees and endless roads.

When he slipped his gaze to the crowd standing below the podium, he swore he could feel his heart stop beating for a moment. A sea of red flooded the area, and that was when he realised the majority of fans that had come to the race were here to support him, Rowan, and Primavera Racing.

Trophies were given to Rowan, Miles, then Thiago, and soon enough champagne was sprayed in the air whilst confetti fell from the sky.

FOOTFALLS ECHOING BROUGHT him back to reality.

He had been sitting on the podium, lingering in the moment, needing a few minutes alone to revel in this reality.

He didn't know how long he had been sitting here, but the

crowd below the podium had dispersed. The track was always open for fans after the race, and most people were walking around.

Looking at the silhouette ever so slowly walking towards him, Thiago couldn't help but smile.

"Hey, you." He was surprised by the sound of his voice—a rasp, a crack through all the emotion that had been consuming him.

"Hey, champ," Kamari said softly. "This lady with an F1 badge allowed me to come up here."

"Miss me much?" He grinned, adjusting the black hat that lay on his head backwardly.

"You wish," she countered with a playful roll of her eyes. "I saw you sitting by yourself from down there."

He sighed. "I needed a few minutes alone."

She pointed behind her. "Do you want me to go?"

"No," he breathed. "Stay. Please."

Almost reluctantly, as if she was scared, Kamari stepped towards the podium, her gaze roaming around. She was in awe, starstruck by the scenery before her eyes. Green and red and white confetti swamped the floor, the view of the circuit ahead utterly mesmerising.

She wanted to sit next to him, but the step was covered in sprays of champagne. The look of resentment drawing upon her face, the scrunch of her nose in contemplation, made him chuckle.

"Come here," he said gruffly, wrapping his hand around her wrist to pull her onto his lap.

Kamari sat sideways on his leg, an arm draped around his shoulders, her wide eyes searching his face, calculating his every move as he intensely scrutinised her features.

"You were so great out there," she murmured. "You make driving an F1 car look so bloody easy."

"Wow," he droned, though a grin was etched on his lips. "Are you complimenting me?"

She teased him by shoving his shoulder, gently. "Perhaps you would like me to insult you?"

"Nope," he replied promptly. "Please, keep the flattery coming."

She glowered. "I think that's enough for today. Your ego's been fed way too much already."

He exhaled, wrapping his arms around her waist. He hadn't realised he was still slightly trembling, and it was only when she rubbed at the spot between his shoulder blades to coax him that the tremors vanished.

Thiago dropped his forehead on her shoulder, eyes closing. She was motionless for the longest minute before sliding her hand to his nape, letting her fingers tangle with his damp hair.

"I miss him, Kam," he whispered, a crack in his voice audible.

Despite the euphoric state he had been in the whole afternoon, the ache in his chest was too overpowering to ignore. The more his grip around Kamari tightened, the more his wound opened. He wanted to keep the bruise hidden, but he couldn't anymore. Not when she was there, ready to receive his pain with open hands. Not when she was there, coaxing him through the anguish with delicate caresses.

"I know," she murmured. "I know."

The tear that had been threatening to escape all day long finally set itself free, and cascaded down his cheek to land on her shoulder. "I wish he was there."

She didn't stop caressing his hair. "He's always there with you, Thiago. Always. He's looking down at you, protecting you and making sure you thrive. Making sure you pass the obstacles thrown in your way. He would be proud of you, of the way you carry his legacy on with such strength and bravery."

The free fall of tears was out of his control, and he hated himself for being so vulnerable in a moment that should've been meant for happiness. He kept his face hidden in the crook of

Kamari's neck, and he held her as though he didn't want to let go.

"Let go of your pain, Thiago," she murmured, her voice holding heavy emotions. "I've got you."

"I'm sorry, baby." Thiago felt like he needed to release the burden he'd been bearing inside his chest for so long. Needed to let go of that affliction. "I don't want you seeing me like this."

"Like what?" She pressed her cheek to his head, sighing softly. "Like a human being? That's how I know you, Thiago. The real you. I think I know who you are, even when you think everything's made to be broken."

Kamari Monroe was the closest to heaven he'd ever be, and he didn't deserve to be in this angel's arms. But she held him so tightly, so tenderly, that he realised that she didn't want to let him go either.

He exhaled shakily. "Thank you for seeing me."

"I see you, Thiago. Your string of light is still bright to me, and I know it's shining in the eyes of millions of other people, too. What you did today is proof that you cannot give up. It's proof that failure is the key to fortitude, and that you'll always manage to rise up after crashing down."

He brushed a kiss to her wet skin—a silent promise, a silent thank you.

He wanted to confess to her what weighed on his heart, wanted to tell her he was willing to catch her, lest she peeled all the layers shielding her heart. But he didn't want to talk about this now. Not when she was listening to him. Not when she was holding him, and acting like the anchor he had yearned for his whole life.

"I've got you, Thiago."

CHAPTER THIRTY

📍 *LONDON, ENGLAND*

W ATCHING AN EARLY 2000s romantic comedy was secretly Kamari's favourite thing to do late at night.

Absentmindedly staring at the television's screen, she wasn't fully concentrating on Anne Hathaway's character trying to drive through the pouring rain in the steep roads of San Francisco. She knew every scene and every line of *the Princess Diaries* by heart, but she felt like watching one of her favourite movies would perhaps lift the uncanny sensation off her chest.

Her phone vibrated on the coffee table. She didn't want to check her notifications because they had been blowing up ever since she had come back from Italy. In the back of her mind, she wasn't regretting this whole deal with Thiago, but sometimes all she wanted was to go back to being a nobody no one had heard of.

She had made sure to avoid all socials after learning pictures of her and Thiago sharing a tender moment on the podium were invading the internet.

Kamari hadn't been able to forget about that particular moment, no matter what she did to distract herself. Brewing coffee? She'd still hear the despair and sadness in his voice. Paying bills? She could see the melancholy in his eyes. She could still feel his lips on her skin, his tears staining her shoulder. She could still feel the ache in her chest when she had heard his cries, and she could still feel how it felt to witness that raw, sincere vulnerability.

Her heart skipped a beat when she checked her device, her breath catching and disappearing.

@THIAGOVALENCIA

Sent a photo.

She frowned and opened the message thread. She clicked on the photo he had sent, the confusion on her face instantly replaced by a minuscule smile.

It was a picture of the white, glowing, crescent moon waning in the dark blue sky, taken from the boat he had rented with his friends.

Thinking of you, he had captioned.

Kamari wasn't sure what to respond. She hadn't really heard from him since she left Monza four days ago.

@THIAGOVALENCIA

Wishing I could be staring at it with you, moonbeam

The others are drunk but I'm just thinking of you

Looking out the window, she noticed the moon peeking behind clouds. She sighed, finally understanding the cause of the weight gripping at her chest.

She hated it. Hated how every wall guarding her heart kept crumbling down to dust whenever she thought of Thiago.

Hated how she couldn't stay away from him. Hated how, amidst secrets and lies, she found solace in silver eyes.

Dialling his number, she took a seat on her windowsill, rubbing her hand on the side of her joggers.

Thiago answered on the first ring. "Hey, moonbeam." A smile was decipherable through his voice.

"Hey, pretty boy. Miss me much?"

A beat passed, distant sounds of chatter and laughter resonating on his side of the line. In a breath, he admitted, "You've got no idea."

CHAPTER THIRTY-ONE

📍 *MONTE CARLO, MONACO*

EXHALING HEAVILY, RAGGED breaths echoing through the room, his chest rose and fell in rapid patterns. Thiago pushed his damp hair away from his face, feeling a bead of sweat falling down the valley of his pectorals.

He inhaled deeply again before pressing the green button, accepting a call he hadn't been expecting since it had been a few days since he last heard from her.

"Hi," he answered, breathless.

There was a beat of silence. "Hey," Kamari said then. "I-I'm sorry. You're busy."

A line creased between his eyebrows. The call muffled the smokiness in her timbre, the malevolence her tone usually held. "Busy? Doing what?"

"I don't know," she rushed. "Doing... things."

Thiago chuckled, using the towel hanging around the back of his neck to wipe the rivulets of perspiration clamming his face. He stepped out onto his balcony, leaned against the doorway, and slipped his stare to the peaceful ocean. "Tell me what I'm doing, Kam. I'm curious."

"You're with someone." Not a question. A statement. "That's, uh, that's fine. You do you. I'll hang up and call later when you're free—"

Throwing his head back, he laughed. "You think I'm busy fucking someone?"

She didn't answer, and her silence was enough as a response.

"Gee, Kam. Why would you think that? Haven't fucked anyone except my right hand in months."

"Thanks for the details, idiot."

He smirked. "I can give you more if you'd like."

"Please, don't."

He chuckled, rubbing the back of his hair with his towel. "Hang on for a sec."

He stared at the screen of his phone and demanded Kamari to accept his request for a video call. He rolled his eyes when she took a few seconds to answer, and he assumed she was either fixing her hair or cleaning the space behind her.

When her face finally appeared on the screen, he couldn't retain his smile from growing. He leaned his head on the doorframe, gaze softening and cheeks heating up as he stared at the woman pushing her big glasses up the bridge of her nose.

"Does it look like I'm in the middle of having sex, Kam?"

She scrunched her nose, but the flush on her tan cheekbones was still evident. "I never said you were busy doing *that.*"

"You implied it very fucking loudly, moonbeam." He grinned, causing her stare to drop to his dimples. "I'm just working out. Gotta stay in shape even when we're on break."

"Oh."

"Where are you?" he asked then.

"My flat." She gestured to her tidy living room behind. To his guess, she had taken a seat on one of the many stools rounding her kitchen island and had deposited her phone against the terrarium decorating the counter. "I just came back from shopping."

His brows rose. "Yeah? What did you get?"

She leaned her chin in the palm of her hand, shrugging coyly. "Just went to treat myself with a few things."

"What's the occasion? Are we celebrating something?"

Thiago moved to sit on the small garden lounge set of furniture he had put on his balcony, placing his feet atop the small table and running his fingers through his hair. Smirking, he observed Kamari's eyes trail from his flexed bicep to the exposed part of his bare chest.

"Actually"—she paused and frowned, darting her gaze away—"that's why I was calling, but now that I think of it, it's a bit silly of me. I shouldn't have bothered you."

"What?" He clenched his jaw. "Where's that coming from? I'll always make time for you."

"How sweet of you," she drawled. "No need to be nice to me behind closed doors, you know that."

Tipping his head back, he groaned in annoyance. "I'm not pretending, Kam. Can you drop the mean girl act for a second? *You* called me, and I'm very fucking happy to hear from you. In fact, I was about to text you. Now tell me what you've been up to for the past few days."

"Okay." She inhaled, and put her glasses atop her head, then wove her fingers together. "Remember the second café I want to open in Soho?"

"The café slash bar slash bookstore?"

She nodded eagerly, and the sight of her excitement made warmth blossom inside his chest, akin to blooming flowers in the spring. "I signed the lease this morning."

His eyes widened as he shifted to move on the edge of his seat. "Wait. It's yours?"

Her smile was as beautiful and unique and bright as a shooting star. "I've signed for a loan with the bank, and I'm still renting the place, but yes, it's mine."

The bliss seeping through his veins was undeniably scorching. He couldn't limit the grandeur of his smile, and it kept growing until his cheeks ached. "Holy shit, Kam! This is amazing."

"I know." She sighed softly, all beaming and peaceful, folding her arms across the counter's edge whilst burying her hands in the long sleeves of her jumper. "It still feels unreal. I got the keys earlier today, so tomorrow I'm on my way to finding a contractor and architect, and all."

"I'm so proud of you," he murmured, sincerely. "You're doing great things, Kam. All your hard work has paid off."

She lowered her stare, her smile falling. He realised it was something she wasn't told very often, and it created an immense pain to skitter around his chest.

I wish I could hug you. Wish I could tell you how amazing you are.

Leaning back in the seat, he rubbed the back of his neck. "Kam?"

Looking up, she allowed him to peer into those green eyes he adored so much, but this time emerald didn't hold that spark he'd been used to seeing. There was a gloom that had made its appearance over her hypnotising irises. Still, she replied with an audible, "Thanks."

"Do me a favour and go out to celebrate with your friends tonight, okay?"

He saw her shoulders tense. "But there's still so much I—"

"Kamari."

She sighed. "Thiago."

"I'm serious. Go out and have fun."

She rolled her eyes. "Fine."

"Good girl," he rasped. "You know you shouldn't fight me."

Kamari didn't answer, only shaking her head. Lost in her thoughts, she started gnawing on her lower lip, causing a low growl to erupt from the back of his throat. He ran a hand over his face, remembering he needed to shower and get ready.

"So," he started, clearing his throat to bring her attention back to him. "The charity gala is this Saturday."

She nodded. "I haven't forgotten. I'll be flying to Monaco on Saturday morning."

"Do you have a dress yet?"

Kamari shook her head. "I'll go sometime this week with Indy. Any colour I should wear?"

He smiled softly. "Green would bring out the colour of your eyes. But anything would look amazing on you. Don't worry about it, just buy the dress that—actually, send me your bank account number and I'll transfer you some money."

She widened her eyes. "What? No. Why?"

"Because I want to pay—"

"No, no, no, you don't have to buy me anything."

"Let me do this for you, Kam. I've begged you to attend this event and the least I can do is treat you with a gown."

"I can't accept this," she argued with a shake of her head. "I won't accept this."

Thiago frowned. This woman was stubborn, headstrong, and goddamned gorgeous. "Spend a few days with me in Monaco then. I don't plan on travelling to London until next week, so spend an extra day with me."

She bit the inside of her cheek, blinking, wide green eyes swamped with uncertainty. "Do I have a choice?"

"Yes," he replied wryly. "Either you let me pay for your dress, or you can spend an extra day with your favourite person in the world."

The roll of her eyes made him chuckle. "I refuse to let you spend money on me, so I guess I'll spend Sunday with you. But I have to—"

"Get back to work on Monday morning," he finished the phrase for her. "I know. I've got you, don't worry."

Just as she was about to say something, a deep crease drew itself between her brows when she glanced at the notification that had disturbed her.

Annoyance was etched upon her expression, and it made confusion cloud Thiago's mind.

"Who's annoying you?" he asked. "I'm the only one who can annoy the shit out of you."

She scoffed, unable to hide her small smile. "It's just Kieran. I need to go. I'm going to call Indy and Diana and see if they're up for a night out."

"Send me a pic of your outfit."

"You wish."

He grinned. "I do."

She grabbed her phone. "Not happening."

"Come on! Just a sneak peek?"

"Bye, Valencia."

"THERE'S SOMETHING DIFFERENT ABOUT YOU," Amelia noted as she placed her wine glass atop the table.

Thiago arched an eyebrow and peered at his mother, thankful she had decided to jump onto this topic when he had already drunk a few sips of Bordeaux Margaux. He closed the menu and set it on the table, observing the setting sun's glow on the side of her face.

Amelia was visiting town and grabbed the opportunity to take her only son to dinner.

Her blonde locks were tied into a neat chignon at the nape of her neck, her timeless fringe falling in soft waves over her forehead.

Le Grill's terrace was full of patrons, chatter overpowering the sound of waves lapping against one another.

Thiago sat back in his chair, dipping his chin in a grateful nod when the waiter came to deposit a ridiculously small bowl of caviar in the centre of the table.

"Merci," Amelia said with a smile that resembled his own.

"Êtes-vous prêts à commander l'entrée?" the waiter asked, hands clasped behind his back.

"Pas encore," Thiago responded. "Merci de nous accorder un petit instant."

"Pas de problème, monsieur." He then turned to Amelia, dipping his chin politely. "Madame."

"Good or bad different?" Thiago then inquired, observing how carefully she unfolded the linen napkin to spread it over her lap.

Amelia smiled softly. "Good. Definitely good."

Amelia was patient and didn't press on the subject, though he was aware she knew the reason for his delight wasn't the podium he had secured last weekend or the positive feedback he'd been getting from his team. His happiness wasn't caused by racing, for once in his life, and it took longer than he cared to admit to realise it.

He reached for his wine glass, bringing the rim to his lips and letting the floral notes of the beverage whiff through his nostrils.

He took a sip, darting his gaze to the horizon where the sun collided with the ocean. A smile drew itself upon his lips when the moon appeared overhead—like it was a sign from the very heavens above.

"I met a girl," he confessed softly, mind travelling to green eyes, a façade made of ice but a woman carrying the purest heart of gold he had ever glimpsed at.

"You meet girls all the time, Tito." There was a knowing smile etched on her rose lips.

His heart was now thundering violently, like rising tidal waves—wild, unstoppable, devastating. The sound of his pulse was loud, deafening, and he barely heard himself say, "This one is...special. Beautiful. She's different."

His mother's gaze was on him—studying, admiring this version of him she had thought had extinguished after her husband's death. "Is she the girl who you've been seen with lately in the paddock?"

Thiago nodded. He couldn't deny it. Had never been able to deny this girl had set him ablaze the moment they'd met. "Yes."

"What's her name?"

"Kamari."

Amelia was silent for a few beats as she stared at her son, a tender gleam in her eyes. "Beautiful name. Pretty girl, too, from what I've seen."

Thiago swallowed tightly, emotions consuming him. "She's the most beautiful woman I've ever seen, Mum. She's—" He had to pause, had to gather his thoughts because he was losing sense of himself. "She's got this light in her soul that she doesn't see. She's got those eyes that look like a forest of vibrant greens, a damned smile that makes a dimple pop next to her lips, a laugh so quiet that you'd think she's scared of being happy. She's independent and strong and witty and cunning and nothing like I've ever seen before."

"There's a but, isn't there?"

He lifted his shoulders in a shrug. "But it's all moving very fast, and I don't think she wants this with me. We only met a few weeks ago, and she's got me feeling some type of way. I can't fathom how rapidly it has become this all-consuming kind of—"

He pressed his lips into a thin line, stopping himself.

"Love?" Amelia suggested, a smile on her lips.

"Call it what you want." He swirled the burgundy beverage in the bottom of the glass. "She's afraid, scarred, wounded by her past. I don't think she wants to trust me."

Amelia extended her hand over the table, silently requesting him to fit his palm in hers. She wrapped her fingers around his own, applying a gentle squeeze. "I don't know her, but I think she'll just want you to be patient. You can draw stars around her scars, you can be there for her; be her friend."

"That's also the thing, Mum." His forehead creased slightly when he noticed the engagement ring his father had given her all these years ago still adorning her finger. "Do you think it's possible to find a unique friendship in someone you barely know? It feels so easy. It's like she really knows me."

Amelia smiled. "Seems to me you've found a treasure in this girl, Tito."

He nodded. "She's a real treasure. She's healed me."

He went on about the time she flew to Monza to help him go through the difficult weekend. Talked about her projects of opening a second café. Told his mother how thrilling it was to teach her about F1.

"Sounds like she cares a bit about you, after all."

"I guess so. I just don't know how to peel the layers guarding her heart. I want to be good for her, Mum, but also for myself. I want to focus on the championship, on renewing my contract, but I don't want to lose her either."

"Why don't you sit down and talk to her about your feelings?"

"Because she'll reject me." He clenched his jaw. "It was only supposed to be a game. I wasn't supposed to fall that far."

Amelia opened her mouth then closed it back as though she had decided not to say what had been sitting on the tip of her tongue. Instead, she rubbed the back of Thiago's hand with her thumb and said, "She's good for you, darling. Don't let her go."

"I won't."

CHAPTER THIRTY-TWO

⚲ *LONDON, ENGLAND*

"WHERE ARE YOU going?" asked Kieran when Kamari stumbled inside the café, a tote bag hanging on her shoulder whilst pulling a small suitcase behind her.

"Monaco," she replied, leaning over the countertop to grab a paper bag to slip a blueberry scone inside it.

She smiled kindly to a customer when the latter retrieved his to-go cup and grinned at the coffee shop owner before stepping outside under the clouds. Kamari huffed at the sight of the dark, brooding sky. If it rained, her flight would be delayed and she'd waste her time waiting whilst she could be doing so much. Peeking inside her bag, she searched for her laptop's charger, emitting a soft sigh of relief when she found what she was looking for.

"Coffee?" her brother asked, his expression hardening at the sight of her fatigued eyes.

She took a seat on a stool after checking the time on her small wristwatch. Her Uber was fifteen minutes away. "Please."

He turned towards the espresso machine. "Why are you travelling down there?"

"There's this charity gala the FIA is organising. Maybe you've heard about it."

Kieran nodded. "Oh, yeah, *that*. It's such a posh event." He slid the foam cup across the wood, the dark liquid creating a cloud of steam trailing lazily in the air. "Since when are you interested in motorsports anyway?"

Ah, there he was with his incessant and intrusive questions. "Since I'm dating an F1 driver? What kind of question is that?"

He shrugged lazily. "I think I like your boyfriend."

Kamari scoffed. It took a lot of willpower not to roll her eyes at his comment. "Of course, you do. You'd get down on your knees for him."

Kieran leaned the small of his back against the countertop behind him. He went to tuck his hands in the front pockets of his jeans, but the small apron attached to his waist created a barrier, so he folded his arms across his chest. "I like him for you. He managed to get you out of your shell. You travel, you go out, you're just living again."

She frowned, trying her hardest to ignore the skip in her once steady heartbeat. "Thanks?"

She took a sip of her coffee, arching a brow when Kieran said, quietly, "But..."

She rolled her eyes. "But what? No need to give me a lesson about boys. I'm not a little girl anymore."

He scratched the side of his neck, uneasiness evident in his demeanour. "James and I agree on the fact he's using you. You've never been interested in motorsports before. Never even looked at a man who brought too much attention to him."

She nearly swallowed her hot drink down the wrong tube. "James?" she echoed, baffled. "So you talk behind my back with my cheating ex about my current relationship instead of sharing your concern with me, your sister? That's a low blow coming from you, Ki."

He lifted his shoulders in a shrug, unbothered by his sister's vexation. "I just want to know why that sudden change in your life. Is it about fame? Money? Do you want to be under the spotlight?"

She stood up, putting the lid atop her cup a tad too aggressively. She wasn't sure why she was so angry all of a sudden, but all she knew was that she needed fresh air. "You are unbelievable. It isn't about fame or dating a rich man, Kieran. It's about what he brings out in me, what he brings *to* me. It's about a connection, about having someone I can count on. I don't fucking care about his money. And for your info, I didn't even know who he was when we met!"

Shit. She needed to stop talking before outing the truth.

"Well—" He sighed, irritatingly, throwing his hands in the air. "You're just trying to piss James off, aren't you?"

"Why would I do that?" Kamari's voice cracked. She pinched the bridge of her nose. Inhaled. Exhaled. "Yes, James hurt me, over and over. Yes, I had a hard time moving on from our five-year relationship. But this isn't about that douchebag. This is about *me,* finally thinking I deserve to be loved the right way. This is about me, searching for what he never gave me and told me I wasn't worthy of receiving. This is about me finally putting him in the past and moving on. He needs to grow up and stop burying his nose in my life, as should you."

Kieran's shoulders fell. His gaze searched her face, eyes filling with sorrow. "Kam..."

Emotions had overtaken Kamari's senses, and she could feel molten rage seep through her veins. "Thiago's good to me, okay? He takes me out, buys me dinner, even calls me beautiful. He asks about my day, which is something you don't even do! He talks to me about the café, he doesn't judge me, and listens to me. He'd fetch the fucking moon for me if I asked for it. So, no,

KANITHA P.

this isn't about scoring a famous athlete or looking for attention."

"I'm sorry," Kieran whispered. "I didn't realise he meant so much to you."

That made her snap back to reality.

Thiago didn't mean anything to her, right?

They were nothing. They just needed each other for PR purposes, and perhaps to relieve the tension that had been building in their respective bodies.

He didn't mean anything, and yet she was ready to jump on the first flight to find him.

Kamari couldn't even think straight. Couldn't even recognise herself.

She had sworn she would *never* let a man inside her heart ever again, but she supposed she had lost sense of herself amidst their games, lies, and secrets.

"I'm leaving," she said firmly, rapidly checking her bag to make sure she hadn't forgotten anything. "Water the plants. Don't make a mess. Make a good turnover."

"You're seriously leaving whilst mad at me?"

"Yes."

"Kam?" Kieran asked when she grabbed her luggage. "Please use the weekend to cool off and relax, and for the love of God, please take it easy."

She didn't turn around, scoffing. "Fuck you, Kieran."

MONTE CARLO, MONACO

"ARE YOU NERVOUS?" Thiago asked, a smug grin gracing his lips.

Kamari's senses were full of him—his charming gaze, his intoxicating scent, his touches he'd been keeping to himself but she desperately longed to feel.

As promised, he had picked her up at Nice Airport, in his matte black Porsche GT3 RS. He had waited in the parking lot, leaning against the hood of the car, phone in one hand whilst the other was buried in the pocket of his trousers.

He made it impossible for Kamari to act like she didn't care about him.

And well, after what had happened in his room before the race in Monza, she knew they were beyond the stage of being acquaintances.

Actually, she wasn't sure what they were. She didn't want them to be *anything*. She needed to keep her freezing walls intact, lest she got heartbroken once more.

But how could she, when he kept glancing at her as though he had never seen beauty quite like hers? How could she, when his fingers twitched atop the gearbox like he wanted to slide his hand to her thigh and touch her?

How could she, when he was all she could think about?

"You wish," she spat, keeping her gaze on the moving horizon. She could recall the unique highways in the South of France with the palm trees on either side of the road.

They were nearly arriving in Monaco, and they had barely spoken. Music had been filling the void, his deep, husky voice resonating on several occasions when he asked simple questions.

She was aware he was slightly nervous to be in her presence; he kept rubbing the back of his neck, kept peering at her not so discretely, kept blushing whenever she met his silver eyes.

"So why aren't you looking at me?"

"Because then you'll look at me and we'll get into a car accident."

Thiago laughed, the melodious sound of his delight making those unwanted butterflies inside her chest wake up.

"Yeah, right."

She drummed her fingers along the rhythm of the song playing in the background, and slightly cleared her throat. "Okay, so don't be mad at me—"

She could hear the confusion in his tone. "Why would I be mad at you?"

"—but I made a reservation in a hotel in Menton. I don't want to invade your privacy nor be a burden, so we can make a pit stop over there to—"

"Woah, hang on, butterfly." She could feel his incredulous gaze scorching her face. "Did you just say pit stop?"

She nodded, her full lips pressed into a thin, firm line as she watched a Ferrari drive past them.

"And why the fuck did you call yourself a burden? And why the fuck did you book a hotel room in Menton?"

"Because—"

They stopped at a red light, and he had pivoted just enough to face her. "You're staying with me. No buts. Think about it, Kam. Even if you're staying in France, it's the closest town to Monaco and fans could still spot you. Don't you think they'll find it weird if you're staying somewhere else but my place?"

She sighed, slightly frustrated. She didn't want to admit he was right. "Thiago."

"Kamari," he droned with equal vexation. "Seriously, why? Are you afraid something might happen? Is that it? Love, you had your lips around my c—"

She glared at him, the lethal gleam in her eyes causing his expression to droop. "Don't finish that sentence or else I'll punch your balls."

"There she is." He grinned. She scowled. "My violent girl."

"Idiot," she mumbled, slipping her gaze to the light still burning red.

"Look at me." He gripped her chin, delicately, obliging her to find silver eyes. "I want you here, Kam. You'll never invade my privacy, let alone be a burden. I've set up the guest room for you because I knew you wouldn't want to sleep with me, and that's fine. You've kept your word and came down here for the gala, and I'm very happy about it."

A line drew itself between her eyebrows. "Did you think I was going to let you down?"

His thumb brushed the corner of her lips—where a dimple would appear if she smiled. "Not for one second."

The instant Kamari knew she was in trouble was when she found herself lingering in the moment. Nearly leaning in his touch, nearly fluttering her lashes when his thumb stroked her lower lip.

A car honked and Thiago raised his middle finger at the driver behind him. "Fucker," he mumbled before hitting the gas pedal. The engine roared loudly, and the sound was starting to become music to her ears.

"What's the hotel's name?" She trailed her gaze from his fingers gripping tightly the steering wheel to his sun-kissed forearms where the veins were prominently alluring. "Dial the number for me."

She blinked. "Now?"

"Yes, moonbeam. Now."

He pointed to his phone resting in the console between them and gave her his passcode. She tipped her lips in a smile at the sight of his home screen's picture: him, standing between Alex and Cal, holding a trophy in hand whilst all three of them bore smiles as bright as the sun's rays. Alex was holding a bottle of champagne whilst Cal was pointing to Thiago, an arm draped around his shoulders.

"That was taken when I won my first ever race my rookie year," he explained, nostalgia in his tone. "Such an awesome race."

She couldn't help but smile. "Looks like it."

"Go to the music app after the call," he demanded.

"Why?"

"I made a playlist for you."

She then dialled the hotel's number, hoping he wouldn't see the blush coating the apples of her cheeks, the loud ringing noise echoing through the car's speakers.

The hotel's receptionist picked up after the fourth ring. "Hotel Vacances Bleues Royal Westminster de Menton, bonjour."

"Bonjour," Thiago said gruffly, causing Kamari to gawk at him, puzzled. He put the blinker on, decelerated, and turned around the corner. "J'appelle pour annuler une réservation, s'il-vous-plaît."

Kamari couldn't even concentrate on the road or the sound of a keyboard clicking on the other side of the line.

"À quel nom?" The lady asked, tone clipped.

"Kamari Monroe."

He even managed to say her name with a French accent, damn it.

She closed her lips that had parted in shock, inhaling to regain composure.

"Je peux l'annuler mais le remboursement ne sera pas possible car—"

"C'est pas grave," he said with a sly smile. "Gardez les sous."

A few more words were exchanged, and Thiago ended the call, draping his left arm on the door panel, grinning smugly.

Kamari gaped at him, curious, bewildered, stunned. "I have so many questions."

A dimple made its appearance on his cheek. "Ask away, baby."

"You speak French?"

He dipped his chin in a nod. "Mum's half French and half British. Dad is—was—half British and half Spanish."

"Interesting. You're driving under the British flag in F1 then?"

"Yeah." He put the blinker on whilst pushing a button on his key to open a garage door that led beneath a tall building. "My dad drove under the Spanish one, though."

Kamari nodded, absentmindedly gnawing on her lower lip as he drove slowly through the underground parking lot. There were expensive cars lined up, piquing her curiosity. Were they all his?

"Did you find that sexy?" he asked, brows pumping when she slid her attention back to him. "My French, I mean. Because I already know you find *me* sexy."

She shoved his arm. "Do you ever stop being arrogant? No, I did not particularly enjoy it. It was whatever. What did the lady say, anyway?"

With the heel of his palm, he turned the steering wheel whilst parking in reverse. "She cancelled your stay, but she can't give your money back. It's not refundable since it's a last minute cancellation."

She frowned. "What! Turn around and let me go have a word with that woman."

A small chuckle rose from his throat. "It's taken care of, Kam. I'll pay you back and there's no negotiating. All I want is for you to stay with me, enjoy your weekend, and try to make you smile."

She scrunched her nose whilst unbuckling her belt. "You're so cheesy."

He grinned handsomely. "You love it."

"I don't. I really don't."

"Whatever," he droned. "Let's get you settled in. Hungry? I know a place where we can get brunch."

The tenderness in his gaze sent a shiver down her spine. She nodded. "Famished."

THIAGO'S FLAT HAD a direct view of the ocean. He lived in a penthouse, certainly too spacious for himself, though he had told Kamari that Alex and Cal practically lived here, too.

She had avoided his gaze in the lifts, all too aware of her unsteady heartbeat and the anticipation coiling in her stomach. Most of all, she was nervous for tonight's gala. They would be exposing themselves to hundreds of people, she would meet important people working in motorsports, and she'd have to pretend again.

Holding her luggage, he led her through the penthouse. He showed her his humongous shelf where trophies and helmets lay, his flat screen television hanging in the centre.

Leading her through a corridor where several doors were closed on either side of the aisle, Kamari halted in front of a frame that had caught her attention. It was a picture of Thiago in his early days. He was wearing a navy-blue racing jumpsuit, holding a helmet, and standing in front of a racing go-kart. A man was crouched next to him with his arm draped around Thiago's frame.

"Is this your dad?" she asked, though she already knew the answer.

"Yeah." He was standing behind her, voice thick with emotion. "I was three. That was my first karting competition."

She smiled softly. "Adorable. You have his eyes. Actually, you look a lot like him."

She heard him swallow the lump in his throat. "So I've been told."

She pivoted, not expecting him to be standing so close. "I'm sorry. We don't have to talk about this—him."

"I don't mind," he murmured. "I want to tell you about him. I know he'd like you."

She tilted her head sideways. "Really?"

"Yep," he said with a chuckle. "Because you keep rejecting me and he would find this totally funny."

"Oh," she laughed, now amused. "Okay. Maybe we'd be besties."

"Definitely. You two would constantly talk shit about me behind my back."

She rolled her eyes. "I'm not always a brat."

He nudged her chin with his knuckles, her skin tingling even when his touch wasn't on her anymore. "I know. But a witch, that, you are on a daily basis."

"So I've heard."

Time stood still when his features softened as he allowed a smile to touch his enticing lips. He scrutinised her face carefully, delicately, as if taking a mental photograph of her at this exact moment and pinning the image in the fore point of his mind.

A lazy strand of hair fell over his brow, and she almost reached out to brush it away from his handsome face. She breathed, slowly finding the control she once had over herself, and dipped her gaze to the door behind him.

"Your room," he suddenly said, voice hoarse and husky as he scratched the back of his neck. "Right. Follow me, m'lady."

She heard him loosen a small, bated breath when he turned on his heel, and she frowned, wondering why he was so nervous around her. She had always known him with an admirable self-confidence, an allure so pristine and enthralling. She'd known him careful, tranquil, and relaxed, yet arrogant and pompous. Therefore, seeing him utterly powerless by her presence was bizarre.

He pointed to a door that was slightly ajar. "My room."

Right at the end of the corridor was the guest room he had set up for her. He pushed the door open, placed the luggage by the wall, and moved aside to let her enter first.

"Alex usually sleeps in this room, but I've changed the sheets and all."

The room was simple, and she assumed Thiago was too busy travelling to put effort into decorating the rooms that weren't of any use to him.

"That's okay," she told him, putting her purse and tote bag on the armchair placed in the corner. "I'm only staying for two nights."

Back turned to him, she ran an idle finger over the silk sheets covering the bed. He stayed silent, though she wished he would have said something—anything. Perhaps ask her to stay longer. Perhaps tell her she didn't need to go so early.

Kamari made a move to peer over her shoulder to take a look at him, but her attention was caught by a turquoise bag sitting on the bureau in front of the window, and the bouquet of white flowers—cosmos to be exact—placed next to it.

Her heart squeezed and she folded her arms across her chest. "I think you put your secret girlfriend's gifts in the wrong room," she pointed out nonchalantly as if seeing these didn't affect her.

"My secret girlfriend," he repeated, tone deep, low, chilling. "I think they're in the right place. Go take a look at the bag, Kam."

She met silver eyes from across the room, her breath hitching when she saw him leaning against the doorway, a smug grin on his face and strong arms crossed over his broad chest.

"Don't tell me you got me lingerie," she bit out, trying to diffuse the tension.

His eyes flashed—turned to stormy grey as he gave her a once-over that made chills rush down her spine. "Not this time, love."

She narrowed her eyes, pushing the idea of wearing lingerie for this man out of her mind, and he chuckled, tipping the corner of his lips into a smile.

"Seriously, Kam." He jutted his chin towards the bureau. "Go ahead."

Heading towards the window, albeit with slight reluctance, she allowed confusion to cloud her senses for a fraction of a second. Why would he gift her something? Why would he spend his money on her?

Kamari sighed softly and grabbed the bag, turning it around to see the shop's name on it. She knew she had recognised Tiffany & Co.'s particular shade of blue.

A small, square box sat at the bottom of it. Warily, she took hold of it. She was cautious, not because she was afraid of mishandling the object, but because she was scared of what might happen if she truly realised Thiago Valencia cared for her.

She glanced at the man whose presence felt so close yet so distant all at once, not knowing how to act when he threw her way a smile full of devotion.

Kamari opened the box, and she didn't know what happened next. She might have gasped softly. Might've become motionless. Might've started to become emotional, uncontrollably and unwillingly, because she wasn't expecting this.

With shaking fingers, she took out a heart-shaped bookmark made out of sterling silver. There was a *K* engraved on its centre, identifying the object as hers.

"Thiago," she heard herself say in a whisper. "What..."

She was totally hypnotised by the bookmark, but she managed to see his silhouette inch closer. When he spoke, his voice was gravel-like. "I know you're passionate about books, and I immediately thought of you when I saw it. I wasn't sure what to engrave on it, so I think your initial was the best choice. I would've put my name on it, but then you would've rolled your eyes at me and all."

Her brows knitted together, and she observed the silver object, a lump forming inside her throat. "It's perfect." She found his gaze, all tenderness and delicacy like always. "You didn't have to get me anything."

A smile drew itself upon his lips. Sliding his hands in the pockets of his trousers, he lifted his shoulders in a small shrug. "I know, but I wanted to. This is your birthday present from me."

"You really didn't have to."

"Stop saying that," he huffed. "I owe you that, okay? I remember you telling me you were planning on celebrating with Indy and Diana on Friday, and instead, you flew to Monza because Alex said I needed you. You've sacrificed a lot for me since we met, and I want to show you how grateful I am for you."

Rising and falling, her chest kept expanding even if she felt as though her breath had gotten lost somewhere deep inside her lungs. "And the flowers?"

His eyes darted to her lips. "To congratulate you on signing the opening of the second café."

Taking in the sight of the bouquet, she let her features soften. "How did you know?"

"What?"

Green found silver—a kaleidoscope of diamonds shining like bright colours in her world that had been painted in grey. "Cosmos are my favourite flowers."

His eyes flashed with surprise. "I had no clue. They just make me think of you."

"Really?"

"Really." He smiled, allowing dimples to adorn his face whilst his cheekbones were coated with a rosy tinge. "The name makes me think of the galaxy, so the moon; you. Their petals are evenly placed, perfectly ordered, just like you are when you do something—always calculated, organised. But above all, they are strong, resilient flowers."

Refusing to show the emotions swamping her eyes, she lowered her gaze to the bookmark she'd been holding in her hands. She wasn't certain why his kind gesture made her feel so vulnerable—paralysed. Perhaps because she wasn't used to receiving presents. Perhaps because she wasn't used to genuine affection, especially from someone who was a stranger only a few weeks ago.

Delicately, Thiago lifted her chin with the side of his index, forcing her to look into starlit moons. "What's wrong? You don't like them?"

She shook her head, emitting a soft sigh. "I love them, Thiago. I truly do. Thank you. I just—I wasn't expecting any of it."

"You deserve all the pretty presents in the world," he murmured softly. "All the flowers and everything you wish for. You deserve the world and beyond. I don't know how you've been treated in the past, and I wish we had met all those years ago so I could erase all your wounds."

He didn't need to belong to the past to be able to draw stars around her scars.

She grabbed his wrist, gently, and pulled his soothing touch away. "Don't say things like that, Thiago."

His sharp jaw tightened. It seemed as though he wanted to say something, as though he wanted to fight and scream at her because there certainly was a heavy weight gripping at his chest, too, that he needed to release. Instead, he said, "I'm sorry. Do you still want to go get brunch?"

"Please," she scoffed, putting the blue box atop the bureau. "I never say no to food."

Thiago's smile had become her favourite feature of his. "There she is."

CHAPTER THIRTY-THREE

⚐ *MONTE CARLO, MONACO*

"THIAGO," KAMARI CALLED from the guest bedroom.

The way his name sounded on the tip of her tongue felt like a caress on his spine, like a serenade meant to envelop his heart in the most devastating way.

"What?"

"Are you busy?"

"Yeah," he groaned, frustrated, brows pinched together. "I can't do my fucking bow tie."

"Oh." There was a pause as he turned on his heel to exit the en suite bathroom linked to his bedroom. "Can you come in here for a sec?"

"Already on my way, pretty girl," he announced whilst securing the last button of his white shirt, letting the bow tie hang loosely around his neck.

He'd been so focused on the steady rhythm of his footfalls and the sound of his dress shoes clicking on the parquet that he hadn't seen Kamari standing before the mirror in the guest room.

Only when he looked up did he feel like losing his breath. Paralysed, he could only blink at the sight of the bane of his existence—a nightmare dressed like a daydream.

Back turned to him, her small hands were reaching to the small of her dorsal, fingers trying to tug the zipper upwards. An emerald gown was clinging to her body, ebbing and flowing like a pool of gemstones behind her.

"Well," she said, tone clipped, dragging him out of his dream. "Don't just stand there. Help me, please?"

"Sure." He cleared his throat at the sound of the husk baritone betraying him, then took a few steps forward until he reached Kamari.

When she dropped her hand to her side, she stood immobile. Thiago took a breath as his fingers found the fly that started at the base of her spinal column. Slowly, he pulled it up until it closed around the middle of her back, her dress exposing her silken, sun-kissed skin to him.

He could've moved away, could've stepped out of the room, though he stayed right here. Meeting her gaze in the mirror's reflection, he felt his knees nearly giving up on him.

Kamari was stunning—like always—and she looked like an enchantress on the cusp of devastating everyone crossing her path tonight.

Thiago dared to brush her dark, curled hair away from her face, purposely touching the side of her neck and shoulder, creating trails of goosebumps to appear in their wake.

"You look breathtaking, Kam," he murmured huskily into her ear.

Her rouge lips fell agape, and she couldn't tear her gaze away from his awe-stricken face. Then, mischief drew itself upon her features. "You've got a bit of drool there," she noted, pointing to the corner of her mouth.

"Very funny," he said sardonically, yet amused. "Very witty."

When she pivoted, her scent enveloped him. Her regard instantly dropped to his mouth, then to his bow tie.

Perfectly manicured fingers grabbed both ends of the black fabric. "You cleaned up nice as well, Valencia."

"I know."

He observed her face stricken with utter concentration, studying the splatter of freckles on the bridge of her nose and dusting onto the tops of her cheekbones. He wanted to touch the small crease between her brows to make it disappear, wanted to trace her cupid's bow and her full lips with the tip of his finger.

He needed to distract himself or else he would do something that wasn't supposed to happen without a crowd watching. "I actually hate ties in general."

"So why are you wearing one?"

"Leo McConnell's commands," he mused. "He says I look good and classy when I wear a tux."

The nod of her head was subtle. "You do."

"I know I do." He grinned then winced. "Don't wrap it too tightly or you'll constrict my airway."

She arched an eyebrow up. "What if I want to get rid of you?"

He feigned hurt by putting his hand above his heart. "What shall you ever do without me?"

A coy shrug of her shoulders. "I'll live in this penthouse, register myself as your wife—well, widow—so I can inherit your fortune, but no worries, I'll mourn and grieve for you on Tuesdays."

"I knew you were a bratty witch." He narrowed his gaze, her amused regard slipping upwards to meet his. "And why on Tuesdays only?"

She let her hands fall to her sides. "I don't know. Tuesday seems like a good day to be sad."

Thiago couldn't help but snort, gently nudging Kamari's chin with his knuckles. "You're an idiot."

"Not as much as you," she retorted, a rosy tinge appearing on her cheeks that could have been mistaken for makeup. "This looks okay to you?"

Turning to face the mirror, he let a smile spread across his lips when he noticed the bow tie was perfectly secured around his neck.

Hands on his shoulders, Kamari obliged him to pivot. She pulled the collar of his shirt down and picked a piece of linen off his chest.

"You ready?" he asked, timbre husky.

"Nope. You?"

God, of course he wasn't. He loved attention, loved the spotlight and cameras, but he was aware he was showing up to the event to seek redemption, so uneasiness was coiling warily inside his stomach. "Nope."

BLINDING FLASHLIGHTS SPARKLED from left and right, the sounds of the outside world muffled for a moment.

Thiago glanced at Kamari, slowly killing the engine of his Ferrari 812. Leaning his elbow atop the console between them, he passed his fingers through his hair, dishevelling his locks that had once been styled to perfection.

She had been silent the whole car ride whilst absentmindedly toying with the ring on her forefinger as she kept her gaze fixated on her lap.

Thiago could see the valet approach the vehicle as other cars started to line up behind him in front of the venue. The sidewalks were cramped with fans and journalists and paparazzi, their attention brought to the people exiting the cars and walking onto the red carpet.

Carefully, he turned her face towards him by cupping her chin. "I'm sorry."

Kamari frowned. "Why?"

"For bringing you into this. For forcing you to be under the spotlight, to be photographed—for faking it all with me."

Something flashed in her eyes, though she didn't let her stone-cold face waver. "Don't be sorry. I wouldn't have agreed to it if I weren't okay with the consequences. I know what I got myself into."

With a feather-light touch, he brushed the corner of her lips, ignoring the scowl she sent him. He wouldn't dare ruin her makeup, hence the delicacy in his caress. "What is it then?"

She shook her head. "It's stupid."

"No, tell me. Is it about the texts you've been receiving?"

A line drew itself between her brows. "How do you know about them?"

"You always check your phone, and I saw you delete a message right after reading it. Who's bothering you?"

She exhaled. "There are two things: the first one is that gossip page that keeps spreading rumours about you cheating, you being dropped by Primavera, you keeping doing things that only stain your reputation, and it's breaking my heart. And the second thing is coming from an unknown number, but I think it's just my ex trying to lure me away from you."

His features hardened. "Can I do something about it?" He knew she was independent and would rather deal with this on her own, but he couldn't fathom the idea of her hiding in the dark and letting this negativity hurt her.

She shook her head. "I keep ignoring him and everything the media says."

"Good. Don't let them get to your pretty head." He lingered his gaze over her facial features he adored so much. "You're nervous, aren't you?"

She tried not to chew on her lower lip. "I've just been so used to being an object, some kind of trophy. So, I'm just afraid of what people might think of me."

How could someone be so selfish to dim her spark? To force her to hide her flame?

His chest tightened. "I won't ever let anyone say a bad thing about you. I will never force you to hide in my shadow." He dropped his hand, curling it into a ball. But the bubble of fury continued to grow, and he couldn't control it. "That dude broke you and it's making me so fucking mad."

Her gaze dropped to his fist to hide the crestfallen gleam shadowing the green around her pupils. "I've been able to mend the shattered pieces on my own. My Nana would always tell me this: if you never bleed, you're never going to grow."

He chuckled. "I think it was Taylor Swift, but maybe your grandma and blondie have the same mindset."

Her lips broke into a small, sad smile that caused his heart to ache as if it had been stabbed.

"Let me take the lead now," he heard himself say in a murmur through the loud thud of his pulse. "I can't stand the thought of you going through that alone. Let me take care of you, Kam. As a friend who owes you everything. Every shattered part of you, I'll repair them. If you can do it for me, then I will do it for you."

She searched his face, his eyes, for a lie, and she only saw raw sincerity. "Thiago..."

He uncurled his fingers, twisting his hand so his palm would face heavenwards—an invitation to place her hand in his. "I promise. I've got you, okay? I understand why you're such an independent woman, why you'd rather be on your own. It's because he made you feel like you're a burden, but you're not. You're the most exciting girl I've ever met. You might be good at hiding behind your cold mask, but I see you, Kam. I've got you."

All she could do was put her hand in his whilst breathing shakily. "Okay."

Weaving their fingers together, he applied a soft pressure around her digits—a silent promise to never let go. This woman had been made for him. He was sure of it. They fit like puzzle pieces and were drawn to each other like magnets gravitating towards their other half.

A tap on the passenger side's window startled the both of them. Rowan stood before the glass, bending his knees to be able to look into the low car, waving and smiling sheepishly. Then, he made a heart with his fingers before blowing a kiss, then turned around to jump onto the red carpet, eliciting a roar of delight from the people attending the event.

Kamari shook her head. "He's something else."

Thiago chuckled. "That he is. Been dealing with that bloke's idiocy for five years."

The moment the valet made a move to open Kamari's door, Thiago rushed out of the car, holding a hand up. He threw the car key to the man. "I've got it. Thanks."

Buttoning his jacket, he rounded the car, rapidly waving at the crowd waiting behind security barriers. He opened the passenger's door, extending his hand towards Kamari.

"Come on, Miss Independent. I've got you."

CHAPTER THIRTY-FOUR

⚑ *MONTE CARLO, MONACO*

" I HAVE A suggestion," Thiago whispered in her ear.

Kamari sipped on her champagne whilst maintaining her gaze on Theodore Singh, the president of the FIA, as he listed and thanked all twenty drivers currently competing on the grid for having donated to a region in Italy where floods had destroyed many lives and homes. There was supposed to be a race over there in April, but because of the weather conditions—unstoppable rain, flooding—they had to cancel it. Out of all drivers, Thiago had been the one to donate the most.

"How about we get out of here?" he continued, tone as low when she didn't give him an ounce of her attention.

Kamari raised her brows. "Are you sure you want to do that? Your reputation is not clean yet."

She ignored the way his warmth felt like a burning flame ready to scorch her body when he draped his arm over the back of her seat, pulling himself closer so his lips would almost graze her ear. "Come on, moonbeam. Don't act like you're not bored."

She narrowed her gaze on the athlete when she turned to him. "I'm having the time of my life."

"You and I clearly don't have the same vision of fun."

"We can't leave," she hissed quietly.

"They won't even notice we're gone."

"What if they ask you to speak on stage?"

"I already did." He caressed her shoulder blade with the tip of his forefinger, causing goosebumps to appear beneath his touch. "Indy texted me. Said she's with Cal and Alex at Buddha Bar."

Only her best friend would ditch an event she'd been invited to.

Kamari huffed. "I know that place."

"You do?"

"Yep." She took a sip of her bubbles. "That's where I was with Indy and Di before going on your yacht the night we met."

"Ah, I see," he mused with a grin that lured her stare to linger on his dimples. "Well, let's go then."

"But—"

"They're going to announce the buffet is open and the rest of the evening is going to be people slow dancing or screaming at the top of their lungs to Celine Dion. We can either recreate that one Titanic scene or just get the fuck out of here and enjoy our night."

Kamari chewed the interior of her cheek. The night had been decent so far—she had spoken to a few people, had complimented women walking alongside other drivers, had listened to speeches, and had posed for cameras with Thiago. It was bizarre, but doing this, and being by his side felt natural.

"Won't you get in trouble?"

His smile only widened. "You're cute when you're concerned. What's the worst that could happen? Receive a call from Leo? He'll yell at me and tell me to get my shit together, so what? Nothing he hasn't done before."

"Thiago," she pressed. "Your behaviour can impact your contract renewal, do you know that?"

"Yes, baby, I do," he mustered with a roll of his eyes. "But they're not going to replace me just because I leave an event early."

His gaze was suggestive, coercing her into following his troublesome attitude.

"I can just go up to Romano and tell him you're not feeling well," he suggested with a sheepish shrug.

"I can't go clubbing in this dress, though."

His smirk was now vicious. "Don't worry, I think Indy took care of that."

"I'm not wearing that!"

"Yes, you are. It's either that or the dress you wore to the gala. Besides, it was the only dress I could fit in my bag for you."

"You cannot call *that* a dress, Indigo."

The loud bass of the music made the walls of the bathroom tremble with its sizzling energy. Kamari glared at her best friend whilst tugging the skirt down and trying to keep her cleavage a maximum covered.

"Stop it." Indy slapped Kamari's bum. "You look hot."

Lifting the emerald dress she had folded, hoping it wouldn't be ruined, she asked, "And what do we do with this one?"

Indy rolled her eyes, but she was amused as small giggles fled her mouth. She had drunk too many glasses with Alex and Cal already. Taking hold of the gown, she smiled coyly. "Let me work my charm and ask the bartender to keep it safe until we leave."

Kamari groaned, her frustration muffled by the loud music. Indy dragged her friend out of the ladies' room towards the famous pub where the light was so dim that they could barely see where they were heading to.

Indy stopped in front of the bar, leaning over as she called a bartender over. The man barely looked 20 years old, though he threw a flirtatious smile at Indy that caused her to giggle.

"Get a grip," Kamari told her firmly.

"Hi," Indy said, ignoring her friend. "Is there a safe place where you guys can hide a dress until we leave?"

"A dress?" the man asked, amused, flickering his gaze to Kamari.

"Don't ask," Kamari mumbled. "Yes, or no?"

He shrugged. "Sure. I'll put it in the lounge room where we hang out during our breaks."

Indy handed him the gown, and he smiled. Moments after disappearing through the backdoor, he came back, placed two small glasses atop the counter and poured an amber liquid in them. "On the house."

Kamari downed the beverage without thinking, causing Indy to cheer loudly before following her actions. The liquid burned her throat as it cascaded through her system, and she couldn't help but wince slightly.

"You look like you needed it," Indy chuckled, looping her arm through Kamari's as she pulled her towards the table she had been sitting at with the boys. "How was the gala?"

"It was fine. Not my cup of tea, but Thiago looked delighted to be there at first."

"Until they started doing long and annoying speeches?"

"Yes. Why didn't you show up?"

"I did, but I left after the red carpet. Socialised a bit, drank two glasses of champagne, and left through the front door."

Kamari shook her head in exasperation. "Typical."

"And how are things going with Mister Hotshot?"

"Well," Kamari started, noticing the thorough skip in her heartbeat. "He refused to let me stay in a hotel in Menton."

"Where?"

"This city in the South of France that's, like, ten minutes away from Monaco. Anyway, I'm staying over at his house tonight."

Indy shoved a man away when he tried to approach them. "Don't you think it's normal that he refused when you offered to stay somewhere else? What if you were spotted by a fan or something?"

"Yeah, I don't know. I just don't want to be a burden to him."

She could feel the concern emanating from Indy's regard upon her face. "Kam, that guy freaking adores you. He loves having you around. I don't know what's going on behind closed doors, and I'm just laying this out there so you can do whatever you want with that piece of information, but Thiago is a really, really good guy. Probably the best man I know."

Kamari's gaze dropped to the floor. "I don't know what you want me to say, Indy."

"Nothing. You don't have to say anything, but just consider looking beyond the deal to—oh, speak of the devil."

The flashes of artificial lighting shone upon Thiago's face as he leaned against a wall, one hand tucked inside the pocket of his dress pants as the other gripped a glass of dark liquor. He had gotten rid of the bow tie and the vest when they had parked the car and had opened the first few buttons of the white shirt to reveal tan skin. He looked dishevelled and rebellious in the best possible way—a stark contrast to the man he was on the red carpet a few hours ago.

"Tell me you've railed this man," Indy whined. "He's such a sight for sore eyes."

"Indy," she hissed, pushing her friend. "Have some manners, please. The relationship I have with Thiago is strictly professional."

Lies. Lies. And more lies.

Kamari had thought of Thiago during the darkest hours of the night more than she cared to admit.

"You're full of bollocks."

"Bollocks?" Kamari echoed with a laugh. "You hang around Callahan and Alex way too often."

"They're fun guys. I like them."

Kamari couldn't fault her friend for that. They were good men—all three of them.

Reaching the table in the corner of the room, Kamari glanced at Thiago, only to see him engaged in a conversation with another woman who, apparently, didn't know what personal space was. Chest almost grazing his arm, she started running her nail on the side of his neck whilst whispering something in his ear.

His gaze met Kamari's, and with an excruciatingly slow yet heady once-over, he travelled his gaze over her physique, his jaw tightening. Kamari couldn't stand that gaze, that dark molten regard because it made her blood boil, made shivers rush down her spine, made her heart thunder ferociously as though it was powered by an invisible string, pulling and releasing, and he was the one controlling the organ.

"Look who's joined the party," Cal mused, standing up to wrap his arms around Kamari.

Startled by this sudden act of—drunken—affection, she patted his back then slid into the booth next to Indy, making sure to accept Alex's kiss on her cheek when he leaned over.

"French people kiss twice on the cheeks to greet each other," Alex explained as he kissed her other cheek.

"In some regions it's three," Cal countered between two sips of his large cocktail.

"We're not in France," Indy pointed out.

"Yes, thank you for that," Alex replied with a sardonic tone. "I'm pretty sure they also kiss in Monaco."

"On the lips?" Indy asked.

"No, Indigo, have you not heard what I said? It's on the cheeks."

Kamari let her friends bicker and drew her attention back to the bane of her existence. Threading his fingers through his hair, he allowed that same rogue lock to topple over his forehead as he grinned to the woman before him.

Her chest tightened as she forced herself to look away and listen to Cal's voice, so she wouldn't realise why she was feeling so angry all of a sudden.

"I'll be right back," Kamari heard the girl talking to Thiago say.

"I'll be right here," he replied with that gruff voice of his.

The next second, he was sliding into the booth right next to her, arm draped on the seat behind them.

His warm breath caressed her cheek. "Hey. Do you want anything to drink?"

"Nope. But feel free to share with blondie who's about to come back, though."

Alex met her gaze from the other side of the table and snickered.

Thiago hummed amusedly. "Do you want my drink?"

"Nope."

"Ah, I see." Pushing her dark curls away from her face, he grazed his lips to her ear then placed a soft kiss on her jaw. "Though green suits you very well, I don't think jealousy looks good on you, Kam."

She scoffed and pushed him away. "I'm not jealous."

"Liar."

Alex, who had been eyeing the pair with amused eyes, raised his glass. "Kam, you look bloody gorgeous in that dress."

"Why thank you, Alexander." She smiled. "I do think it makes my boobs look amazing."

Alex dropped his stare to her cleavage, and she rolled her eyes. His brows raised, and a suggestive smirk splayed across his lips.

But before Alex could say anything, Thiago's low voice echoed. "What the fuck is wrong with you, Myers? Don't look at her like that. In fact, don't look at her at all."

Kamari turned to look at the athlete whose wrath emanated like a wildfire. Jaw clenched, gaze dark with fury, knuckles whitening as he gripped his glass tightly. "Careful, Valencia," she murmured for him only to hear. "Jealousy doesn't look good on you."

Silver clashed with her eyes, though usually starlit eyes were now ashen with vexation. His lips parted as though he was ready to say something. Thiago was an honest man, and she knew he wouldn't hide his blatant jealousy from her.

A perfectly manicured hand slammed two shots of tequila onto the table alongside a tiny bowl of salt and another with lime slices.

It was the woman who had been flirting with him earlier. She popped a hip out, her short blonde hair falling like a curtain around her beautiful face. "Want to take a shot with me, Theo?"

Kamari scoffed softly.

"It's Thiago," he corrected wryly. "But sure."

"What about us?" Indy asked, waving a hand. "Hello. Hi. Bonjour."

"Hola," Alex chirped.

The other blonde barely looked at them. "Didn't see you guys there."

"Bitch," Cal muttered under a scoff.

Kamari narrowed her gaze when Thiago reached out to grab the small glass. Licking the back of his hand, he allowed the girl to sprinkle salt on it, and waited for her to be ready. Ignoring their entourage, they clinked their glasses together.

Kamari was totally enthralled by his movements. She watched as he glanced at her before wiping the salt off his hand with his tongue, tipping his head back when he drank the liquor. His face didn't contort into a grimace, didn't break. She watched his throat work as he swallowed, and the moment he grabbed a slice of lime, he turned to face her.

"Open your mouth," he demanded gruffly.

Speechless, she only followed his request. He placed the lime between her lips then cupped the back of her neck, leaning forward to suck onto the slice. His hooded gaze was hypnotised by her plump lips wrapped around the piece of citrus.

Smirking, Thiago pulled away and wiped the trickle of juice dripping down her chin with the pad of his thumb. His lips were gleaming, calling for her to taste the sourness etched on them. She moved—finally—and took the green citron out of her mouth.

He brushed her lower lip then. "The only lips I want to taste tonight are yours, moonbeam."

Kamari felt a surge of both confidence and relief seep through her system. Leaning in, she collected a droplet of tequila running down his chin with the tip of her tongue, slowly backing up until her lips brushed his in a light-feather way that made his breath catch. Then, she felt him smirk against her mouth as he slid his hand towards the back of her head, pulling her in to slant his mouth on hers.

The kiss was brief but enough to make her breaths stagger, enough for her to crave more. He angled her head so he could kiss her deeply and slowly, and she heard a moan trying to escape free from the back of his throat when their tongues brushed against one another. He nibbled at her lower lip, and when he pulled away, he winked.

"That's my girl," she heard Indy praise.

"Faking it, my arse," Cal muttered, though amusement was lacing his tone.

"Damn," Alex murmured. "Anyone want to make out with me like that?"

Draping an arm around Thiago's waist, she pulled herself closer to his side whilst he wrapped his own arm around her shoulders, his upper body vibrating with the chuckles he tried to keep quiet. Kamari offered a faux, dangerous smile to the woman who had been staring at them with bulging eyes.

"You have two seconds to walk away from my boyfriend. I'm not scared of breaking a nail."

Thiago chuckled, nuzzling his nose to her cheek. "So violent."

"She bites," Alex said. "I'd listen to her and run."

With a dramatic scoff, the blonde walked away.

"Her face was epic," Cal snorted. He tried to pout then to appear shocked, causing the table to mock him with loud laughter. "You're such a heartbreaker, Tito."

"Sorrow, sorrow. That's because my heart's taken," Thiago pondered, unbothered, and straightened himself. Grabbing Kamari's wrist, he pulled her away from the booth. "You, come with me."

Before she could be dragged away, she took a large gulp of the drink he had left on the table. He stood behind her as he guided her towards the dance floor, one hand holding hers and the other resting on her hip—he was claiming her, and something told her this wasn't part of the act they needed to display for the world to see.

"Keep walking in front of me," he ordered.

"Why?" She squeezed his hand, thinking he was starting to get anxious. He applied pressure in response but there was no tremor in his touch.

"Because I have a raging hard-on right now, and you're making it impossible not to drag you into the nearest bathroom and take you against the wall."

"Why don't you?"

His gaze dropped to the swell of her breasts when she pivoted to face him, and he smirked. "Feeling bold, aren't you, pretty girl? I'm not taking you back there because one, I'm not fucking you in some random washroom, and two, we're both tipsy. And the first time I get my hands on you, Kamari, I want you to remember every. Single. Thing. I do to you."

Her chest heaved, and she wasn't sure how she managed to breathe through the wave of desire. Thiago made her spin around again, causing her back to collide with his front.

They could barely see anything under the dim lighting and

through the cramped space, could barely hear anything with the loud bass of the music reverberating off the walls. But she could feel him everywhere: hands on her hips, toned torso pressed to her back, breath fanning across her jawline. Could feel his desire for her straining against the zipper of his trousers, pressing into her backside and causing her core to stir with arousal.

"You drive me fucking insane," he whispered huskily. "You don't have a single idea of what you do to me, Kam."

Weaving her fingers through his as they glided towards her waist, she leaned into him as they swayed to the rhythm of the music.

Drunken words are sober thoughts, Kam. Stop finding an excuse to run away from him.

"The way you make me feel," he continued, that gravel in his timber making chills arise on her spine. "Madness. Complete madness."

"Should I apologise?"

She heard his chuckle, low and everything but amused. "No."

She shivered when his palm descended the side of her hip, her thigh, only to graze warm fingertips at the skin below the hem of her skirt. "So what do you want, Thiago?"

"I think you know the answer."

"I want to hear you say it."

Swiftly, he obliged her to face him. His whole physique was shrouded in darkness, though she knew his gaze was dark, devastating. Wrapping her arms around his neck, she let a smirk touch her lips when his perusal dropped to them.

"Say it, Thiago." She wanted him to give in.

He fluttered his lashes when her fingers twined with his curls, his enticing lips parting slightly. She wondered where he was losing himself, what he thought of whenever she touched him. The sliver of distance between their chests was minuscule, and she wished they were alone. Wished they hadn't consumed alcohol tonight.

His chiselled jaw ticked. "You're going to ruin me."

She leaned closer, and even through the loud music, her voice was a smoky whisper. "Does that scare you?"

He nodded, subtly. "Terrifies me."

"Good."

Tucking a strand of hair behind her ear, he let his other hand travel to the small of her back. "But here's the thing; I'd tear myself apart for you."

Her heart stopped beating. "Don't say things like that."

"I mean it, Kam. You've just corrupted my soul."

She couldn't help but chuckle, sucking in a breath when his nose grazed hers. "Evermore the poet, Thiago Valencia."

His tone was coarse and gravelly and raspy. "I want you, Kamari."

She already knew it, but hearing those words out loud again made the hazy fog that had taken over her senses dissipate.

Thiago gripped her chin, his mouth millimetres away from colliding with hers. "But I want to have that conversation with you when we're sober."

She swallowed tightly. "I don't have a choice, do I?"

"You don't, because I refuse to let you hide in uncertainties, awake with what ifs, comparing your ex with me. I'm not him, Kam, and you know it. I'd give you the entire galaxy if you asked for it."

"BUT WHAT ABOUT THE CAR?"

"I'm *waaaay* too smashed to drive, and I can't crash the Ferrari," Thiago retorted, words slurred and incomprehensible. "We'll come back tomorrow."

"Is it safe?"

He lifted his thumbs up, grinning. "Their parking lot is the safest."

Thiago had managed to take a half-consumed bottle of

champagne with him when they left the club, leaving their friends over there. "Let's get out of here," he had said, an arm around her shoulders.

"God, you can't stay put tonight. Is everything okay?"

"I just want to go everywhere with you." He took a sip straight out of the bottle of champagne and handed it to her. "Actually, I want to show you something."

She didn't know how long they had walked, but they ended up at the beach right under the building he lived in.

Kamari had taken her shoes off and was now walking behind Thiago through the quiet and empty shore.

Everything was hazy, a blur, but she could still decipher the way the moonlight spilled on the side of his face like a splatter of stardust.

She watched him in awe when he took his shoes and socks off, rolling the hems of his trousers up to his shins. Taking his phone and wallet out of his pockets, he tossed them onto the sand, unable to control his widening grin. Depositing carefully the bottle of bubbles, he groaned when it toppled and spilled its contents onto the shoreline.

"Come on," he called, stars glimmering along the edges of his pupils.

"Where?"

He smiled broadly. "In the water, Kamari. Where else?"

She chuckled at his sardonic tone then sighed softly. Palm turned towards her, his eyes demanded for her to take his hand. He wouldn't let go, she knew that.

"You're alive," he started, offering her that grin that had managed to pierce her ice barriers. "But are you really living?"

It was at that exact moment that Kamari asked herself why the universe hadn't introduced him to her earlier. Why they only collided recently. It was at that exact moment that she understood he was genuinely, willingly ready to draw stars around her scars.

Dropping her shoes next to the items he had left on the sand, she shook her head. Kamari ran into the sea, a soft squeal erupting from her throat when the cold water came into contact with her bare feet. She didn't know why, but with him she'd dance in a storm, in her best dress, fearless.

Thiago was following her lazily, hands in the pockets of his trousers. And when she turned to fully look at him, she wished she would be able to remember the way he looked. The ocean's breeze caressed his face, like a lover's touch, blowing his dark locks away from his forehead. Beneath the silvery glow of the moon, she was able to decipher the tinge of rosy that had drawn itself upon his cheekbones, and the way his pupils were expanding as he looked at her as though she was more beautiful than the starry night sky.

"Fuck," he breathed, stepping towards her, the waves lapping at their feet gently. "You're exquisite, Kamari."

"You're drunk," she stated, smiling.

In the blink of an eye, he was standing before her, hand cradling her face. The delicacy of his touch made her shiver when he ran his thumb over her small dimple. "I might be, but my thoughts about you don't change despite my state of mind."

Kamari only flickered her gaze between his, trying to comprehend the meaning behind that starlit gaze of his. Those constellations in his eyes.

She could feel the sparks coursing from his fingertips towards her skin, like he wanted to set her ablaze, too.

There was a strange look on his face as he whispered, "I feel like I've known you my whole life."

She couldn't control her thoughts, her words. "Me too."

"Yeah?"

She nodded. "That connection. I feel it, too."

"Good," he murmured, relieved, happy. "I would have died from embarrassment if my affection was unrequited."

She huffed. "You're dramatic."

"No," he argued, hand on his chest. "I would have been deeply wounded."

"Yeah, sure."

"I want to kiss you," he whispered. "Can I?"

She held his gaze. "You don't have to ask."

"Nothing to say about rules and a contract?" he teased.

She couldn't help but roll her eyes amusedly. "Not today."

He looked at her lips, ever so slowly making the sliver of distance between them vanish. "I'll always make sure you're comfortable with everything we do. I'll always put you before me, Kam. Always."

Thiago cupped her jaw and pecked her lips. Kissed her again. And again, and again, until time stopped, and the universe was a simple haze. She could feel his smile against her mouth, could feel the zip of electricity burning her veins and making her feel alive. She felt her mind go into overdrive. Felt her heart race. She was so powerless and helpless, but she was starting to accept the fact Thiago held power over her.

She pulled away, a laugh flying past her blood-rushed lips. Turning around, she started running further into the water, body numb, and mind clouded with thoughts about Thiago Valencia.

"Running away from me?" she heard him call out, a smile evident in his tone.

Yes, because the way you make me feel frightens me.

A smile touched her lips. "Catch me if you can."

She heard the water splash as he made haste to catch up after her. Strong arms locked around her waist, lifting her off the ground and making her spin around. She squealed, and she could hear his soft laugh blending with the waves gently crashing with each other.

Accidentally tripping over his own feet, they fell into the water. Kamari managed not to get all her hair wet whilst Thiago plunged his whole body underwater. He emerged to the surface, and they only looked at each other for a few seconds before bursting into a fit of uncontrollable laughter.

"You pushed me," he exclaimed, eyes wide, pushing his hair back.

"I did no such thing, Valencia. Not my fault if you can't keep your balance."

"Brat."

"Jerk."

He grinned. "Witch."

"Arsehole."

He tugged her by the hip, and her chest collided with his. She looped her arms around his neck, and she could feel his fingers running over her back, delicately and tenderly, whilst his eyes studied her features.

"Kamari," he whispered softly. Every murmuration felt like a lover's caress against her barriers, slowly yet surely tearing them down.

She had once believed love was black and white, but perhaps Thiago would be able to show her that it was golden, burning red, and beautiful.

"Yes?"

"I'll catch you, I swear I will. I don't care if I get hurt in the process of picking the thorns shielding your heart."

She was pristine moonlight in ever harmony with him; he was an ethereal, radiant star shining just for her. And under the starry glow of the heavens, they were infinite.

CHAPTER THIRTY-FIVE

📍 *MONTE CARLO, MONACO*

H ER PULSE DRUMMED against her temple—loud and scorching and painful.

Waking up, Kamari winced when she felt the migraine fog her mind detrimentally. It took a few minutes to realise where she was, who she was.

When she finally managed to blink the haze of fatigue away, she pushed herself onto her elbows, causing the duvet that had been covering her body to drop. She was in Thiago's living room, and she had slept on his large yet extremely comfortable sofa. She knew she was at his place because:

1. She didn't forget what had happened last night. In fact, every moment came to the surface of her mind like a whirlwind —the gala, the Buddha Bar, the beach.

2. All the trophies and helmets adorning his shelf were attention-catching. She would have to wait until her headache vanished to take a closer look at these items.

3. A familiar musky smell was invading her senses. She supposed he was already awake and had taken a shower.

Sitting up, she couldn't help but groan softly. She hated the aftermath of a good night out. As she looked down at herself, her eyes widened when she saw she wasn't wearing the pyjama set she had packed, but one of Thiago's large t-shirt. She blinked. Kept her eyes closed. Tried to remember what had happened after dancing and running and laughing under the starry sky.

Nothing.

Not one single memory surfaced her mind.

Kamari inhaled, exhaled, remaining calm and collected despite her spiralling thoughts.

Set on the coffee table was a large glass of water and a box of painkillers. She allowed a small smile to take over her features and took small sips of the beverage. She hated taking medicine, even on her worst days, so she left the box untouched and looked around for her phone only to realise it was nowhere in sight.

"I've plugged your phone into its charger in your room."

His deep voice startled her. When she looked towards the source of that coarse sound, she heard her own breath hitch.

Thiago was leaning against the doorway, one hand in the pocket of his grey joggers as the other held a cup of steaming coffee. Only wearing a pair of joggers, his tan skin gleamed with droplets of water. He was all muscles, hard ridges and enthralling physique, and for a fraction of a second, she wondered if this man was a figment of her imagination.

When she found his gaze, he was smirking behind the rim of his cup, though he made no comment about the way she had been checking him out, blatantly and unashamedly so.

"Morning, sunshine," he drawled lazily. "How are you feeling?"

She yawned. "How do you think? What time is it anyway?"

He glanced behind his shoulder to look at the clock hung in the kitchen. "Almost nine."

"Oh." She looked away from his enticing gaze and tucked an

untamed strand of hair behind her ear. "Did we, uh—where did you sleep? Why am I on the sofa?"

She heard him chuckle before his footfalls covered the sound. He took a seat beside her, the smell of his coffee lingering in the air.

"You're pretty funny and unhinged when you're drunk," he started. "We came back from the beach around one, and you were very insistent on wanting to sleep on the sofa."

She met his amused stare. "Really?"

"Yep." He sipped his coffee. "You bit me, too. Violent little thing that you are."

"Me? I bit you?" She blinked. "Why would I do that?"

He was laughing, which sent a wave of relief through her because he wasn't judging—he never was. "Because I tried to carry you to your bed but you *really* wanted to sleep on the sofa. I stayed with you."

She grimaced. "Did I force you to?"

He flickered his gaze between hers. "All you had to do was ask me once and I was by your side."

Chewing the inside of her cheek, she tried to ignore the flutter inside her chest. "And did we..."

He looked down at the shirt she was wearing, his eyes flashing. "No. I just gave you my shirt. Actually, you're still wearing Indy's dress underneath it. I would never take advantage of you like this."

Her chest rose and fell. "I know."

She trusted him. With everything.

His features were soft, eyes still hooded with fatigue, but then he offered a smile that made all her walls crumble.

"I'm sorry, by the way. For being so...clingy."

He reached out towards her to gently push her shoulder. "Don't be. It was cute. And funny."

"Not cute," she grunted, batting his hand away. "I smell like the ocean."

Thiago chuckled and stood up. She couldn't help but follow

his motions with her eyes, surveying the flex of his bicep when he ran his fingers through his hair, the prominent v-muscle on his lower abdomen, pointing and leading towards an area she shouldn't be thinking of.

"I'll run a bath for you in my bathroom. Make yourself at home. There's coffee, fruits, cereals, and other things in the kitchen if you'd like to eat."

Kamari stood up after pushing the blanket off her thighs, causing his stare to drop to her bare legs. "Thank you."

"No worries. I've got you." He pivoted, and she sucked in a breath at the sight of his back muscles. When he faced her again, she tipped her lips into a tight smile that made him chuckle. "Weird question, but did you pack a swimsuit with you?"

She arched a brow. "Strangely, yes."

"Good. How does a boat day sound to you?"

"Sounds perfect."

THE SUN'S RAYS shone softly on her skin, procuring her the serotonin she desperately longed to feel after her eventful night. Knees tucked to her chest, she had tipped her head back so she could feel every inch of her face being kissed by the sun. Hair flowing behind her, the salty air of the ocean whiffed through her nose whilst the late September breeze caressed her cheekbones.

She could feel the intensity of a scrutiny upon her—observing, studying, remembering.

Opening her eyes, she met Thiago's gaze. His lips broke into a soft smile, and he shook his head whilst looking back at the horizon. He'd been adjusting his backwards cap on top of his head whilst his other hand rested on the steering wheel of the boat. Standing there, in the incandescence of the blue sky, he looked heavenly. Devastatingly beautiful. Perfectly crafted from the hands of the Gods above.

Kamari had expected them to take the yacht on which they had met a month ago, but he had led her towards a smaller boat that looked like it had cost over a million pounds, too.

"So, where are you taking me?"

Thiago was wearing swimming shorts and a linen shirt. Rolling a sleeve up to his elbow, he allowed a smile to spread across his lips. "There's this small island about an hour away from Monaco. I usually go there with Cal to run and train. It's, like, my secret spot."

She leaned her chin atop a knee. "How many girlfriends of yours have you taken to that secret spot?"

"You're the first girl I'm taking there, Kam." He peered at her, expression serious. "Besides, I've never had a girlfriend."

"Never?"

His brows shot upwards. "You look surprised."

"I am."

Thiago shrugged nonchalantly. "A two-month fling isn't anything serious to me. Sure, I've had a few flings here and there, had my fair share of one-night stands, but I've never been serious about a girl before."

There was this uncanny feeling stirring inside her chest as she felt a sudden wave of protectiveness wash over her. Like she wanted to wrap her arms around him, ask why he was afraid to give his heart away, and she understood why. He didn't want to have his heart broken either. But she also wanted to tell him she would never hurt him, that she'd give him the world just like he'd already given her an entire galaxy.

"Is there a particular reason why you never settled?" she heard herself ask quietly.

He rubbed the back of his neck, glancing her way whenever he wasn't watching the horizon. "My rookie year, I just wanted to focus on racing and not be distracted. Two years later, I lost my father, and I completely lost myself along the way. I didn't want anyone to bear that weight with me because, you know, I wasn't doing okay at all. I didn't want my girl to feel like it'd be a burden to be with someone who's grieving. And now... well, I guess I'm just waiting to meet *the* girl."

She inhaled when his silver gaze collided with her. "She's out there, somewhere. And she's going to love you so much."

Time came to a halt. She knew that tender regard, those constellations in his eyes. She watched as he swallowed tightly, holding her gaze. "And I'm going to love her so fucking much that it'll physically hurt. She's right around the corner, I just know it. I'm just waiting."

She felt like she couldn't breathe. "For what?"

"For her to be ready. Because, Kam, the moment I have her, I'm never letting her go."

"ARE YOU AWARE the land is, like, not here?"

Thiago chuckled as he rose after checking the anchor had fallen to the bottom of the water.

"Thank you for letting me know." He sat next to her and pointed to the expanse of the ocean before them. "We're just stopping for a moment so you can take in this view."

Behind them was the island he had talked about, very few tourists walking along the shoreline, but there wasn't any other boat in sight. It felt as though he had taken her into another universe, another realm, where it was only them.

"This place is very pretty," she acknowledged, meandering her gaze around.

"Yeah, it is," he replied in a murmur, though she could feel his stare on her face.

She looked back at Thiago, enthralled by his dimpled smile. "Thank you for taking me here."

"I owe you that." He winked, then his fingers flew to his shirt to undo the buttons he hadn't secured. "You jump, I jump? I bet the water's really nice."

She narrowed her eyes. "You did not just quote *Titanic*."

He grinned. "I did."

He had reached his navel, and she grabbed his wrist, instantly releasing it when she felt a jolt of electricity course through her veins. "Wait."

She slightly pivoted in her seating position, dropping her feet to the floor. Her knee was touching the side of his thigh, and she felt heat crawl up her spine when his gaze dropped to her collarbones, the swell of her breasts, his pupils expanding until his eyes became stormy grey.

She ignored the vehemence in his perusal and gathered her long hair on a shoulder. "You said earlier that you didn't want to be a burden to someone whilst grieving. Why would you think it's a burden to feel this way? Who hurt you?"

Deep down, she was angry. Angry at the thought of Thiago getting hurt by someone. Angry because he deserved to be listened to. He deserved the world.

The corner of his lips curved upwards into a small smile. "The only woman who has ever broken my heart is you."

She rolled her eyes. "I would do no such thing."

"I'm messing with you," he teased, putting his hand on her knee then pulling it back. "Is this okay?"

Kamari nodded. "It's perfectly fine."

Delicately, he placed his hand back on her knee, thumb gently brushing her bare skin. He could feel the goosebumps rising beneath his digit, like a glacial sequence of chills caused by his corrupting touch.

"You don't talk often about losing your dad, do you?"

His jaw tightened. "Never. Sometimes with Mum, but she's having a hard time coping, too. Alex and Cal are my best buddies, but they don't really understand what I go through."

"I don't either," she whispered sorrowfully. She wished she did. Wished she could help him.

"That's where you're wrong," he said, applying pressure around her knee. "You get me, Kam. I know you feel sorry for me, but you hold me through the pain. You're here to listen, and you're not scared of saying things and reaching out at the same time. I really wish we had met earlier. I wish you had been there to hold my hand on the hardest day."

She placed her hand on his. "I'm here now. You're not alone, Thiago. Don't bottle those feelings inside, okay?"

His eyes were swamped with emotions. Still, he was able to throw her a beautiful smile. "I won't."

Kamari's heart ached at the sight of his nostalgic, crestfallen eyes, but it was evident he didn't want to talk about this topic further. She only wanted to let him know he could find a friend in her, and he knew it.

He nudged her chin with his knuckles. "You're so cute. Thank you for caring."

When he stood up, he fully unbuttoned his shirt and threw it atop the bench she was sitting on. He then slid towards the swimming platform, then plunged into the lukewarm water.

She watched him emerge to the surface, pushing his dark hair away from his forehead, a single ray of sunshine glowing on him, creating a halo above his head—like he was a divine being, like he knew how to attract sunlight.

"Join me."

"Later. I'm going to read a bit."

He glared at her, swimming towards the boat. Draping his arms on the platform he asked, "Seriously? What are you reading?"

She reached into her bag and pulled out her novel. "This sweet romance."

"Sweet," he parroted, followed by a scoff. "I know those cute covers hide pure filth."

Heat threatened to coat her cheekbones. "How do you even know?"

"Might have gone to the bookstore," he said. "I wanted to make you a book bouquet, but I wasn't sure what genre is your favourite. I skimmed through a few books in the new adult section, and... yeah."

She was feeling bold. Tilting her head, she demanded, "Did you imagine yourself doing all of those filthy things to me?"

Silver eyes instantly darkened as he clenched his jaw. "Be careful with what you ask me, Kamari. But yes, I have. I'll be needing all the time in the universe, though, because I will be taking my sweet, sweet time with you and your perfect body."

Her heart thundered, skin pebbling at the sound of his hoarse voice. "Oh."

He chuckled then and cleared his throat. "Anyway. You'll have to give me a list of your favourite books so I can start reading them."

She blinked. "Are you serious?"

He nodded. "Yes. I want to immerse myself into your world as well."

Kamari smiled, then shrugged as if needing to appear indifferent. She reached to the hem of her dress and pulled it over her head. "Okay, I'll send you a list later."

Lying herself down into a comfortable position, she opened her book and discreetly glanced at Thiago. His gaze was sauntering over her physique, jaw slack. He rolled his tongue over the interior of his cheek, scoffing under his breath.

"Fuck me," she heard him grumble before disappearing into the water.

"KAMARI, IT'S BEEN TEN MINUTES."

Rolling her eyes, she shut her book closed and propped herself onto her elbows. "What?"

"Come in the water," Thiago whined. "Please."

She couldn't see him, but from the volume of his voice, he was nearby. She sat up and met his mischievous gaze as he swam to the side of the boat where she was at.

"You've been annoying me for the past ten minutes and I barely got one chapter done."

He snickered. "Yeah, well, you're ignoring me so you deserved that."

She sighed. "I promise I'll jump in later."

"Fine," he huffed. "Help me get up, then."

"No."

"Please?"

Bothered by his incessant annoyance, she faced him, leaning forward. She saw him drop his gaze to her cleavage, but he then extended his hand. As naive as ever, Kamari grabbed it, but he was too quick and swift. Easily, he pulled her into the ocean, causing droplets of water to splash around.

She had anticipated the fall and held her breath underwater before kicking her feet to push herself to the surface.

"You're such a piece of shit," she breathed out.

Thiago laughed. "You had it coming, witch."

She pushed water into his face. "I hate you."

He smiled broadly. Beautifully. "No, you don't."

As they held gazes, she watched his smile drop, features hardening and eyes switching to a darker, tempestuous shade of grey.

She swam towards him—because that invisible string obliged her to gravitate towards Thiago wherever he was, whether he was at arm's length or in another country.

"Don't look at me like that," she warned.

"Like what?" He caught hold of her hip, pulling her into his broad chest.

Her breath lost itself somewhere inside her lungs, but she wanted to play his games. Wanted to touch him. And so, she put her hands on his shoulders, feeling the taut muscles beneath.

"Like I want you, Kamari?" he continued when she didn't respond fast enough, eyes fixed on her lips. "Like I'm ready for you to ruin me?"

"What happened to having some self-preservation, darling?"

He smirked, one arm looping around her waist as the other hand travelled up and down her ribcage. "Apparently I have none."

Shaky breaths escaped her lips when his fingers reached the hem of her bikini top.

"Are we going to talk about what happened last night?"

She could barely recall what had happened at the club, though she remembered him admitting, blatantly, that he wanted her.

She watched his mouth, tracing the curve of his cupid's bow. "Nope."

"Are we really avoiding the topic?"

For some reason, Kamari couldn't stand the sudden absence of malevolence around the edges of his irises. Couldn't stand that look of pure concern and weariness as he was ready to lay his heart open.

She wasn't ready. Wasn't certain she was strong enough to hand him everything she's worked hard for to guard her heart.

And so, she slammed her mouth on his, eliciting a mixture of a surprised moan and a relieved sigh to rise from his throat. The kiss instantly turned fiery, desire emanating from both of their burning bodies.

He slid his hands to the back of her thighs, urging her to lock her legs around his waist. As she wrapped her arms around his neck, brushing her breasts to his hard chest, she moaned softly when he bit her lower lip, hands finding her arse.

A groan vibrated in his throat when he started kneading at her flesh. He turned them around so she could lean against the boat. Despite supporting himself against her and the boat, he was still kicking his feet, trying to swim, which caused the kiss to be messy and sloppy. He chuckled, and she couldn't help but mirror his delight against his mouth.

His lips found her jaw, her neck, her shoulder. She wanted him everywhere. Her breathing had started to become heavy, and she needed some friction. Some release.

"Thiago," she breathed.

"Let's go inside," he demanded huskily.

They swam towards the platform, and he jumped up first.

He pulled her up, swiftly, easily, and just as he was dragging her towards the cabin, he stopped.

"Give me a sec to just look at you, Kam."

She felt so naked and exposed beneath his dark gaze even with the few layers covering her most intimate body parts. He had threaded their fingers together, eyes not knowing where to settle as he catalogued every single inch of her physique.

"God," he rasped, "You're so fucking sexy."

She smirked. "You're not too bad yourself."

"Not too bad, huh?" He grabbed her jaw, angling her head so she could stare up into his stormy eyes. "Just you wait until I make you scream my name. You won't be thinking of me as 'too bad' anymore."

She grazed her lips to his. "Always words, Valencia. Show me some action now."

Jaw tightening, he nodded slowly before finally pulling her inside the cabin. She didn't have time to look around now that his mouth was on hers again, tongue claiming dominance over her own.

Her hands were on his muscular biceps, his pectorals, his abs. Thiago whimpered when her nail grazed the route of his v-line, inching awfully close to his prominent, hard bulge.

They didn't break the kiss when he sat down on the bench, pulling her onto his lap. Instantly, they started rolling their hips, heavy breaths twining between vehement kisses.

She tangled her fingers through his hair, gently pulling at the roots, causing him to buck his hips upwards. Thiago let his head fall back against the headrest, his blood-rushed lips agape. He held her hips and guided her against his erection, eyes rolling when she applied the perfect amount of pressure to make the both of them writhe.

"Feel how hard I am for you, Kam? Does this feel fake to you?"

She looked at where the outline fitted between her thighs as she grinded on him. He was big, thick, throbbing. She could still remember how she had barely been able to put him inside her mouth. She could feel herself grow more and more slick with arousal, and she needed all those barriers between them gone.

Their breathing was in sync, heavy and staggered. As he let his lips trail down her jaw, he peppered kisses on her neck, and throat, and collarbones, until he reached the swell of her perky breasts. He licked a path down the valley of them, causing her to tip her head back as she let a breathy moan out.

"How long have you been waiting for this moment, Thiago?"

"Since the moment I laid eyes on you. You have no idea how much I think of you when I shouldn't."

"Do you now?"

"Yes, but this, right now, isn't about me."

He grabbed her by the waist to pull her off his lap, and told her to sit on the bench. She watched him in confusion when he rose, but when he kneeled before her, she was starstruck.

"Don't you look handsome begging on your knees for me, Valencia?"

He scoffed. "Enjoy it whilst you can, baby."

He pushed her knees apart, draping her legs over his shoulders whilst his calloused hands ran over her shins. He started peppering her inner thighs with small kisses whilst a hand started caressing her ribs, always halting below her breasts.

"Tell me what you like, pretty girl," he asked as his lips inched closer and closer to her core.

Her mind was suddenly blank. "I—"

His stubble tickled her flesh. "Hm?"

"I'm not sure."

He glanced at her, a small frown on his brows. "What? Has no one ever gone down on you before?"

Unable to voice her words, she only shook her head.

Thiago blinked before rising up until he could cradle her face, gently putting her feet on the edge of the bench. He brushed her lips to hers. "Could your ex make you come?"

Another shake of her head.

"Ever?"

"Ever."

"You've never—"

"I have," she cut in, slightly embarrassed. "On my own, you know."

His eyes flashed, like he was imagining Kamari touching herself whilst thinking of him. His burning fingers slid down her stomach to rest on her covered core, middle finger pressing small circles on her clit, causing a gasp to build in her throat.

"You're a little slut, aren't you?"

She smirked. That mouth of his would ruin her. "Only for you."

"Fuck, Kam." Hand baring her throat, he tipped her head back and kissed her slowly yet deeply, causing a soft moan to echo inside the small cabin whilst she started rolling her hips against the hand buried between her thighs—slow, torturous. "I'm going to make you scream. Going to make you come so hard that you will crave my touch, my tongue, and my cock. Going to ruin you for every other man." Kneeling again, he held her gaze. "Are you sure you want this?"

"Yes, Thiago. Make me feel something."

"Anything for you, baby."

Pulling her flimsy bikini bottom aside, he groaned at the sight of her bare, gleaming core. "Even your cunt is perfect. And look at you soaking wet for me."

She bucked her hips forward. "Hurry up, Thiago."

"As much as I love seeing you so desperate for my tongue, I'm going to ask you to be patient, love."

Her despair was his greatest entertainment. He smirked when she huffed. Slowly, as he draped her legs over his broad shoulders, he kissed her inner thighs, and finally latched his lips where she needed him most. She instantly leaped her pelvis upwards, the pleasant surprise of warmth and wetness on her clit making her squirm.

"Oh," she moaned softly, her brows knitting together.

He looked up at her whilst licking a flat stripe from her entrance to her clit. "Do you think you can be quiet? I don't want the whole ocean to hear the sounds you make because they're all for me."

She nodded, threading her fingers through his hair. "Yes."

"Good girl."

His tongue found her clit again, sucking and licking. He moaned at the taste of her arousal coating his tongue, sending vibrations throughout her body.

"You taste even better than what I've imagined."

She started rolling her hips against his mouth, the sound of her arousal mixing with his saliva resonating in the small space. She threw her head back, pulling at his hair, back arching.

Thiago knew how to work his expert tongue, sometimes licking flat and slow stripes along her folds, sometimes sucking at her clit, causing her breaths to grow heavier.

"Eyes on me, baby."

She looked down at dark grey eyes as he sucked on her clit. Maintaining her gaze, he inserted a finger in.

"You're so wet and so tight," he murmured huskily. "I'm going to destroy you."

She didn't care if he would be the reason for her ruination.

"Shut up," she breathed, bucking her hips.

"God, you're so hot," he mumbled between breaths before going back to devour her with abandon—like a man starved.

She grabbed his free hand and put it on her breast. "Touch me, Thiago."

He groaned against her. Slipping his hand under her bikini top, he cupped her breast, grunting at the feeling of her full flesh in the palm of his hand. He focused on pleasuring her by thrusting his finger in and out, sucking on her swollen bud. Pinching her taut nipple, he rolled it between his thumb and forefinger before grabbing her breast again. She put her hand on his, her breathing ragged as he moaned softly against her clit.

"Come for me, Kam. Let me see you fall apart."

She could feel that familiar bubble rise deep inside her core, the pleasure intensifying when he added a second finger. Curling his digits upwards, they brushed at the spot that caused white stars to blind her vision.

The pace of his thrusts became rapid, falling in rhythm with the lapping of his tongue on her wetness.

She felt her legs tremble, her walls clenching around his fingers. Reaching the pinnacle of pleasure with breathy and staggered moans, Kamari came undone, hard. Her hand flew to her mouth to muffle her cries whilst he helped her ride down her high by sucking every last drop of her arousal.

Her chest rose and fell as she tried to regain her breath. She cradled Thiago's face, forcing him to meet her lips. Rapidly, she wiped the trail of saliva and excitement dribbling on his chin, and he whimpered when their mouths crashed as he kept on palming her breast, like he couldn't get enough of her. Like he needed to realise she was real. She moaned at the taste of herself on his lips and tongue, craving more.

Gliding her hand down his muscular torso, she started palming his hard erection, but he grabbed her wrist. "This was about you, Kam. But keep in mind that from now on, you're mine."

She couldn't admit it verbally, but Thiago had ruined her for any other man, and therefore, she supposed it made her his.

CHAPTER THIRTY-SIX

⚑ *MARINA BAY, SINGAPORE*

"How nice of you to join us, Thiago. A big standing ovation for the Crown Prince of the paddock, please."

Suppressing the urge to roll his eyes at the condescending tone of the reporter, Thiago pressed his lips into a tight smile and took a seat between Huxley and Beaumont.

Thursdays during race weekends were called 'Media Day', during which all twenty drivers had to attend press conferences, interviews, and other PR activities around the circuit.

Racing in Singapore was one of Thiago's favourite moments of the season for three reasons:

1. It was a street race, meaning they'd be driving through the roads of Singapore.

2. It was a night race, which made the thrill of speeding under the glow of street lamps even more exhilarating.

3. Marina Bay was one of his favourite tracks.

"I'm five minutes late," he drawled, leaning back in his seat, arms folded across his chest.

The small room was filled with a dozen of sports journalists with the Head Reporter of F1 sitting at the front, asking questions to the drivers who usually came into the room in groups of three or four.

"Well, how about I address the first question to you? Since, you know, we've been waiting for you and all?" Franklin Harlow was a man full of vices Thiago couldn't stand.

He waved a hand in the air, then took hold of a microphone. "Sure, go ahead, Frankie. I'm here for that, aren't I?"

Standing in the back of the room was Leo next to Ava, both of them watching him with pinning glares. He looked at them, shrugging coyly before offering a sheepish smile to the reporter.

Franklin glanced at the tablet resting on his lap. "We are six races from the end of the season and your contract with Primavera hasn't been renewed yet. What are your personal plans? Do you still want to race for them?"

Thiago's jaw ticked. "A lot can happen during those upcoming weeks."

"Are you saying there is a possibility of you signing with another team?"

"That's not what I said."

"Are you in touch with another team?"

"None of your business."

"Let's suppose you and Simon Romano can't agree on a contract renewal—"

"I'm keeping an open mind," Thiago snapped. "But my future remains with Primavera."

"Is that all you have to say?"

"Yep."

Primavera Racing was his family, his life, his father's legacy. He didn't care what it would take to stay with them.

"Okay," Franklin trailed, brows raised. "You've brought

upgrades to your car last week. What result are you expecting for Sunday's race?"

"What do you think, Frankie? Which driver doesn't want to finish P1?"

Miles leaned towards him, baring his microphone with his hand. "You're going to make him cry."

Thiago scoffed, depositing his own microphone on the table. "Good. He's already a crybaby anyway."

Beaumont's snort was audible, and Huxley only shrugged, unimpressed by Thiago's indifference.

The rest of the press conference was a blur to Thiago because the instant he understood Franklin wouldn't address questions towards him, he only stared ahead and blocked the rest of the world out. He thoroughly ignored Leo's gaze, and peered at Ava who was rapidly typing on her phone—always ready to defend him, always ahead of everyone else to see what the media would say about his behaviour.

Not that he cared, anyway.

But he needed to start caring. He needed to put effort into being a good person outside of racing.

When the signal was given for the three drivers to be dismissed, Thiago rose from his seat, bowed at his waist, and said, "Have a lovely day, gentlemen."

He walked past Ava and Leo, bracing himself for the storm that would wind itself into his face.

"In here, Valencia," Leo asked firmly from behind. "Avery, come in, too."

Thiago threw his head back, groaning.

"I don't want to intrude," Ava said quietly.

"I need you to be there so I don't murder this little piece of shit."

Thiago watched Ava walk into the room, albeit reluctantly, and he followed closely, shutting the door behind him. Leaning against it, he buried his hands in the pockets of his trousers and met Leo's wrath-filled eyes.

They had entered a room in the FIA's building where there were only a few tables and chairs.

The silence was heavy for a moment, and he jutted his chin towards his agent's chest. "Go ahead, Leo."

His agent threw his hands in the air. "What's the matter with you?"

Thiago shrugged.

"Arriving late at the press conference—again? Talking like this to Franklin? Leaving the charity gala early to go make out on the beach? Did you forget you're on the verge of losing your seat?"

The athlete huffed. "Look, I arrived late because I was chatting with a fan outside the building. It's not like I was busy taking a nap or some shit. And the gala was boring as fuck! I saw you fighting your yawns before they invited people to join the dance floor, so don't be a fucking hypocrite, McConnell. I was with Kam, too, not with some random chick."

"Are you aware Romano is looking at options to replace you?"

He wasn't. Thiago knew he wasn't. Leo was only trying to get a reaction out of him.

He lifted his shoulders in a nonchalant shrug. "He can replace me for all I care, but he can say goodbye to another constructor's title then."

Leo took his glasses off to put them on top of his head and rubbed the bridge of his nose. "Okay, tone it down with defensive behaviour and sarcasm. What is going on?"

"Nothing, Leonard."

"It's Leopold."

"Same shit." Thiago exhaled, frustrated. "You need to stop beating my arse. All I saw about the night of the gala were pictures of Kam and I, having fun, and nothing linked to my future with Primavera."

Leo gestured to Ava who was glancing at everything but

them. "Yes, 'cause your amazing PR officer has managed to take all those posts down."

"What do you mean?" He looked at Ava. "Ave, what is he talking about?"

Her brown eyes collided with his. "It's nothing bad, I promise. Just a few posts on gossip pages where people think you're distracted."

"Distracted?" he echoed, bemused.

Leo sat on the edge of the table behind him. "Kamari's a distraction."

Molten rage started seeping through his veins as he furrowed his eyebrows. His hands curled into fists in his pockets, and he tightened his jaw. "What the hell do you people want from me?" he smouldered with resentment. "If I'm seen with a model, I'm distracted. If I'm seen with my best friends on my boat, I'm distracted. If I'm seen with my actual girlfriend who happens to be the most amazing, supportive woman to ever exist, I'm distracted? Sorry to break it to you, but I know how to dissociate personal life and racing."

"Yes, but you left with her—"

He pushed himself off the door. "Are you saying she influenced me into leaving the gala? She didn't. Don't bring her into this. She would never ask me to choose between her and racing."

"I never said that," Leo said with a shake of his head.

"Yeah, but you implied it very fucking loudly."

Leo swallowed thickly. A beat passed, and he sighed. "You're falling in love and I fear it's distracting you from your goals."

"Why don't you start being happy for me instead of coercing me into thinking she's a bad influence? She's the best thing that's ever happened to me, Leo. I need you to see that." He turned on his heels, still trembling with rage. "Now, if you'll excuse me, I have to shoot a video with Rowan for the YouTube channel."

Aggressively, he opened the door and left the building, Ava following closely.

"I'm sorry, Tito," she said softly. "I thought it was best to take those posts down."

He glanced at his PR officer, his fury slowly dissipating. "You did the right thing. Thank you."

She nodded. "I've got your back."

He smiled, draping his arms around her shoulders. "And I've got yours. I'm going to make a quick call before joining you in the motorhome to shoot the video, yeah?"

"Sure, whatever you have to do." Parting ways, she turned to look at him. "Are you aware she did the impossible?"

He knew who Ava was talking about. He frowned. "What do you mean?"

"All those rules you set for yourself, you broke them for her. I know you don't talk to anyone about your feelings, the way you've been dealing with your father's death. But I do remember you telling me you didn't want to bring any girl into the paddock unless you were sure of her. I know you were convinced that no one would love you because the rest of the world sees you as ruthless and cold-hearted. She sees you, and she's good for you."

Before he could answer through the lump stuck in his throat, Ava walked away after sending him a soft smile.

> **@THIAGOVALENCIA**
> Are you busy?

It would be eight in the morning in London, but he knew she was already working, or at least awake.

Her response was instant.

> **@KAMARI.MONROE**
> Getting ready to meet with an architect

> **@THIAGOVALENCIA**
> Can I call you?
>
> I miss the sound of your voice.

That was something Leo couldn't understand—the fact Kamari kept him grounded. That she managed to make his inner turmoil go away with a mere smile. That she would never be a distraction, but rather, his salvation.

All those people thought their love was for show, but he'd die for Kamari in secret.

"Hey," she said as soon as he answered the call. "Is everything okay?"

"All grand." A smile spread across his lips. "Weird question, but what's your favourite planet?"

A beat passed, and he wondered if she, too, was looking at the sky. "Saturn."

He grinned. "Mine too."

CHAPTER THIRTY-SEVEN

📍 *LONDON, ENGLAND*

"SPECIAL DELIVERY FOR Miss Kamari Monroe."

Peering up from the tablet in the palms of her hands, Kamari frowned when Diana approached the counter with a bouquet of flowers in hands.

"Are these from you?" she asked her friend, putting the tablet down to grab the flowers.

"Have you looked at me?" the redhead scoffed. "I don't gift flowers."

"Grumpy," Kieran said as he passed by them, a tray filled with teacups and pastries in hand. "Got a secret admirer, Kam?"

"Secret-not-so-secret," she said, admiring the white cosmos.

A smile touched her lips as she grazed the petals with her fingertips. Finding a note attached to it, she grabbed the small card, and she felt like her heart was ready to burst at the seams, dividing itself into millions of irreparable pieces. Still, even if she was convinced a broken heart could never be mended, she thought of silver eyes, knowing the man who bore that starlit gaze had been able to repair those shattered fragments.

To the moon, and to Saturn.

-T.

She wasn't sure what the meaning behind his written words was, but she felt warmth blossom inside her chest—something she had longed to feel for a very long time.

"Are you blushing?" Diana asked, snapping her out of her daydream.

"God, no."

She was.

Rapidly going into the backroom to retrieve a vase, she came back to the front of the café to see Diana snapping a picture of the bouquet with her phone.

"There," Diana said coyly, putting the phone back next to the register. "I put the photo on your story and tagged your beau."

Kamari rolled her eyes. "Thank you for your service."

"Anything for my bestie," Diana teased, helping herself to a chocolate chip cookie when she sat on a stool. She watched Kamari put the bouquet into the water before asking, "So, what's the deal with him, anyway?"

Kamari made sure Kieran was out of sight. "Nothing."

Diana pointed her biscuit at the cosmos. "That's not nothing to me, Kam. Unless it's part of the, you know,"—she lowered her voice into a whisper—"the plan."

Kamari shook her head, slightly frowning. She grabbed the vase, rounded the counter and placed it on the centre of the biggest table which was currently unoccupied. "I don't know what this is. But you know all of this is over once he renews his contract."

"Well, what if it didn't have to end?"

For some uncanny reason, Kamari could feel her chest tighten. She sat next to her friend. "I don't think he wants something more. He just wants to win the championship."

"Are you sure about that? This man has changed you, Kam. You're so different now."

A few heartbeats passed. "Good or bad different?" she asked, voice cracking unwillingly.

"Definitely good," Diana replied softly. "You smile easily, you go out, you travel. You've got that glow that had faded away when you were with James. He's really good to you, Kam. Even your brother thinks that."

She darted her gaze towards where Kieran stood, the empty tray cradled to his chest as he chatted quietly with a blonde woman whose face looked familiar.

"And look, I don't follow gossip within the F1 world, but if you ask Indy, I'm sure she'll say everyone thinks Thiago has changed as well. Outside of racing, I mean."

Amidst those rules and games and secrets, desire had managed to be more powerful, and craving for something as utopian as love had brought daylight to the darkest corners of her soul. Amidst the certainty she would never feel loved again, she realised she had broken her rules for Thiago, and that he had managed to find his way to her heart through the tangles of brokenness and the unyielding thorns that had once protected her.

To conceal the way she was reacting to the realisation, Kamari scoffed. "Since when are you a love expert, Di?"

Her phone chimed, causing her to ignore Diana's retort.

@THIAGOVALENCIA

I didn't send those flowers for you to put on your story

Though I appreciate the effort

I sent those to you because you deserve all the flowers in the world

@KAMARI.MONROE

You're a charming man

Thank you

I love them

@THIAGOVALENCIA

I'm glad

I'm sorry I can't make it to Kieran's bday party tonight.

Have fun

Pls don't overstress yourself with organising and all. xx

@KAMARI.MONROE

I'll try.

Good luck for quali

He replied with a fingers crossed emoji, and she smiled.

MUSIC WAS BLASTING, the notes reverberating off the walls of Dawn's Café. Kamari peered behind her shoulder with empty bottles of liquor in her hands, smiling when she watched Indy and Diana stroll through the kitchen door, their eyes full of glee and raw happiness.

"For someone who hates her own birthday, you sure do know how to throw a party for your brother," Indy noted as she hopped to sit on a counter.

"Off," Kamari urged firmly, gently nudging her friend's thigh with a bottle. "Who knows where your arse was before sitting on the table where we make our croissants every morning."

"Party pooper," Indy drawled before getting back on her high heels.

"Are you hiding?" Diana asked, plunging her hand into a packet of crisps. "People are having fun out front."

Kamari put the bottles on a table before leaning the small of her back against it. "No, I'm just making sure everything's perfect. I'm about to bring the cake out."

"We barely saw you," Indy whined, then took a large sip of her beverage. "Everything is amazing, Kam. Come and have a drink with us."

"Can't."

Diana rolled her eyes. "You need to relax," she said between two mouthfuls of crisps. "And stop overworking."

Indy snorted softly. "Did you take a proper look at Kam? That bitch can't relax unless she's with her boyfriend."

The redhead cupped her hands around her mouth, and whispered, "Fake boyfriend."

Kamari made sure to glower at her two friends, just to hide the way her cheeks started to redden. "Are you two here to annoy me or what? If yes, please go back to getting shit-faced."

Indy elbowed Diana, blatantly ignoring Kamari's presence. "Look at the stars in her eyes. Look at her small smile. Faking it, my arse."

Kamari was about to defend herself but her words got stuck inside her throat when a shadow loomed in the doorway. She narrowed her gaze on the intruder, folding her arms across her chest, instant irritation rushing through her veins.

"Party's out front," she bit out, coldly.

James lifted his empty bottle of beer. "Here to give you this. Heard you were collecting trash."

"Talking about yourself, are you? I'm glad I threw you away."

She watched her ex-boyfriend's expression harden as he maintained her chilly stare.

"What is he even doing here?" Indigo asked Kamari.

She shrugged, nonchalant. Still, resentment was flaring inside her gut. "Apparently my brother is still friends with him."

"That's so shitty," Diana said. "After the way he treated you? Kieran needs to sort out his priorities."

James waved his hand in front of Diana's eyes, causing her to bat him away. "I'm still here."

"And you shouldn't be," Diana countered aggressively. "I'd suggest you leave before I vomit on you."

"There's nothing sexy about vomiting, Diana."

"And there's nothing sexy about a cheater," she retorted, causing the room to fall silent for a few heartbeats.

Kamari's shoulders tensed as she dropped her gaze to James' unfastened necktie, noticing his flushed cheeks and hooded eyes. "What do you want?"

"Can I have a word with you?" he demanded quietly. "Alone?"

Though Kamari was holding his gaze, she saw Indy move from the corner of her eye, like she was ready to push James out. But for some uncanny reason, she felt like she needed to have this conversation. Felt like she needed some sort of closure—the one he didn't give her, the one she deserved.

Despite the misplaced bitterness flooding her veins, she said, "You have ten minutes before I throw you out."

Indy and Diana glanced at each other.

"You sure, Kam?" Diana asked.

Kamari nodded. "I can defend myself. You two go out and have fun. I'll join you in a bit."

It was only when they were left alone that James rolled his tongue over the front row of his teeth. He stayed in the doorway, far away from her. "Where's that boyfriend of yours? You know, the race car driver who appeared out of nowhere, who started dating you when you swore you'd never go out with a boy again."

A scoff rose from the back of her throat. "Listen to what you just said. I said I'd never date a boy like you, but he's a man. And for your information, he's in Singapore, and about to win a Grand Prix."

His eyes narrowed. "Since when are you looking for attention? Dating a famous athlete? F1 isn't even a sport—"

"Save your breath with your irrelevant facts." She would defend Thiago with her life, but also his passion, his universe. "You should do some research before saying things like that."

He ignored her remark. "This isn't going to last. Look at you, he can't even commit to a family event and be there for you. He's going to leave you for someone who's not a control freak. Who doesn't spend her evenings buried under blankets with a stupid book. He's going to leave you for someone else like I did because he'll be bored."

His words didn't hurt her. Not anymore. He was just trying to get a reaction out of her, and she refused to give him that satisfaction.

He continued when she didn't react, placing his bottle on the table to his left. "He's playing you, you know. Did you see the pictures of him partying whilst he travels without you? All those gorgeous, sexy women in his arms? You're nothing compared to them."

She didn't believe him. Didn't want to. She trusted Thiago. But she couldn't help but feel small and insecure at the thought of not being enough—again.

She scoffed softly then. "You know what your problem is, James? You can't move on, and you can't stand the fact that I have. You can't stand the fact I found someone better than you. He loves me despite my flaws, he pulls me back up when I'm at my worst, and he doesn't treat me like shit. He doesn't have the superiority complex you have. You always had to bring me down, never cared about me, and I don't know why it took me so long to realise I was simply a trophy to you."

His pupils flared with fury, but when he opened his mouth to speak, no sound resonated because he knew she was right.

"I truly loved you," she said. "But I was young, naive, and I let you tarnish my flame. I never wanted your downfall, you know, because I think I gave you the world. But I wish you were a better man who could've sat down and told me what wasn't working in our relationship, but instead, you walked away like a coward and kept being a pathological liar. I feel sorry for you. I really do."

"Kamari—"

She held a hand up, pushing herself off the table. "And whilst I'm at it, I'm going to twist the knife in the wound because you deserve to endure the affliction you put me through by cheating on me, repeatedly. Thiago makes me feel things you've never given me in five years. He encourages me to burn bigger, to shine brighter. You can try and spread every rumour you can, but I won't believe you. He's a better man than you'll ever be. So please, grow up, and move on."

Her heart thundered erratically, her head was spiralling, and molten anger was stirring within her.

"Bitch," he muttered resentfully, then took long strides into the room. She didn't move. Didn't look away. "I can't believe I ever dated you. You're such an attention-seeking whore—"

"What's going on in there?"

Kamari had never been more grateful for her brother to appear during a moment of distress like this one. She took the opportunity of James looking behind his shoulder to step to the side—to feel less suffocated.

"Just catching up like old friends," James explained, a faux smile on his lips.

She scoffed. *Boys never grow up.*

"Really?" Kieran flickered his gaze from James to his sister, uncertainty shimmering in his alert regard. "Why did I just hear you call her an attention-seeking whore then?"

James shrugged. "Cause she is one. Come on, man. You even told me yourself that you didn't know where that new relationship was coming from."

Kieran stepped into the kitchen whilst glaring at his friend.

"Yes, and? You don't need to insult her. I was concerned because I'm just scared he'll break her heart."

"I'm not insulting her. I'm trying to pry her eyes about the truth of her relationship. That guy is going to leave and find someone better."

"Do you even hear yourself, James?" Kamari's voice cracked because she was so goddamned tired of this situation. "Can you just please walk away?"

"No." He stood his ground, pivoting towards Kieran. Then, he gestured towards Kamari as if she weren't standing there. "Aren't you going to say something about the way she's been acting and dressing ever since she started dating that bloke?"

Kieran frowned, disbelief etched on his expression. "She's a big girl, James. And actually, I'm happy for her. Thiago's a good man. He treats her the way she deserves to be treated. Yes, the sudden change was random. Yes, it was weird to see her date a famous F1 driver—my idol. And so, what, man? There's no point in hiding ourselves from the truth."

James scoffed. "Which is?"

"That she's finally happy. That she's getting out of her shell, that she's not scared of falling in love again after you made her feel like she wasn't enough. You might be my friend, but I'll never forgive you for cheating on my sister. You're so fucking lucky she's a good woman for not giving you shit about your behaviour. For moving on and putting distance between the two of you whilst respecting the fact us two are still hanging out."

James was speechless. He opened his mouth and closed it back, knowing all too well he wouldn't have the last word when it came to the Monroe siblings.

"Leave my party," Kieran demanded quietly, yet firmly.

James didn't need to be told twice. He exited the room, making sure to grab a bottle of Brandy. But before he could be out, Kamari called out for him—because *she* would be the bigger woman tonight.

"Oh, also, Thiago can make me come which is something you've never been able to do. Not even once. Goodbye, James."

Kieran slammed the door shut when her ex-boyfriend was out of sight, slight disgust on his expression. "That last comment was so unnecessary."

Kamari narrowed her eyes. "You've got nothing to say because I've heard you and Tillie shag too many times for the past decade."

A small smile spread across his lips, but he swallowed tightly when Kamari didn't let her guard down. She was trembling with fury, her temper still on the verge of cracking.

"I'm sorry, Kam," he murmured, frowning.

She swallowed the lump in her throat. "For what? For agreeing with him that I was looking for attention? For letting yourself be manipulated by his words and for believing I wanted to get back at him whilst I was moving on?"

"For not believing you. For not seeing how much you actually love Thiago and his world; that your relationship isn't fake or a meaningless fling. And I'm sorry for still hanging out with James after he cheated on you."

As she held her breath, trying hard not to crumble to pieces, she accepted her brother's embrace and wrapped her trembling arms around his waist.

"I love you, Kam. You're the strongest woman I know. I'm proud of the woman you are, of everything you've accomplished on your own. And you might not see it yet, but the whole world loves how Thiago Valencia is when he's in your company."

She sniffled. "I know."

"What can I do for you to forgive me?"

She tightened her hold around him. "Can we hide in here and eat your birthday cake alone?"

Delight could be heard in Kieran's tone. "Took you long enough to ask me that. Just like old times, right?"

CHAPTER THIRTY-EIGHT

📍 *MARINA BAY, SINGAPORE*

"WHAT THE HELL is Rowan doing? Don't let him overtake. I'll give him shit."

"He's faster than you," Luke communicated on the radio. "We need to go with plan A."

"There's nothing to talk about," Thiago bit out as he checked his rear-view mirror to see car number 33 get closer. He narrowed his eyes, then focused back on the route ahead of him. "He's on softs, so of course he's faster than me. If he passes in front, he'll stay in this position for, like, seven laps until he has to pit. That's useless."

"Copy."

"What's my position?"

"Still P3. Twenty laps to go. Gap to Huxley three point five seconds."

Racing under the dark sky and the bright glow of the street lamps, Thiago breathed heavily as he could feel sweat dampen his suit. The humid, warm air didn't help with the combination of the weather and the heat of the circuit.

Rowan was right behind Thiago's rear wing, but the latter managed to escape his teammate before hitting the brake milliseconds before taking the turn.

Turn 13 was the trickiest of the track; short, narrow before leading towards a long straight line.

Thiago saw Rowan attempt an overtake, his front rear wing nearly colliding with his as they took the turn. Thiago was driving on the inside of the corner, Rowan to his right, a wall to his left. Wanting to escape his teammate's trap, Thiago tried to widen his trajectory to force Rowan to stay on the outside. But Rowan, not being able to anticipate Thiago's move, didn't give either of them enough space, causing his front wing to come in contact with the side pod of car number seven.

Thiago braced himself for the impact as his car crashed into the wall.

Time stopped for a fragment of a second.

His heart was battering like uncontrollable tidal waves.

His pulse was deafening and out of control.

And then, he slammed his hands on the steering wheel, repeatedly so.

"Fuck! Fuck. Fuck. Fuck."

Thiago inhaled. Exhaled. Tried to collect his thoughts as the buzzing in his ears vanished.

"You okay, Tito?" Luke's voice resonated in his earbuds.

He breathed shakily. "Yeah. Fine."

Tipping his head back, he lifted the visor of his helmet and shook his head in thorough disappointment.

He had it.

He didn't think he would win, but the podium would've been his.

Unbuckling his seat belt, and taking the steering wheel out, he pulled himself out of the car with the halo's help, shrugging off the stewards that had come to help him and Rowan. He noticed the debris from their collision laying on the concrete. The yellow flag had been brandished, and the cars passing by them were driving slowly, avoiding the scattered pieces.

Thiago glared at his teammate as the latter watched their cars before walking off the track. Anger thrummed through his veins, causing him to quiver with molten wrath.

All eyes were on him as he walked hastily towards the garages. Before he could take his helmet off, he closed the visor back. "Fuck!" he shouted, his dismay muffled as he threw his gloves on the ground.

Cal emerged from the garages, one towel in hand with a bottle of water in the other. Thiago dragged his helmet and bala-clava off and gave them to his physiotherapist, not saying a single word as he kept clenching and unclenching his jaw.

"Are you fucking stupid?" Thiago snapped at Rowan when his teammate showed up a few seconds later, unzipping his suit.

Rowan's chest heaved. "You're the idiot who can't take a fucking turn, Valencia."

"Oh, right, because obviously I'm the one who caused the collision. Who taught you how to drive? You had all the space to take the turn and you had to be on my arse."

"I was faster than you."

Thiago threw his hands in the air. "How's that relevant right now, Rowan? God, I'm about to punch your stupid nose."

Rowan emitted a shallow laugh, curling his fingers in a 'come here' motion that made Thiago's blood boil. "Come on, then."

Thiago took a step forward, untameable fury searing through him. Cal put a firm hand on his shoulder, dragging him backwards. "Easy, Tito. He's not worth it. Not now. There are cameras everywhere."

Thiago scoffed. Gesturing towards Rowan, he groaned. "He's smirking, for fuck's sake."

Emerson's cocky, signature smirk didn't falter, though Thiago knew it was just the façade he liked to put on instead of showing his real emotions. "Keep Valencia on a leash, mate."

Thiago clenched his fists, holding his chin high. "Walk away from my garage."

Rowan bowed at his waist. "You got it, *Your Highness.*"

Not having the patience to deal with Rowan and the rest of the team, he turned on his heel, pushing Cal's hand off his arm.

Finding his engineer's gaze, he swallowed. "I'm sorry, guys."

THIAGO'S THUMB HOVERED the call button for five minutes before clicking on it.

Kamari answered on the third ring. "Hey, pretty boy." There was a pause, then a sound of cutlery colliding. "Hang on a sec."

He couldn't help but smile when she video-called him. Her face appeared on his screen, though she wasn't looking at her phone. Seeing her, even with thousands of kilometres standing between them, felt like a breath of fresh air. A cocoon of solace embracing him. He shifted in the bed, propping an arm behind his head as he watched her talk to someone. Her humongous glasses were falling down her button nose, and her hair was tied into a bun—she was about to eat dinner, he supposed.

Finally, green met silver. "Hey, hotshot."

"Hi, pretty girl." His voice was rough, hoarse. "Who are you with?"

She raised her phone and turned to show the people behind her who were busy in the kitchen. "Kieran, and that's Tillie,"—she pointed to a brunette standing in front of the stove—"his fiancée. Indy and Diana are here, too. We're just having dinner."

"What are you having?"

"I made lasagna and a tiramisu for dessert."

His brows raised. "You'll have to cook for me one day."

She winked. He still wasn't used to that playful, taunting side of her, but he loved it. "That can be arranged."

He cleared his throat. "Did you all watch the race?"

A sad smile touched her lips. "Yeah. Wait."

She walked away from the living room and entered, what he supposed was, her bedroom. She took a seat on her windowsill, and when she looked at Thiago, he noticed the gleam of anguish swimming along the edges of her irises.

She sighed heavily. "How are you feeling?"

"My neck is a bit sore, but I've been through worse. The G-force is insane when we crash. I mean, the crash wasn't even that bad, but you get me."

Kamari brought her knees up to her chest and leaned her chin atop one of them. "I got scared, honestly."

"For me?"

"No, for the car."

He rolled his eyes, amused by her sardonic tone. He was certain he could build a whole castle out of all the sarcasm she'd been throwing at him. "The car's fine."

She was staring absentmindedly at something ahead of her. "Felt like my heart stopped beating when I saw your car go into the wall. It looked brutal."

His lips tipped into a smile. "You were worried about me."

"Was not."

"Was too."

"Maybe a little." She started nibbling on her lower lip, concern flashing in her forest green eyes. "Are you sure you're okay?"

Thiago sighed. "Physically, I'm fine. But mentally? I feel like shit. I had it, Kam. I would've finished P2 or P3, and now I'm, like, so far behind Huxley in the drivers' standings. I hate being the pessimistic dude, but right now it feels like I won't be able to win the championship."

"There's always next week, and the four races after that. You can bounce back, Thiago. You always do. You're an impressive driver. Look at your weekend: you struggled during FP1 and FP2, qualified fifth and managed to gain two positions at the race start. It's okay."

The lump constricting his airway was uncomfortable, but he managed to swallow it. "You always have the right words to say."

A beat of silence. Then, her voice softened into a feathery melody. "Keep dancing through your storm."

He frowned. "Is that something from your grandma?"

She nodded subtly. "Good guess. She'd say this to me when I would struggle to push through hard times. I have a tattoo of it."

His eyes flashed with surprise. "Really? Where?"

"My ribcage."

"I haven't seen it."

Her cheeks flushed. "You were too busy doing something else. But anyway, keep dancing through your storm, Thiago. The tempest eventually settles down. I'll hold your hand the whole time."

He smiled. "Thank you, moonbeam."

"I've got you," she murmured softly.

Heartbeats passed by, and he couldn't detach his gaze from her. She was the most exquisite woman he'd ever laid eyes on, and he wondered what he had done for the heavens to send an angel like her into his life.

"Kam?"

She pushed her glasses back up the bridge of her nose. "Yes?"

His jaw tightened. "I know I shouldn't, but I really miss you."

He watched as her features softened whilst she dropped her gaze to the ground. She chewed the inside of her cheek as though she was refraining herself from saying something. In the meantime, he could feel his heart race, his stomach churn, preparing himself for the rejection.

"Thiago..."

"I know," he said, voice cracking. "I know. I can't help it."

He heard Kamari breathe out, tremulously, and he didn't want to scare her away. Didn't want to lose her because he couldn't control his feelings.

"Tell me about Kieran's party," he pressed then, shifting

onto his side and putting the phone against a pillow to free his hand.

She was silent for a heartbeat, her expression closed off for an unknown reason. "It was fun."

"Yeah?"

And as Kamari went on about the party she had spent hours organising, he couldn't help but smile until his cheekbones hurt and until he could feel his heart fill itself with her—her voice, her smile, her spirit. He listened and listened, never letting his grin falter, and she talked and talked until he finally fell asleep to the sound of her voice.

CHAPTER THIRTY-NINE

⚐ *LONDON, ENGLAND*

"S o, Mister Valencia, you're on pole. Are you feeling confident for tomorrow's race?"

Kamari heard shuffling on the other side of the line, like he was moving around in his bed.

The husky timbre of his voice was muffled by the call. "It's going to rain, and wet races are always crazy. I'm definitely excited."

She tucked the phone between her ear and shoulder as she arranged her coffee table, making sure the candle was perfectly centred. "You'll be careful, right?"

He chuckled. "You act like you don't care about me but you're as concerned as my mother. I will be very careful, Kam. I'm good in the rain."

She hummed. "Yes, I saw it during qualifying."

"Look at you," he said, smiling audibly through his tone. "Being all interested in F1 and watching every chance you get."

"I did a thing, actually." She straightened herself and walked towards her kitchen, feeling like a glass of wine would be much appreciated after this long, exhausting week. "Wanna know about it?"

"Of course. Tell me everything."

She opened her fridge to take out the bottle of white wine Indy had left. "I'll have to show you when you come by, but I made this sort of catalogue with F1 slang, information about the tracks you race on, regulations I should know about and all."

A beat passed. His words were strangled in his throat when he said, "You're joking?"

"Absolutely not. I just feel like you're embarrassed to be seen with someone who knows nothing about motorsports, and F1 especially."

"Kam," he groaned. "I could never be embarrassed. You're a literal treasure, the most fucking beautiful woman to walk the paddock. I'm very happy you're finding more and more interest in my world."

She was glad they weren't video calling because the blush coating her cheekbones was scarlet.

"I owe you that."

"You don't owe me anything."

"Well, I wanted to."

"Thank you," he whispered. She could imagine the way his throat would work as he swallowed, the way his features would soften into tenderness. "It really means a lot."

She opened a cabinet and took a wine glass out. "I think it's ten p.m for you, so I'm going to let you go to sleep. You have a long day ahead of you."

"Wait." She heard him move. "What are you doing right now?"

"Pouring myself some wine. Why?"

A second of silence passed. "I'm not tired."

Had his voice turned huskier?

She stopped in her tracks as she was ready to uncap the bottle, a frown on her brows. "Why? What's on your mind?"

"You."

Her heartbeat sped up. "Me?"

"Yeah," he breathed. "You, Kam."

She leaned against the counter, tucking a strand of hair behind her ear. She could feel her body become warm. "What about me?"

His tone was gruff. Demanding. Punishing. "Go into your room."

She felt like she couldn't control her own body anymore. Once she was in her room, she closed the door and leaned against it. "Done."

"Lie down on your bed."

She kicked her slippers off and sat against a mountain of pillows, anticipation coiling inside her stomach.

"I can't stop thinking about you," he admitted gruffly. "Your soft skin, the way you taste, your body, the sound of your moans."

Oh.

"Are you touching yourself, Thiago?"

"Not yet," he said hoarsely. "But I'm so fucking hard just by thinking of you."

She pressed her thighs together. "Go ahead. Touch yourself for me, pretty boy."

She heard his heavy breathing through the phone as she imagined him sliding his hand into his boxer briefs.

"Tell me how you think of me," she asked in a sultry whisper.

"Right now, I'm imagining you sitting on my face and riding it. I'd be grabbing your perfect arse, I'd be devouring you until you came hard."

Her chest heaved. Closing her eyes, she tried to think of how it would feel to have his lips on her again. His hands. His teeth.

"Kam?"

She sucked in a breath. "Yes?"

"FaceTime me right now. I want to try something."

She knew what was coming, and just the thought of it made her core slick with arousal.

He instantly answered the call, and all she could see was his handsome face and the flush on his cheekbones. She almost smiled when his features brightened at the sight of her, despite the dark regard he had given her.

"Set your phone down and strip for me."

She narrowed her eyes. "Say please."

His jaw tightened. "Please, Kam. Be a good girl and take your clothes off."

She smirked. "I love it when you beg."

"Brat."

She clicked her tongue on the roof of her mouth. "Careful, or I'm ending the call."

He threw his head back and groaned in frustration. "Sorry."

"That's what I thought."

The way he looked at her gave her a spark of confidence she didn't know she possessed. He was praising her with his intense scrutiny, was worshipping her.

Grabbing a pillow, she set her phone against it, offering him a view of her, still sitting in bed. She shifted onto her knees and pulled her jumper up.

She heard Thiago suck in a breath. "Did you wear this for a particular reason?"

Kamari looked at herself in the small rectangle in the upper right corner, smirking at the sight of her breasts nearly spilling out of her white lace bra.

"Just for myself."

He rubbed his jaw, eyes wandering over her chest. "God, you are the hottest woman alive."

The sound of his verbal applause gave her assurance. Made her feel powerful.

She tugged her cotton shorts down, showing him the matching underwear as she lied down, prying her legs apart. She let her phone rest on the bed, offering him a full view of her body, but then decided to shift to lie on her side, grazing her nail on the outline of her bra.

He was biting on his lower lip, trying to keep his breaths even and quiet.

"Show me, Thiago."

A whimper fled past his lips—perhaps because of her authoritative tone or because he was already edging himself. He flipped the camera around, and she stopped breathing for a second. His veiny hand was wrapped around the base of his long, thick shaft, stroking it slowly.

"Keep going," she demanded. "Think of me riding you."

"Fuck," he breathed. "That's unfair. Touch yourself too, baby."

She had never done this before—self-gratifying in front of someone else. But the thrill of experiencing new things with Thiago made frissons jolt through her body.

Palming her breasts through the lacy fabric of her bra, she could already feel her peaked nipples straining against the flimsy piece of clothing. She heard Thiago's staggered breaths echo, causing her to clench her thighs together and seek friction. She watched as he pleasured himself, slowly, torturously, to make the moment last.

She turned to lie on her back, one hand tugging the cup of her bra to the side to expose her breast.

His breath hitched. "I love your tits. They're perfect."

She cupped her cleavage. "They're kind of small."

"They're really fucking perfect, Kam. A handful. Soft. Perky. Fucking adore them. Imagine my hands on you—all over you."

She closed her eyes, trailing her other hand down her stomach.

"Right now I'm thinking of taking you from behind," he said. "You'd be on all fours, squirming and writhing under my touch, begging for my cock to fill you up."

Her fingers ran along her folds over her underwear, already damp from excitement. "God, the mouth you have, Valencia."

She could see the smirk on his face. "What about it?"

"I want it on me. Your tongue especially."

He groaned, and she glanced at her phone to see his pace had picked up. "I can't fucking wait to see you."

Dragging her underwear to the side, she gathered her arousal on the tip of her middle finger before circling her clit with it.

"Show me your perfect cunt, Kam."

She moved, spreading her legs in front of the camera, and leaned back on a hand. She went back to circling her clit with two fingers, her motions already fast as she needed to release the pent-up tension.

"Perfect," he praised sultrily. "You're so wet. So sweet."

She moved her hips, throwing her head back when the pleasure started intensifying, breathless gasps flying past her lips.

"I'm going to be thinking about you like this, touching yourself for me, thinking of me, every time I jerk off."

Her breaths were bated, heavy. "What do you usually think about?"

"You. Always you. But now I have a visual image to help me come harder." A groan caught inside his throat when he swiped his thumb over the leaking head. "Do you think about me?"

She picked up her pace. "More than I care to admit."

A soft groan rose from his throat. "I can't wait to fuck you."

"Thiago," she moaned quietly. "Show me your face. I want to see you when you come."

"Fuck." He flipped the camera, and she circled her clit hard, fast. His cheeks were flushed, his lips parted, a small crease between his brows evident. "Say my name again."

She rolled her hips against her hand. "Thiago."

"F-fuck," he whimpered. The sound of his bliss made her legs shake, made stars whiten her vision.

He came with a hoarse moan, throwing his head back whilst his mouth fell agape. His brows knitted even further, unwavering pleasure etched on his features.

The sounds of his quiet whimpers sent her into the pinnacle

of pleasure as she unravelled. Shaking, she fell on her back, soft mewls echoing in her room. Riding down from her high, she pinched a nipple to intensify the pleasure, hips bucking and fingers working in small circles until she stopped spasming.

She lay there, listening to both her heaving breaths and Thiago's as she blinked until the small stars vanished.

"You are definitely the sexiest woman I know," she heard him rasp out after a moment. "Mine."

Kamari scoffed softly, shaking her head whilst adjusting her underwear. She grabbed her phone to look at Thiago, her breath catching when she saw utter awe and adoration in his once lustful gaze.

"Whatever pleases you," she teased, knowing all too well where her heart was gravitating.

He grinned broadly. "Stubborn witch, aren't you?"

She chuckled. "That's why you like me."

His voice softened as he said, "I fucking adore you, Kamari. So much."

Her heart was battering so hard that she felt like it would explode. His gaze was tender, bright, telling her everything she needed to know.

"Thiago?"

"Yes, baby?"

"Come home soon."

CHAPTER FORTY

📍 *SUZUKA, JAPAN*

T HE RAIN DIDN'T stop pouring down for over an hour. Thiago had rarely seen a deluge so violent that they had to delay the start of the race.

Warm coat atop his racing gear and headphones on, he sat on the floor of the garage, bopping his head to the rhythm of the music as everyone waited for the weather conditions to get better.

Cal came to crouch down in front of him, obliging Thiago to pause his music and drag his earphones down.

"There's only a slight drizzle now so they're saying they're going to start the race in fifteen minutes. You'll probably start behind the safety car for a few laps to dry the track out."

"Okay."

Needing to be wrapped in his own bubble for a few more minutes, he put his music back on. Thiago was aware everything was at stake now. There were five races left and he was currently fifth in the drivers' standings. He hadn't talked contract renewal with Simon Romano yet nor hadn't been approached by another team for a possible deal. He wasn't sure what he was doing wrong, but he wouldn't give up.

The next song instantly made him think of Kamari—The Archer by Taylor Swift. He took a screenshot and sent it to her, before skipping to the next song, needing an uplifting rhythm to help him find the right mindset.

> @KAMARI.MONROE
>
> Been awake since 5:45 to watch the race
>
> Hope you guys can go out soon
>
> Be safe xx

HE'D BEEN LEADING the entire race until lap twenty-nine where he lost control of his car whilst taking corner seven. With a trajectory too wide and not enough downforce on the car, he slipped out of the track limits and spun on himself. Thankfully, he managed not to collide into barriers.

"You okay?"

Two cars passed in front of him and he grunted.

"All grand," he answered whilst checking his rear-view mirror. The coast was clear, so he hit the throttle and turned his wheel to go back out on the circuit. The grass was slippery, but nothing too threatening to keep him from chasing the first place.

"It's still a bit wet out there."

"Thank you for the information."

HUXLEY LOCKED his front wheels in the chicane, causing him to hit the protective barrier.

The safety car was deployed for five laps.

The green flag was brandished, and Thiago took the lead back as soon as DRS was enabled.

THIAGO VALENCIA WON the Japanese Grand Prix, setting him into fourth position in the drivers' standing.

It had started pouring again during the podium. Perhaps it was a sign that his father had been watching over him, shedding tears of pride from the heavens.

Drenched to the core, Thiago lifted his trophy to the sky. And when he looked down, Simon and Leo were watching him with wide smiles.

He wouldn't give up on his dreams.

He would prove them wrong.

He would keep dancing through his storm.

CHAPTER FORTY-ONE

📍 *LONDON, ENGLAND*

A BEAD OF sweat cascaded down her temple. Wiping it away with the back of her hand, Kamari sighed, slightly frustrated by her lack of energy. She had spent the whole day here, so it was only evident she was growing tired.

Lowering herself into a crouch, she grabbed the paintbrush and dipped it into the large bucket of white paint. Just as she started drawing a line on the corner of the wall, a loud knock on the window startled her.

Hand on her chest, she exhaled and laid the paintbrush down before strolling towards the door. To keep her new shop a secret from prying eyes, Kamari had draped curtains over the large windows. Warily, she peered behind the veil, her shoulders slumping with relief at the sight of Thiago.

He was standing under the pouring rain, a coy smile on his lips. Instantly, a lump built itself in her throat, and she swallowed it. She could feel her hands tremble as she went to twist the key before opening the door.

Face woven with awe, Thiago meandered his gaze over her face, a soft sigh escaping his mouth. "Hi."

"Hi." Immobile, hypnotised by his presence, she observed his wet, dark locks falling over his brows, droplets streaming down the bridge of his nose. His white shirt stuck to his chest, revealing the outlines of his abs and muscular pectorals. She hadn't been aware he was back in town. "What are you doing here?"

"You need to stop greeting me like this."

She rolled her eyes, causing him to laugh. "Oh, cry me a river."

"You're tense," he observed. "Aren't you happy to see me?"

She was. God, she was so happy to see him despite the reluctance clouding her mind.

She felt suffocated without him. Felt so alone.

But her self-preservation had to kick in. "It's whatever."

Narrowing his gaze, he let her remark slip away, as if he knew he'd be able to tear her walls down soon enough. He lifted a paper bag then. "Hungry?"

She sighed, knowing he wouldn't leave. "Starving, actually."

The corner of his lips turned into a smile. "I had a feeling."

Stepping aside, and with subtle hesitancy, she allowed Thiago to enter the chaos the new shop was in. The space resonated with every footfall and every note of *Fade Into You* by Mazzy Star playing in the background.

The smell of fresh rain lingering on the concrete curled with the scent of his musky cologne, and she felt herself being tugged into an embrace of solace only he could procure, even when he wasn't touching her.

"It might be a bit colder now because I originally stopped by your place, then Kieran told me you were here. And parking around here is so shitty."

She locked the door behind him. "Why didn't you tell me you were back? I would've made myself a little bit more presentable."

She was wearing jeans and an oversized jumper with stains of paint on it.

Thiago chuckled and deposited the bag on the only table in the room, pushing his wet hair back. "You're effortlessly breathtaking, Kam. Besides, it's just me. You know you can be yourself around me."

"Such a flirt," she mustered, indifferent; trying to conceal the slight blush on her cheeks.

"You know it," he said with a grin. Then, his features dropped, a line drawing between his eyebrows. "Are you here by yourself? Doing all of this alone?"

She shrugged. "Yes. I didn't hire anyone to do the painting, so I'm doing it."

"Kam," he whispered, shaking his head. "Don't do this to yourself. You can't bear all that weight and pressure on your little shoulders. You know you can reach out for help, right?"

She pressed her lips into a line. "I know. But you know how I'd rather do everything on my own."

Grabbing her shoulders, Thiago obliged her to sit down. He frowned when he sensed her taut muscles under his palms, then sat beside her and reached for the bag. "My overworking, overachieving girl. Eat something first, then we'll get back to work."

She gaped at him. "We?"

He hummed, smiling softly as he placed a container of pad-thai before her. "A Formula 1 driver knows how to paint."

She accepted the chopsticks he gave her. "I never doubted that."

As they ate, they caught up on each other's past weeks—like two friends, two lovers unable to look away from the other. Unable to realise there was a world outside.

Thiago's regard made flutters grow inside her chest, made her cheekbones burn with an unfathomable timidity. She couldn't push him away if she wanted to. Even if she kept her answers short, cold, clipped, he knew how to treat her with delicacy.

She noticed he was shivering, cheeks coated with a splatter of scarlet blush, goosebumps arising on his forearms.

"Are you cold?" She put her chopsticks down, frowning.

"No," he replied softly, smiling. "I'm good."

"But you're trembling."

He swallowed tightly, the gleam in his eyes foreign yet reassuring. "It's just my body's reaction to your presence. I promise I'm okay."

She wanted to close the sliver of distance between them. Wanted to kiss him because it had been so long since she had felt the softness of his lips, the devotion in his magnetising touch. But she wasn't sure where they were standing, even after everything that had happened between them.

And she couldn't. Not after what she had seen. She needed answers first.

"Good," she said then, taking a sip of water as if it would help calm down her racing heart.

"You're acting weird," he noted, a frown etched on his brows.

Of course, he had been able to see right through her. "I'm not."

"You are."

"You're being delusional."

"Okay?" He peered around the enormous yet empty space. "Tell me what you want to do with this place."

She blinked and stood up. Gesturing with her hands where they were sitting, she explained, "So, the counter is going to be here. It'll be big because it will be the bar, too. Imagine Dawn's vibes, okay? Plants hanging from the ceiling and pretty much everywhere." She walked to the other side of the room. "Over here, shelves upon shelves filled with books and vinyls. Chairs, oak tables, velvet armchairs."

The vision she had in mind was clear and thrilling. She felt like grasping another dream of hers in the palms of her hands.

Thiago was now standing, hands in his pockets as he watched her with tender amazement.

"Come with me," she called, gesturing with her hand for him to follow.

She opened the back door and stopped in the doorway when she noticed the rain crashing down on the terrace. He stood behind her, the heat emanating from his body casting her the warmth she'd been craving.

Screw it, she thought before stepping under the downpour.

"What are you doing?" he chuckled, leaning against the doorframe.

She opened her arms, spinning on herself. "This is my favourite part. I'm going to hang lanterns overhead, put small tables all around, make a cosy place for people to hang out during the day and the evening."

She couldn't care less if she got sick, if her clothes were soaked. Because at that exact moment, Kamari felt free. Happy. At peace with all the choices she had made on her own, with where her future was going.

Thiago met her in the pouring rain. He was the kind of reckless that should have sent her running from the beginning, but she knew she wouldn't have gone far.

"Do you have any idea of how much of an amazing woman you are, Kamari Monroe?"

Gently, he cradled her face in between his large hands, brushing her cheekbones, dusting away the rivulets of rain crashing down her skin. Kamari lost sense of herself instantly as she leaned into his touch, trembling. It was only now that she realised she had missed him—everything about him.

She blinked up at him. "Do you truly mean that?"

A crease made its appearance between his brows. "Yes. I'm in awe of you. Have been since the moment I laid eyes on you. You're so special, Kam, and it's breaking my heart that you can't see it because of someone who has extinguished your flame. Step out of that shadow. Show the world how bright you shine."

Words were stuck inside her throat as she held his starlit gaze. He was sincere, honest, and it caused her heart to burst open.

"Why do you keep running away?" he asked quietly. "What are you scared of?"

Forever is the sweetest con. There's nothing such as eternity.

"I'll take your pain away," he continued when she didn't respond. "Lay your heart open, Kam. I'm here to receive it all."

She exhaled, disliking the lump that had barricaded her airway. "You partied in Japan after your win."

His expression fell, and his eyes instantly misted over. She was so scared of what he was about to admit. Scared of throwing it all to waste. His hands left her face. "You saw pictures of me clubbing?"

She nodded because she didn't trust her voice.

"Kam," he murmured, voice thick. "Nothing happened with those girls. You know I would never do that."

She folded her arms across her chest. "I never doubted you, but James raised my suspicions, and those photos confirmed my doubts—"

"James?" He was nearly roaring with anger now. "When did you see him?"

She closed her eyes, sighing. "At Kieran's party. He said you'd leave me."

She felt his fingers lift her chin up. "Look at me." Green clashed with silver, and his eyes were swamped with undeniable sincerity. "The only woman I want is *you*. James is trying to get to you, he's trying to distance you from me. Those were just pictures taken at the wrong moment. A girl was leaning too close to me, when another was saying something in my ear because the music was too loud. But I didn't touch anyone. Barely looked at them."

"What's stopping you from hooking up with someone else?"

"You! Because I don't want anyone else, Kamari. I know we're not exclusive. I know you don't want us to be, and that's fucking fine. I'll be patient. But I'm also an athlete who loves to party. I attract attention, I attract other people, and you need to be aware of that. I need you to trust me."

He'd been so patient, so loving with her. He deserved nothing but the truth—to see her scars, to look at her demons. "I'm scared of getting hurt, Thiago. You already know I don't do things halfway. When I love, I give my all, and I've been destroyed over and over. I'm just scared of loving again because I know I'll end up having my heart shattered."

Thiago swallowed tightly, carefully listening to her and studying her crestfallen expression. "You know it's different with me. You know I'd never hurt you."

"I know."

"I'd get down on my knees and beg to be loved by you. I'd do anything for you."

A slight shake of her head was perceptible. "You're a fool, Valencia."

"The biggest fool for you, Monroe."

The pad of his thumb brushed her under eye, and before she could say anything, he placed a delicate kiss on her forehead.

Grabbing her hand and lifting it up above their heads, he made her spin around. She felt herself relax under all those uncertainties he'd been able to blow away.

"What are you doing?" she asked between two soft chuckles.

He smiled. "I've heard all hopeless romantics dreamed of dancing in the rain."

Sparks by Coldplay had started playing in the background just as he guided her hands to the back of his neck. He looped his arms around her waist, pulling her towards his chest—tethering the drum of their heartbeats, binding their souls together.

"I always think of you when I hear this song," he admitted softly, brushing his nose to hers.

Kamari fluttered her lashes, accepting his devotion. Accepting the fact she couldn't shield her heart any longer. Her fingers wove through his damp curls, and she couldn't believe she was dancing in the rain with Thiago, standing there with open hands and an open heart. Couldn't believe how much he had managed to change her and wipe her fears away.

"Is this the way you feel about me?"

A dimpled smile graced his features. "It's beyond what you make me feel, Kam." He tucked a strand of hair behind her ear. "You ruined me the moment we met. But you're everything to me now; my peace, my solace, my personal trophy."

"A trophy?" she echoed. She closed her eyes, feeling a fissure in her heart because she didn't want to be that woman to Thiago.

"Kamari." Her gaze found silver, and she observed the adoration swirling around the edges of his irises like shimmering stars shooting through a pool of starlight. "I couldn't have asked better to have a woman like you by my side. Having you trust me with your heart feels like winning everything I've ever wished for. I'm so fucking proud of you that I want to hold your hand and tell the world I'm yours. I'm going to put you on a pedestal. On a fucking podium and let you shine your light."

"Thiago—"

His voice cracked when he murmured, fiercely, "I know. I know you're not ready, and I'm going to wait for you, okay? However long it takes for you to take your armour down. I will fight for you, and I will hold your hand. I will wait for you because you're it for me. I am utterly yours, but I don't want any barrier between us. So please, take your time to tear your walls down. I'll be holding your hand along the way. And fuck your contract, fuck your rules. No matter where I finish at the end of the season, no matter where I'm going next year, I'll still want you. Every day. You're as important as racing to me; you're the only exception."

Fragment by fragment, she felt her heart mend itself back. Shattered pieces by shattered pieces disappeared, now allowing a place for a new love. A new beginning. Something good. Something alive. Something burning like an all-consuming fire, yet thrilling to experience the free fall from the cliff, knowing he'd be there to catch her.

Kamari leaned forward and placed her lips on his, causing him to gasp in slight surprise. She poured all of her feelings within the slow, passionate kiss, letting him know through the entwining of their breaths how much she adored him, silently giving herself to him. He cupped her face, returning her kiss with equal affection and devotion and longing. He kissed her as if tomorrow wasn't promised. Kissed her like she was his salvation.

Breathless, they parted ways.

"Come home with me, Kam," he demanded. "Come home with me and let me take care of you."

CHAPTER FORTY-TWO

📍 *LONDON, ENGLAND*

THE ATMOSPHERE WAS sizzling with burning embers ready to combust into lethal flames.

Kamari was shivering, not only because her whole body was drenched and her clothes were clinging to her wet skin, but also because of the glances Thiago threw at her whilst his hand rested on her thigh, the other on the steering wheel of his McLaren.

Absentmindedly, his thumb brushed slow circles over her clothed skin, sending shivers up and down her spine. She still hated the way he managed to hold a power so devastating over her. No one had ever been able to make her feel this way.

The car ride from Soho to Kensington lasted for less than ten minutes, though it felt like an eternity.

Kamari used the given time to dwell on her sentiments. She understood why she'd never felt like this until Thiago. With James, it felt like it was inevitable because they had been child-hood friends—as though it had been meant to be. But, she barely had that connection she found with Thiago. Barely experienced the thrill of falling in love. Barely learned how to love herself whilst loving her other half. Perhaps she had stayed with James out of obligation, as if they had to owe Kieran something.

She put her past relationship in the furthest corner of her mind, ready to forget about all the affliction she had been through.

It was Thiago's light pressure upon her thigh that made her come back to reality. "We're almost there."

His tone was gruff, a hoarse rasp. She understood he was as nervous, anticipating whatever would happen the moment they'd walk through his front door.

"Can't believe you're taking me to your house without even introducing me to your mother," she teased, trying to ease her hammering heart.

Thiago peered at her. "I'd love to introduce you to her soon. She would adore you."

Kamari looked at the block of houses around, the bubble of nervousness in her stomach growing continuously. He parallel-parked easily, causing Kamari to watch him in awe.

"What?" he chuckled, turning the engine off. His hair was a mess from the rain and the amount of time he had passed his fingers through it.

"I can't parallel-park. You, people who know how to do it, are impressive."

He snorted. "Do you even have your driver's licence?"

He got out of the car before she could respond, rounding it to open the door for her. She scowled, and he grinned. Still, she accepted the hand he extended out.

"I do have it," she answered his question as he laced their fingers together, leading her towards his house. "I just prefer taking the tube because it's easier. I can't stand the traffic in this city."

He grimaced. "Yeah, they're pretty awful."

Unlocking his door, he stepped to the side to let her enter.

He didn't even flick the lights on, didn't let go of her hand even when they took their shoes off. He brushed a kiss to her knuckles before leading her upstairs, not giving her a chance to visit his small house.

She followed him up the narrow staircase and through the dimly lit corridor. He pointed to a few rooms: his gaming room where he had a simulator, a guest bedroom where Alex practically lived when he was in town, his own bedroom, and the bathroom which he led her into.

Kamari inhaled when he slammed the door, letting go of her hand and switching the lights on. She stood in the middle of the bathroom, but her eyes were on him—they always were.

She watched his chest rise and fall as he travelled his gaze from her face down towards the rest of her body. When their gazes collided again, his irises had turned into that shade of molten grey that could ruin her. Their breaths echoed in synchronisation, and when he took one step forward, she met him halfway.

His mouth fell on hers—demanding, punishing, claiming. She instantly wrapped her arms around his neck, pulling herself as close as she could. Warm hands slid beneath her jumper to rest on the small of her back, setting the rest of her body to an unrestrained inferno.

She gasped softly when he pulled her lower lip with his teeth. Blindly, Thiago reached into the shower cubicle and turned the water on, letting it heat as he kissed Kamari's jaw. Sucking on the spot below her ear, she arched into his touch, moaning quietly.

"I need you, Thiago."

"And you're going to have me," he whispered, fingers finding the front of her jeans to unbutton them. "All of me."

Tugging at the hem of his shirt, she allowed him to pry his lips away from her skin to take the piece of clothing off. Her hands skimmed his hard abdomen, nails grazing the outline of his abs, causing him to breathe heavily.

She pressed her lips to the crook of his neck, placing gentle kisses on his throat. "You're every girl's dream, did you know that?"

A laugh escaped as he took hold of the bottom of her jumper. "You're doing wonderful things to my ego, pretty girl."

She smiled against his skin. "Enjoy it whilst you can."

Thiago pulled her jumper off along with the t-shirt she was wearing in a swift motion. His gaze instantly fell on her cleavage, and she made a move to cover herself, but he grabbed her hands.

"You don't have to hide from me. Ever." He lowered himself to brush his lips over the swell of her breasts, hands moving towards her back. "You're perfect to me, Kam. Words can't describe how beautiful you are. Your body, your mindset, your spirit—all breathtaking."

Unclasping her bra, he tossed it away, lips immediately latching around her hardened nipple. Kamari sighed in pleasure, throwing her head back and threading her fingers through his hair. He was already looking at her when she peered down, his tongue flicking against the taut bud, before switching to her other breast whilst palming the other with his big, expert hand.

"Been thinking about these for weeks."

"Really?"

"Yeah," he breathed, grazing his lips at her nipple. "You haunt my dreams, my thoughts."

"Good."

She rapidly unbuttoned his jeans, pulled them down along his boxer briefs, and wrapped her hand around his erection that sprang free.

"Ah, fuck," he exhaled, dropping his forehead on her chest, bucking his hips into her hand. "Been dreaming about your hands and your mouth, too."

"You think of me a bit too often," she teased, her murmur salacious and wicked as she stroked him slowly.

"You've got no idea."

As he tried to push her jeans down, he laughed. The fabric,

still damp from the rain, stuck to her skin, which made it difficult to take off.

"Sit down," he ordered whilst pushing the last pieces of his clothing down.

As Kamari tugged her jeans down, her mouth watered as she drank in the sheer size of him. She rubbed her thighs together, finally sitting down on the edge of the bathtub.

"Patience, pet," he murmured, kneeling before her. He helped her out of her jeans, giggles and chuckles blending with the loud sound of the water crashing down in the shower.

Once she was out of it, Thiago slowly found her gaze, his own eyes dark with desire. He licked his lower lip, hooking his fingers in the band of her underwear to take them off, too.

He trailed feathery kisses on her shin, holding her gaze. She knew she was looking at him with equal intensity. Equal steady and unhesitating longing. "Look at me being on my knees for you. Being at your complete mercy."

She smiled like a triumphant queen. "Such a sight to behold."

He pulled her to stand up, guiding her lips towards his. Their tongues brushed against one another, his hands grasping firmly her arse, his fingertips digging into her flesh. Pulling her chest into his, he moaned at the sensation of her bare breasts crushed against his torso.

Thiago led her into the shower, clouds of steam curling around them. Her back collided with the wall and a soft moan escaped the back of her throat, but he swallowed the sound—like it belonged to him.

He touched her everywhere, as though remembering the feel of her. Then, his fingers slid down the valley of her breasts and her stomach, finding her aching clit. He rubbed his digits along her slick core, causing him to grunt, and finally circled the swollen bud, making Kamari tip her head against the tiles.

She gripped his biceps, digging her nails into his skin, gasping softly.

"Let me hear you tonight," he rasped out against her neck. "It's only the two of us."

Her breaths were staggered as she rolled her hips against his hand. He entered two fingers, eliciting a moan from her mouth, and used his thumb to circle her clit.

"Oh, God," she breathed, wrapping her hand around his throbbing shaft. The head was already leaking pre-cum, and she gathered his arousal on the pad of her thumb.

He sucked on the skin of her breast until he left a mark. "I'm going to make you come so many times tonight, pretty girl."

"Please," she cried when he picked his pace up.

"Please, what?"

"Make me come. I need more. I need you."

Tongue on her nipple, fingers thrusting in and out of her core, other hand palming her arse, Kamari started to tremble when he curled his digits upwards. She came fast and hard, pleasured sighs echoing through the room.

He grazed their lips together. "Good girl."

It took a few seconds for her to come down from her high. In the meantime, he peppered her neck with soft kisses and turned the shower off.

"We'll come back to this later. Come here."

Stepping out of the shower, he grabbed the back of her thighs, hoisting her up until she wrapped her legs around his waist. Their lips crashed into a fiery kiss, messy and sloppy. He walked them into his bedroom and set her down gently on the bed.

He was kneeling between her legs, hands on her thighs, softly caressing her wet skin. He flicked the lamp on and sat there for a moment, admiring her as she lay before him, bare, gleaming, ready.

Thiago's grey eyes found hers as his lips parted. His chest rose and fell, and Kamari couldn't stand that look in his eyes. She didn't want to hear those words yet, and so she motioned for him to inch closer.

Hand bracing her throat, he plunged his tongue into her mouth, punishing her with another kiss that left her breathless and speechless. He trailed his lips on her cheek, neck, and shoulder, down her breasts, where he took the time to take both pebbled nipples into his mouth, before travelling downwards her navel.

His lips on her skin felt like poetry, a poem of unspoken passion, of intense desire she knew he solely possessed for her.

His lips on her skin felt like salvation, a trail of stardust lingering on every inch of her burning flesh.

The sequence of his lips on her skin was a prelude to the song he wanted to ingrain in the back of her mind, a whisper, a promise that echoed, "*I am yours. To the moon, and to Saturn.*"

Kamari gasped when he buried his head between her thighs, tongue flat out against her wetness and collecting every drop of her arousal. Still sensitive from her recent orgasm, she trembled, instantly tangling her fingers through his wet curls. She bucked her hips towards his mouth, causing him to grin smugly before sucking on her clit. He devoured her with abandon, tongue lapping fiercely against her clit, switching between licking and sucking.

"Just like that," she encouraged, panting.

She arched her back when he started palming her breasts. He was breathing heavily against her but was intent on sending her to the stars again. He placed his other hand on her stomach, pressing her into the mattress, and forcing her to stay still. Kamari looked down at him, and when he met her gaze, she came undone again with a loud moan and a tremor in her legs, pulling at his hair.

He sucked her clit until she stopped trembling, until her vision stopped wavering, praising her by emitting soft groans and watching her catch her breath.

"You're going to be the death of me," he droned hoarsely as he crawled back up.

"Good." She wiped the arousal staining his chin, pulling his mouth towards her.

She moaned at the taste of herself on his tongue and reached down to grab his hard, pulsing shaft. Pumping it a few times, she listened to Thiago's heavy breaths before bringing the tip to her entrance. They gasped at the same time when she coated the head of his cock with her wetness.

Thiago broke the kiss, lowering himself onto his elbows whilst grinding against her. He brushed her hair away from her face, and whispered, shakily, "Are you sure about this?"

She flickered her stare between his, nearly melting at the sight of stars shimmering around his dilated pupils. She noticed he was trembling, so she coaxed him by caressing his cheekbones. "Never been so sure of something"—*someone*—"in my whole life."

"Me too," he murmured. "I'm so fucking sure about you. I haven't been with anyone in months, so I'm clean."

"Me too."

He kissed the tip of her nose. "I want to feel all of you, but did you want me to wear a condom or—"

"I'm on birth control. I want all of you, Thiago. No layers in between, no barriers."

He swallowed thickly. "There's only you for me from now on. Always."

She pushed his tip into her entrance. "And you for me."

Slowly thrusting in, Thiago dropped his forehead against hers, brows knitting together. He whimpered, kissing her lips once. Twice. Three times to coax her through the uncomfortable sensation.

"You're so big," Kamari cried out as she felt his shaft stretch her out.

"Keep feeding my ego." He chuckled and kissed her forehead, helping her relax. "I know, baby. I'm sorry. You can take it."

He buried himself to the hilt, dropping his face in the crook of her neck whilst grunting in pleasure.

"Are you okay?"

She nodded. "Move."

Pulling out to the tip, he pushed back in gently. She was already used to his size, caressing his back muscles until her hands rested on his tailbone. Whilst he found a lazy rhythm to bask in the moment, she bucked her hips to meet him halfway.

"I won't last long if you keep doing that," he said, already breathless. "You're so tight. So perfect. Made for me."

"It's okay." She gasped when he slammed in more roughly. "I'm not made from glass. Fuck me, Thiago."

He didn't need to be told twice. Hooking a leg around his hip, he plunged in and out of Kamari, slow yet deep, causing the tip to hit the spot that made her drown in pure bliss. His breath was warm, and she writhed beneath him, arching her back, searching for friction.

"How do you want it, baby?"

She watched his brows pinch together, lips parting and pupils expanding. "The way you've always wanted me. Hard, fast."

He wrapped his hand around her throat. "I'm going to ruin you."

You already have. "Go ahead before *I* ruin you."

"Fuck," he whimpered, lips pressing to the crook of her neck.

He sat back on his heels, holding her hips whilst he picked up his pace, slamming hard and fast into her. Her eyes rolled back when she felt the tip of his cock brush against her sweet spot, fingers tightening around the bed sheets.

"Eyes on me, baby."

She opened her eyes, finding stormy grey irises worshipping her silently.

He groaned. "I can't hold it for too long. I need you to come with me."

His thumb found her clit, applying little circles on the already sensitive bud. Kamari grabbed her breasts, rubbing her nipples, chasing her high as she felt the familiar bubble grow in the pit of her stomach.

"So damn sexy," he rasped, breathless, aggressively thrusting in and out of her drenched core, gaze settled on her bouncing cleavage. Sounds of skin slapping filled the room, yet all she could hear was his claim. "Mine."

"Thiago," she moaned. "I'm so close."

He groaned, satisfied. "Come for me, pretty girl."

The pleasure was even more intense than being fingered or receiving oral sex—it made her whole body spasm, her vision blinded by stars. She and Thiago came in perfect harmony, and he spilled his release deep inside her, collapsing on her chest and stilling. With sloppy, uneven thrusts, he helped her ride down from the high. He kept moaning raspily in her ear, trembling. Slowly, he continued to thrust until every last drop of his cum dripped on the inside of her thigh.

Kamari couldn't breathe properly as her chest heaved, her body quivering after the three orgasms he had given her.

Thiago was the first man to ever send her into the pinnacle of pleasure, and she wanted to cry at the thought. He was the first man to make her feel things she had yearned to experience her whole life.

He pushed himself onto his elbows and looked down at Kamari. His eyes were shining, his face was flushed, and strands of hair were sticking to his forehead.

"You okay?" he asked softly, brushing her fringe away from her brows.

She nodded, unable to retain her smile. "Never been better. You?"

He grinned, and her heart swelled at the sight of his dimples. Of the adoration alighting his clear irises. "Best sex of my life. I'm keeping you, Kam. I swear I am."

She placed her hand above his thundering heart. "I trust you."

Petal by petal, layer by layer, Thiago had found the treasure that was her heart with the delicacy of a feather, the tenderness of a lover. With her, he wasn't the man other drivers feared; he wasn't as ruthless and cold-hearted as he was known to be. Wasn't the careless man who only thrived for success and champagne sprays. With her, he was the embodiment of a radiant star whose purpose was to show her daylight—like a lighthouse through the darkness and the danger of a wave-swept reef in the reckless sea. To Kamari, he was the one who showed her she deserved to be loved at her fullest, and he was the one who gave her the world and its infinity beyond the galaxy.

CHAPTER FORTY-THREE

⚲ *LONDON, ENGLAND*

T HIAGO HAD READ very few novels in his life, but he knew how writers would describe love. He was aware that everyone fell differently—at a different pace, a different strength. And God, had he fallen hard for this woman.

He wasn't sure when he had realised Kamari Monroe was the love of his life. Perhaps she'd been the one the very moment he had laid eyes on her. Perhaps he'd lost himself in the middle of their games. All he knew was that he was absolutely mesmerised by her—captivated, magnetised by the heavy gravity between them.

He would do anything to see her smile, to see the way the corners of her eyes would crinkle whenever she laughed. Would do anything to keep her.

"Why are you looking at me like that?" Kamari asked, a smile touching her lips as she entered his living room, only wearing one of his shirts.

He grinned. "You know why."

She placed the cup of coffee she'd been holding on the table and came towards Thiago. He tugged her onto his lap, bunching her untamed curls in his hand as she leaned in to kiss him tenderly.

This was a new version of Kamari he loved. The softness in her gaze, the delicacy in her touch. But somehow, someway, he had always been able to glimpse the sweetness in her soul.

"I can't get enough of you," he mumbled against her lips.

"Get a grip, pretty boy. I need to leave soon. One of the contractors is visiting the new shop."

He groaned, slipping his hand beneath her shirt to take hold of her hip. "And I need to go to the Headquarters to train on the simulator."

He slowly unbuttoned the shirt when they pulled away, exposing her already hard nipples and her toned physique. A shaky breath fled past her lips when his thumb grazed the side of her breast, and he watched as she parted her lips. He brushed her tattoo, smiling at the sight of the fine-lined petunia flower.

"My Nana's favourite flower," she had explained. *"Strong, difficult to get rid of."*

"A bit like you?" he taunted with a smirk.

"Yeah." She smiled up at him. *"A lot like me."*

"Keep dancing through your storm," he read out loud.

Kamari placed a kiss on his chest—right above his thundering heart. "I'll hold your hand through it."

Cupping her jaw, he brought her lips back to his. "To the moon, and to Saturn."

He was addicted to her lips. To everything about her. He kissed her slowly, pouring out all the feelings he was scared to admit out loud. Kissed her with a vehemence that made her sigh into his mouth. Kissed her, promising he was hers.

Her eyes had turned into a dark shade of green when she pushed herself onto her knees, sucking in a breath when Thiago tugged her lace to the side.

They exchanged a shaky breath when she lowered herself down him, a guttural groan catching in his throat.

She was divine.

Made for him.

He cradled her to his chest, allowing their erratic heartbeats to pulse in perfect harmony, like two metronomes in sync.

I love you. I love you. I love you. He swore he could hear it, but he didn't know whose heart was screaming those words—his or hers.

He held her gaze as she moved up and down at a slow, excruciating pace, pushing her hair out of her face, kissing her nose, her lips, her jaw, her cleavage.

He dug his nails into her silken skin when she clenched around him, a shaky moan evaporating into his mouth.

And through the symphony of their mutual desire, the cries of their desperate hearts, their souls collided and their stars aligned, tethering them into an eternal remembrance of passionate devotion.

Thiago had fallen off the cliff and, unexpectedly, she had caught him. He never wanted to get back up.

"You have ruined me for everyone else, moonbeam." She had erased every other kiss he had ever shared with other people. Had obliterated every souvenir of girls who had never been able to steal his heart like she did. Had eliminated the whole world until it was reduced to her, and solely her. "You've brought me to my knees."

CHAPTER FORTY-FOUR

📍 *AUSTIN, UNITED STATES OF AMERICA*

T HERE WERE FOUR Grand Prix left before the end of the season.

More rumours were circulating about Thiago ending his career, more fans were to believe he'd been chosen as a reserve driver for another team because Primavera Racing was set on letting him go.

And Kamari did not like this. It was evident the lack of response coming from his team principal was destroying him, even if he acted like everything was sorted out.

He'd been silent on social media, not responding to the inquiries about his future. Not reacting to any of the speculations.

She wasn't one to pry in others' businesses, but the more time passed by, the more she realised how much she felt for Thiago. *About* Thiago. She was protective of him. His pleasure was her salvation. His smile was her solace. His heart was her home. And so, his pain was her detriment.

A silhouette passing by in the motorhome caught her eye. She looked away from her laptop, surprised by Thiago's affection when he hovered over her to plant a brief kiss on the crown of her head.

"I'm going to warm up," he announced, a towel and bottle of water in hand.

She smiled up at him. "Good luck, champ."

He nudged her chin with his knuckles. "Where are you going to watch quali?"

"In the garage. I'm just waiting for Indy to come back from her interviews or whatever she's doing around the paddock."

Thiago took a seat opposite her, the soft glow of the sun shining on his sharp profile. "Did she tell you the news?"

"About her and Huxley?"

"No— What?" he gasped after blinking a few times.

Kamari closed her laptop, smiling coyly. "Forget I said anything. You were saying?"

Thiago narrowed his gaze before shrugging her off. "About her applying to be an F1 broadcaster."

Her mind was blank for a second. By the look of his mischievous smirk, it was evident he knew Kamari was unaware of the news. "Excuse you? How come you know about it before me?"

He winked, standing up. "I'm apparently best friends with *your* best friend."

"You're such a piece of shit," she muttered.

He rounded the table, grabbed her jaw and grazed his lips to the shell of her ear. "That's not what you were saying when I had my cock buried inside your tight little cunt this morning."

She batted him away, a rosy tinge flushing the tops of her cheekbones. "I hate you."

He laughed and kissed her cheek. "I know you do."

"Alex is my bestie now."

Thiago waved a dismissive hand in the air and jogged towards Cal who passed by, riding a scooter. "He's all yours, darling. Fair warning, he's the most disorganised dude to ever exist."

Kamari released a sigh, shaking her head. She observed Thiago interact with fans who had the privilege of walking through the paddock before entering Primavera's garage to warm up before qualifying.

"Hey, Kamari," Leo McConnell greeted as he was ready to step inside the motorhome.

"Leo." She stood up, holding her laptop to her chest. "Can I talk to you?"

A frown settled between his brows. "Sure."

He led her towards an all-purpose room in the motorhome, pocketing his phone. He gestured for her to take a seat, and she refused with a small shake of her head.

"Alright, then." He cleared his throat and sat on the edge of a table, crossing his legs at the ankles. He already had a set of headphones around his neck. "Is this about Thiago's contract renewal?"

She nodded, glaring at him. "Any progress?"

"Does he know about this?" About this secret meeting, he meant.

"No, he doesn't, but he'll know about it. I'm just concerned about him and his future."

Leo shrugged. "Well, Romano's just taking his time to consider his options."

"What options? Thiago's the best driver they've had in years."

Leo nodded. "I agree."

Kamari raised her eyebrows, slight annoyance flaring inside her chest. "Then why aren't you doing anything to help him? Aren't you supposed to be his agent? Defend him?"

He sighed heavily. "I'm doing my best, Kamari."

"What more do you need from him to prove he's a good guy? He really wants to continue racing, he's fighting to finish every weekend with good results, and that's not enough for you? Are you all still blaming him for the mistakes he's done in the past? Can't you see he's doing his best? He won two races out of five this second half of the season, he has pushed his car to its limits. And seeing him in the points, on the podium is still not enough?"

Leo's eyes were swamped with emotion as he exhaled. "I am doing everything I can to keep him at Primavera because I know how much this team, this family, means to him. We see the efforts he's been making, I promise we have. But as much as I know how much Tito means to you, I'm going to have to ask you to step back from the situation."

"I know," she said, nodding. "But what am I supposed to do, Leo? I can't stand seeing him so hopeless. I don't want him to give up on himself and his dreams."

For a moment, Leo searched her eyes, her features that were threatening to break. But she kept her composure, chin held high. "You know," he started, "I wasn't sure about you when he first introduced you to us. Because he claimed to be in a relationship out of the blue when I was convinced he didn't want to be serious about anything—dating and racing. But now I see why he's waited all those years to bring a girl into the paddock. All his life, he's waited for someone like you—who supports him, loves him despite his darker days, who will fight the battles with him even if he thinks that's not what you're made for. And I know you won't believe me, but Thiago's my friend before anything, and seeing him happy is all that matters to me."

A lump was constricting her throat, a heavy weight gripping at her heart. "Help him, then. Please."

***

KAMARI HELD INDY's hand as silence reigned in the garage. Starting P3, Thiago waited to hit the throttle.

Her gaze was fixated on the five lights that were, one by one, lighting up to bright red. Nine seconds felt like an eternity. Frozen on the spot, no one could blink as they waited for the lights to go out. And when they did, the garage roared with excitement, blending with the prolonged sounds of engines zipping.

Kamari watched as Thiago slipped in between Emerson and Huxley, claiming the lead within the start.

"That's a good start," Cal exclaimed, clapping into his hands. "Come on, Tito."

"For your dad, man," Alex murmured. "Evan's watching over you."

———

DUE TO POOR STRATEGY, Thiago's team of mechanics wasn't ready with the tyres when he entered the pit lane to box. A pit stop that should have lasted two seconds lasted seven, so when Thiago drove back out onto the track, Huxley and Emerson had been able to overtake him, putting him back in third position.

There were only fifteen laps left.

"*Bande d'abrutis*," Thiago said on the radio, voice stricken with raw anger whilst he pushed his car to the maximum to catch up to his teammate.

"What does that mean?" Indy asked.

"Bunch of idiots," Cal translated.

"They *are* idiots," Alex said. "They called him to box, and they weren't ready and now Tito is losing everything."

Kamari shook her head, deception searing through her veins.

Indy leaned towards her ear. "I didn't know he could speak French. Does he talk dirty in French to you?

Kamari pushed Indy away. "No."

Her friend threw her an amused glance. "You wish, though."

FALLING OFF THE CLIFF

"Who wouldn't?" Alex interfered with a sheepish grin.

BY THE LOOK on his face, it was evident Thiago wasn't happy with the results. He stood on the smallest step of the podium—P3—hands locked behind his back, gaze settled on the horizon.

Kamari's entourage was a blur. She didn't listen to the British anthem as Miles Huxley was claiming the biggest trophy. Didn't clap when Rowan received the second's place medal. All she could do was look at Thiago's face: hard with deception, stricken with self-affliction. He clenched his jaw, shook his head, and sighed heavily.

He put a smile on when Miles started spraying champagne around, minuscule droplets falling towards the crowd. He grabbed his own bottle of champagne, shook it, and started drizzling the other two drivers with the bubbles whilst confetti engulfed them into a cosmos of celebration.

That smile hid the deepest pain.

That smile concealed the hardest reality.

People thought standing on the podium would be the most exhilarating, refreshing feeling, but being on those high steps didn't always mean they had won.

KAMARI OPENED THE door even if he didn't answer. Her heart shattered into an infinity of fragments, scattering into dust in the very bottom of her stomach.

"Can I come in?"

Sitting on the edge of the large bed and facing the window, his head was hanging low between his shoulders.

"You don't have to ask, Kam," he said quietly, a crack in his voice audible. "It's also your room."

For a fraction of a second, he was a blur, and she rapidly blinked her vulnerability away. She closed the door, kicked her heels off and rushed towards the bed. She came to sit behind him, legs on either side of his body, arms wrapped around his midriff. Pressing a soft kiss to the back of his neck, she listened to the tremulous exhale he released, then leaned her cheek between his shoulder blades.

She listened to the steady rhythm of his heart, felt the tension in his physique, the muscles taut with anger beneath her hands.

"I have a feeling you're not happy about today's results."

He scoffed softly but didn't say anything.

"Talk to me, Thiago," she whispered. "It's killing me to see you like this."

He grabbed her hand, lacing their fingers together. She could feel him quivering, but he tightened his grip—anchoring himself to her. With her free hand, she caressed his torso, coaxing him through that wild storm of anger and sorrow.

"I'm just so fucking tired," he whispered. "I feel like I'm the only one fighting. I feel like they purposely want to give up on me."

She knitted her brows together. "They'd be fools to let you go. Your efforts don't go unnoticed, your talent doesn't go unappreciated. I'm in awe of how much you are loved in the racing world, of how many young kids look up to you, of how much you are an inspiration to the future generation. What happened today was not your fault, and I know you made sure to show how angry you were with your team. But look at you, you still secured another podium. You pushed the car to its limits. Pushed yourself to your limits. Keep fighting."

She heard Thiago swallow the lump in his throat, his fingers tightening around hers. "I'm not enough, Kam. I'm not enough and it's driving me insane."

Her heart broke again, and she let go of his hand to move until he allowed her to sit on his lap. He was looking down, refusing to meet her gaze. Delicately, she cradled his face, bringing her favourite colour towards her.

A sorrowful gloom had misted over his eyes, causing the grey to look like a pool of molten crystals, veiled by sadness.

"You, Thiago Valencia, are more than enough. You have a unique string of light, a heart made of pure gold. You fight for the ones you love, you hold onto them and tell them they, too, are enough. You've been fighting like a fierce soldier, and now it's their turn to see how important you are to them. They'll be making a huge mistake if they let you go. They'll lose their best driver—both on track and as a human being."

His lower lip quivered, and when he blinked, a tear escaped. And another one. Another one. Until his cheeks were stained with teardrops which Kamari wiped away with the pads of her thumbs.

Gingerly, she wrapped her arms around his shoulders, and he returned her embrace. He held her tightly, trembling as he buried his face in the crook of her neck.

"I've got you," she murmured, threading her fingers through his hair, and coaxing him through this moment of anguish. "It's okay. You don't have to be the best all the time. You don't have to act like it's easy, and okay, all the time. You're the strongest person I know, Thiago, but I'm going to ask you to let it all out. Don't bottle your feelings inside. Let go of your pain. I've got you."

All she could do, at that moment, was hold him. Listen to his muffled cries. Be there for him.

She felt a tear of her own fall down her cheek, because hearing his sorrow felt akin to being stabbed countless times in the heart.

"Tell me how I can help," she asked when his cries became quieter. When he had let go of his affliction.

"Just hold me. Hold me and don't leave me."

"I won't." She closed her eyes and gave him every ounce of love she possessed and found deep within her soul. "I promise."

He had helped her come to the surface. Had helped her breathe. Because for years, and without realising it, she had been drowning and trying to overcome the bruises her past had marked upon her heart.

And Thiago had held her hand the whole time, finding a rhythm that matched her pace to finally heal. Together.

Naturally, she'd help him, too.

CHAPTER FORTY-FIVE

H IS CHEST ROSE and fell in steady patterns as he traced the contour of Kamari's face with his lazy gaze. Drawing intricate shapes on her bare back, he observed the chills rising on her skin. Studied the way her lips were slightly parted whilst small puffs of air escaped. Catalogued the features he'd always been attracted to and thought about her fiery spirit he had fallen in love with.

"Moonbeam?" he whispered.

She didn't so much as move.

He could hear it in the silence—those three words that needed to escape.

"You're my best friend, Kamari," he whispered as the tip of his forefinger traced a light-feather route between the sprinkle of freckles dusting over the bridge of her nose, like he was drawing constellations on her skin. "My everything."

He let a beat pass, waiting for a reaction, but she looked so serene beneath the moonlight's glow. He sighed, unable to take his eyes off her.

"I don't know where I would be today without you. I think I would have lost sense of myself, trying not to drown under all that pressure. Mere weeks ago, I was convinced redemption would never be mine, but you've guided me towards salvation, towards light. You showed me that winning isn't everything. You gave me a purpose outside of racing."

Her lids fluttered, but her gaze was still hazy with fatigue as she barely kept her eyes open. "What is it?" she asked, almost inaudibly.

He traced the outline of the lips he was addicted to, listening to the deafening thrum of his heartbeat. He waited until her breathing became steady again, and he finally found the courage to say, "Loving you. You are the essence of my devotion, my heart's salvation. You're everything I have ever dreamed of."

CHAPTER FORTY-SIX

📍 *MEXICO CITY, MEXICO*

"VALENCIA, COME IN here."

Exchanging a confused glance with Cal, Thiago entered the room Simon used as an office in the motorhome.

Leo slipped in behind, causing the cloud of turmoil inside Thiago's head to grow bigger.

"Close the door," Romano asked.

Thiago did so, and instead of taking a seat at the bureau with his agent and team principal, he leaned against the wall, tucking his hands in the pockets of his trousers. He had just changed out of his racing suit and was ready to leave the circuit after this exhausting day.

"I know my results during FP1 and FP2 weren't the best," he started, holding his team principal's gaze. "But I've talked about the issues on my car with the mechs and we'll be testing with the upgrades tomorrow during FP3. I know I'm not living up to your expectations, and—"

"You're a hard-working man, Thiago," Simon interrupted. "The spitting image of your father. Ruthless and rough on the edges, skilled in the rain, heartless whenever it comes to the trophy that's supposed to be yours. You don't give up easily. Isn't that right?"

Thiago clenched his jaw and dipped his chin in a nod. "Yes, sir."

Simon blinked. "Why are you calling me sir? We've known each other since you were a baby; I'm like an uncle to you. Cut your crap for a second."

"I don't know what I'm supposed to be calling you nowadays, Simon."

The man in the red polo sighed. "You know I consider you like my own. You've been with this family long before you started racing in F1. I taught you the best tricks at karting, I got you into Primavera Academy. You owe me everything."

"I've never been ungrateful to you, Simon. You know I'd never be here without your help."

Simon cast a glance towards Leo who had been sitting in silence, admiring the back of his hands like they were the most interesting thing to look at in the room. "What are your plans for next season, Thiago?"

He refrained from the urge to scoff. "Are you seriously asking me that? You know I want to stay and race with Primavera. You know it. I don't understand why you're hesitating to renew my contract. I had a few slip throughs, bad results at the beginning of the season, so what? Did you not see how I got back on top those past few races? How much effort I'm making into proving I'm worthy of that seat?

"You know, Simon, it's breaking my heart to know you've lost faith in me. I lost my father, who was my hero, who was a brother to you. Along the way, I lost myself whilst mourning. Yes, I won the championship that year, but that didn't mean I wasn't struggling and not battling my demons. Last season was tough because of the new car regulations, but I still finished P2 in the drivers' championship.

"Do you think I've been able to grieve properly? I haven't, and I'm still working on that. And yes, this year I might've DNF'd more than one race. I might've acted like I didn't care to end P10. I might've spent too many nights clubbing. I might've been hard on my mechanics and engineers because they can't go with a proper strategy. But I always try to bounce back. I try my fucking hardest, okay? I don't want to give up. I don't want to throw my dreams away because of some reckless mistakes I made."

He felt like he couldn't breathe after his monologue. Still, a weight had been lifted off his shoulders, relief seeping through his veins.

Simon gestured for him to move. "Come here, son."

Swallowing, Thiago came to sit next to his agent.

Simon slid a stack of papers towards his driver.

"What is this?" Thiago asked warily, feeling his stomach drop.

"Next season's contract," Leo finally said, a smile on his lips. "A multi-year deal."

Shocked, Thiago glanced from his agent to his team principal, to the contract, and back to Simon. "Seriously?"

Simon chuckled at his baffled tone. "Listen, we know winning the championship this year is not possible—let's stay realistic. But we're going to work hard for you to win your second title next year. Your efforts don't go unnoticed—they never have been. We just needed you to find a purpose and to be focused again like you used to be."

Thiago gaped at Leo when the latter offered him a pen. "Did you negotiate with him?"

Leo shrugged sheepishly. "Unfortunately, your salary stays at 30 million but—"

"I don't care about the money," Thiago bit out.

"I didn't have to say much," Leo said with a small smile. "All I had to do was to talk about possibilities and show Romano your progress over the past few weeks. You're a good man, Tito. We all wanted you to get better."

His head was spinning. He wasn't sure he was realising how drastically the situation had changed in a matter of minutes.

He frowned slightly. "Thank you. The both of you."

Leo tapped the athlete's back. "I know you said you didn't want to mix racing and love life, but I do think your girlfriend is good for you."

His heart skipped a beat at the mention of Kamari. His whole body was a tornado of emotions. "Did you talk with her?"

"She made me realise how much she loves you, how much millions of people love you. But above all, she made me realise how passionate you are about racing."

"HOLD YOUR POSITION."

Thiago had just been given the order to stay in front of Rowan despite his teammate having a faster pace.

"How many laps are left?" he asked, foot pressing onto the brake before turning in the chicane. He was panting, the rhythm of his pulse out of control. "My water system is broken."

"Full push," Luke said, causing Thiago to roll his eyes. He was getting closer and closer to Huxley's car. "Full push."

"Answer my question."

"Five more laps."

Thiago had been racing through the heat without any water, and he could feel his head spinning.

He was nearly there, though. He had to keep pushing.

"Gap to Huxley is one point two seconds."

Sometimes, racing felt like a game of chasing. Anytime he'd get closer to Huxley's rear wing, his rival would fly away, putting more distance between them.

He was currently P2, and Thiago was slowly starting to accept the fact he wouldn't win the championship, even if it felt like the sharpest blade was cutting through the wounds that hadn't healed yet.

Wheel to wheel, Thiago overtook Huxley in turn 17, braking late. His trajectory was wide, but Miles gave him enough space to take the inside of the corner. Thiago slipped past him, then flew down the long straight ahead of him.

"Good job, Tito," Luke praised on the radio. "Keep pushing."

His breaths became heavier, and he focused on winning the race.

"You've got a five-second penalty."

He roared with anger and shock. "What? Why?"

"Breached the speed limit in the pit lane. Get as far away from Huxley so you don't lose too much."

Fuck. He'd driven too fast before stopping for the change of tyres.

"I know what I'm fucking doing."

"Copy."

The chequered flag was brandished fast enough, yet Thiago didn't feel the exhilaration of crossing the finish line first because he knew he would be standing on the second highest step, yet he was treasuring every moment. This felt like a victory to him.

That's enough. That's more than enough. Don't be too hard on yourself.

———

THIAGO'S HEAD WAS SPINNING, but not because of the drinks he had consumed, but because he could still feel the stranger's touch burn his skin. Because all he could think about was Kamari who would stumble upon those pictures in a matter of minutes. Could still see the flashing lights capturing a moment he hadn't anticipated nor wanted.

There was nothing he could do to turn back in time and erase his mistakes.

Hell, it hadn't even been his fault. He hadn't initiated anything. He had pushed that woman away the moment she had attempted to kiss him.

All he could feel was regret. He shouldn't have gone clubbing. None of this would have happened if he had stayed at the hotel.

"Okay, you need to breathe," Cal said from his side.

The car was moving, but Thiago wasn't even sure where he was. What time it was. All he needed was to get back to London.

He shook his head, blinking that burning feeling in his eyes away. "I can't. She's going to hate me, and I can't lose her."

Cal emitted a loud scoff. "She couldn't possibly hate you even if she tried. Mate, it wasn't your fault. You know that, right? Kam trusts you, and I'm sure she knows you pushed that girl away and had zero interest in her."

A painful sensation was stirring inside his chest. The thought of hurting Kamari was so agonising he could barely inhale and exhale properly. "She's been through so much and all I did was betray her."

Cal sighed. "Get your shit together."

Thiago's knee started bouncing up and down whilst he ran clammy hands through his already tousled hair. "I can't lose her," he repeated shakily.

"You won't," his friend assured. "Deep breaths, Tito. Having a panic attack now won't make you cross the entire world faster."

"You're right." He leaned his temple against the window, allowing its coolness to soothe his nerves. He released a heavy sigh before trying to call Kamari again, only for her to decline the request. "She won't answer me."

"Let her cool down a bit," Cal suggested.

Swallowing the lump inside his throat, Thiago tried to hold a semblance of control over those unbearable emotions—just because the possibility of losing Kamari was obliterating his heart. God, she was his salvation. He wouldn't live a life without her. Not a single lifetime.

"I think I love her," Thiago murmured.

"You think?" his friend echoed, baffled. "No, man. You're head over heels for that woman. You're in love with her. I've never seen you act like this with any other girl before, and I have no doubt that you're going to fight for her."

"Damn right, I will." Kamari was an evidence to him. She'd always been the brightest star in his galaxy; she'd always been everything. "I don't know what to do."

"Just breathe." Cal turned to the chauffeur, tapping on his shoulder. "Hey, man. Look, I don't really condone law violations, but could you maybe speed a little bit? We need to get that big guy on a plane before he loses his damn mind."

CHAPTER FORTY-SEVEN

⚲ *LONDON, ENGLAND*

SOMEHOW, SOMEWAY, HE was even more beautiful than the last time she'd seen him, and she hated him for that. Ruggedly handsome, she realised his features were striking in a way meant to devastate her soul. He was crafted from marble, created by the hands of the most beautiful, powerful star above.

"You've been avoiding me," he said. "Not answering my messages. Not returning my calls."

Kamari's body betrayed her. She swallowed, tightly, and blinked. She couldn't break down today. She wasn't even sure if she had tears left to cry.

"I have every reason to ignore you," she seethed bitterly as her grip tightened around the doorknob.

She saw instant sorrow flash around his pupils, and the moment he took a step forward, she stepped backwards—creating a distance that would destroy the both of them. She could feel her heart shatter, minuscule piece by minuscule piece as if the pain she had endured yesterday was nothing compared to this because he was right there, standing in front of her.

"Don't. Don't come near me."

Expression falling, he attempted to reach out, causing her to march backwards until she stood in the middle of her small kitchen. His features were stricken with fatigue, red-rimmed eyes that made her believe he was hurting just as much.

He closed the door but respected the distance. "Kam..."

She folded her arms across her chest, ignoring the tremors in her hands. "It's Kamari to you."

A crease drew itself between his brows. "Moonbeam—"

"Kamari," she pressed coldly. Still, her voice had wavered. "What do you want, Thiago? You can't show up to my flat and act like you didn't do anything."

She watched his throat work up and down. Watched his jaw tick. Watched his eyes mist over. "I wasn't going to address the situation by text or call. I needed to see you to explain myself."

She took a deep breath in, shaking her head. "I can't do this, Thiago. I trusted you. I gave you my heart—I gave you *everything*. I trusted you with my entire heart and soul, and you broke me. You did the only thing you had promised to never do, yet you still abandoned me." Her voice was thick with tears whilst rage gripped her. "You know I've been cheated on before. You know how hard it has been for me to open up and trust you. Why did you have to hurt me?"

"I never wanted to hurt you." This time, she didn't move when he took one single step forward. It was when she saw a tear escape his eye that she felt a detrimental weight push at her chest, aggressively. "I did not kiss that woman, Kamari. She came onto me, and I pushed her away."

Those photos of him clubbing in Mexico were haunting her dreams, her thoughts.

"I want to believe you," she whispered.

As he passed his fingers through his hair, he tugged at the

roots. His lips trembled, his voice breaking as he said, "You know I would have never done that to you. I'm yours, Kamari."

"We're not exclusive. We're nothing," she bit out through gritted teeth. Every word hurt. Every look caused her scars to burst open. "But I was such a fool to think everything could change."

"We are *everything.*" His hands fell to his sides, shoulders shagging. "My heart is exclusively yours, Kam! You know it. *Fuck.* Women, men want me, and you know it damn well. But I don't want any of those people because they aren't you."

She felt a tear roll down her cheek, and she wiped it away furiously. She diverted her blurry gaze to the door behind his head because she couldn't bear that look in his eyes. She wanted to believe him, but it felt as though he had thrown her trust to waste in the blink of an eye.

"Call Callahan," he demanded.

She sucked in a breath. "Why?"

"Call him."

Kamari felt numb. Couldn't think through that thick cloud fogging her mind. With shaky hands, she grabbed her phone that she had left on the sofa. Ignoring all seventy missed calls from Thiago, she dialled Cal's number, pressing the device to her ear. She draped an arm across her stomach—shielding herself again.

Cal answered rapidly, and she could hear slight confusion blended to his tone. "Good evening, Kam. I wasn't expecting your call. Everything okay?"

She closed her eyes, letting another tear fall. "Is it true?"

There was a beat of silence. Too long for her liking. "Tito didn't cheat on you. He would never hurt you—not in a million years."

"But he did."

"He loves you."

She could barely manage to speak through the large lump constricting her throat. "He doesn't."

"Kam," Cal said in a whisper. "That woman came onto him.

And he instantly pushed her away and told her he was taken. Said he wasn't interested when she kept being insistent. We left the club immediately after that, and he looked for the first flight back to London whilst we were in the Uber. Listen to him. I'm begging you."

"Why should I?"

"Do you know what the first thing he told me after that party on the yacht in Monaco was?"

She didn't answer. Couldn't answer.

Cal continued softly. "He said he was in love. He might have been buzzed, but he told me he fell in love with that beautiful, fiery woman. His words, not mine. He even said that despite that attitude of yours, he'd find you and make you his. Listen, Kam, you two are so good for each other, and—"

Cal didn't get a chance to finish his phrase because Thiago had grabbed her phone to end the call. She felt her breath catch as she realised he was now standing right in front of her. He threw the phone on the sofa, and she didn't move even if her heart screamed to run away.

Grey eyes were veiled by a layer of tears. "You heard him. I didn't want her. In fact, I don't want anyone but you. I came home to you. I'll crawl home to you. I'll drop to my fucking knees and beg for your forgiveness. You hear me?"

She batted another rivulet of tears away. "This is hurting me." It was destroying her. She'd never felt so betrayed and broken-hearted.

"I'm sorry." He then fell to his knees, a sob erupting from the back of his throat. Raking trembling fingers through his hair, he looked up at her, incessant teardrops staining his face. "It's killing me, Kamari. I never wanted to be the man who broke your heart. I have wanted you every single day for the past three months. You are the one for me, and I never doubted that—not for one second. I'm sorry I ruined it by going out. I only wanted to celebrate the podium and—and—"

"Get up, Valencia." He refused by shaking his head. She

sighed then. "I can't stop you from being you. You like to party. You like attention. And I grew okay with those facts. I grew into your world, your lifestyle even if ninety percent of the time I'm scared for your life, but mostly for mine because you knew I couldn't bear getting hurt again."

He swallowed, the line between his eyebrows deepening. "I know. And I'm sorry, okay? I shouldn't have gone partying. I shouldn't have allowed those random girls to enter our VIP section, and I shouldn't have accepted the drink she bought me. She probably thought it was my green light or whatever but it was not. It was me being nice. Kamari, I cannot lose you. I refuse to accept the fact you want us to be over because of my reckless decisions. F1 and you are the constant things in my life I'm sure of, the things I wouldn't trade for anything. And I know for a fact that I make you feel the same. Please, please tell me what to do to be forgiven."

She felt dizzy. Exhausted. Felt like her knees were about to give up on her. A sob rose from her throat. "I don't know."

His voice was thick with tears, and his eyes—God, his eyes were filled with weariness and raw sorrow that made her heart crack. "I'll put out a statement on all socials about the party. I'll tell the world I'm with you. I'll face the media—"

Finally, she met him at his level, kneeling before him, causing a whimper to fly past his lips. He lifted his hands to touch her, then noticed her reluctance. He only curled his fingers into fists, shaking with anger. "This love isn't for show, Thiago. I don't want it to be—not anymore. You know I'd die for you in secret. I just need to know where your heart lies."

"It lies with you. Within the palms of your hands. And I know you have the ability of suffocating it, of crushing it to dust, and I don't care. I can't stand the thought that I hurt you. I'd rather be stabbed or even lose my seat with Primavera than—"

"Don't say that, Thiago. Don't you dare finish that sentence. Primavera Racing and F1 are the essence of your existence. Your daily dreams. I will not allow you to say you'd rather have me than racing. No, I refuse. Your career comes before me."

He held her gaze, and she desperately wanted to wipe away the teardrop marring his soft skin. "See how much you mean to me, Kam? You're on the same level as racing, if not higher because I can envision a lifetime with you. Do you know how many times a girl made me feel that way? Zero. None. You're the first and only woman I will give my heart and soul to. Already done so."

Kamari's eyes were already prickling with tears. And when she couldn't push away that powerful wave of sadness, she cried out, putting her hand over her mouth to muffle her despair.

"Kam," he whispered, voice thick. He sighed sadly, heavily. "Can I touch you? Please. I feel so fucking suffocated without you."

For a few heartbeats too long, she blinked the tears away and looked at him. Searched for the lie. Looked for the truth. And when she only saw pure adoration, unwavering affliction caused by the situation, she nodded. Because she realised he was her anchor, and she couldn't stay away from him.

His eyes flashed with a glint of hope, but he didn't move. "You know I need your words."

For some uncanny reason, her mind was blank. So, she made the first move by reaching out to him, and he met her halfway by looping his arms around her waist. He sat down and pulled her on his lap, a heavy, loud sigh of relaxation fanning across her neck when he buried his face in the crook of it. He trembled, cried, offering his unbridled vulnerability.

"I'm sorry, baby," he murmured. "I'm so sorry for all of this. It was killing me to know you had seen the photos and that you wouldn't answer me. I was so worried about you. Indy couldn't get a hold of you. Kieran even texted me, begged me to come home because you didn't go to work today. I'm sorry for causing all that pain, Kam. I will do anything for you to trust me again."

She felt his whole body shake underneath hers. "Give me time."

He nodded. "All the time you need. You know I'll be patient. But I'm not walking away."

"Okay," she whispered when he leaned back.

His finger found the underside of her chin, lifting her head up to oblige her to look into silver. "You're it for me, Kamari. You're so beautiful—everything about you is."

She threw him a sad smile, and his features softened. When his lips broke into a broad grin, she nearly cried out in relief. "I'm a crying mess."

"You're still exquisite," he whispered. For an eternity, his perusal meandered her face—remembering, cataloguing—as a soft sigh escaped his mouth. "Were you about to have dinner with your hair down?"

She sniffed, nodding. "I can't find my hair tie."

"Come on," he said gruffly whilst pushing her off his lap. "Turn around."

Warily, she turned her back to him, bringing her knees to her chest. Her body was still taut with irritation, but she relaxed when he put his hands on her shoulders. His delicate touch was her favourite thing.

Gently, he gathered her hair whilst putting his legs on either side of her hips. "Is it weird that I went to the store to buy a bunch of hair ties for, like, two pounds?"

Purposely, he brushed the back of her neck with that light-feather caress that made her knees buckle. Then, he started parting her hair into three sections.

"Why did you buy these?" she asked, voice caught in her throat, still hoarse from her fading sadness.

She imagined him lifting his shoulders in a shrug. "I don't know."

"What are you doing?"

"Braiding your hair because I know you can't eat without

having your hair tied. I don't know how to make buns, so a French braid it is."

A smile spread across her lips, but she dropped it before he could hear the delight in her tone. "Where did you learn to do this?"

"My mum taught me," he explained softly. "I so desperately wanted a sister because Alex has one, and he used to braid her hair every time we'd go out to the skate park."

She let her imagination fly to a young Thiago begging his mother to braid her hair, and the thought raised her spirits. "That's sweet."

They stayed silent for a moment, and she wondered if he could hear how loud her heart was thumping. Then, she ceased to breathe when he wrapped his arms around her shoulders, pulling her into his chest. Kamari closed her eyes, lungs tightening.

"Can we stop pretending?" he asked hoarsely. "I think about you all the time."

"I know." She sighed. "I think about you all the time, too."

He pecked her jaw and leaned his chin on her shoulder. "What's going on in that pretty head of yours, Kam?"

She breathed, shakily, sliding her fingers through his. He squeezed once, letting her know he wasn't going anywhere. "Do you know why I despised you so much when we met?"

A glacial sequence of chills followed the route of his lips when he grazed his mouth above her thundering pulse. "Why?"

She refused to give herself to him—not yet. "You were able to make me feel something from the moment you looked at me with those eyes, and I hated it. I hated how much power you had over me. How much you were able to tear down my walls when I've worked all my life to guard my heart. I just hated you so much, Thiago."

"I know you did, baby." He pressed a kiss to her temple, because even if she was intent on closing herself off again, he wanted to coax her through that storm of emotions. "I loathed you just as much, and for the exact same reason. I've never felt this way about anyone before. And it terrifies me how much I adore you because no one gets me like you do. To the point it physically hurts not to be close to you; to the point I can't breathe when I don't have you in my arms. God, Kam, I'd tear myself apart for you."

Kamari was scared to give her heart out again, and she had every right reason to.

"I know what you're trying to do." He gently asked her to turn around again. Cupping her face, he allowed green to clash with silver—allowed her to come home. "You're hiding behind that tough façade again because you don't want me to see the real you. But I see you, Kam. I've seen you since the moment we collided into each other. You're terrified to be loved, to love again. You're terrified to show your vulnerability because you think it makes you weak, but you know it doesn't. You're shielding yourself because you're scared, and that's alright, but I refuse to walk away from you, Kamari. Push me away all you want, hate me all you want, but I'm not leaving. I'll take your anger and your pain and your love. I'll take it all."

Thiago was a blur, but his words felt like a summer breeze, gently blowing away the clouds of sorrow fogging her thoughts —her heart.

Kamari swallowed. "I'm just so, so scared to lose you."

His expression softened. "I'm not going anywhere."

"Why not?" Her brows creased. "I'm nothing like these women, Thiago. I'm not always available to attend your races, I'm just a simple girl who can't afford an expensive bag unless she works hard for it. I'm just a girl who owns a small business, who could never buy you a Patek for your birthday. I'm just—"

"You're Kamari Monroe," he interrupted gruffly. "You're you, and that's why I'm in love with you. You're hard-working, passionate, cunning, witty, a brat sometimes, but you're the strongest woman I know. You put everyone else's happiness and well-being before your own. You work day and night so you can treat yourself with luxury goods, because your hard work always pays off. You are a bright constellation amongst a sky full of stars, but you're the one who stands out the most to me."

Her chest rose and fell, and with trembling hands, she grabbed his wrists—finding her anchor. "You love me?"

He smiled broadly, handsomely, tenderly, thumb delicately brushing her cheek to collect a teardrop. "I love you so fucking much, Kamari. So much it hurts. I've loved you since the moment I laid eyes on you. You had to stumble into my world and tilt the universe onto its axis, because that's the impact you have on people; you change their lives. You're a fiery ball of anger but you weren't scared of defying and challenging me. You weren't scared of beating me at my own game. You weren't scared of me, and I instantly fell in love with you."

"Thiago," she choked out.

He was the love she had been waiting for her whole life.

The love she deserved.

The love that provided her the rush, the adrenaline, the thrill of falling off the cliff.

"You don't have to say it back," he murmured softly. "I'm patient, and I will wait for you."

She leaned in to place a kiss on his lips. When he returned her gesture with equal devotion, slowly, tenderly, lovingly, she finally felt all the shattered fragments in her heart disappear, like he'd been able to run a finger over the rough edges of her soul and mend the indentations her past had created with a lover's caress.

"I have something else to tell you," he whispered. "I didn't want to tell you over text."

She frowned. "Should I be scared?"

His smile grew as he shook his head. "On the contrary. Guess who has signed a multi-year deal with Primavera."

Widening her gaze, she could feel shock ripple through her veins. "You?"

He nodded eagerly, silver eyes swamped with emotions. "Yeah, baby. Me."

Kamari was electric with happiness—because of that news, because of his promise. She leaped forward, wrapping her arms around his neck, causing him to laugh loudly. He didn't hesitate to return her embrace, and she felt like crying all over again.

"I'm so, so proud of you. You've proved them that you haven't lost your spark."

His lips brushed her neck, causing her to shiver. "All I needed was someone to hold the match for me to burst, like a moth to a flame."

"Such a poet," she chuckled. They embraced each other like they couldn't bear having distance separating them any longer. "This is amazing, Thiago. Second chances are always given to the most deserving. You just have to seize the opportunity and do the right thing with it."

He pulled away to look into her eyes. "I want you to give me a second chance."

"You don't have to doubt me because I will."

"Thank you." He pecked her nose. "Leo told me you spoke with him."

She sighed, drifting her gaze behind his head. "I shouldn't have done that. I'm sorry."

"I'm not mad," he said gently. "I ended up pouring my heart out to Romano, and he just, like, gave me the contract. I think he was waiting for me to release my anger."

"That's good," she murmured. "Your actions mattered, but maybe all he needed was verbal proof that you don't want to give up."

"What if we hadn't met, Kam? What would've happened?"

"You would have found your purpose, you would've gotten a grip with Cal, Alex, and your mum's help. What happened here, the renewal with Primavera, isn't because of me. It's all you, Thiago, because you're more than enough and worth it and deserving of this opportunity. You are enough, and I'll tell you every day until you believe me."

"Gosh," he started, tone cracking as he sauntered his gaze over her face, all tenderness and unyielding devotion etched on his face. "I love you."

When his lips sealed another unspoken promise with hers, he smiled, and she couldn't help but mirror the action.

"Do you want to hear a poem?" he mumbled against her lips. She chuckled. "Sure."

"You remain infinite deep inside my soul, tethered to my heart from the very moment I laid eyes on you. You're the moon in my universe—the only source of light in darkness. You're the delicate touch of starlight I've longed to feel on my rough edges. You're everything to me, Kamari. Everything I've ever wanted. Everything I've ever loved."

She'd never smiled so widely. Had never felt so loved than at that exact moment. "Evermore the poet, Thiago Valencia."

CHAPTER FORTY-EIGHT

📍 *LONDON, ENGLAND*

H ER LUNGS WERE depriving themselves of oxygen whilst a needle started to puncture her heart, obliging it to cease beating.

She couldn't breathe. Couldn't bring herself back to reality.

She felt Indy catch her hand, squeezing it. Could hear, somewhere in the distance, Kieran call out her name. But everything felt like a blur around her.

Kamari couldn't look away from the television, body shaking with undeniable fear.

It was raining in Sao Paulo—more like heavy drizzle, but still dangerous because of the poor visibility around the circuit. Because of the weather conditions, the twenty drivers had to put wet tyres on. It was evident it would be a tricky race because driving in the rain was never easy despite the thrill it procured.

Thiago was starting at the front row, in second position

behind Huxley. When the lights had gone out, Thiago had made a perfect start and was ahead of Huxley in a matter of milliseconds, rushing down the straight line before decreasing his pace to take the corner.

Taking the first turn on the inside, Huxley had been following closely, driving on the outside whilst Denver was right behind Thiago.

The chaos unravelled behind at first: a driver who had started at the back of the grid had lost control of his vehicle, causing him to slip then collide with the car in front of him. Said car hit the one in front, pushing it into the driver trying to escape the strike. The collisions had been brutal—at least from the public's view —but when Denver's rear wing got touched, he spun, and drove into Huxley, who sent Thiago's car flying metres away when his front wing collided with the side pod of his car.

Time had come to a halt as Kamari watched Thiago's car spin and tumble and whirl at over one hundred kilometres per hour. She'd been holding her breath when she realised there was nothing he could do to stop the car, and her heart stopped when the vehicle flipped upside down, sliding down the concrete on its halo.

"That's bad," Kieran had whispered, causing Indy to tell him to stay silent.

It had been a minute, yet it felt like an eternity as everything stopped. Kamari's hand flew to her mouth as she waited for something. Anything.

The red flag was brandished.

The cars that had been able to escape the chaos ran a slow lap before going into the pit lane. Whilst the impacted drivers stopped where they were, Kamari could only look at car number seven surrounded by debris.

Huxley, Denver and even Emerson ran towards Thiago's car whilst the safety car arrived, stewards dressed in fluorescent orange desperately trying to help Thiago out.

"He's not moving," Kamari choked out between a pained

sob as she felt her chest ache. He wasn't getting out. Indy draped an arm around her shoulders, but her friend was just as nervous.

The box where they broadcasted the radio exchange appeared.

"*Tito?*" Luke asked, panic evident in his tone. "*Tito? Can you hear me?*"

Indy squeezed Kamari's hand.

"*There's smoke,*" Thiago replied after a while. "*I can't get out. Get me out. Get me out.*"

Indy gasped when small flames burst from the engine.

Stewards were trying to extinguish the fire which was spreading too rapidly, whilst another one was risking his life, crouched next to Thiago and trying to help him unbuckle his belt.

After what felt like an endless eternity, the steward rose to his feet, hands under Thiago's armpits, and pulled the driver out just as the fire started spreading towards the cockpit.

"Holy shit," Indy cried.

All Kamari could see was a hazy mass of colours, an entourage made out of blurs. Her thoughts were spiralling, her lungs tight.

"He's okay, Kam," Kieran assured from the other side of the sofa. "He's okay. Look."

She wiped her tears away, angrily, and focused back on the screen. Thiago was kneeling on the gravel, chest heaving, metres away from his ruined car. The fire had been doused, thick smoke curling in the air. Rowan came to crouch down next to him, a comforting hand on his back. They exchanged a few words, and when she saw Thiago shake his head, she knew he was devastated. She could hear his cry of frustration. Could hear the loud crack in his chest.

She needed to be ready to receive his anger.

She realised she couldn't do this without him. Couldn't live a life without him.

She had nearly lost him.

Everything could change in a matter of seconds, minutes.

She needed to tell him she loved him more than anything.

CHAPTER FORTY-NINE

⚲ *ABU DHABI, UNITED ARAB EMIRATES*

"LOVING YOU WILL kill me one day, Valencia."

The glow of the burning sky cast an ethereal glow upon the side of his face when he turned towards her. Hair blowing away from his forehead, the crease between his eyebrows immediately disappeared when silver clashed with green.

His chest heaved, and he blinked, as though he couldn't believe she was standing there. The ocean's breeze brushed his jawline, his hair, sending his addictive scent towards her.

"What are you doing here?" Thiago breathed hoarsely.

A lump got stuck inside her throat. She couldn't believe how heavenly he looked. "Is this a proper way to greet me?"

The lips she hadn't been able to get out of her mind tipped into a smile, revealing devastating dimples on both his sun-kissed cheeks. "How I am supposed to greet you, Kamari? Bowing before my queen? Falling to my knees like I'm at your complete mercy?"

Dropping her sandals into the sand, she shook her head. "You're an idiot."

He fell silent as he revelled in the view—her presence. "Are you sure you want this with me? If you say yes, I will never let you go. If you say yes, you have to understand what is at stake; my pain, my grief, my anger, and my injuries are inevitable. But I'll give you the moon, all the love you deserve."

She didn't have to think. "I'm sure. Two hundred percent in. I want everything, Thiago."

His eyes searched her face for a fragment of a second—cataloguing and remembering. "Come here, baby."

They reached for one another at the same time, like neither of them could fight that powerful, magnetising force pulling them together. He looped his arms around waist as she winded her hands behind his broad neck.

He lifted her off the sand, embracing her tightly—cocooning her into that cosmos of solace she'd been calling home. Lips grazing at her skin when he buried his face in the crook of her neck, she sighed in relief at the feeling of him.

She hadn't been in touch with him for two days—since the crash.

He had texted her he was alright and needed to rest before flying to Abu Dhabi on Tuesday. It was now Wednesday.

"Seriously," he said, putting her down, cradling her face. "What are you doing here? I thought you were only flying here on Friday night after FP2."

"I needed to see you, needed to make sure you were okay." She sighed heavily. "I was so, so scared. I felt suffocated, breathless. I couldn't sleep, couldn't think properly. God, I was so scared for you."

"You dropped everything for me?" His eyes were swamped with emotions—awe, amazement, adoration.

Kamari nodded. "I always do. Always will."

He brushed her cheekbones, traced a route over her face with his gaze—drawing constellations between her prominent freckles beneath the setting sun's glow. "I'm okay, moonbeam. Just still a bit sore from the impact and tired from all the travelling, but I'm perfectly fine."

Her hands descended his pectorals, and she could feel the hammering of his heartbeat under her palms. "What were you doing all alone on the beach?"

"Waiting for you to close up the café so I could call you. Waiting for the moon to show up so I could associate you with the beauty of the world."

If this was how it felt like to be loved by Thiago Valencia, she never wanted it to end. There was a single thread of gold tying her to him, and she never wanted it to break.

"You're obsessed with me," she teased, nudging his shoulder.

"I am." He chuckled, shaking his head. A few rebel strands fell over his brows, his cheeks had turned into a soft tinge of pink, and his smile never once faltered. He was so beautiful. "You bring out the best version of myself."

"I'm glad," she murmured.

He tucked a strand of hair behind her ear. "My one and only. My best friend, my everything. There isn't a lifetime where I'm not made for you. You've corrupted my soul, you've put a spell on my heart. And the only love I want is yours because you, Kamari, are the love of my life."

Their lips brushed, ready to seal with an unyielding devotion. "I love you," she whispered. "I love you so much, Thiago."

He smiled broadly, sliding his hands to the side of her neck, thumbs brushing the outline of her jaw. He could feel her thundering pulse—like he could control it and continuously send it into overdrive. "I know."

"Thank you for welcoming me into your world with open arms and an open heart."

He left a lingering kiss on her forehead. "No, thank you. For everything. For trusting me with your heart. I promise I'll be gentle."

To the moon, and to Saturn.

CHAPTER FIFTY

⚑ *ABU DHABI, UNITED ARAB EMIRATES*

"THIS SUNDAY IS the last race of the season, and your whereabouts about next season have yet to be determined. Is there a reason why nothing hasn't been announced yet?"

God, if Thiago could wipe that smirk off of Franklin's face.

Leaning back in his seat and threading his fingers behind his head, he smirked, then met Rowan's gaze as his teammate sat beside him in the conference room. Kamari, who had been allowed into the room, stood at the back with Leo. The both of them smiled proudly back at him, and it took every ounce of willpower for Thiago not to cross the room and grab his girl. He then took hold of his microphone, twirled it between his fingers, and of course, let it drop as it slipped away from his grasp.

"This is what I have to deal with on a daily basis," Rowan announced whilst Thiago leaned forward to grab his mic.

"Says the most annoying guy on the grid," Huxley interjected.

"At least I can maintain a reputation," Rowan countered coyly.

"Big reputation, big reputation. Oh, you and me we got big reputations," Huxley started singing, causing a few chuckles to erupt in the crowd of reporters.

Miles Huxley was the most reserved, quietest, grumpiest driver on the grid, yet he knew how to entertain his entourage and bring a smile on people's lips.

"Would you look at that?" Franklin said. "The current top three in our drivers' standing. Miles, you're leading with 25 points ahead of Rowan. Rowan, Thiago's only two points behind you. Do you feel threatened?"

Rowan scoffed. "My teammate is not a threat. Other drivers on the grid are. It's not a secret that I'll be receiving a five-place grid penalty because of my gearbox change, so I'll be starting behind Valencia. Unless he fucks up. But we'll see." He lifted three fingers in the air—index, middle, and ring ones—and whistled the Hunger Games melody. "May the odds ever be in your favour."

Thiago met green eyes when her soft laugh echoed, standing out amongst the other sounds of delight. He winked, and she winked in return.

"Thiago?"

He lifted his shoulders in a shrug. "May the man best win."

Reflecting back on his season, he could only be proud of his achievements. From losing hope because of the engine failure, the poor results, and the lack of self-confidence before the summer break, to climbing back to the top despite the obstacles and struggles. There was a lot to work on, but now that he knew where he'd be next season, he was okay.

"Still nothing to say about next—"

"Frankie," he sighed, putting an ankle atop his opposite knee. "Would it shut your obnoxious mouth if I told you I'm staying with Primavera? The multi-year deal has been signed, so now you can sleep peacefully."

ACCEPTING THE PATS on his back, he smiled at the car mechanics whilst wiping the sweat off his temple.

"Good job, man. Good qualifying result for the last one of the season," Tim cheered.

Thiago winked. "P2 isn't too bad."

He entered the garage, high-fived other team members, and rushed towards the motorhome. He saw Kamari standing in the paddock, in the middle of a dynamic conversation with Indy and Alex, and when green met silver, her features instantly brightened.

"Congrats," Indy beamed, clapping her hands and bouncing on her heels. "That was a mega lap."

Thiago grabbed Kamari's hand, pulling her away. "Thank you, Indy. I'll be right back, I just need to have a conversation with Kam."

Kamari looked at him incredulously. "About what?"

"Don't ask questions and follow me."

They walked hastily into the motorhome and into Thiago's personal room. He slammed the door shut, turned the lock, and pushed Kamari against the wall. A mischievous smirk broke on her full lips, and he groaned. She instantly grabbed his damp racing suit, pulling him towards her. Their lips collided, tongues battling for dominance. She moaned softly into his mouth, fingers working to unzip his suit.

"Quiet, baby," he ordered before trailing his mouth on her jaw, pecking it. "Did you really think I would have let you walk around in that dress and not fuck you?"

She pushed the suit off his shoulders, helping him out of the sleeves. She untucked his fireproof shirt, nails grazing his abdomen. "I've been waiting all day for this moment."

He smirked. "You're so naughty behind your pristine allure."

"You know it, pretty boy."

Their lips fused again, moulding perfectly despite the heavy breaths entwining together. Thiago bunched her dress up to her hips, hands finding the generous curve of her backside, down to her arse. He groaned, bucking his hips into hers before marching them towards the small bureau against the wall.

"We've got to be quick," he rasped out. "I need to shower afterwards and go into debriefing with the engineers."

Kamari chuckled, tugging his fireproof shirt off. "You really couldn't wait until we got to the hotel room, could you?"

"No." Hands on her hips, he made her spin around. He pushed her chest onto the desk, kicked her feet apart with a brusque motion. "I got a semi all day by just looking at you walk around like you own the fucking paddock. That arse of yours, those tits of yours. I could come just by looking at you."

She only whimpered, which made him chuckle quietly. He rubbed her bum, then slapped it.

"Hurry up and fuck me, Thiago."

"So desperate to come," he mustered, followed by a *tsk*.

He kneeled on the ground, hands travelling her calves and the back of her thighs before pushing her already-damp underwear to the side. He smirked at the sight of her lace red thong and almost came into his jumpsuit at the sight of her aroused, gleaming, bare cunt. His lips latched to her wetness, causing her to fall forward onto the bureau. He sucked on her clit and dragged his tongue flat against her drenched core, humming against it. She moved against his mouth, doing an excellent job at keeping her mewls quiet. He kept his eyes closed, devouring her, tasting her, collecting every single drop of her excitement on his tongue.

Hurriedly, feeling like he would explode, he pushed his suit down his thighs, along with the other layer of fireproof underwear, letting his shaft spring free. He wrapped his hand around his throbbing erection, pumping slowly.

When he heard Kamari's bated breaths become uneven, he stopped, causing her to whine.

"You're going to come when my cock's inside you."

She turned around, and God, she was so electric with the lust in her gaze and the flush on her face. He rose to his full height just as she sank down to her knees.

He bunched her hair around his fist and traced her lower lip with his thumb. Keeping her gaze locked on his, Kamari spat onto the leaking tip of his hardness, causing him to whimper.

"Quiet," she demanded.

Full lips wrapped around the head whilst two hands stroked the base of his shaft. He threw his head back, already panting. She did that thing with her tongue, where she flicked the slit, causing him to tremble in pleasure.

"That's enough," he said, pulling her upwards. "I can't come yet."

He turned her around again, and as she leaned over the desk, she offered him a heavenly view of her backside. "Perfect," he murmured, guiding the tip of his shaft to her wet entrance. "Whose slut are you?"

"Yours."

"That's a good girl."

They both breathed heavily when he slid into her tight core, her walls already clenching around him. He didn't give her time to adjust that he started thrusting deeply, holding her waist. He watched as she tugged the fabric of her dress down to rub her breasts on the bureau, and the sight made him whimper out loud. She reached out to grab the edge of the small table, knuckles whitening.

"Oh, fuck," she moaned quietly. "Yes. Yes."

"Shut up." He pulled her upwards against his chest, hand baring her throat, applying just enough pressure to make her gasp for air. His other hand slipped towards her front, pushing the lace to the side to find her swollen clit. "Stay quiet, baby."

He felt her walls tightening, so he drew fast circles on her clit as she met his rapid thrusts by rolling her hips. "Holy fuck, Kam. You feel so good. So goddamn good."

She tipped her head back, lips forming into a silent *o*. She supported herself against him with a hand on his bum, the other playing with her breasts and hard nipples. He nibbled at her earlobe, grazed his teeth at her pulse, tightening his fingers around her throat.

"Good girl," he praised when she whimpered. "Taking my cock so well."

"I'm coming," she breathed, nails digging crescent moons into the skin of his arse.

"I'm right here with you, baby."

Thiago had to put his hand on her mouth to muffle her cries as he buried his face in the crook of her neck. He sped his pace up, flicking her clit as his thrusts became punishing, deep, uncontrollable.

He came hard, with a muffled grunt, white stars spreading across his vision as his head spun with pure bliss. He stilled and spilled into her, panting.

"Fuck," he breathed, kissing her shoulder blade. "You're going to ruin me, but you're my good luck charm."

"YELLOW FLAG IN SECTOR TWO."

Thiago hit the brake and clicked on a button to set his pace at 80 kilometres per hour.

"Is everyone okay?" he asked Luke, tightening his grip around his steering wheel.

Miles had been leading the race for the past 47 laps, except for the two after his pit stop where Thiago was at the front.

"Yes, just Beaumont and Denver colliding again. Beaumont has a puncture on his front left."

"These rookies," Thiago mustered, zig-zagging to keep his tyres warm.

Miles was driving slowly behind the safety car, causing Thiago to catch up, but he was forbidden to overtake.

Luke's voice came through again. "Box, box. We're going with plan B."

Thiago frowned. "What? No. Plan B is a double pit stop! You're going to fuck the race up. I've got this, Luke."

"Box, box," he repeated. "Trust us. Huxley is going to pit, too."

"There are only ten laps left," Thiago countered. "What the fuck are you guys doing?"

"Box, box."

"Bloody hell," he whispered. "That box I'm shoving up your arse."

A beat passed. "Radio is still on."

"Exactly."

Thiago needed to trust his gut, and weirdly, his instincts told him to listen to his race engineer. He drove into the pit lane, observing in his rear-view mirror a few other drivers doing the same. His team was ready with a set of soft tyres. Two seconds later, his new compounds were on, and he left the pit lane, falling back into fourth place. He caught a glimpse at Rowan coming in afterwards, and he smiled when the double pit stop succeeded.

"Good job," he praised his engineer.

"Now go get that trophy, Tito."

There were seven laps left when the green flag was brandished. Easily, Thiago overtook two cars with a full push on the throttle, late braking before the turn.

The smell of burnt rubbers was whiffing in the air, the heat radiating off the circuit having the same effect as the summer sun's rays. His heart was thumping as he overtook another driver, the drum of his pulse as deafening as the roar of his engine.

"DRS is enabled," Luke announced then when Thiago was racing behind Huxley, less than a second distancing them. Pushing on the green button on his wheel, he caused the superior flap of the rear wing to open. With less dragging in the straight line, he was able to drive at top speed.

Catching up to Miles, he pushed the car to its limits, braking late when they turned in the corner. He could feel his car vibrate, sending jolts through his bones. Could feel the time stop as his front wing grazed Huxley's left rear tyre as he rushed the inside of the corner. Could imagine the roar of excitement in the crowd when he overtook his rival, flying down the straight line and putting distance with Huxley.

"Yes!" Luke shouted. "Full push, baby, full push. Four laps left."

Thiago kept checking his rear-view mirror, grinning at the sight of Rowan chasing him. Miles had pitted, he supposed.

Two laps before the chequered flag could be brandished, Miles caught up. He was chasing the win, but Thiago wouldn't let him.

The finish line was right in front of him, and Huxley was less than a second away.

Hitting the throttle, racing at full speed, Thiago crossed the line first, fists brandished in the air as he saw his team cheer against the fence.

"You did it!" Luke cried, emotions lacing his voice. "You're P2 in the drivers' standings, and Primavera finished second in the constructors' championship."

For a moment, during the cool-down lap, as he waved at Miles driving past him, he took a moment to breathe. He was wild with joy, overwhelmed with pride, intoxicated with emotions.

Miles was World Champion because he had too many points ahead of Thiago, and even if Thiago finished the race first, he still couldn't beat the Lion.

"Can I do doughnuts?"

He heard Luke chuckle. "The world's only waiting for you to do them."

Engulfed in thick clouds of smoke as his tyres were being

dragged on the asphalt, Thiago turned his wheel whilst creating doughnuts with other drivers.

When he parked his car in front of the panel dedicated to the race winner, he killed the engine with a full heart and tears threatened to escape his eyes. He tipped his head back against his seat, listened to the happiness unravelling around him. Lifting the visor of his helmet, he pressed his fingertips to his eyes, smiling so widely under his balaclava. He got out of his car, stood on the halo, and praised the stars for having been on his side this weekend. Finally, he jumped down whilst tearing his helmet and balaclava off. He rushed into his best friends' arms, Primavera's mechanics tapping his back.

Alex ruffled his hair. "That's our man."

"You're a champ," Cal smiled, grabbing his helmet.

He could only laugh at his friends, accepting other embraces. He got pulled away for the post-race interview and to monitor his weight, though he could only search the crowd for green eyes and a devastating smile.

In a crowded place, Thiago could always find Kamari. She stood at the back with Indy, smiling widely, gaze shimmering with happiness.

He winked, and she winked back.

HE LISTENED TO the British anthem he knew all too well, standing on the highest step of the podium. He smiled at the sky —at a particular star.

After his moment of glory, he looked down at the World Champion who would receive his trophy at the FIA's ceremony at the end of the winter. He high-fived his rival, a broad smile set on his lips. "Congratulations, man. Second consecutive title. That's grand."

Miles grinned brightly. "You fought brilliantly, too. Have you ever been told you have your father's driving style?"

"Only a few times."

HE PUSHED PAST THE CROWD, barely glanced at people begging for a photo, barely returned the smiles.

All he could see was Kamari.

His moon.

His anchor.

The love of his life.

His home.

She was walking away from Indy, Alex, and Cal, a radiant smile on her lips. Just as she reached for his shoulders, he grabbed her waist, lifting her off the ground and making them spin around. Soft giggles fled past her lips, and the sound of her delight added to the excitement rushing through him, causing him to be slightly dizzy with bliss.

"Hey, champ." She tangled her fingers through the hair at his nape, pecking his nose. "I'm so proud of you, Thiago."

When he looked into her eyes whilst setting her down on her feet, a gloom had misted over, but it was genuine happiness. He had worked hard to see her true façade, and now that he had her, he was intent on spending the rest of his life with her.

"I couldn't have done it without you," he murmured, joy sparkling inside of him—as bright as the fireworks exploding in the night sky.

She shook her head slightly. "I didn't do anything except hold your hand."

"Winning the championship was my goal, yes, but in the meantime, I won your heart over. It's my most prized possession, Kam. You gave me a purpose outside of this universe, and I'm thankful for that. I refuse to never, ever let you walk away because being loved by you is giving me the same adrenaline rush as hitting the apex at full throttle."

Her gaze dropped to his lips, hand slipping to his chest. "I don't plan on walking away."

"So, you want to do this again? Walk by my side in the paddock next season, and the ones after that?"

Her eyes flashed with joy. "How about we do this again without all the pretending, the fake dating, and the rules?"

He raised his eyebrows, taunting her. "Are you sure you want to get rid of the rules?"

She shrugged, rolling her eyes playfully. "Okay, maybe we'll have to set a few rules."

"Like what?"

"Like no falling in love."

He couldn't stop smiling. "Too late. Too fucking late, Kam. You had me on my knees on the first day."

Their surroundings didn't matter. The horde of photographers stealing pictures of their tender moment was a blur. The champagne sticking to his hair was a simple detail. All he could see was Kamari.

She took a step back, extending her hand. "Do we have ourselves a deal, pretty boy?"

He laughed loudly and grabbed her hand, tethering himself to her once again. "The deal of a lifetime. That okay with you, pretty girl?"

"Perfect. I'll send the contract to your agent first things first in the morning."

He grabbed her face, grazing his lips to hers. "You're such an idiot. An idiot I love with every fibre of my being."

And when their breaths entwined, he felt plummeting into the deepest abyss, felt his world tilt onto its axis before the stars aligned. Felt like falling off the cliff, but only now, there was a safety net at the very bottom to catch him.

FIN.

EPILOGUE

📍 *LONDON, ENGLAND*

Five years later

"DON'T MAKE ME drop to my knees and beg for your attention."

"You know I love it when you beg, Valencia. Though, you always have my undivided attention."

"No, I don't."

"You do."

"You're not even looking at me right now."

Thiago nearly laughed at Kamari's exasperated expression when she pivoted to face him, brows raised in defiance. Even when her features were stricken with raw anxiety, she was the most beautiful star to him.

He leaned his hip against the counter, folding his arms across his chest whilst letting his lips break into a smirk.

"Stop looking at me like that," she bit out, returning to her previous occupation, which was making two margaritas.

"You're terribly sexy when you're mad."

She pinned him with a glare. "Stop flirting with me."

He lifted his shoulders in a coy shrug, a grin touching his lips. "Can't help myself, love."

Whilst he listened to the catchy rhythm of the music that resonated through the place, he watched Kamari's agility, expert hands, and elegance as she slid the two cocktails on the counter, offering a radiant smile to the customer who had ordered them. Complete awe was slowly etching itself upon his face, as though she had been able to bewitch him without so much as meeting his gaze.

"Go and have fun with the boys," Kamari said then, running a clean cloth over the oak counter. "And tell Alex to stop flirting with my waitress. She can giggle at his foolish jokes when she's done with her shift. I need a hand over here."

Thiago peered behind his shoulder to look outside, witnessing Alex throw a roguish smile to a nervous, blushing Sara as she struggled to smoke her cigarette because she was too busy chuckling.

Thiago threw a thumbs-up at his best friend when the latter met his gaze, before turning back to look at Kamari. "Moonbeam, can you look at me?"

Begrudgingly, she set her cloth down and faced him. He could see her shoulders taut with stress, could nearly hear all her racing thoughts ricochet inside her mind. But when green fully met silver, her features softened.

He grabbed her upper arms, then slowly slid his touch down her soft skin until he wrapped his fingers around her hands. "Can I get ten minutes of your time?"

Her expression was blank as she blinked, and her voice lowered when she hissed, "I'm not having a quickie with you again, Thiago. I'm busy right now."

"You weren't complaining when you were almost biting my

hand to keep you from screaming my name the other night." He chuckled when she widened her eyes, slipping his gaze down her body. "I wasn't even thinking about that, but since you're suggesting..."

"Don't make me step on your foot so you come back to your senses."

"So violent." She stared at his dimples when he smiled broadly. Gently squeezing her hands, he pulled her away from the working space. "Come look at this."

"But—"

He placed a kiss on the crown of her head. "Kam, everyone has been served by the best manager. Everyone is enjoying their drink and busy having a great time. Take a small break and come with me. Please."

He heard her sigh heavily but still listened to his command. He pulled her towards the centre of the room where no one was paying attention to them—where, even in a place filled with other people, they still managed to find themselves in a world alone.

Guiding her to pivot until her back collided with his chest, he wrapped his arms around her waist so she wouldn't run away.

She leaned into him whilst he put his chin atop her shoulder. "Look around you, Kam. Look at the people loving your hard work."

He tried to follow the route of her perusal as she scanned the room. All tables were occupied by friends catching up around a drink or two, whilst a group surrounded the pool table as they waited to take turns in trying to win the round of eight-ball. Some were watching the television as their undivided attention was brought to the captivating game of football. And others were dancing, singing, and smiling.

Kamari's second café was her treasure, something more special than Dawn's. Maybe because she had accepted Thiago's help when he wasn't racing. Maybe because they had spent hours painting and constructing and deciding on pieces of furniture together away from prying eyes—supporting each other's dreams, building an eternity together.

"Dusk 'Til Dawn is the world's favourite place," he murmured as he led her to sway to the rhythm of the now slow music. Still, patrons were screaming the lyrics at the top of their lungs. "You need to stop worrying and relax. Look, Sara is back from her date with Alex. No one's queuing to get your famous drinks. You can breathe."

"I want everything to be perfect," she countered, exhaling softly when he placed a kiss behind her ear.

"Everything has been perfect since we opened four years ago, Kam." He tightened his hold around her. Even after all these years, he knew his heart would always batter erratically in her company. Knew he kept plummeting and falling each day, harder. "I have a suggestion."

Her hands found his, fingers entwining together like the steady rhythm of their synchronised heartbeats. "What is it?"

His thumb started rubbing soothing circles on her hip, and he swore she started shivering. "I need to go back to Monaco, and you're coming with me."

"Sounds more like an order than a suggestion to me," she huffed.

He kissed her temple. "You love taking orders from me."

"Really?" she mused. "I think it's the other way around, pretty boy, but whatever makes you happy."

"Well, what would make me super, extra, mega happy, is that you'd take a small break. We can go to Italy, stay over there for a few days. There are two more weeks of summer break left, and I intend on spending every minute with you before I leave for the triple-header."

"I don't know," she trailed with uncertainty, sighing softly.

"Everything's taken care of," he pressed. "Kieran is going to manage Dawn's. Sara will stay here—and Alex is supposed to be travelling, too, so he won't be here to distract her. Everything is under control."

Slowly, she turned to face him, looping her arms around his neck. The moment her fingers tangled with his hair, he smiled softly.

He flickered his gaze between hers. "Please? I'm willing to get down on my knees in front of those people."

She shook her head, exasperated, but she looked at him amusedly. "You've got no sense of self-preservation. Fine. I think I need that break, anyway."

"Yeah, you do." He cradled her jaw with a hand, still not caring about his surroundings. She was his getaway, his favourite place. "It's killing me to hear you cry out of stress, to see you so anxious without being able to see all the good things you do."

She blinked, a small line appearing between her brows. "I'm sorry."

"Don't apologise for having emotions. For being a human being. Never with me."

Green irises appeared lighter when a veil of emotions misted over. Dropping her gaze, she grabbed the silver chain around his neck, toying with the pendant.

Three years ago, Thiago had gifted Kamari a set of matching necklaces—only hers was made of pure gold—where he had engraved words with their handwriting on the pendants. Whilst he had "*To the moon*" embedded on his, she had "*and to Saturn.*"

"*You're so fucking cheesy,*" *she had said after opening the gift.*

He grinned. "*You love me for it.*"

"*Unfortunately,*" *she teased. Still, she took the piece of jewellery out of the box, unable to contain her smile.*

"*Brat,*" *he snapped, obliging her to turn around to drape the necklace on her.*

"*Arsehole.*"

"What are you thinking about?" he asked softly, grabbing her hand to twine their fingers together.

"Two things." She smiled, and he suddenly felt weak in the knees. "How amazing you are. You still know how to coax me through my moments of anguish. You can still see me and read my mind when I desperately try to push you away because I don't want to hurt you. You're just incredible, Thiago."

"Keep feeding my ego. I love it." Warmth flooded his chest as he sighed. "I'll always see you. Always."

"I know."

He raised his brows. "And the second?"

He knew that glint of mischief swirling around her pupils all too well. "Still up for that quickie?"

Throwing his head back, he laughed but tugged her towards the backroom by the hand. "Thought you'd never ask."

When Kamari opened the door to the small lounge room reserved for employees, she gasped, turning around to bury her face in Thiago's chest.

Thiago was laughing loudly. He waved at Rowan and Ava, snickering as he observed the latter drag her skirt back down her thighs.

"Come on, you two," Kamari huffed as she turned towards the pair, trying to scowl despite the small smile playing on the corner of her lips. "That's where I take naps between two shifts."

"Enjoying ourselves, are we?" Thiago asked at the same time, leaning against the doorframe.

Ava grabbed the purse she had left on the coffee table. "As if you two weren't about to do the same."

Rowan followed his girlfriend out, not bothering to fasten the buttons of his shirt, leaving his tattoos on display. He blew a kiss to Thiago. "Revenge for all the times you shagged in your room whilst I was literally next door."

📍 *MONTE CARLO, MONACO*

HE SWALLOWED HER breaths like they belonged to him whilst threading his fingers to hers above her head. Slowly, passionately, he thrust in and out, causing Kamari to gasp softly, arching her back whenever he was about to send her towards the pinnacle of pleasure.

"Eyes on me," he demanded huskily.

His favourite colour collided with his gaze, making his features soften in a fraction of a second.

"You're beautiful," he whispered.

She smiled. "That's all you."

He started shaking, his thrusts becoming uneven and nearly uncontrollable when he observed her brows pinch together, pleasurably, as he felt her walls clench around him.

To keep their symphonic cries of pleasure quiet and private, he placed his lips on hers as they unravelled in perfect harmony. Kamari trembled beneath him, catching her breath whilst he continuously moved to ride them both down from their high.

Thiago lay down next to her, pulling her into his chest. He placed a soft kiss on the crown of her head before darting his gaze towards the starry sky. He didn't know what time it was. All he knew was that he had spent countless hours stargazing with Kamari on the roof of his yacht.

"Do you remember our first kiss?" he asked, smiling.

"It's a blurry memory, you know that." She wrapped an arm around his stomach, cheek pressed to his chest. "I wish I hadn't drunk anything that night."

"Things would've been different if we had been sober."

Her voice was a euphonious caress along the edges of his soul, cocooning him into a cosmos of solace. "Do you really think so?"

He hummed. "I think I wouldn't have had the courage to kiss you. You'd have rejected me, let's admit it. But I do think I would've fought and ran after you to get your number."

"I'm not surprised," she chuckled.

"I would have done things the right way. You know, take you out on a few dates, bring you to the paddock, introduce you to Mum, all that."

He felt her gaze on him. "Are you saying you're regretting we did everything in the wrong order?" she teased.

"Never," he replied with a broad grin. "I love how we did our thing on our own terms—our own rules."

The moment he looked down at Kamari, he felt his heart go into overdrive, its pulse rising like wild tidal waves. Her tender gaze catalogued his features, something new, unique brightening her irises—something that promised forever, eternal adoration.

"Marry me," he blurted out.

Surprise etched upon her face as she slowly rose to sit. She cradled the thin blanket to her chest, her dark hair spilling on her back as her lips parted.

"Marry me," he repeated more firmly as he sat up, too. Grabbing her left hand, he watched where a diamond—or whatever stone she'd love—would adorn her finger. "I didn't plan this, so I don't have a ring yet, but I want forever with you, Kam. Be my partner for life. Be my queen. Be mine for eternity."

A beautiful smile spread across her lips. "Took you long enough."

Thiago cradled her face, brushing his lips to hers. She inhaled shakily. "Is this a yes, Monroe?"

"I'll go by Monroe-Valencia from now on, thank you very much." She winded her arms around his neck, nodding eagerly. "Yes, Thiago. I'll marry you."

When their lips touched, he felt as though their hearts were tethering themselves together, in perfect synchronisation with the stars aligning overhead. He smiled against her mouth. "Took you long enough."

MONZA, ITALY

Five (more) years later

"Well, that was a mega lap you did there, Thiago. How does it feel to be on pole again?"

Thiago's chest heaved as he lifted the microphone, one hand on his hip as he rapidly glanced at the camera to his left. He waved to the crowd chanting his name before returning his attention back to the sports journalist.

"Why, thank you, Indy," he smiled. "It does feel very nice. Especially since we struggled a bit yesterday during FP2 to find a perfect balance between agility and rapidity after the engine failure last weekend. But I'm super happy to see we've managed to fix the issue. Running one single lap in the two last minutes of Q3 was risky, but who I am if I don't take risks?"

His friend grinned proudly. "You're already a five-time World Champion, and with all the points you have ahead of the other drivers, you could already claim your sixth title tomorrow. How do you feel about that?"

He exhaled, pushing his hair away from his face. He chuckled when cheers coming from the grandstands echoed. "Feels unreal. Every day still feels like a fever dream, but I'm so thankful for everyone—the fans who have been supporting me for over 15 years, the new fans; my team, my family."

"You could win the same number of championships as your father."

"I could," he said, and when he held Indy's gaze, she dipped her chin in a subtle nod—encouraging him to continue talking. "But I am about to do something that will piss off my PR officer because she told me we had to wait another week to announce this."

The whole circuit fell silent, and whilst Thiago was used to having cameras pointed at him, he couldn't help but feel nervous at that moment. This announcement would change the course of his life, but he was sure of his choice. He had talked through it with everyone—his wife, his team principal, his engineers, his friends—and even if thorough disappointment had overcome his entourage, they all knew his personal happiness came above all.

He took a deep breath in and faced the camera. "I hereby announce my retirement from Formula 1 by the end of the 2032 season." He ignored the lump that had built inside his throat. Ignored the gasps full of shock resonating. Ignored everything, and only accepted Indigo's friendly hand when she offered it to him. "I love this sport. It's been part of me my entire life. It's been the essence of my existence since I was born, and I don't think I will ever be able to leave this world. Life on track is the most thrilling and exhilarating thing I have experienced to this day, but life outside of racing is something I long to live to its fullest."

He slipped his gaze towards his team of mechanics where Kamari stood amongst a sea of red between Alex and Cal, all of them smiling proudly back at him. "Today, my gorgeous, wonderful wife is in the company of our little Evan who has just turned three, and soon enough we'll have a new addition to our family. I'm a devoted man to my wife, and I want to be a hero to our son and his little brother or sister. This is not me saying goodbye—I think this is just a see you later because one way or another, I will come back. Besides, we still have a few weeks of racing before I bid you farewell, so let's make the most out of it."

He embraced Indy before giving her the microphone back. Running towards his team, he waved at the crowd, his vision ever so slightly blurring.

"We're all so proud of you," Cal said, fist-bumping the athlete.

Alex sighed, sadly, despite the smile he put on. "Can't believe this is the end of an era."

"It's the beginning of a new one," Thiago stated with a wink.

The driver jumped over the fence and reached out to Kamari, instantly pulling her into a bone-crushing hug, feeling that invisible bubble of comfort build itself around them.

"I'm proud of you," she murmured before placing a kiss on his cheek.

"Thank you for being my amazing, supportive wife."

They chuckled when Alex and Cal came to wrap their arms around them. "When are you going to compliment us?" asked Alex. "Say things, like, we're the most awesome people in your life."

Thiago pushed them away, only keeping an arm draped around Kamari's shoulders. "Never."

"Dickhead," Cal mustered, turning on his heel.

"Absolute bellend," Alex taunted.

The physiotherapist snickered. "That's what becoming a father does to you."

"Cretins, the two of you," Thiago droned as he pulled his wife away from the crowd.

Gently, he rubbed her stomach where a small bump was noticeable beneath her sundress. "Where's Ev?"

"Napping with Kieran in the motorhome."

He traced the contour of her full lips, the route of her nose, sighing softly at the sight of her features stricken with complete awe. She was electric. Enchanting. As per usual, he was speechless and starstruck. "Are you feeling good?"

She nodded. "Yes, you?"

"Perfect," he admitted before nudging her chin with his knuckles. "Do you want to go and lie down on the track and watch the sunset?"

"Like old times?"

He nodded and brought her hand to his lips before kissing it. "I hope you won't grow tired of me because I'm so ready for this new life with you."

She taunted him with a nonchalant shrug. "Might need to set a few boundaries and rules."

"You're such an idiot."

"Arsehole."

"Brat."

She raised an eyebrow. "Is this a way to talk to the mother of your children?"

Rolling his tongue on the interior of his cheek, he scoffed and obliged her to follow him towards the track. "I could put another child in you right now."

She scowled, and he grinned. "Behave."

"You love me."

"I do." She smiled. "Come on, pretty boy. Let's do this."

ACKNOWLEDGMENTS

To Mary—Without your unconditional support and love, I would have never taken the leap.

To Ivy—The very first person who has ever read FOTC. Thank you for cheering me on, supporting me, and mostly for making this gorgeous cover. And of course, for being an amazing friend. I love you. The second book in the series is for you.

To Nyla—Thank you for everything. From beta reading to proofreading to giving me helpful suggestions to make this story better. Thank you for always answering all my questions, for all the times you've reassured me in moments of doubt, for cheering me on, for loving Kam and Thiago as much as I do, and for being my friend. This book wouldn't be as good without your help. You're now stuck with me for the rest of my author journey.

To Deidre—Without your thorough excitement for this book, I would have drowned under all the uncertainties and moments of self-doubt. Thank you for beta reading, and for always screaming at the top of your lungs when I run an idea by you or send you sneak peeks. Your support means the world.

To my beta readers—Anna, Eevi, Em, Daeja—Thank you for helping me make Kam and Thiago's story better and unique.

To Hannah, my amazing editor—Thank you for everything. Your help was and will always be so appreciated. You've helped me perfect this book in so many ways. I'm so grateful for you.

To the Wattpad community and the friends I made on there —Thank you for making my author journey so special. Who knew writing fan fiction would get me here a year later? Honorable mention to my friends who have never stopped showing their support: Rocio, P, Arushi, Mal, Annie, Kirtsy, Cassie, Nyx, Saph, Eren, Marine, Athena, Lucia, Laibs—Kisses to you all.

To my little family at the bakery—Thank you for everything and for always being my cheerleaders.

To you, my readers—There isn't a right word to express my gratitude towards you. Publishing a debut is scary, but you all made this experience extra special, welcoming, and heart-warming. I hope you all fell in love with Kam and Thiago, and the Full Throttle universe. So much more is coming your way regarding the rest of the series. Thank you for sticking around, and for supporting and loving my work.

And to Jeremy—I love you. Thank you for being my Thiago. For being my anchor. For giving me a hand to hold and a shoulder to cry on when clouds are calamitous on darker days. For being my biggest supporter, my number one fan.

ABOUT THE AUTHOR

Kanitha P. is a twenty-something sports romance author, slowly emerging in the world of publishing with the release of her debut, Falling Off the Cliff.

She has been writing since her early adolescence, and has always had an unconditional love for books. Lover of romance and fantasy, she's an avid reader, but she's also a passionate author. Her mind never settles down; always creating new, thrilling, fun, swoony stories.

Find Kanitha (also known as Kay) on her socials for news and updates about her upcoming releases.

Made in the USA
Monee, IL
03 January 2024

51130531R00272